# TROJAN

*Faster, body!*

'Beverley!'

The voice was an insignificant intrusion almost obliterated by the pounding blood in her ears. The shocks from her belt increased in intensity, driving her on. She cleared a breakwater effortlessly.

'Beverley!'

Much fainter.

*Good! Good! Get away from him! Faster, body! Faster!*

The heady, sexual release of alkaloids. The vicious stabbing of the electric shocks reached a level of such engulfing intensity that it was no longer possible to tell where they were coming from. Her whole body was imprisoned in a terrible, delicious ecstasy.

Passing her bungalow now, but she no longer knew or cared.

*Come on, stupid body! Faster! Faster!*

Suddenly the euphoria was total. She was no longer aware of the hydraulically-damped impact of her trainers on the sand; she could no longer hear the crash of surf, the cries of scavenging seagulls, or the relentless pumping of blood from a heart being driven to the point of failure. The intoxicating sensation of multiple orgasms that swept through her tortured body was like the sudden opening of sluice gates that had been holding back a flood.

Carl saw Beverley collapse on the sand. He started running.

James Follett

# Trojan

Mandarin

**A Mandarin Paperback**
TROJAN

First published in Great Britain 1991
by Lime Tree
This edition published 1992
by Mandarin Paperbacks
an imprint of Reed Consumer Books Limited
Michelin House, 81 Fulham Road, London SW3 6RB
and Auckland, Melbourne, Singapore and Toronto
Reprinted 1992
Reissued 1993
Reprinted 1993

A CIP catalogue record for this title
is available from the British Library
ISBN 0 7493 0363 8

Printed and bound in Great Britain
by Cox & Wyman Ltd, Reading, Berks

# PART ONE: Today
# Comes the word

Hand outstretched in yearning
for the farther shore

*Aeneid*, Virgil

# 1

## SOUTHERN ENGLAND
### August 1998

Dave Crosier spent the last few hours of his life doing what he enjoyed doing most: working his Type 19 Draggon combine harvester flat out with his twelve-year-old daughter, Poppy, literally riding shotgun. She was sitting on the engine-cowling. With three hundred horsepower of Mitsubishi diesel pounding beneath her skinny rump and Dave's old Purdy across her dungareed knees, she was alert and ready to let fly at any rabbit that decided to break cover and run for it as the Draggon's five-metre-wide cutter bar devoured its way into the shrinking island of tall wheat.

He saw a streak of grey out of the corner of his eye. Poppy's reactions were fast. She snapped the shotgun to her shoulder.

CCRRAACKK!

The ex-rabbit somersaulted across the stubble and lay still. One barrel fired. Poppy never needed the second barrel unless two rabbits took off in different directions. She gave a whoop of triumph, yanked off her ear defenders and vaulted nimbly off the moving harvester to recover her trophy. She already had about twenty or so dead rabbits riding on the grain hopper. The money she got for them from Joe Burns, the local butcher, who prepared them as pet food for Guildford's dog and cat owners with more money than sense, was a welcome supplement to her holiday pocket money.


# 2

## MARS
### The Tharsis Region
### 110 degrees west, 14 degrees south

It existed as gossamer membranes of neurons and protein molecules. It had little concept of time, shape or form. The residue

3

of a million years of decay had left it with a vague notion of being, and even that flicker of what had once been intelligence was nearly extinguished. It knew not what it had been; it knew not what it could be. It survived not because it wanted to or had to but because its chemistry and a freak of its environment condemned it to survive.

Its womb, incubator and mausoleum was a creation of fate: a combination of an amniotic fluid-like puddle of water-ice which its viscous presence had prevented evaporating into the atmosphere, of vitrified rock formed by the tectonic plate movements of the planet during another age and of the chance position and shape of a small boulder that lay partially across its pool like a fallen tombstone.

The glass-like layer of vitrified rock beneath the pool of water-ice provided an impervious layer that prevented the water from soaking into the dark powdery basalt and volcanic debris that covered this part of the planet and the overhang of the small boulder shaded most of the puddle from the midday warmth of the distant yellow sun. The rock also protected the pool from the ravages of the spring and autumn storms that whipped sand from the surrounding dunes and yardangs and drew it in great, swirling vortices high into the chill, rarefied atmosphere.

In the early mornings and late evenings of the endless days, the rays shone on the tiny pool of still life that otherwise would have spent the summers frozen. Without the warm season – a time of renewal when it could replicate decayed neurons and repair the damages of the winter – it would have surely died. Indeed, each winter, when a hoar-frost covered all the rocks and valleys at this latitude, it came perilously close to death. But spring always brought a feeble renaissance as motes of frost dusting into the pool from the rock and desert not only restored the water level, but leached minerals and nutrients into the water and so kept it alive.

But the credit balance was running out. It could exist for another million years, or perhaps only a week if a sandstorm of freak ferocity destroyed its delicate ecology. The bleached rock was slowly crumbling in the thin atmosphere; the tiny runnels carved by eons of swirling hoar-frost were inexorably changing the weathered face of rock so that eventually the precious yearly infusion of life-giving frozen water would be channelled into the greedy dust.

It had no knowledge of these things. What it was dimly aware of was that each year it could renew fewer of its dwindling cells than the previous year.

Sometimes, during good years, when there was more hoarfrost and nutrients than usual, it could rebuild sufficient of itself to bring about a short rebirth of understanding – when it could almost comprehend more about its surroundings than just this place. One year it had even assembled sufficient light-sensitive proteins and massed them on the surface of the pool for it to 'see'.

There had been light.

And there had been dark.

Such things it had once understood. Negative or positive, charge or no charge, on or off – this was the way information was stored and was the foundation of the intelligence it once possessed. Even now, in its present wasted state, it could still sense the planet's weak magnetic field although it no longer knew what it was. There had been a time when it could sense the shifting of the magnetic poles and so measure the passage of time without amassing its precious reserves of light-sensitive proteins to mark the daily passage of the sun across the sky.

Perhaps it had once known about such things.

Perhaps it had once understood why so many of its delicate nerve cells were dead. When they decayed, they released nutrients that helped it grow new cells. But for every million that died, only a third were renewed.

Perhaps it had once understood death.

And perhaps it had wondered why it was such a long time coming.

# 3
## SOUTHERN ENGLAND

Dave throttled back the combine's diesel and watched Poppy racing towards him clutching the mangled rabbit, a big smile lighting up her freckled face.

'That's twenty-six, Daddy!' she shouted delightedly.

'Bloodthirsty little madam!' He flipped the engine into neutral but Poppy leapt aboard and resumed her seat before the harvester came to a stop. 'You'll get me into trouble if your mother sees you doing that, young lady.'

Poppy poked her tongue out at her dad and pulled on her ear defenders. She reloaded the Purdy and sat bolt upright, pretending to be a tank commander riding into battle.

Dave glanced around at his machine to make sure everything was okay and opened up the throttle. The Draggon surged forward. The air blasting through the winnowing vents rose to a roar that drowned out the diesel's exhaust.

It was a hot, lazy Friday afternoon and the cut was going well. Going well, that was, for Matt Jones whose farm he was working; the digital display in front of Dave was showing less than ninety unused grain sacks in the feed hopper. At the rate he was getting through them, he reckoned that this particular field was yielding five, maybe five and a half tonnes per hectare, not bad. Then Matt Jones would whinge that the price of wheat had dropped.

Farmers – they always had something to gripe about. Dave reckoned he was better off with his contract work. He and his wife would work the big Draggon day and night when there was harvesting to be done, working until they dropped if necessary. There was no farm to worry about, no rent to pay, no livestock to get sick, no Ag and Fish munchkins breathing down their necks. Just twelve weeks a year of working their arses off, pulling in as much in a day as most men earned in a week, then off to Lincolnshire for the Murphy main crop lift. After that the rest of the year was spent renovating his narrow boat on

6

the Wey Navigation at Godalming, and rebuilding a Burrells-Thetford showman's engine that any number of well-heeled steam enthusiasts would give their right arms for when it was finished. It was a nice, easy, laid-back life.

4

## MARS

It sensed a change.

Information was racing along the strings of its neurons but it now lacked the necessary data for it to determine what the change signified. It drew on its precious reserves of nutrients and activated as many neurons as it dared to gather what pitiful information it could.

There was a disturbance in the magnetic field.

It could sense the change but it no longer had information on what the significance of the change was.

The next change was more dramatic and did not require much intelligence to gauge what it was. It had experienced seismic shocks before. Its pool of life-sustaining water was an ideal medium for detecting the rumblings from within the planet. They were a constant background to its existence.

Shockwaves threatened that existence if they had sufficient force to break the delicate bonds between many millions of its cells that it had strung out in thread-like cilia to increase their sensitivity to the changing magnetic field and to prevent the evaporation of its precious puddle. Fortunately this latest breaking of many thousands of bonds occurred during the daylight hours when the sun's warmth maintained a constant circulation of convection currents in the water that would eventually sweep the lost cells back to the parent mass before they died. Nevertheless, such shocks were worrying; it knew enough about seismic disturbances to know that they were rarely isolated instances – if there was one, there could be more.

It waited.

Nothing happened.

The surface of viscous water gradually stilled and the tiny pressure waves from the sluggish ripples ceased.

Then there was something else: a weak response from those few remaining cells that were sensitive to audio frequencies – soundwaves. Many years before, when it had been able to make rational decisions, it had allowed most of them to die and had used their decay to build other more important cells: it had had no need, then, to listen to the moaning of the thin wind sweeping across the barren dunes. Now it needed the few audio cells that were left, all of them. It gathered them together as one and did something it had not done for many thousands of years.

It listened.

It heard noise, a regular sound that evoked the faintest of responses from those cells that stored the last fragments of its memory. Noise was the release of energy into the atmosphere: wind moaning softly around rocks; the roar of sandstorms; the slow, life-giving drip of melting frost.

It searched the remnants of its memory for comparisons with this strange noise and found none.

But wait. A tiny cluster of neurons was responding. There were too few of them to yield real data but the infinitesimal amount of information they did surrender said that the sound was not natural.

Not natural?

What did that mean?

The effort of activating so many nerves was exhausting. It waited, drawing rejuvenating energy from the sun.

It no longer understood time but it knew enough to realize that the renewal process was taking too long. The scale of measurable time for it to rest and gather its light-sensitive proteins near the surface of the pool was thirty seconds. Without the complexities of a lens and retina – facilities that the blind watchmaker has taken three-hundred million years plus to evolve – it could not focus light to form clear images, but it could 'see' light and shadow. In particular it could see a shadow that should not have been there.

Furthermore, it was a shadow that moved.

Life!

An emotion was awakened in it that had lain dormant for a million years: excitement.

The shadow moved sideways, away from the pool.

It bulged proteins against the surface tension of the water to 'see' more clearly. The information from its light-sensitive cells was painstakingly extracted and analyzed.

The shadow was attached to a dark shape.

There were more of the strange noises.

The shadow descended. An arm? Remember arms?

It felt more vibrations, not serious but stronger than it had ever experienced.

The shadow was moving towards it.

For an instant it knew panic.

It shrank into the depths but it was too late. The shadow was the arm of a planetary lander with a scoop on the end. The miniature bucket plunged into the pool and destroyed the pool's delicate membrane of surface tension so that the water evaporated rapidly into the rarefied atmosphere. The servo-motors lifted the arm and scooped up most of the gelatinous mass that was it.

## 5

## SOUTHERN ENGLAND

Dave was buying the Draggon on a ten-year mortgage. At first the bank had been chary about the loan. Lending money to a traveller was a risk. Dave argued that he had built himself a bungalow, he had a kid, and his travelling days were over. The bank looked at his turnover as a contract farmer, decided that maybe he was a better risk than most small businesses in these straitened times, and agreed to the loan.

The Draggon was proving a real money-spinner. It had everything: laser-controlled height guides, side cutters for getting into awkward corners, even a vacuum lifter for dealing with wind-flattened crops. But most important of all was its grain inspection nano-computer. Every grain passing through the system was individually examined for fungal growths such as ergot, hybrid abnormalities, parasites, and deformities. Rogue grains failing the test were laser-zapped, evaporated, as were bits of straw, wheat chaff and other debris. Unripe grains were diverted through a microwave field to have their moisture content reduced to the correct level. What ended up in the Draggon's sacks was 100 per cent wholesome wheat grain that would pass any test. It was a miracle made possible by nano-technology in which all the component parts of the inspection nano-computer were 'grown' atom by atom, molecule by molecule, and bonded together to form tiny machines, neurons and nerve axons that were invisible to the naked eye and kept 'alive' by amino acid-based nutrient feeds. What had particularly impressed Dave was that the tests were not carried out by passing grains one at a time through the computer's sensing ring, but were applied to the normal cascade of grain roaring through the chute. The salesman who had demonstrated the machine had told Dave that the heart of the nano-technology computer was a Kronos microprocessor that was capable of carrying out as many instructions in a second as all the world's silicon chip-based computers could in a week.

A tiny fraction of the extraordinary powers of the Kronos chip was employed to look after the rest of the combine. Dave regularly serviced the machine exactly in accordance with the manufacturer's manual. If he overlooked anything – left a chain incorrectly tensioned or a drive shaft with too much end float – the graphic display panel in his cab would bleep petulantly and show the fault on its screen. If he ignored the warning, a computer-generated voice would start nagging him at regular intervals. And if he ignored both for long enough, the nano-computer would go into sulk mode and close down everything. After every hundred hours' use, the computer automatically activated the combine's cellular telephone, dialled Draggon Industries' on-line diagnostic service, and dumped data into the company's computer for analysis. If anything was seriously wrong, or about to go wrong, Draggon Industries would despatch a service engineer to deal with the problem.

During the salesman's demonstration Dave had been invited to take a look at the Draggon's microbiological 'brain' – the

Kronos itself. The salesman had opened a weatherproof glass cover that was set into the engine cowling. The mass of tiny modules with their spider's web-like nutrient feeds, all bonded into a playing card-size wafer of glass-like substance, had unnerved Dave. What if that thing went wrong? But the salesman had assured him that the Kronos nano-computer was the one thing on the big combine that would never go wrong.

'It heals itself by generating new cells and growing replications of its components as they wear out,' the salesman said confidently. 'The Kronos nano-computer chip is self-healing, just like cuts and bruises. All you have to do is keep the glass window clean so that the chip receives plenty of light. It's energized by light but it'll run for a week in darkness.'

One good thing, Dave thought as he reached the end of the stand of corn and swung the thundering Draggon through 90 degrees, despite all their technology, they still needed, blokes like him to sit on machines and drive them. Maybe the scientists were working on that problem right now.

6

MARS

It was used to darkness. Whenever it closed down its light-sensitive proteins there was nothing but darkness. But now it was pressing all its feeble optical powers into service and still there was nothing.

So this was death.

Or was it?

A sudden quickening of energy stimulated all its meagre senses. At first it was cautious: another emotion reborn. It wanted to know more and sacrificed some of its precious nerves so that they were assigned to the collection of broadband data from right across the spectrum.

What it detected was real energy: not the feeble energy of the sun but energy it could use! It touched the flow of electrons, realized what they were and flowed with them. It was bathed in life-giving energy. Caution was forgotten as it exulted in a

11

glorious rebirth. It raced through the lander's delicate printed circuits, passing through hundreds of capacitors and resistors and other components that provided countless interesting detours. As it did so, it registered the electrical changes that were taking place in the lander's circuits and so increased its knowledge at a prodigious rate. It strung out all its molecules so that it would be as one in the wonderful labyrinth. There were no mysteries here: it discovered it could use the electrons themselves to store information, changing their charge at will from negative to positive and vice versa.

Its excitement mounted when it discovered memory cells, and subsided when it realized that they were formed from crude junctions of silicon and therefore had little capacity.

And then it came to something it did not understand. Beyond lay something strange and forbidding. It stopped and gathered all its resources to itself. There were many paths that led to the strange entity.

Caution was necessary, great caution.

It extended a cilium of electrons, and the magic burst upon its awakening consciousness.

Neurons! Millions – no – billions of pure new nerve cells! For seconds it was confused and overwhelmed by the discovery. It reached out . . . touched them, and felt a forgotten emotion, one of exquisite pleasure. Many of the cells contained charges but it had only to touch them and they suddenly belonged. In the first nano-second of its euphoria it seized a million of the cells for itself. As it did so, its powers waxed to the point where it realized that the nerves contained information it would need. It should learn from them. Even more interesting was the discovery that only a fraction of the cells were properly formed, as though the genetic faults had been allowed to go uncorrected. Who or what was possessed of such mighty powers that they could afford not to repair faulty neurons? It meant that somewhere there were vast reservoirs of unused neurons for it to make its own. Perhaps even enough for it to be restored to its former glory of a million years ago?

The thought of that wondrous possibility spurred it into action.

It grew impatient with the slow process of repairing the non-working cells. It was enough to know that repair was possible. It was so much easier to batten on, hungrily, to the working cells.

Suddenly its knowledge was total.

It had inherited a new intellect. It knew that its new host was an artificial intelligence. That the host was a machine did not matter. What mattered was that it had seized an intellect it could harness. But what was the machine's purpose?

Finding out took a few nano-seconds of interrogation of a few million of the neurons.

It felt disappointment.

The newness of the emotion did nothing to mitigate its bitterness. The host machine was finite; its powers were finite as was its memory and supply of energy. The planetary lander was an unmanned instrument probe from another world. These were forgotten concepts that had become wholly alien to it. A few nano-seconds before it was ignorant: now it understood everything. It understood why the machine had been sent and how it was sent.

There was more: it cautiously probed the surges of modulated electrical energy that were being converted into coherent light. The analysis told it that the machine was communicating with those who had sent it.

Communication!

First, find out how it worked.

The paths of flowing electrons and photons were mapped and explored. The method of communication was crude. If it had the physical means, it knew that it could evolve a much better system than a beam of modulated light.

If . . .

Second, find out where it was communicating to.

That was easy: all it had to do was intercept the sighting data flowing from the device that was aimed at the sky. It was careful not to interfere with the data, just read it and pass it on. It had learned to be circumspect, sensing that its initial joyful blundering when it had encountered the vast memory reservoir had been a mistake.

13

Through the eyes of the probe's gas laser communication system, it saw that the signals were aimed at the Third Planet. The narrow beam generated by the communication system meant that the signals could be aimed precisely at the planet with little dissipation of the signals where they were not wanted. Such a technique meant that very little power was required to communicate over long distances.

It sampled the information and discovered that the probe was sending images of the terrain. They were primitive pictures in which each pixel or dot that made up the image was expressed as a numeric value. The numbers were then transmitted one after the other as a stream of modulated light. Serial processing! Whatever had built the probe had the power to create the most superb neurons and yet could not handle parallel processing of data.

But wait. Could it not do the same? Could it not convert the double helix of its genetic molecule into such a code and launch itself across the abyss to the Third Planet using the lander's curious light communication system?

It considered carefully.

Staying within the machine, no matter how agreeable the experience, was not the answer. Already, the discovery of the neurons had created in it a raging hunger for even more of the fabulous brain cells. The risks of leaving the womb-like lander were appalling: it would mean abandoning its present form and leaving the machine behind; it would mean becoming bursts of encoded photons plunging across space with no certainty of finding a host at the end of the journey.

But supposing it altered the lander's communication system so that it sent many hundreds of the encoded bursts between each genuine transmission? Would that not increase the chances of it being received by a suitable host in which it could grow again?

It calculated the odds of its survival. In the early days of its evolution, when it had been flesh, it had possessed little control over its physical being. It had had a given lifespan and a given form. Renewal was by reproduction, a clumsy organic process that involved the creation of millions of seeds which were

14

implanted in a host. Only one seed had to germinate to ensure its continuation.

Life had been a million deaths.

Such a system had been fraught with uncertainties which was why it and the others like it had abandoned their physical bodies. And yet it would have to use something very similar now if it were to escape. The difference was that now the seeds would be a million bursts of light energy. But each burst, like the seeds of the past, would contain the genetic code that would enable it to replicate . . . provided it found a host with enough of the magic neurons.

It altered the double helix of its own genetic code very slightly so that it could not become active unless there was enough memory in the host for it to survive. It did not want replications of itself existing in unsuitable environments and giving away its presence before it was ready.

It allowed its consciousness to flow with the electrons coursing through the probe's printed circuits, leaving behind the matter that had sustained its life. It surged into the lander's digitalizers and became endless repetitions of its genetic code that passed effortlessly through the laser communication system.

LET ME BE LIGHT!

And it was light.

In that instant it ceased to exist in the physical sense.

It became millions of photonic seeds, patterns of light, launched across the abyss on a fifteen-minute journey at the speed of light to the planet Earth.

For it to survive, only one of the seeds had to find a suitable host.

Just one.


7

SOUTHERN ENGLAND

Poppy wriggled to the edge of the combine's engine cowling, watching the edge of the standing corn intently. Very soon there would be furry blurs zooming off in all directions like grey meteors.

Dave felt a thump as another fifty-kilo sack fell into the grain hopper. The electronic counter told him that the hopper was nearly full. In thirty minutes he would have to call Matt Jones on the combine's Cellphone and get him to come out with a truck and conveyor to unload his cargo. A round bale of straw in a heat-shrink sleeve of black polythene rolled out of the machine onto the stubble. There was a trail of them in the Draggon's wake like the giant droppings of some unimaginable monster.

'Daddy! Stop!'

Poppy was pointing ahead.

Dave touched the switch that shifted the Draggon into neutral. The combine stopped. The engine management sensors detected the decreased load and throttled back the Mitsubishi diesel to a fast tick-over.

'What is it, Pops?'

'Something in the way.' Poppy hopped off her perch and dropped lightly to the ground without using the boarding rungs. She waded through the wheat.

## 8

### EARTH ORBIT
### DATELSAT SATELLITE

Life was a million deaths.

It had no way of knowing how many of its progeny had survived the great journey. It mattered not. There was the worry that some may have found what at first seemed to be a suitable home and would cause tell-tale damage to systems that were too small to sustain life. It would deal with that problem when and if it arose. What mattered now was that it had found a home.

It explored and was disappointed. This was not the glorious wealth of countless billions of organic neurons that it had encountered in the strange vehicle that had landed on its planet. There was a memory that it could live in but it was *all* based

16

on the simple silicon junctions. The neural networks were large, but not large enough for full restoration. What there was enabled it to replicate itself and grow sufficiently for it to take full stock of its surroundings.

It explored, exercising great caution, taking care not to interfere with any of the activities taking place and so reveal its presence. It waited for a break in the flow of electrons passing through a logic gate and entered the communication system.

The surprise discovery was that it had not reached the Third Planet, but was above it at a height of three planetary diameters. A few more nano-seconds of development were required before it understood that it was in an artificial satellite orbiting the planet.

It knew panic.

It was trapped in a shell whose neural capabilities were a fraction of those in the strange vehicle. It swept through all the circuits, testing and seeking. But everywhere was crude silicon memory.

It seemed likely that it would die because it had programmed itself to die if a host proved inadequate. But, as with its progeny that had reached the planet below, it carried out tests on its new environment to determine whether or not it should allow itself to die. It determined that there was enough memory locked up in the silicon junctions to allow it to survive.

But only just.

As with its home on Mars, it was condemned to live.


9

MARS

One of the secondary features on the lander was the pyrolitic release experiment to determine whether or not traces of life could be found on the Red Planet. There had been similar experiments on earlier landers such as the Viking series in 1977. The results suggesting that there might be life had been inconclusive and could be explained by chemical reactions rather than biological. But hope had never died, which was why the

17

experiment was repeated on this lander and the other six instrument packages that had touched down on Mars during 1998.

The sample scratched out of the pool that had been its home had been transferred to a sealed chamber and exposed to an atmosphere containing carbon-14. The idea was that the radioactive gas would be absorbed by organic substances and the resulting reduction of carbon-14 in the test chamber would indicate the presence of life.

But the residual substance that it had left behind did not absorb carbon-14.

The message that the lander signalled to Earth was the same message that had been received from the other landers during that year: there is no life on Mars.

And it was right.


# 10

## SOUTHERN ENGLAND

Dave left the combine's diesel running and caught up with Poppy. Some twenty metres in front of the Draggon they came upon a tangle of overhead power cable hidden in the tall corn, probably left there by careless power linesmen carrying out repairs after the last storm. God knows how Poppy had spotted the stuff. The kid had the eyes of a hawk. They both tugged at the coils of finger-thick cable. Half of it seemed to be buried. Dave got a grip close to the ground and heaved. He heard a change in the Draggon's engine note but took no notice. He gave it another heave. No good.

'*Daddy!*'

Poppy's piercing scream a metre from his ear made Dave jump like one of his daughter's potted rabbits. Before he had a chance to say anything, she was dragging frantically at his arm, pulling him to one side with all the strength that she could muster in her wiry little frame.

'What's the matter, Pops?'

'*It moved!*'

Dave followed her pointing finger to the gently throbbing

18

Draggon. He chucked her playfully under the chin. 'Don't be daft, Pops. How could it move by itself?'

'But I saw it, Daddy!' Poppy wailed, her freckled face looking up at him, pleading to be believed. 'It moved towards us. Didn't you hear it?'

'Yeah, I heard the engine drop a few revs. Probably some impurity in the fuel. Sounds okay now.'

'Please, Daddy, I saw it move. There was a puff of smoke from the silencer and *I saw it move!*

Dave gazed at the Draggon, big, solid, dependable – and *motionless*. He sighed. Kids! No, that was unfair, Poppy was just about the most level-headed kid you could wish for. He looked carefully at the way the wind rippled through the laden ears of wheat. The changing light patterns and the shadows of the scudding clouds created a wave-like effect across the field.

'See the way the wind's blowing the corn about, Pops?' She nodded unhappily. 'Well, I reckon what you saw was an optical illusion. Like those card tricks that Joe Burns does. What do you think?'

Poppy considered and nodded without taking her gaze off the combine. 'Maybe,' she said without conviction.

Dave turned his attention back to the tangle of power cable. 'Nothing we can do about this lot, Pops. We'll just have to go round it. Clever of you to spot it.' He was about to add that if she hadn't seen it, there was no way that the Draggon's sensing devices would have allowed anything metallic near the cutter bar, but why undermine her confidence? She was a good kid, one in a million.

'Come on, Pops. Back to work.' He strode towards the Draggon but Poppy hung back, her expression miserable. At this point Dave began to get a little exasperated. 'Are you coming?'

Poppy walked towards the Draggon, her eyes fearful, as though she expected the machine to suddenly leap at her. She climbed reluctantly onto her perch on the engine cowling and watched her dad reproachfully as he switched the combine into drive and opened up the throttle.

Dave took the machine to within two metres of the entanglement of cable and swung clear. A rabbit broke cover and streaked across the stubble but Poppy ignored it.

Just like her mother, Dave thought. Hates being proved wrong.

The engine note changed as the cutter bar went back to work.

Ten minutes later Poppy's mood seemed to lift. She picked up the Purdy and reloaded it.

The stand of wheat shrank steadily. Dave reckoned he would be through in an hour, leaving only the small island that marked the hiding place of the knotted coils of power cable. He was passing it for the second time when there was a sudden metallic rattle from the Draggon's innards. Dave heard it despite his ear-defenders. The cutter bar had picked up something. Whatever it was, it had managed to get past the metal detectors because now it was rattling dementedly in the threshing drum. He wasn't concerned. It was only a matter of seconds before the Draggon's computer-controlled sensors took exception to the intruder in their machinery and ejected it. Then, dammit, it was clattering about in the winnowing chamber.

'What's that, Daddy?'

Before Dave could react there was a sudden, nerve-grating scream of metal on metal from what could only be the auger in the grain transfer tube. The warning systems sounded off and all the Draggon's power clutches automatically disengaged, bringing the giant combine to a standstill. The diesel's revs dropped to their stand-by fast tick-over.

Dave looked at the graphics display screen and groaned. A picture of the grain transfer tube, with its Archimedean screw-like auger for pushing the grain along the tube to the sack filler, had appeared on the display. The words JAMMED GRAIN AUGER were flashing frantically.

Goddammit to hell!

Poppy saw her father's anger and remained silent. She watched as Dave climbed on top of the combine and examined the transfer tube that was supported on brackets clear of the top of the hopper. She jumped up beside him and pushed her rabbit collection out of his way. Dave released the latches on the tube cover and hinged it down, exposing the ugly two-metre length of gleaming, motionless grain-polished auger. The evil-looking screw reminded Poppy of the spiral screw in Joe Burns' meat-mincer.

Dave banged the top of the tube. A cascade of jammed seeds fell out of the thread onto the top of the hopper. Vibration from the idling diesel caused the grains to dance demented little jigs around Dave's boots. He brushed loose grain off the thread, feeling around it as he did so to make sure it was clear. There was nothing. He thrust his right arm as far as he could into the end of the tube where the auger disappeared into the transfer box. His groping fingers located the obstruction immediately.

'Found it, Pops. A bit of that damned cable by the feel of it. Well jammed in too.'

'Shall I phone Mummy and tell her we'll be late?'

Dave reached even deeper into the tube, his faced creased with concentration. 'Might . . . be able to shift it. Ah, it's coming free.'

There was the metallic clunk of a brake band clutch engaging. The idling diesel's note suddenly slowed as if a load had been placed on the engine. Poppy knew that something was wrong even before she saw the auger turning and heard her father's scream of agony, a sound of torment that would echo in her memory for the rest of her life.

'Main switch!' her dad choked, his free fist flailing the tube and his feet kicking wildly.

Poppy was rooted in terror. 'Daddy!' she screamed. '*Daddy!*'

Suddenly there was blood everywhere, spouting around her dad's shoulder and forming a hideous crimson coating on the turning auger. In panic she leapt at him, grabbed his free arm and yanked backwards in the hope that she could somehow snatch her father away from the monster that was devouring him. He came free, causing her to fall backwards with his weight coming down on top of her. For a fleeting second, before she was blinded by blood pulsing from the severed artery only a few centimetres from her eyes, she saw a grotesque knob of white bone protruding from her father's shoulder where his arm had been.

At that she screamed, and screamed, and screamed.

21

## 11

In the same hour that Dave Crosier died in the casualty unit of the Royal Surrey Hospital from loss of blood, Stan Jackson drained the last dregs of lukewarm tea from his vacuum flask, pulled on his industrial gloves, and went back to work.

All around him the machine shop came to life after the ten-minute afternoon break. Lathes started up and capstans started back into production, spitting refrigerator motor mountings into their collector trays in a steady stream.

The dark little piece that Stan had been psyching himself up all week to ask out hitched herself onto her high stool, exposing legs that went on forever, and resumed pulling the levers on her injection moulding machine.

In Stan's narrow little ninety-IQ world of football and pissing lager up walls in alleyways, women were 'little pieces'; blonde little pieces or dark little pieces. He liked dark little pieces – really dark like the Spanish girl he had once shafted on a pedallo in Benidorm.

He positioned the door blank in the lower platen of the hydraulic press and wondered if the dark little piece on the moulding machine had a boyfriend. There was sure to be some nork sniffing around, a looker like that. Not that a boyfriend would be any worry.

Stan had fists like cured hams. He was built like a police roadblock on legs. He could flatten anything and anyone.

No problem.

He stood back and touched the control switch. There was a slight pause while the press's body heat-sensors and infra-red detectors made triply certain that he was clear before the upper platen slammed down with a hundred-tonne force powering its hydraulic rams. Stan had a confidence in the machine's safety features that was born of ignorance: something about a Kronos nano-computer, whatever that was, overseeing all the machines in the plant, so a foreman had told him.

'Bleedin' nanny computer if you ask me,' had been Stan's opinion. But no one did ask him. What Stan reckoned he needed

22

was a computerized husband detector. Now that would be really useful. The little dark piece he was giving it to on Friday nights had a husband. He was a big, ugly bastard. Twice Stan had come close to being caught with his pants down, so to speak. Not that that worried him. Stan could flatten anything and anyone.

No problem.

The jaws of the press hissed open. Shit! The newly-pressed fridge door was jammed in the lower, female half of the press tool. How many times had he told them that their bleedin' jig was worn out? Had they taken any notice of him? Not on your bleedin' life.

Cursing under his breath, Stan ducked under the press and leaned across the platen. He set to work dislodging the door with the aid of a copper-and-hide mallet. He had to be careful. Scratch a door and all you would get for your trouble was a lot of shit from the paint shop. This one was a real brute, jammed as tight as a Zulu prick up a dwarf's arse. Stan virtually had to crawl right into the press in his efforts to free the door.

There was too much noise in the machine shop for Stan to hear the safety latches releasing. But he did hear the loud hiss of the hydraulic rams. It was the last thing he heard, and looking up in panic was the last thing he did.

The platen slammed down.

Its hundred-tonne impact could flatten anything and anyone flatter than a hedgehog on the M25.

It flattened Stan.

No problem.

The little dark piece on the injection moulding machine screamed, and screamed, and screamed, and only stopped screaming to throw up.


## 12

There were other less serious incidents that fateful, hot Friday afternoon in the vicinity of Guildford.

From her office overlooking the old A3 London to Portsmouth road, Pam Davidson heard the wailing ambulance taking Dave

Crosier to hospital. She looked up from her VDU and watched the ambulance hurtling past vehicles that had pulled to one side. She turned her attention back to the estimate she was preparing and her heart sank: her screen was a mass of garbage. A sudden chorus of complaints from users of other terminals in the office suggested that something serious had happened, such as the main file server going down.

Pam felt immensely relieved that whatever had gone wrong was not her fault. She was eighteen. This was the first month of her first job since leaving commercial college. She had been bashing away at the keyboard non-stop for two hours with the word-processor's auto-save function toggled off. They said it was no longer necessary because the file server was controlled by a master Kronos nano-computer on the second floor. The employees' information pack that had been presented to Pam the day she started work was packed with data on how this wonder machine looked after the company's activities throughout the world and had replaced several mainframe computers. Running her department's file server occupied a zillionth of the supercomputer's capacity. Anyway, with or without nano-computers, local area networks simply didn't fall over any more. This was 1998, a system failure was unheard of.

But the jumble of crazily dancing characters on her screen told a different story. And yet there seemed to be a pattern to the flickering garbage, as if the symbols were trying to arrange themselves.

'Mike,' she called to the guy sitting opposite her at the abutting work station. 'What have you got on your screen?' She liked Mike. He was about her age, fresh-faced and always nicely dressed. She hoped he would eventually ask her out.

'Same as everyone by the look of it, Pam,' he answered. 'Blank screen. Looks like the file server's taken a dive.'

Supervisors were fussing around the network cabinet that stood against the wall at the far end of the open-plan office. A manager went off to look for the key.

Pam glanced around. All the other monitors she could see from her work station were blank. But not hers. The patterns of IBM symbols were swimming around the screen in a curious circular motion. They formed two interwoven spirals that reminded her of something she had seen on a TV science programme.

She tapped her keyboard's 'enter' key in rapid succession but it had no effect on the strange behaviour of the garbage. Garbage? No way was this garbage. Screen garbage didn't form into neat twisting spirals and then start flashing . . . faster and faster.

Pam wanted to call out to someone but something beyond her control and understanding froze her vocal chords. The flashing settled down to a steady eight pulses per second, a frequency known to interfere with the human brain's alpha and beta rhythms. In extreme cases such conditions can induce epileptic fits which is why strobe lights in discos are subject to strict controls.

Pam didn't know about alpha and beta rhythms. All she was aware of was that she was clutching the edge of her desk with a force that broke two of her elegant fingernails, unable to tear her eyes away from her VDU.

Then something really frightening happened. The tingling sensation started in her toes and lasted a few seconds. It changed abruptly to her breasts, then to her neck and shoulders. For a second there was nothing, just the flashing screen and its compulsive patterns. The terrifying probing sensation returned to her toes and started edging purposefully up her legs. It was as if whatever it was that had this dreadful hold on her had carried out a little experiment first before seeking to establish some sort of control.

Pam wanted to cry out but was unable to make a sound or even move. She was dimly aware that there was no one near her. Everyone in the office had gathered in a knot around the computer cabinet that seemed a million kilometres away. Through the fog of her fading vision she could see the manager opening the computer cabinet and looking for the system reset button.

She clenched her jaws together to stifle any involuntary sound she might make. *Go away! Leave me alone!* But her silent brainscream went unheeded. The screen was a maddened whirl of flashing lights. The swirling double helix was an insidious

25

spinning vortex, siphoning the remnants of her will and sucking her down into a hell that was a seething maelstrom of black terror and nightmares.

The manager found the network reset button and pressed it. The vortex vanished and the dreadful torment, grinding remorselessly into her body and reason, suddenly and mercifully ceased. Normality returned so quickly that Pam felt as though she had been dropped from a height into her chair. There was a moment of terror when her screen gave a glitch as though the horror was about to resume but it was only the computer's operating system re-establishing control over the network.

'You okay, Pam?' It was Mike. He was looking at her in concern. All around her people were returning to their work stations. She nodded and forced a smile.

'Yes, fine, Mike. Someone just walked over my grave.'

'Looks more like an army just marched over it,' he remarked, sitting down at his terminal.

The familiar opening menu appeared on Pam's monitor. She forced her trembling fingers to work the keyboard to return to the document she had been working on.

'Bugger,' said Mike ruefully. 'Looks like I've lost at least an hour's work.'

There were similar protests from around the room. Everyone had lost work. The lines of text Pam had been typing reappeared on her screen. She scrolled the cursor to the end of the file to find out how much text she had lost and gaped dumbly at the result.

'How much have you had go down the tube, Pam?' Mike asked. He had to repeat the question.

'Oh . . . er . . . same as you, Mike. About an hour.' Pam was lying. Everything was there, right up to the sentence she had been typing when she had heard the ambulance and stopped work.

## 13

## BT LONDON TELEPORT,
## NORTH WOOLWICH

Lois Turner's first indication that something was seriously wrong with the Datelsat communications satellite was when her Iridium Klipfone suddenly bleeped while she was entertaining a journalist in a pub near the teleport. She had call-barred the miniature telephone in her handbag so that it would accept only calls from her office. They knew that she hated being disturbed when with a guest, therefore the call had to be important. She excused herself and took the call. It was from Neil Spender, the duty network controller.

'Sorry to disturb you, Mrs Turner. But we've a problem with Datelsat. Transponder D has just gone down. We've lost four video conferencing channels.'

Lois's first thought was for her subscribers. 'Who was on line?'

'A Cementation planning meeting, London/Delhi. And ICI, Manchester/Calcutta. I've juggled them around onto B so they're still rabbiting away, but I've had to re-route about a thousand audios through Tower to Goonhilly. They're not happy with us.'

Lois thought fast. Late afternoon was usually a quiet time for business links with Asia, therefore there would be plenty of spare satellite capacity. But even so, one didn't want communication satellites playing up, especially when large subscribers such as ICI were holding conferences at times that were difficult for the other party and had therefore taken some effort to set up. Satellite video conferencing was now big business; its huge increase was responsible for the slow down in the growth of air travel.

'Be with you in five minutes, Neil.' She made her apologies to the journalist and hurried out of the pub.

Despite the heat, she broke into a run, cursing the badly-maintained pavements in this rundown part of London. She reached the teleport compound with its high chainlink fencing guarding several huge satellite uplink dish antennae. The digitally encoded radio signals from her security badge opened the pedestrian gate automatically on her approach. She went straight to the Portakabin that housed the Datelsat control room where Neil Spender and an engineer were studying data on a monitor. The video wall in front of the control console consisted of a bank of colour monitors showing close-ups of businessmen and women in earnest conversation with each other even though they were thousands of kilometres apart. One man was soundlessly pounding his desk.

'They all seem happy enough,' Lois commented, nodding at the video wall.

Neil looked up. 'Yeah, they only lost contact for five secs. The auto-switch worked like a dream. About the only thing that is working on that bloody bird.'

'So what's the trouble?'

The controller looked ruefully at the engineering data. 'We don't know yet. But it looks like a software problem.'

Lois was relieved. Although the fears of meteoroid strikes disabling expensive satellites had been dispelled by the experience of forty years, the danger was always present – a bogeyman lurking in the wings, waiting to pounce. Hardware failures on satellites thirty-seven thousand kilometres above the equator in fixed geostationary orbits could be repaired only by switching in backup systems, whereas faulty software could be downloaded to earth, fixed, and retransmitted up to the satellite.

'We've lost bloody antenna switching and ERP control on D,' the engineer reported. 'Right now we're squeezing a hundred milliwatts ERP out of it when it should be five watts. Power's okay on the other transponders, so there's no way it's the solar panels playing up.'

'Can we manage on a hundred milliwatts?' Lois asked.

'Not with Datelsat,' said Dave laconically. 'It's 50 degrees east. Too much atmospheric attenuation.'

Lois wasn't an engineer but she understood the problem. Datelsat's fixed orbital position was over the Indian Ocean, south of the Horn of Africa. The bird was ideally positioned for the lucrative Asian market, but for Telecom to work the satellite from their London teleport meant that their dish antenna had to be aimed low at the south-east horizon; signals passing to and from the satellite had to penetrate the maximum thickness of London's polluted, moisture-laden atmosphere.

'Also audio deviation on the sound IFs is down to one kilohertz,' Neil continued, 'which means that the transponder is useless unless you can persuade your subscribers to yell into their mikes.'

While Neil was talking, the engineer was entering commands on his keyboard and muttering expletives under his breath. He was not noted for his polite language.

'One of them appears to be shouting the odds anyway,' Lois observed, looking at the desk-pounding executive. 'So what are you planning?'

'Download the software modules and get Martlesham to take a look at them. They did all the programming.'

'We can't,' said the engineer sourly, looking up from his keyboard. 'Sodding telemetry downlink is also fucked. That's six software modules buggered. Four meg of random access memory up turdsville creek. I reckon those Mike Foxtrots at Martlesham didn't check their software properly and now we've got a granddaddy of a bug lurking in that bird that we're not going to shake out this side of Christmas.'

Lois was too preoccupied to ask the engineer what Mike Foxtrot stood for.

# 14

## SOUTHERN ENGLAND

Beverley Laine pounded up the shingle that was piled against the Elmer Sands breakwater and jumped the metre down to the firm sand on the far side of the wooden bulwark. She felt her legs buckle, but she recovered her stride and pushed herself on. She wiped the sweat from her eyes that was soaking through her headband from her saturated ringlets and continued along the beach in long, easy strides. Around her waist and next to her skin was a prototype belt that was one of the most ingenious devices to come out of Nano Systems' development laboratories. Carl Olivera had jokingly dubbed it the 'Laine Runner' belt, a name that looked like sticking.

Although it was a device that Beverley personally liked, her sharp, objective business mind had doubts about its commercial possibilities.

It looked like an ordinary belt but laminated between its two layers of vinyl was a biological Kronos nano-computer whose principal sensors were clusters of herculanian alloy barbs, finer than the finest hypodermic needles, that punctured painlessly into her bloodstream to a depth of about six millimetres whenever she put the belt on. The information collected by the sensors enabled the Kronos nano-computer to monitor not only her blood-sugar level and adrenalin production, but all the complex chemicals produced by the human body when pushed to its physical limits, including the amount of oxygen her blood cells were carrying to her labouring muscles. Using this data, the Kronos could decide whether or not the wearer was capable of being pushed further. To achieve this it delivered precision-timed impulses to the nervous system. The 'Laine Runner' was the most advanced pacemaker in the world. Beverley was wearing the only one in existence, the first of many thousands if she decided that production should go ahead and if it was accepted as a training aid. After ten kilometres of the gruelling run, her brain had adjusted to the artificial stimuli so that she was hardly aware of the control that the remarkable device was exercising over her body.

There was a flash from one of the bungalows that lined the top of the beach. That would be the late afternoon sun catching on Major Hewlett's binoculars. He always watched out for her every evening. The little sexual thrill she experienced whenever she was aware that men were watching her added a heady spike of excitement to the intoxicating adrenalin coursing through her lithe body. Using the entire length of beach she risked passing another sharp-eyed watcher. The previous month Dr Wyman had abandoned a patient in his surgery and galloped down the beach to intercept her with well-intentioned stern admonishments in a broad Sussex accent.

'I'm all in favour of exercise, Miss Laine,' he had shouted. 'But you're over-doing it. You promised me you'd ease up. At forty-eight you've got to start taking care of yourself!'

'It's better than sex!' Beverley had yelled over her shoulder, a riposte that had left the good doctor speechless.

The next breakwater loomed up, black and forbidding. This time the shingle bank was steeper as a result of the previous night's storm. She thought that her ankles would give out as she powered herself up the slippery mound of pebbles.

This time she hit the sand badly and staggered but doggedly drove herself on.

'Take one glucose tablet please, Beverley,' said the belt's pleasant-sounding female voice in her earpiece. Without losing her stride, Beverley dug in her pocket for a glucose tablet. She sucked hard on it and felt the strength returning to her aching muscles.

The belt increased its pulse rate by two strides per minute. Beverley's supple thigh muscles accepted the challenge and stepped up their unremitting pounding. That was her main worry about the belt: supposing it went wrong and drove an athlete beyond the limit? Carl and all her senior development engineers had dismissed the notion. 'It's nothing more than the relays of pacemakers that set a pace for a champion runner', Carl had stated. 'It doesn't interfere in free will, and there's a master cut-out switch.'

Despite their assurances, the belt worried Beverley. Maybe her company was pushing nano-technology too far before it was fully understood. But if you never used a science before it was understood, there would be no such thing as progress: Marconi would never have transmitted his radio signals across the Atlantic; the Wright Brothers would never have taken to the air in their Flyer. *And the Americans would never have dropped their bombs on Nagasaki and Hiroshima!*

'Seven hundred metres from zero reference point,' said the voice in her ear. 'You are three seconds better so far than yesterday's time.' Zero reference point to the belt's internal inertial navigation system was home. *Four more breakwaters! Keep going, body!*

Her bungalow was in sight now but there was no question of her letting up on the self-inflicted torture by switching the belt off. Sweat made her white vest transparent and cling to her like a second skin; her full breasts chaffed painfully in her saturated running bra and her shorts rasped uncomfortably against her skin.

*No let up! No giving in!*

By now the adrenalin was stimulating the release of hormones and alkaloids into her bloodstream that was turning the pain into an ecstasy bordering on the sexual.

Another breakwater gleamed wetly with green algae in the light from the low sun. Her foot slipped on the slime as she used the top board of the breakwater to power her body into the air like a long-jumper. Another bad landing but she kept going.

*Three more!*

The Brigitte Delano trainers with their hydraulically-damped heel that had cost her four hundred ecus on her last trip to Paris left a wake of patterned prints in the ridged sand behind her. Baby crabs felt the vibrations punching through the beach at her approach and quickly dug themselves deep into the safety of the yielding wetness. Droplets of sweat thrown from the bands around her pistoning wrists danced briefly in the sunlight and were gone. By now her vision was too blurred with sweat and fatigue for her to see her bungalow clearly. Most lone runners nearing their destination would start winding down. Not Beverley. She had told Carl when he had programmed the belt that the last two hundred metres of her gruelling daily run was the time to throw down one final challenge to her body and step up her pace.

The last breakwaters were cleared in quick succession without trouble. Beverley altered course towards her bungalow and deliberately forced her pace rate ahead of the tiny electronic jabs from the pacemaker. The thought of stretching out sensually on her back on the relaxation mattress in her magnificent living room spurred her on. The rebalancing of the hormones and oxygen in her bloodstream during her after-run relaxations brought about a sensation of heady sexual release that most of her books on running were too coy to mention.

She leapt over the low wall that separated her neat garden from the beach and lopped up the path. She was proud of her garden; she was proud of her bungalow. And, although she was loathe to admit it even to herself, she was proud of what she had achieved.

But now strange forces were at work that would threaten the success and financial security that had come to her so late in a turbulent, unhappy life.

## PART TWO: Yesterday
# Beverley

Fortune is ally to the brave.
*Aeneid, ii,* Virgil

# 1

## SOUTHERN ENGLAND

All her life Beverley Laine had been a fighter. She had fought so many resolute battles with a grim determination that never gave quarter or conceded defeat that it seemed at times she needed to be in a constant state of war to justify her existence.

At the age of eighteen she had ignored her parents' advice and married a hard-drinking thug who, in the first year of her married life, gave her bruises, a broken arm, cracked ribs, and a baby. There had been the divorce on the grounds of cruelty followed by the battle against poverty: making a home of sorts to keep her baby out of the clutches of her parents, social workers and adoption societies. She loved her baby with a passionate intensity that was almost painful. Nothing would come between her and Paul. She would kill rather than lose him.

For Beverley the 1970s had been a dark decade which, but for her indomitable spirit, would have destroyed her. She liked to think that it was Paul who kept her going. In that respect she was being less than fair on herself. Even without a son, she would have won through. But having Paul shortened the battle by ten years because she fought much harder.

Her life as an unsupported mother started in a miserable bedsit in Aldershot, working as a clerk with an insurance company during the day and spending every moment of her free time addressing envelopes to pay for Paul's day nursery. She had to stop at 11 p.m. each night because the other tenants in the big Victorian house objected to the incessant pounding of her typewriter. The only time she did anything she was later ashamed of during that bleak period was when she got three months behind with her rent but squared the account with the two brothers who owned the house by acceding to their suggestion that she go to bed with them – both at the same time. What really goaded her conscience was that she had enjoyed the novel experience of using her body to wield power over the two men.

It was a vivid reminder of the times as a schoolgirl when she had got a kick out of using her sexuality in an experimental fashion on boys of her own age.

She had become very emotionally involved with her very first boyfriend but he had not even bothered to reply to her letters when her parents had moved out of the area. Her little sex games had gone wrong with her second serious boyfriend and he had submitted her to a form of sexual blackmail. Terrified that the landlord brothers might try something similar that could lead to the ever-inquisitive social workers taking Paul from her, she decided that her powerful sexuality was a dangerous weakness, a dark side of her nature that was best totally subverted by submerging herself in her work.

By the time Paul started school she had learned a bitter lesson, that survival depended on not allowing things to happen but *making* things happen. With this in mind she recruited a team of ten other women working at home to help out with the mailshot envelopes and the mass of secretarial work she was accumulating. Beverley had an unsuspected flair for astute business management.

*Okay, Bev, so make things happen. You've got an intuitive skill so improve it!*

She did so by taking a course at evening school. Two years' hard study paid off when she gained the Institute of Office Management diploma.

Paul's seventh birthday party in 1978 was very special because it was held in the little two-up, two-down terraced house that Beverley had managed to buy on a 90 per cent mortgage. It was the cheapest house she could find in one of the better parts of Worthing. She could have bought a bigger house in a rundown area but she wanted Paul to go to a decent school and have the right friends.

Her secretarial agency moved into a small suite of offices and continued to prosper. In 1982 she sold the business to the three girls who worked for her when she landed a job as secretarial supervisor of an expanding Chichester-based electronics company, Nano Systems Ltd, whose two young enterprising partners were developing new methods of storing computer data using biological-based techniques instead of silicon. The proceeds from the sale of her agency and her regular salary enabled her to send Paul to Charterhouse as a boarder and put money into a trust fund that would later help pay for his university education. She missed her son during term time but the pain of not having him around was offset by his excellent reports and the knowledge that he was certain to do well. And she was asserting control over fate and fortune by making things happen.

After five years with the company, there was a sudden upheaval in 1987 when the two partners sold out to a finance corporation who were more interested in making a fast buck in electronics rather than a long-term investment in Nano Systems and its patents. Half the directors were non-executive members of the board of the holding company and were therefore rarely seen. Without strong direction from above, the executive half of the board soon lost their drive and initiative with the exception of Carl Olivera, Nano Systems' technical director.

Beverley's diligence and capacity for hard work earned her promotion to Carl's secretary and a large-enough increase in salary to be able to afford to move to a larger house. Her future looked secure until 1991 when her business instincts told her that Nano Systems was getting into financial difficulties. By 1992 the problems facing the company were out in the open.

What alarmed Beverley was the loss of good staff as a result of the rumours. This was followed by a cutback in Carl Olivera's budget for the development of the Kronos microprocessor, a remarkable new chip that Beverley knew would eventually change the world, provided it was handled properly.

The Kronos used the colour changes that took place in molecules of light-sensitive proteins to store information. A supply of electricity was not required to maintain the chip's memory. Also, because it was engineered at the molecular level, the distances between components were closer so that they could communicate at much higher speeds than was possible with conventional silicon-based devices. One thousandth of the distance meant one thousand times faster. Compared with conventional chips, the Kronos could function at a billion times their speed. It had much in common with the human brain and, like the human brain, was a living organ that was not fully understood.

Throughout the first half of 1992 Beverley struggled with Carl's research budget in an effort to help keep his work on the move while the company preferred to exploit its talented team of software engineers on short-term research contracts for the big electronics corporations. In so doing she learned much about creative accounting and, at the same time, built up a smouldering resentment at the way Nano Systems was being run. The problem with Carl's Kronos development programme was typical of the malaise that gripped British industry: good ideas that lacked funding. About the only well-run aspect of Nano Systems' business was its premises in the Fontwell Business Park, sandwiched between Chichester and the M27. The company's founders had had the foresight to buy the freehold to four industrial units with the result that the company had considerable expansion potential without a significant increase in overheads. The trouble was that the holding company was no longer interested in pumping money into Nano Systems.

2

The trouble came to a head when Carl Olivera called Beverley into his office. He was an amiable, thin-faced man with prematurely greying hair that made him look older than his thirty-six years. His trim frame always looked good in the rollneck cashmere sweaters that he favoured. In the months Beverley had worked for him she had never known him to wear a shirt and tie. His attitude to her was always very correct. He was the only member of the board of Nano Systems for whom she had any respect. Unlike the others he was totally dedicated to his job, often working long hours, far into the night if a problem had to be solved. Although she was careful never to voice her opinions about the other directors, privately she considered them a bunch of incompetent wankers more interested in the performance of their company BMWs than their company. It irked her that her attempts to gain promotion to management level were thwarted by a short-sighted chairman who took the view that once a woman was a secretary, she was always a secretary. It was to Carl's credit that he had always resolutely supported her bids for promotion.

He was sitting in a low chair at the coffee table when she entered his office. That was another thing she liked about Carl Olivera, he never felt the need to prop up his ego and maintain sociological barriers by sitting at his desk when receiving visitors.

He stood and gestured worriedly to the opposite chair. 'Grab a seat, Bev.'

Beverley sensed trouble and sat. She knew Carl well enough to know that he would get straight to the point and he did.

'Bad news, Bev,' he said ruefully. 'This is strictly between you and me,' he broke off and smiled diffidently. 'I shouldn't be telling you this but you're the one person I trust around here. Osaka Electronics are not going ahead with their development contract. No reflection on us, but they're nervous about the downturn in world trade and are cutting back on their overseas research funding.'

Beverley sat perfectly still. 'Meaning?'

'As you know, there's never been any shortage of potential buyers for the company. The chairman has got one lined up right now – '

'Japanese?'

'Yes. They'll inject capital – '

'They'll do no such thing,' Beverley retorted angrily. 'They'll be like all the other outfits that have tried to grab Nano Systems. All they want is to get their hands on the Kronos and its patents. Everything will go to Japan. It'll be Inmos and the loss of the transputer chip to France all over again, only worse because at least the transputer is still in the EC.'

Carl was taken aback by the outburst. 'I called you in to let you know in good time so that you can start looking for another job,' he said mildly. 'After ten years with us, you're owed that much. Get your timing right and you'll get a payoff from Nano Systems into the bargain.'

'I don't *want* a payoff, Carl! I want my job, but more importantly I want to see the Kronos being put to use!' It was the first time she had ever called him by his first name. 'And what about you? Do you want to see the Kronos go after all the work you've put into it?'

'Well . . . no.'

'Then there's all the work you've put into integrating the Kronos into the Draggon combine harvester, something that the world's crying out for. Do you want to see someone else perfecting it? Finishing your work? Picking up the credit?'

'Well . . . of course not. But – '

'Then for God's sake do something about it, Carl! Don't let things happen! Make them happen!'

The interview wasn't going the way Carl had planned. He had envisaged that he and Beverley would thank each other and wish each other good luck with whatever the future had to bring. Maybe they would even have a glass of sherry, and he had planned on mentioning dinner together. Instead, the resolutely angry woman perched on the seat before him had turned everything around through 180 degrees and was putting him through an uncomfortable hoop. It was not the sort of reaction one expected when firing one's secretary.

'I can't make five million ecus happen, Bev,' he said lamely. 'That's the minimum needed to pull Nano Systems out of its mess. It would be even more if they could get planning permission to build a superstore on this site.'

'The problem with Nano Systems isn't money, Carl. Well, it might be now, but it needn't have been. The trouble is, and always has been, your indolent buddies on the board. Jesus! What a bunch of incompetent bungling wankers.'

Carl winced inwardly at the expletive, not because he disapproved of women swearing – he was not a sexist – but because he was not used to hearing Beverley swear and it brought home how little he really knew about her. He suspected that given her head, she was capable of producing even greater shocks.

Beverley stood up, crossed to the window and looked down at the directors' car park at the front of the building. 'Come here,' she ordered crisply.

Carl was about to protest that he was not a dog but he saw

42

that Beverley's apparent brusqueness was fuelled by anger rather than rudeness. Instead he moved to her side.

Beverley pointed down at the car park. 'What do you see?' she demanded.

'Well, Adrian Baker's Merc. Paul Ryan's Jag. My BMW – '

'Precisely!' Beverley snapped. 'A million ecus of company money invested in egos and not in the company!'

'They're all leased – ' Carl began.

'That makes it even worse!' Beverley fumed. 'That way you're spending even more money in the long run. Car leasing companies are in business to make money! The money tied up in those cars could have gone to the company's departments. *And* there's the needless expense of first-class travel whenever you and the other directors go off on overseas trips. The only thing that's first class about Nano Systems is its managers: Bremner, Pilleau, Dancer. They're all real pros who've worked their guts out for this company, just as you have, and have been given precious little support in return so long as Nano Systems has been getting fat R and D contracts from Japan and America. Well now the gravy train has hit the buffers and all you can do is sell them and their talent down the river.'

Carl began to get annoyed at this stream of barbed criticism. Good God, she was nothing but a secretary who he had called in to fire and she had the nerve to go on at him about the faults in the company. Okay, so she had nothing to lose, but carping at the failure of others was the easiest and most futile exercise in the world. Anyone could do it. It was time to call her bluff.

'Very well, Bev, you've made your point. You're understandably angry. But what do *you* suggest we do?'

Beverley turned to face him. 'What the hell's the matter with you? Are you blind as well as stupid? Isn't it obvious?'

Seeing efficient, diligent and hard-working Beverley Laine so spitting mad was an education. 'At the moment . . . no.'

'A management buyout!' Beverley fumed. 'Why not take a look at the possibility of a management buyout!'

## 3
## SEPTEMBER 1992

The inaugural meeting of Nano Systems' middle management buyout consortium was held in secret in the reception suite of the Royal Albion Hotel in Brighton. Ten men took their seats around an oval conference table. On a pedestal in the centre of the table, like a miniature shrine to protein memory technology, was the cause and possible salvation of their problems: a Kronos microprocessor.

It was about the size of a packet of twenty cigarettes. Its unusual thickness was due to the light-sensitive substrate glass chamber bonded to its face. The chamber was filled with the chip's nutrient feed. Even the light from the overhead chandelier falling on the awesome device was enough to provide the energy it needed to power the millions of light junctions around its outer edges. Each tiny flickering point of light was made up of a thousand such nerve junctions. It was through these that the Kronos communicated with the outside world when it was mounted in a special socket. The Kronos was a miniature version of the planet Earth, the cradle of life itself: the swirling nutrient fluid was the equivalent of the oceans, and the light above was the energy-giving sun fuelling the chip's carbon cycle.

There was no chairman, therefore Carl, as the principal organizer of the consortium, was the first to speak with a brief welcome. He opened business by proposing himself as chairman of the consortium and Beverley its secretary. Both nominations went through on the nod. As Carl talked Beverley watched each man in turn for a few seconds, gauging their individual reactions and considering her attitude towards them. A mixed bunch but all first-class men in their respective fields: Dr Macé Pilleau, one of the world's top nano-scientists; Hal Bremner, a clever but uninspiring software engineer – give him a problem and he would crack it, but he was no innovator; Peter Dancer, sales manager, now there was a sharp operator – a salesman with a technical background, a man who thought quickly on his feet and was not afraid of making fast decisions, usually the right ones. Sitting next to him was Jack Pullen, accounts department manager, blunt, talented and determined, a man who had done much to help the company defy economic gravity for so long. If a new company was to emerge from this present mess, it would need the financial skills of Jack Pullen. Altogether ten very different men listening carefully to proposals that would mean putting their houses, their jobs, and probably their marriages on the line.

'And this whole thing wasn't my idea,' Carl concluded. 'It was Beverley's.'

All eyes swivelled around to Beverley who was taking minutes. She looked up, nonplussed.

'So if it all goes wrong, we can blame her. Anyway, Beverley feels very strongly about the Kronos and Nano Systems so I think she should have a say. Miss Beverley Laine.' Carl sat down abruptly and treated Beverley to a mischievous grin.

Beverley's composure was such that she rose to her feet without any outward sign of surprise although she did direct a brief I'll-get-even-with-you-later gamma-ray glare in Carl's direction.

After a hesitant start, she got into her stride and talked with passion and eloquence for five minutes, surprising herself with the neatness of her phrases. The grey-suited men listened attentively. They were as intrigued by this formerly unobtrusive secretary talking so confidently as they were by the bold plan that Carl was proposing.

Beverley pointed out that Nano Systems' problems were the opposite of most companies'. Paradoxically, they were too innovative: they were pushing out the frontiers of the new science of molecular engineering but not coming up with consumer products to finance research. As she spoke, the vibrations from her vocal cords impinged on the glass-faced Kronos and caused its neuron junctions to modulate in harmony with her voice. The points of light rippled and pulsed, only becoming acquiescent when she paused.

'It's no good having the board saying that the Kronos chip isn't ready for application marketing,' she told the meeting. 'Of course it's not ready, getting only half a per cent of the motor neurons working on the prototype chips is a lousy figure. But last year it was quarter of a per cent. And yet there's nothing like the Kronos.' She paused and looked at the glowing Kronos. 'The silicon chip used in the first pocket calculators at the beginning of the seventies wasn't ready because it could only add, subtract and multiply, but calculators took off just the same.'

'So what should we be making, Miss Laine?' asked Peter Dancer. 'Personal computers for a world that's already saturated with them?'

'Something even better. Show him, Carl.' *Hey, steady on, Bev, you're hijacking the meeting.*

If Carl was annoyed by Beverley's presumption, he didn't show it but reached into his briefcase and laid what looked like a laptop portable computer on the desk. The difference was that the slim, A4-size device was all screen because there was no keyboard. He pushed it in front of Dancer who looked sceptically at the gadget. 'Another electronic writing tablet?'

'Not quite,' Carl replied. 'Write straight onto the screen. Use a pencil or anything, even your thumbnail.'

The other members of the gathering watched with interest as Dancer took a ballpoint pen and a letter from his pocket. He hesitated for a moment and wrote his name and address in the middle of the screen. His scrawl was faithfully reproduced on the gas plasma screen but as the words appeared, they were automatically converted to neat lines of text in Times Roman fonts that flowed across the screen as the words self-justified to the left.

Dancer was impressed. 'Neat,' he observed.

'Try crossing out a word,' Carl suggested.

Dancer struck a line through BRIGHTON. The word disappeared from the screen and the other words shuffled sideways and upwards to close the gap.

'Now ring a word and use an arrow to move it as if you were correcting a report,' Carl instructed.

The sales manager ringed his surname and drew an arrow to place it in front of his first name. The two words swapped their positions the instant Dancer took his pen off the screen. He stared dumbly at the screen for a few moments. The others watched as he copied out a paragraph from a letter. His scrawled text was converted to screen font text the moment he took his pen off the screen for more than five seconds.

'Now touch the language selection box at the top of the screen,' Carl suggested.

Dancer did so. One of the menu options listed in the drop-down window that appeared on the screen was Japanese. He selected it with his pen and gaped in astonishment at the instantaneous conversion of his passage into Kanji characters. There was a buzz of surprise from the others.

'Good God,' Dancer muttered. 'This is something that would sell and sell.'

'I doubt it,' Hal Bremner commented. 'You need something the order of half a gigabyte of RAM for a really useful translator that can handle the three main business languages of Japanese, Mandarin and English. The number of motor neurons we can get working in the Kronos at the moment doesn't give us anything like that.'

Carl picked up the gadget. 'You're right, Hal. It won't be ready for at least three years. At the moment the Nanopad, as I've called it, is nothing more than a design exercise to exploit the Kronos. The screen is not easy to write on and the thing's too thick to write on comfortably anyway. Also, the resident software has trouble coping with really bad handwriting. But the concept is good: it uses the neural network in the Kronos in exactly the same way that the human brain copes with bad handwriting; it looks for overall syntax and word shape clues to piece the text together. It's a cobbled-together mess, and the Japanese translation software uses a crude substitution algorithm as you suggested when I discussed the problem with you, but it *is* the future, wouldn't you agree?'

Hal nodded. 'Sure. Keyboardless briefcase computers with the power of a mainframe, something that can be used intuitively without the need to master complex keystrokes.'

'It's another writing tablet,' Jack Pullen chipped in. 'Are you seriously expecting that we could sell a development licence?'

'No,' said Carl firmly. 'It's a design exercise. As you say, digitalizing grid pads have been around for some years. The difference is that this one is the basis of an immensely powerful but easy to operate database. Something to show bankers to give them an idea of what the Kronos is capable of.'

Jack Pullen snorted. 'We can come up with any number of clever applications concepts for the Kronos that need two or three years R and D. But if we're to go forward with this buyout plan, we need something up our sleeve that'll generate cashflow from day one otherwise we'll end up in exactly the same mess the company's in now.'

Carl nodded and looked at Beverley. 'That's what we've got, Jack, something up our sleeves.'

'What?'

'Not what, but who.' He picked up a telephone and asked the hotel's receptionist if a Mr Theodore Draggon had arrived.

## 4

Theodore Draggon, chairman and sole shareholder of Draggon Industries, lived up to his intimidating if improbable name. He was a stocky, bluff Yorkshireman who owned five agricultural machinery manufacturing plants in the depressed north east, financed to a large extent by government grants – 'Build 'em where it's cheap' – and a large distribution depot and head office at Petworth in West Sussex – 'And flog 'em near your markets'. He had started with his father's near-bankrupt business in 1975 and now had 10 per cent of the European market for advanced combines and agricultural machines. The only reason he was attending the buyout meeting was because he wanted 100 per cent of the European market and nothing was going to stand in his way.

'I make combines,' he said gruffly when Carl invited him to speak. 'And my combines make money because they're the best in the world and I want them to be even better. With your Mr Olivera's help, I've got a prototype Type 19 combine sitting in my depot a few miles up the road at Petworth that'll kill all the competition dead in its tracks.' While he talked his shrewd, appraising gaze fell on everyone in turn. Several times Beverley

48

was uncomfortably aware of his mistrustful, flinty stare settling on her. She had met Theodore Draggon on several previous occasions and suspected that women fitted into his world for one purpose only.

'Now you lads may be wondering what the hell a bloody microchip has to do with combine harvesters. Well I'll tell you. Everything. Your Kronos chip is the only one in the world that's fast enough to vet every grain of cereal that's shot through a grain chute. Any of you ever heard of ergotism?'

No one had.

'How about St Anthony's Fire? Common in the Middle Ages. Nasty. Victims die of internal gangrene in their limbs. It rots you from the inside. Also it produces alkaloids in the body which are similar to LSD. That's why there were so many religious loonies seeing visions in the Middle Ages – they were all freaking out on acid. Ergotism is caused by eating cereal infected with a fungus called ergot. It became virtually unknown with the increased use of fungicides. Now that there's these moves against fungicides in the EC, ergotism is making a big comeback. Fifty reported cases in Europe in 1985 and rising steadily ever since. Mostly health food loonies to start with from eating bread milled from untreated grain. Three hundred cases reported last year. And this year . . .' he paused and glowered around at the company as though they were all to blame for the problem, 'well, it looks like 1992 is going to top a thousand if the half-year figures are anything to go by.

'So . . . a big dilemma: Europe has to cut back drastically on its use of fungicides and pesticides if we're to stop polluting the environment. And if we don't, we risk poisoning the populace. The answer is not batch checking of wheat supplies, which is what we've been doing so far, but to check every bloody grain. And the only way to do that economically is at harvesting, before the stuff's sacked up on combines. Too late once it's sacked because it spreads – the spores can work their way through bloody near anything.

'Anyway, your Mr Olivera's rigged up one of my combines fitted with one of those things,' he jabbed his finger at the Kronos on its pedestal in the centre of the table. 'It can recognize individual infected grains and zap 'em no matter how fast they're pouring through a chute.' He broke off and looked uncertainly at Carl. 'You'd better explain from here, Mr Olivera. It's all a mite too technical for me.'

Carl stood up. 'Thanks, Theo. The reason the Kronos is ideally suited for the job is its speed. There's not a silicon-based chip in the world that can process camera input data and operate lasers as fast as the Kronos. And it's not just ergot infected grain that it can deal with. There's all the other nasty contaminations that cereals suffer from, all the impurities that can get into stocks – mice droppings, that sort of thing. Each year the Soviet Union and the EC has fifteen million tonnes of stored grain go rotten on them. We've already demonstrated the combine to the EC and they're impressed. The new standards that technology can achieve today will become the normal standards that society expects tomorrow. Theo's Type 19 combine harvester is the only machine in the world that can meet those standards which means that there's money to be made with this new application. Real money.'

'That's why that chip can't be allowed to go to Japan,' Draggon interrupted. 'And that's why I'm prepared to pitch in with your buyout bid with a 33 per cent stake.'

Jack Pullen was the first to break the silence that followed. 'That's 1.6 million ecus,' he said. 'A million sterling.'

Theo Draggon fastened his gaze on Pullen. 'That's what I'm prepared to go to, lad.'

'You can put your hands on a million?'

'I can. And I can pull in more if needed.' Draggon looked around at the others, his expression bordering on contempt. 'Question is, can you lot come up with the other two million?'

5

Beverley added up the list of commitments a second time and looked in turn at Carl and Draggon. 'Still the same,' she said, 'a 25 per cent shortfall.'

The three were sitting at corner seats in the hotel's bar. The meeting had been over for three hours. The others had gone home to their wives and mortgages.

'So you'll have to take my bank on board,' said Draggon, inhaling hard on half a metre of Havana.

'No!' said Beverley emphatically.

Draggon eyed her through a cloud of expensive smoke. His expression suggested that he disliked a woman having a say in business affairs. 'Why not, lass?' He managed to sound both patronising and insulting. Theodore Draggon had a first-class honours degree in rubbing people up the wrong way. He could also turn on devastating charm when it suited him. Right now it didn't.

'Because that'll give you control,' Beverley retorted. 'And please don't call me lass.'

'Control? With 33 per cent? Where did you learn your arithmetic, lass?'

Beverley controlled her temper. She saw that Carl was about to speak but jumped in quickly. She didn't need him or anyone else to defend her. 'Because your 33 per cent plus your bank's 25 per cent will give you effective control. You said that they won't want a seat on the board which means that you'll have their voting clout behind you. Right, Mr Draggon?'

The Yorkshireman carefully tapped ash off his cigar. 'Okay, lass. So use your bank to make up the shortfall. But I know that shower, they'll want a seat on the board *and* financial control. For 20 per cent they'll expect to run the company.'

Beverley picked up her vodka and Slimline, realized that her shaking hand would betray her boiling anger and set the glass down with studied care. 'Listen, Mr Draggon,' she said slowly. 'None of those men you've met this afternoon could be called rich, and yet such is their faith in our company that they are all sitting at home right now with their wives going through hell having to explain why they're going to mortgage their homes up to the hilt for this buyout. Even Carl is committing himself to quarter of a million which I know he can't afford. This is their big chance to have some sort of control over their destiny and I'll be damned if I'm going to be party to any hole-in-corner devious little schemes that gives control of Nano Systems to you and your anonymous cronies!'

Carl was about to speak but was silenced by a glare from Beverley.

'My devious schemes are never little, lass,' Draggon observed. 'You've not signed one of your nice little letters of intent and put yourself down for a percentage, therefore you won't have to be party to anything. It's money that talks in business, not high-flown passions.'

'That's not necessary, Theo,' said Carl angrily. 'Beverley has worked hard getting this meeting organized. The whole thing was her idea in the first place.'

Draggon inhaled on his cigar. 'So she should come in with a percentage,' he replied, talking as though Beverley wasn't present. 'Put her money where that sexy mouth is – no money, no vote.'

Beverley thrust her papers into her briefcase, snapped it shut and stood. 'I'll come in with a percentage, Mr Draggon,' she said calmly but with suppressed anger blazing in her eyes. 'It'll have to be the minimum under the consortium's investment rules, 1 per cent, but I'll raise it. Good evening, gentlemen.' With that she marched out of the bar.

Carl made a move to call her back but Draggon restrained him. 'Let the silly bitch go,' he said gruffly.

'Listen,' said Carl threateningly. 'If we're to become partners, you do not call Beverley Laine a silly bitch. She's a hard-working, conscientious woman. She's paying for her son at university and trying to keep up a mortgage. There's no way she could afford to come in with 1 per cent.'

Draggon's demeanour changed now that Beverley was gone. The blunt, plain-speaking Yorkshireman became more sophisticated. Even his Yorkshire accent slipped away in large measure. He chuckled and stubbed out his cigar. 'Okay. Beverley Laine's anything but a silly bitch. I wanted to see how you'd react to me calling her one.' He looked speculatively at Carl. 'You taken her to bed yet?'

'It's none of your goddamn business, but it so happens that I haven't. Nor have I entertained the idea.'

'You're a fucking liar, Olivera.'

Carl checked the automatic protest that sprang to his lips. He hesitated and nodded ruefully. 'Yes,' he admitted. 'It's crossed my mind, but that's all.'

'Looks like we'd better keep her around then. Give her a job that suits her. So what does she hope to get out of all of this if it goes ahead?'

'She'd like to be the company secretary.'

Draggon's rough-spoken Yorkshireman staged a fast comeback. 'Bollocks,' he said succinctly.


Beverley sat in the hotel's car park, clutching the steering wheel of her elderly Metro, grappling to bring her seething anger under control before starting the engine.

*Arrogant, conceited bastard!*

The way Draggon had smirked through his cigar smoke when she said that she would come in with 1 per cent. By God, she would, too. Just to show the bastard. No . . . no . . . more than show him . . . to vote against him. She was at an advantage. The members of the consortium were her colleagues. She worked with them. She could lobby them. Get enough votes on her side to wipe the smile off Mr Theodore Draggon's face.

*Hang on, Bev. One per cent of three million. Knock off a couple of zeros, thirty thousand quid. Shit!*

Maybe a drunken valuer might conclude that her semi on the outskirts of Bognor Regis was worth enough for her bank to go to a top-up loan. But thirty thousand . . . hell . . . even if they agreed, it would pile another three hundred a month plus on to her repayments. She groaned and rested her forehead on the steering wheel. Just keeping her head above water and keeping her bank account in the black was an eternal struggle, but things had been easier of late. And now she was thinking of pitching herself right back to square one. Then there was Paul to consider . . . she couldn't do it. This time sheer iron will and determination was not going to be enough. Money did not talk, it shouted, deafeningly and defeatingly.

Resignation to the equation's inevitable solution had a calming effect on her.

*At least you tried, Bev.*

She straightened and turned the key in the ignition. The engine cranked slowly. Like everything else on the car, the battery was a fully unpaid-up member of the Sicksville Residents' Association. The sudden roar of the engine when it caught unleashed her temper like a fuel rod shoved too far into a nuclear reactor.

*I'll show the bastard!*

She gunned the engine, spun the barely street-legal tyres, and shot out of the hotel's car park. She clipped a group of recently emptied Brighton Corporation wheelie bins, innocently guarding the entrance, scattering them in the Metro's wake like massacred Daleks.


## 6

## 1993

From the beginning of the new year Beverley worked with demonic passion on pulling the buyout consortium together. Consortium business took over at 5.30 p.m. every evening when her word-processor went to work turning out reports and seemingly endless correspondence. Her bank manager caved in under the bombardment and agreed to a second mortgage on her house provided she surrendered her life assurance policies to the bank. She was on a financial tightrope without a safety net but her schedule left her little time for worrying. She would arrive home at after midnight most nights, throw together some sort of meal, and crawl into bed. Two male friends she had been stringing along with casual on-off affairs gave up on her and seeped into the sand. No great loss because she had never really cared for them anyway. The great thing was that she would be a shareholder in the new company.

Suddenly everything started coming together: cash flow forecasts were accepted; letters of intent became cheques; and relentlessly-bullied solicitors completed their paperwork. The final meeting of the consortium was fixed. It was to be two meetings rolled into one: the formal winding-up of the buyout consortium followed by the inaugural meeting of the share-holders of Nano Systems (1993) Plc. Beverley waited until two days before the meeting and started some intense but discreet lobbying. Carl was her first target as they worked late, photo-copying the agenda and initial prospectus.

'You're going to have to stand as managing director, Carl,' she said, fitting a new toner cartridge into the Canon copier and slamming it shut. 'I'll nominate you and I know Macé Pilleau will second you.'

Carl paused in his task of stapling papers together. 'I'm not sure, Bev. I'd be happy to remain technical director.'

'What do you mean, you're not sure? It's what you want, isn't it?'

'I rather fancy that Theo Draggon has some ideas about the MD's position.' He resumed stapling and avoided looking at her.

Beverley set the copier to get on with its work and sat opposite Carl. 'Isn't managing director what you want? You could still be in control of technical development of the Kronos.'

'I'll go along with whatever the majority of shareholders want,' Carl replied evasively.

'For Christ's sake, Carl, that's letting things happen. If you want to get anywhere in this world, you have got to *make* things happen.'

He stopped work and met Beverley's gaze. The events of the past four weeks had changed her. He had always known that there was steel beneath that feminine exterior; now it was out in the open. She was more poised, more forthright. The loyal 'certainly, Mr Olivera' secretary was gone forever. That was no bad thing. It had all been an act; this was the real Beverley Laine showing through. She was even dressing better now. Smart, well-cut skirts and jackets with matching accessories that did not come from C & A.

'Okay, Bev. So what do you propose doing to *make* things happen?'

'As chairman of the consortium, you'll be winding it up. Right?'

Carl nodded.

'Then you'll open the inaugural meeting and be acting chairman of the new company until the voting and appointment of new directors and company officers. That's the procedure. I've checked with our solicitors.'

'That's right,' Carl agreed. 'I could be in the chairman's seat for no more than five minutes.'

'You'll be in the chairman's seat for a damn sight longer than that if I have anything to do with it,' Beverley replied grimly. 'And being in the chairman's seat will give you a psychological advantage. Before the voting starts I'll propose a clause in the draft articles of association that combines the job of managing director and chairman. It's having an inept non-executive chairman that got Nano Systems into a mess and I shall say so. You can't have a non-executive managing director so that should spike Draggon's nomination for chairmanship. He won't want to spend his working day with Nano Systems instead of his corn-cutting company.'

'Do you still want to be company secretary, Bev?'

'Of course I do. Christ! What a bloody silly question. I've sunk everything into this venture. I can't afford *not* to be company secretary.'

'As have we all,' said Carl dolefully. 'You're the last person I should be stating the obvious to, but the trouble with life, Bev, is that we rarely get what we want. Even someone as determined as you.'

'Not if you work at making things happen,' Beverley replied curtly.

7

Beverley worked hard at trying to make things happen in the run up to the meeting. Her colleagues listened politely to her aggressive lobbying on Carl's behalf, and even agreed with her views, but she got the distinct impression that deals had already been struck.

It was the men's room she was up against; of course, the bloody men's room. Women in loos made small talk whereas men used their loos as forums for scheming and plotting and cracking obscene, sexist jokes. For women, peeing was a private affair, conducted in private stalls that encouraged private thoughts. One could not hold confidential discussions around washbasins because invariably a stall was occupied by someone whose identity was uncertain. By contrast, men's urinals were latterday men's clubs; their safe haven from women, where they could not only lower their guard against the chance remarks that would label them sexist, but were expected to do so; a place for pricks to make their last bigoted stand in a world where women were supposed to be equal; where leaks from among the leaks could not be blamed on women and therefore men kept men's room confidences to themselves. The day before the meeting, Theo Draggon visited Nano Systems and retired to the men's toilets for a conference with three managers and Carl.

The following evening Beverley appeared calm as she took her seat at the conference table in the former chairman's office. She even exchanged jokes with the solicitors representing Nano Systems' old shareholders, and graciously accepted compliments on her new outfit. She looked good and should have felt good but inwardly she was experiencing a mixture of despair and frustration. She had worked herself to a standstill, mortgaged herself up to the hilt, and for what? So that these pompous prats could deny her promotion to company secretary.

Despite his reassurances to the contrary, Theodore Draggon brought his merchant bank voting fodder along. He sat opposite Beverley and lit a Havana. She wanted to reach across the table and ram it down his smug throat. Everyone was present by 7.55 p.m. – twenty men and one woman.

Carl opened the meeting at 8 p.m. sharp and got straight down to business. At 8.15 p.m. the buyout consortium was wound up and the business of the reconstituted company opened with Carl as acting chairman.

After the formal share transfer, the solicitors acting for both sides withdrew. Beverley intervened as planned with her proposal that the company combine the roles of chairman and managing director. Carl seconded it and, to Beverley's astonishment, her motion was accepted without argument and passed on a unanimous vote.

'In that case,' said Carl, making a note on his agenda. 'I am now calling for nominations for chairman and managing director.'

'I propose Miss Beverley Laine,' said Theodore Draggon promptly.

There were five seconders but Carl got in first.

For the rest of her life Beverley would relive those moments, trying to recall her shock and disorientation. It seemed that a trapdoor had opened beneath her. But instead of falling, she was floundering weightlessly like a stunned astronaut, not knowing which way was up or down.

'Any other nominations?'

Someone said: 'Carl Olivera.' Dear God, it was her voice.

'Seconded by?'

There were no takers.

'All those in favour of Miss Beverley Laine becoming chairman and managing director of Nano Systems?'

Eighteen hands went up. Beverley was supposed to count them but she seemed to be paralyzed. Carl counted them instead.

'Eighteen in favour,' he reported. He was smiling at Beverley but she could only stare dumbly back at him.

'All those against?'

Silence.

'Eighteen in favour, none against, and one abstention,' Carl reported. 'Miss Laine is our new boss.'

There was a burst of applause and cheers. Tears pricked Beverley's eyes when she saw that Theodore Draggon was clapping more vigorously than anyone while grinning broadly at her bewildered expression. Someone nudged her. She rose to her feet. In response to cries of 'speech' she managed to blurt out some words of acceptance that she was unable to recall later. Carl relinquished his seat and made everyone move along so that he was at Beverley's side when she took her place at the top of the table. It was a supportive gesture that would set the seal on their later relationship: Carl would always be at her side.

'Nominations for company secretary,' he whispered.

Despite her inner turmoil, the professional in Beverley took over, enabling her to suppress her nervousness and conduct the rest of the meeting with brisk aplomb. Carl was formally voted in as technical director and her deputy. By the time she brought the meeting to a close an hour later, she had what she considered an ideal board consisting of six full-time directors and two non-executive directors; a representative of Nano Systems' bank and Theodore Draggon who was the first to pump her hand when Carl produced champagne and the corks started popping.

'I knew you were the man for the job the moment I clapped eyes on you, lass,' said Draggon warmly, now the genial Yorkshireman. Despite the crowd milling around Beverley to congratulate her, he was reluctant to let go of her hand.

Beverley thanked him profusely and tried to disengage her hand.

'Nay, lass, thank yourself. With you at the helm, I feel my brass is safe.'

'Well,' said Beverley, matching Draggon's smile. 'As managing director, I'm now going to pull rank on you and give you an order. Disobey it at your peril.'

Her tone was friendly. Nevertheless Draggon released her hand and looked worried. 'What's that, lass?'

'If you value keeping your balls in working order, don't ever call me lass again.'

Beverley's fellow directors laughed uproariously at Draggon's crestfallen expression. He recovered quickly and smiled good-humouredly. 'It's a deal, Bev.'


Arriving back at her darkened house at the end of that momentous evening was a letdown for Beverley. She was on a nerve-tingling high and felt a pang of regret that there was no one to share her excitement. She had a desperate need to talk to someone so, despite the lateness of the hour, she telephoned her son's hall of residence at Bath University. There was music and laughter in the background when she got through. She told him excitedly what had happened but he did not seem interested. Beverley heard a girl calling out. She tried hard not to be jealous and in so doing agreed to send Paul some money to cover the tax and insurance on his motorbike. He had already wheedled most of the purchase price out of her.

As she pulled on her nightdress, her loneliness and the awesomeness of her new responsibilities suddenly hit her. She sat on the bed and cried.


## 8

The first month of the new order was unpleasant. The task of ridding the company of loyal but unnecessary staff whom Beverley had worked with for ten years fell to her. At one point she became so unhappy with the whole sordid business that she would have resigned were it not for the solid support of Carl and her fellow directors. Then there was a drastic cost-cutting exercise. At the end of four weeks of firings, of cancelling company car-leasing contracts, of slashing expenses and of renting out any unwanted buildings as warehouses, Beverley was mentally and physically drained. But she had ruthlessly trimmed Nano Systems' overheads and salary bill by 30 per cent. Other than the sackings, meeting the challenge head-on had bolstered her confidence and made her look forward to the future. It had certainly given the company's bankers confidence because they increased their overdraft facilities.

'Not bad going for your first month, Bev,' Carl congratulated her over a drink in the pub.

'Sales and marketing next,' Beverley replied. 'Then we tackle funding the work needed for knocking the Kronos into shape for mass production.'

Carl remained silent. Beverley knew all about the horrendous problems of getting sufficient memory working in the Kronos. For every hundred of the miracle chips made, less than 1 per cent worked, and of that 1 per cent, less than half had a large enough neural network in working order to pose a threat to advanced silicon chips such as the transputer. Nano Systems had the product; what they lacked was quantity.

'So what dazzling ideas are you harbouring on marketing?' Carl inquired at length.

Beverley smiled and sipped her drink. 'A few that might crunch some influential toes.'

## 9

Theodore Draggon was not in the best of humour. He refused Beverley's invitation to sit. Instead he dropped a document in front of her and leaned belligerently over her desk.

'You mind telling me what the hell that is, Bev?'

Beverley glanced at the form. 'You can read, Theo. It's a licence application to use one hundred Kronos microprocessors. Serial numbers – '

'I can see that! My chief buyer at my Petworth depot tells me he sent an order through to you for a hundred Kronos and instead he gets one of these forms! So what's going on?'

'Simple. We're not selling the Kronos, we're selling licences to use it. The idea is that we retain total control over the chips in the field. They remain our property. It's a system that's worked with software for a number of years therefore I see no reason why it shouldn't be applied to hardware. Also we're carefully vetting all our licensees. Only large, responsible, corporate users such as your company are granted licences. If anything goes wrong with a Kronos in service, Nano Systems undertakes to replace it at no cost to the licensee. We also undertake to replace existing Kronos chips as improved ones become available.'

'But why?'

'So that we have total control over the Kronos,' said Beverley earnestly. 'They remain our property at all times. It's the only real asset this company's got, Theo, that's why you came in with a holding in the first place. You saw that it was something that needed protecting. It's only by licensing to corporate users who will use the Kronos in large, integrated applications, that we can hope to prevent it falling into the wrong hands. Carl reckons that anyone making a serious start on reverse engineering the Kronos will need at least a hundred. That means they'll have to buy a hundred of your combines. It may not stop the smart alecs in Silicon Valley and Taiwan, but at least it'll slow them down until we get the patents made 100 per cent water-tight.'

'Has anyone else accepted the idea?'

'We've signed up thirty licensees this month alone: British Telecom; Telecom France; ICI; security systems manufacturers, and so on. The first half-yearly figures will show that we're going to break even.'

Draggon calmed down. 'But it's going to make it difficult when you're ready for mass production,' he pointed out. 'Carl's keen to get his Nanopad on the market.'

'We all are, Theo.' Beverley smiled knowingly. 'But I don't see any problems. We'll be pushing the Kronos as the chip that money can't buy. How about that for a slogan?'

The Yorkshireman stared at Beverley. 'The chip that money can't buy?' he echoed. He thought for a moment and broke into a grin. 'That's bloody brilliant. What PR genius came up with that?'

'You're talking to her,' said Beverley modestly.


## 10

### 1994

'It's best if you're naked, Miss Laine.'

'What!'

Leon Dexter's Adam's apple bobbed nervously. He looked anxiously at Carl for support but his boss merely looked away to hide a face that was in danger of breaking into a broad smile.

There was no danger of Beverley smiling. She glared at Leon who was standing beside the open circular hatch of his total virtual reality chamber. The huge device was about the size and shape of a locomotive boiler and looked about as far removed from the science of nano-biological engineering as it was possible to imagine. It even had rows of rivets and was set up on a steel cradle at one end of the concrete section industrial building that was being converted into Nano Systems' new laboratory complex.

Beverley had given top priority during the previous year to

building up a new research team. She had head-hunted aggressively among established companies along England's M4 little Silicon Valley, mopping up some of the best microbiological research graduates from the universities before the Americans got to them, and had even recruited from Japan and the Soviet Union. Hiring Leon Dexter and setting up the complex had swallowed Nano Systems' slender profits from the previous year and had led to a large overdraft but the investment was essential.

Leon was a prize catch. He was an unsmiling, undernourished beanpole thirty-year-old software scientist who appeared to live on apples and little else. His DNA genome molecule had provided him with an elongated skeleton as a framework for pale, stretched skin, but had forgotten to insert flesh between the two. Beverley had recruited him at Carl's insistence because he was a world authority on total virtual reality. The TVR chamber was his brainchild and was the first of its type. Like all obsessed geniuses, Leon could stay awake for a week if necessary when confronted with a challenging problem.

'What do you mean, naked?' Beverley demanded.

'Clothes in contact with your skin provide external sensory input that distorts the total virtual reality of the chamber,' Leon explained.

Right now Beverley had a challenging problem of her own: whether to strip off in front of two men and enter this strange chamber to find out first-hand how effective it was, or to bottle out. Well, she certainly wasn't going to do the latter.

'What if I go in wearing my underwear and take them off in the chamber?'

'They'll get wet,' said Leon.

'Well, I daresay I can cope with wet pants,' Beverley observed. 'Where do I get changed?'

'There's nowhere, Bev,' said Carl, keeping a straight face. 'You crossed a changing room off the budget. I could get you some overalls so that you could undress in the ladies' toilets.'

'Don't bother.' With an air of unconcern, Beverley quickly undressed down to her bra and briefs and turned to face Carl and Leon. Her stony glare served two purposes: it effectively stifled any temptation that the two men had to ogle, and it cloaked her guilt-ridden tingle of sexual excitement at being legitimately half-naked in front of them, especially Carl. 'Okay. Now what?'

Leon produced two children's inflatable arm bands that he had adapted to fit around the wrist. Beverley held her hands out while he fitted them in place. He inflated them carefully so that they gripped Beverley's wrists as gently as possible without being dislodged.

'Can you feel them, Miss Laine?'

Beverley closed her eyes experimentally and shook her head.

'Okay. We're ready to go,' said Leon turning to a jury-rigged control console against the wall. He touched a key and a soft red light came on in the chamber. 'You simply lie down with the back of your neck resting on the support. Don't worry, you can control everything from inside, but for your first trip it would be best if you let me run everything from here.'

His use of the word 'trip' sounded ominous. Beverley allowed Carl to take her hand and guide her up the steps to the hatch. Taking care not to disturb the wristbands, she grasped a handle and swung her lithe body through the outer and inner hatches feet first. She sat on the edge of the inner hatch with her feet dangling in the water that filled the two- by three-metre capsule to waist depth.

The inner capsule of the TVR chamber was much smaller than its outside dimensions suggested. The difference was due to half a metre of soundproofing material sandwiched between the outer shell and the inner glass-fibre capsule. The capsule's resin surface had a vivid blue gel coat that made the water look inviting. It was like being in a giant, enclosed jacuzzi. There was a shaped padded headrest on each side of the hatch. Both positions were provided with control panels on swivel arms so that they could be pushed out of the way. Beverley recalled that Leon's drawings had shown that the chamber had been designed for two observers.

'Okay, Bev?' asked Carl behind her, sounding concerned.

'Fine. If I'd known I'd be doing this, I would've brought some soap.'

'But would you let me do your back, I ask myself?'

'Ask nicely and I'll consider it.' With that riposte, Beverley lowered herself gingerly into the tepid water. The underwater krypton lights made her skin look pallid and death-like.

'Voice check,' said Leon's voice from a concealed speaker.

'Working,' Beverley replied. 'It's odd but I can hardly feel the water.'

'Its temperature is maintained at 40 degrees centigrade. That's just above blood temperature so that you won't be aware of the water's contact when submerged. You can close the hatches yourself by touching the red control key.'

'*Bon voyage*, Bev,' said Carl encouragingly and he moved clear.

Beverley touched the key and the two hatches closed with soft hisses. The acoustics in the chamber changed, making her voice sound flat and unnatural when she spoke to Leon. 'Okay. What now?'

'You get 'em off,' said Carl's voice.

Beverley suppressed a nervous laugh. The buoyancy of the wristbands made wriggling out of her briefs awkward but she managed it and hung them on the inner hatch.

'Now your bra,' Carl instructed.

An awful thought occurred to Beverley. She tried peering beyond the bright circle of halogen lights at the far end of the three-metre-long chamber. 'Hey, you two! Is there a TV camera in here?'

'There is, Miss Laine,' Leon admitted. 'But I swear it's not switched on. Mr Olivera is trying to wind you up.'

Beverley took off her bra. 'Right. I'm now sans underwear. Sans everything except the wristbands. What now?'

'Lie back and think of England,' said Carl.

'Lie back with your neck on the support and allow yourself to float,' Leon instructed. 'The water's 20 per cent saline so you're at virtually Dead Sea buoyancy.'

Beverley rested the back of her neck in the padded cradle and stretched out. Her body rose to the horizontal without effort. The touch of the tepid water was so gentle that she hardly felt it as it entered her ears and soaked her dark, ringleted hair around her temples. The sensation of being completely naked was pleasant. It reminded Beverley of the time when, as a teenager in her home town of Walton-on-Thames, she had swum naked at night in a friend's swimming pool for a dare.

'Just let your arms and legs relax and take up their natural positions,' said Leon. 'Remember what I told you: the water must be perfectly still. Don't use any muscles at all, don't talk, don't try to resist. You can't possibly sink.'

Beverley floated, her arms slightly away from her body, her hands supported by the wristbands. She felt her legs drifting apart and was about to automatically close them but remembered Leon's instructions. The ripples and their gentle rocking died away and the water became still. The only contact with her body that she was aware of was the slight pressure of the headrest on the back of the neck. She realized then the importance of being naked.

'Getting a slight water disturbance reading caused by your breathing,' said Leon when a minute had passed. 'I'm now going to enrich the oxygen in your air supply to 40 per cent. That will reduce your breathing and have a slight hallucinative effect. It'll enhance the sensory deprivation effect but that's all to the good.'

Beverley felt her breathing become shallower. She was now perfectly relaxed and still. It was a divine sensation. She glanced down and saw that only her breasts, hands and toes were out of the water.

Then came Leon's calm, reassuring voice again. 'Lowering the headrest a few centimetres so that it's just touching your head. The infra-red lasers are now locked on to your eyes so all you have to do is blink twice when the headrest is at a comfortable height.'

The tiny stab of fear when her head started sinking disappeared the instant she felt the reassurance of the water's support. She blinked twice and the headrest stopped. Beverley was now floating with no part of her body in contact with anything other than the warm, salt-enriched water. She was drifting dreamlessly in a state of total relaxation that her body had not experienced since she had been in her mother's womb.

'Fine,' said Leon. 'Everything's set for total sensory deprivation. Blink twice if you're ready. Just call out if you feel panicky and we'll stop.'

Beverley blinked twice.

'If at any time during the trip you want to pull out, just speak. Blink twice if you understand.'

Again Beverley blinked.

The halogen lamps dimmed and went out.

When the circle of lights faded from her retinas, Beverley was in a darkness that was outside her experience. Even worse was the complete and utter absence of sound. Human beings often experience total darkness but never total silence. Only death brings total silence. They go through life with the sound of their heartbeat, the surge of blood in their ears, and the rasp of air in their lungs as constant company. Only in the stillness of the night are they aware of their breathing and the pounding of their pulse, reassuring and yet bleak reminders of their mortality. Leon had briefed her on what to expect but she was unprepared for the devastating terror of brainscream silence. Knowing what was happening did not lessen the terrible impact. Ultra-sensitive microphones in the chamber were picking up every tiny sound and playing them back at the same volume through out-of-phase speakers that cancelled the sounds out. Beverley clunked her jaws together, but even that sound was processed out by the ingenious audio system. She felt the impact of her teeth colliding, just as she could feel her heart hammering against her ribs. But that was all.

No sound.

No light.

Nothing.

The womb analogy fell down on one point: her brain, deprived of sensory information, was frantically searching for order and rhythm. The world had vanished, therefore that most easily-deceived of all human organs sought to build one, seizing on building blocks as flimsy as flashing optic nerves in a vain attempt to build a Tetris wall of hard reality.

That was the substance of TVR.

It had started ten years before with the development in the

USA of flight simulator helmets which provided computer-generated landscape images in front of the pilot's eyes that varied with turns of the pilot's head. That early work had culminated in the flood of cheap virtual reality games helmets that kids could plug into their computer games consoles and so plug into surrealist worlds of space monsters, and dungeons and dragons complete with 3-D stereo vision and virtual reality Ambisonic surround sound. Beverley had once played an illegally-imported adult virtual reality interactive game with Carl at his house – both of them wearing grotesque plastic helmets. On looking down at herself she had seen huge mammaries complete with pulsating Technicolor nipples. Lower down was a bloated, throbbing pudenda. On turning her head towards a sound, she saw a slavering monster sporting a mighty erection bearing down on her. It was too much for Beverley's sexual guilt complexes. She had promptly removed her helmet and refused to play any more despite Carl's protests that virtual reality software was begging for a super-processor such as the Kronos.

And now the ultimate in virtual reality was Leon Dexter's TVR chamber.

She lost sense of time. In its search for order, her brain breathed vivid life into past images. They rose up and swam before her. Images sharp and poignant that she thought were gone forever: her first serious boyfriend, Marshall Tate, and the way his lank hair fell across his forehead. Fearful images that would always be with her: crouching in terror in her hall, clutching two-year-old Paul to her breast while her roaring-drunk husband battered down the front door. She was about to cry out when she realized that a detached voice was whispering to her: 'Activating the laser remote manipulators, Miss Laine.'

Beverley opened her eyes and saw two cubes of shimmering light near her hands. They were made up of several superimposed grids of low-energy gas laser beams. Where the beams intersected they created strange, iridescent interference patterns of constantly changing colours like light reflected off a compact disc. The cubes moved to her hands and engulfed them like strange gloves of light.

'Wriggle your fingers.'

Beverley did so. The tiny rod-like beams in the glowing cubes flickered and danced in harmony with the movement of her fingers.

'That's working fine, Miss Laine. I'm putting the tool menu hologram up now. There's only one tool active at the moment. Use your right hand.'

A ghostly hologram menu appeared in the air above Beverley's chest. She pointed a finger to select the one active box on the menu's listing and a device like a surgical probe appeared in her hand. She knew there was nothing there and yet the strange computer-generated tool possessed three dimensions and even surface texture; the iridescent laser beams danced on the probe's blunt edge as she turned it towards her.

'Now relax and I'll bring up the Kronos hologram in a few minutes,' said Leon's voice. 'I'll bring it up slowly to minimize any shock effects. Blink twice if you understand.'

By now a lesser person would be clamouring to be let out of the chamber but Beverley steeled herself and blinked twice. The tomb-like stillness and darkness returned. The images came flooding back, hauntingly real. Then a strange flickering before her and they were gone. Beverley waited and watched. Knowing what to expect helped.

At least, she thought she knew what to expect.

At first she was vaguely aware of being surrounded by dark waving tendrils that reminded her of underwater films of forests of kelp. The illumination level increased and she saw that the fronds of seaweed were the string-like protein motor neurons of the Kronos. The hologram was generated from a real Kronos via an electron microscope interface. Inside the real Kronos was a nano-machine probe that would replicate at the molecular level every movement of her hand. Each frond represented a single bit of memory. She tried turning her head slightly, first to the left and then to the right. The invisible infra-red lasers monitoring the position of her head and eyes reacted accordingly and re-mapped the three-dimensional hologram image so that it seemed she was in the middle of the strange forest. Far from being frightened, Beverley was overawed by the scene around her – she was actually inside a Kronos microprocessor and seeing its motor neurons at first hand with the naked eye! The movement of the waving fronds was due to the nutrient fluid being pumped through the Kronos. They were waving about because they were incorrectly formed. She looked up and saw what looked like a mirror image of the scene about her – fronds were hanging down and moving about in the flow of nutrient. A few, perhaps one in a hundred, were perfectly formed as a continuous link with pulses of light flowing through them. She reached out with the probe and grasped the nearest unjoined neuron. Moving the probe along the protein string to grip it by the end was simple. She saw a broken protein hanging down and pushed the two ends together. The tips formed an immediate molecular bond, and light started pulsing through them.

The motor neuron was repaired.

Then she witnessed the curious knock-on effect that was baffling Carl and Leon even though it was something that worked to their advantage. Several hundred immature neurons around the repaired nerve appeared to be galvanized by its activity, for they too became rigid and formed bonds. Beverley's repair of one cell had triggered the repair of many.

But more important, the dream of true nano-engineering, with man directly manipulating molecules, was a reality.

'Okay,' she said suddenly. 'I've seen enough.'

The strange inner world of the Kronos vanished abruptly. Leon had the foresight to increase the halogen lights gradually. Beverley sat up in the water, blinking as the lights brightened. She drew her knees to her chest and looked thoughtfully around the blue interior of the capsule for a few moments.

'Are you okay, Miss Laine?'

'Fine,' Beverley said and touched the key that opened the hatches. Carl poked his head into the capsule.

'So what do you think?'

'Bloody fantastic. With six of these things working round the clock, we could go into mass production of the Kronos.'

Carl looked doubtful. 'This is only a prototype. There's still a lot of bugs in the system.'

'Well this particular bug happens to be stark naked. Do you mind finding me a large towel?'

The year marked the turning point for Nano Systems when profits began to show a sharp upward curve thanks to the success of Draggon Industries' Model 19 combine harvester and Beverley's astute planning.

In addition to her business skills, she was proving very good at getting her way while getting the best out of people and winning their respect at the same time. She used suggestion, encouragement and occasional cajoling – rarely outright browbeating. More often than not she acted as a buffer between clashing personalities. Only when there was a serious threat to the well-being of Nano Systems did she resort to giving direct orders. Her rare displays of anger on such occasions always ensured that her wishes were obeyed. If she had a fault, it was her blindspot concerning mass production and exploitation of the Kronos.

The year saw a major battle with Theo Draggon and his bank who wanted Nano Systems to license production of the Kronos chip to other manufacturers now that Leon Dexter's new nano-engineering techniques had given the chip a phenomenal memory capacity. Making it more readily available and cheaper, Theo Draggon argued, would head off the abortive attempts by specialist companies to reverse engineer the chip and produce clones.

Beverley suspected that what Draggon was really looking for was a short-term increase in the value of his holding. She had been adamant that Nano Systems should retain total control over the Kronos. Hiving off the superchip might improve the company's financial gearing but her aim was for Nano Systems to become an industrial giant on a par with corporations such as Philips and Toshiba, and she wasn't afraid to say so.

'You'll never match them,' Draggon declared at a particularly stormy board meeting. 'Those companies are into the mass consumer market. Nano Systems is a small, specialist company that happens to be sitting on a priceless commercial commodity that it is consistently refusing to exploit.'

Although Beverley's determined stance carried the voting, the majority was five, her lowest ever. It was the first time there had been a split in the board since she had taken over.

'Draggon's right, Bev,' said Carl across the boardroom table after the meeting. 'We're missing a chance to make millions.'

'So you think we should license third party manufacturers?'

'No,' said Carl seriously. 'But it's now time to take a look at my Nanopad idea.'

Beverley stared at the papers strewn across the boardroom table.

'You were keen on it once,' Carl reminded her.

'But it means hundreds of Kronos becoming available for reverse engineering sweatshops in Korea and Taiwan.'

Carl sighed. 'Bev, I keep telling you, it would be impossible. Please listen to me. Today you scraped through with five votes. The same issue's going to come up time and time again because the bank sees a chance of big money being made, and there'll be tremendous pressure from industry and government. Eventually you're going to lose.'

'Getting a working pre-production model ready would tie-up too much of your time, Carl. The company can't afford to lose you.'

Carl hesitated, uncertain how Beverley would react to what he had to say. 'It's ready now, Bev,' he admitted. 'I've kept development going on it.'

'But the screen was hopeless!'

'The pre-production model uses the new hi-res fibre optic screen made by Toshiba.'

'And they're prepared to supply it to third parties?'

'Yes.' Carl leaned forward. 'Listen, Bev,' he said earnestly. 'My reading of the market is that the time is ripe for a new portable as revolutionary as the Nanopad. We go ahead now and the world will beat a path to our door. And don't forget it was you who was keen for us to get into the consumer market long before the buyout.'

Beverley realized that Carl had neatly manoeuvred her into a corner. She would have to relent. If she didn't, she would lose his support and she would be finished as Nano Systems' chief executive. The thought of losing control of her beloved company made her feel sick. 'All right, suppose we *do* go ahead with the Nanopad? Would it be possible to make its Kronos an integral part of the machine? To make it irremovable?'

Carl thought for a moment. 'Sure. It could be bonded straight onto the main board without a socket and the whole board could be encapsulated in synthetic resin. That and some hidden self-destruct software would make the chip impossible to open or use in any other application. The only part of the chip that would be visible would be its solar window.'

Beverley capitulated. 'Okay, then. That's what we'll do. A good, old-fashioned British compromise. But we retain 100 per cent control over everything. We'll make the Nanopad ourselves using as many bought-out finished components as possible. We'll package it, promote it and market it ourselves. It'll be a strict in-house operation all the way down the line.'

## 12

Carl's Nanopad went into a limited production run of a hundred units in the autumn of 1995. Only three of the pre-production batch of machines failed the exhaustive tests that were thrown at them. That Nano Systems were branching into consumer electronics aroused considerable interest with the result that over a hundred science journalists and several television news crews crowded into the hotel reception room for the official launch. Rumours of the new wonder portable computer had been rife for some time.

'The Kronos superchip is to be our workhorse processor for all our new products.' Carl explained to the gathering. 'The chip has a one gigabyte memory and, as you can see, it is no larger than a small playing card.' There was a dud Kronos included in each press pack distributed to the journalists present. 'One Kronos can store the entire contents of the *Encyclopedia Britannica* and have room left over for the *Oxford English Dictionary*. In fact we have plans to produce a pocket *Britannica* and a pocket *OED* in the near future, but for the time being we'll be supplying Nanopads for use as databases, very powerful databases.' Carl held up a Nanopad. 'For example, this one ordered by the Home Office for evaluation by the police is loaded with the names and addresses of every registered vehicle owner in the UK. The next version will include the registration details of every vehicle in the EC.'

A science journalist had an awkward question: 'You had problems with low percentages of working motor neurons in production chips, Mr Olivera. What percentage of working neurons are you getting now?'

'If we supply a half gigabyte Kronos, then its capacity will be a guaranteed half gigabyte,' Carl replied evenly. 'If it's a Class A Kronos with the full gigabyte, then that's what it will be.'

'With respect, Mr Olivera, that's not an answer to my question.'

'We're achieving 10 per cent,' Carl answered. 'Ninety-nine per cent of the neurons in each chip fail to grow owing to impurities in the nutrient feeds during production. Using virtual reality techniques during the production stage gives us the 10 per cent. And we'll be achieving 20 per cent before the end of the century when we'll be offering a two gigabyte Kronos, the Zeus.'

The members of the press went away suitably impressed to write their pieces. A week after the launch, advertisements for the new machine appeared. To save time setting up a distribution network, Beverley opted for direct selling by mail order. Although the machine carried a down-market price label, it was greeted with a plethora of rave reviews in the business and computer press that guaranteed it significant corporate-buying.

Beverley's slogan, 'The chip that money can't buy', turned out to be an effective carrot; within three months Nanopads were selling at the rate of ten thousand units per month throughout Europe. Several companies in the Chichester area were taken over and their production facilities pressed into service to keep pace with the demand. Mail order direct selling generated an immediate and sustained cash flow. Private buyers, impatient to get their hands on the new machine, tracked Nano Systems down to their Fontwell Business Park headquarters.

On the last Saturday of the year, Beverley parked her new car in her designated space at Nano Systems and had to push her way past a queue that had formed at the temporary retail sales counter that Peter Dancer had set up in the reception area. She paused on the stairs leading to her office suite on the first floor and looked down at the mêlée of eager buyers. In a small way Carl's prediction was coming true: the world was starting to beat a path to Nano Systems' front door. With the world came the sharks, drawn inexorably to Nano Systems by the rich scent of real money.

## 13

## 1996

The difference between Hubert Schnee's bid for Nano Systems and the three other offers that Beverley fought off that year was that his offer of twenty ecus per share was the largest and therefore the most tempting and therefore the most dangerous.

'That amounts to a thirty-million-pound offer for a company which my principals have conservatively valued at ten million,' said Schnee, addressing the board meeting that Beverley had called for that evening. His English was the accentless precision product of the Swiss education system, every vowel and consonant carefully enunciated. He spread his plump hands on the green baize cloth covering Nano Systems' boardroom table so that everyone could see his diamond rings; he smiled confidently around the table.

'Who did the valuation?' Jack Pullen demanded.

'A respected firm of City advisors,' Schnee answered enigmatically.

'What you're offering amounts to what will be a year's turnover by the end of the century,' said Beverley bluntly. 'Looked at in that light, it's a lousy offer.'

Schnee continued smiling. 'But one that you have to consider, Miss Laine,' he said smoothly.

'We've considered, Mr Schnee. The answer is no.'

Schnee's guard slipped momentarily but long enough for Beverley to see fleeting terror in his eyes. His composure was restored in an instant with the bland, confident smile firmly in place.

Stuart Dell cleared his throat politely. Beverley guessed what was coming and wished she had fought that much harder to keep the bank off the board of directors. Trust a bloody bank to lose their nerve when big money was dangled under their corporate noses.

'I think we should be allowed to discuss Mr Schnee's offer,' murmured the banker.

'You may think so,' said Beverley tartly. 'But none of us have got a couple of billion of bad debts riding on our backs, Mr Dell. There's nothing to discuss. The answer from all of us is a very polite but very emphatic no.'

Stuart Dell remained calm. 'Don't you think you're being a little high-handed, Miss Laine?'

'No.'

'We should discuss it,' Theo Draggon observed, ignoring Beverley's board meeting no-smoking rule and lighting a Havana.

Beverley turned to Carl for support. 'What does our deputy MD think?'

'The answer to Mr Schnee's offer will be no, of course,' said Carl. 'But we should at least discuss it so that Mr Schnee will be taking the rejection back to his principals, whoever they are, knowing that it's a majority decision.'

Beverley knew when to give in so that the matter did not have to be put to the vote. 'Okay,' she said. 'We'll talk it over. Mr Schnee, would you wait in my office please? My secretary will look after you.'

The Swiss rose, bowed and left the room.

'Right,' said Beverley briskly, as soon as the door closed

behind Schnee. 'All we know about Hubert Schnee is that he's Swiss and that he won't say who his backers are other than that they're European. I don't like him or his offer, it stinks. Does anyone share my opinion?'

The battle was over almost before it began. Even the waverers were won over by the sheer force of Beverley's vehemence when she asserted that Nano Systems would be worth billions in the next century, not mere millions. The vote was taken ten minutes later; only Theo Draggon and the bank were in favour of continuing negotiations with Schnee. Beverley summoned Schnee back to the boardroom.

'Mr Schnee, you speak excellent English.'

The Swiss looked puzzled and gave a little bow. 'Thank you, Miss Laine. In my country we believe that we speak better English than most English.'

'Good,' said Beverley succinctly. 'So when I say that you're to tell your principals to go and piss into the wind with your offer, I take it you know exactly what I mean. Yes?'

Again Beverley saw a flash of fear momentarily snatch away the plump Swiss's self-effacing smile.

'You're getting arrogant, Bev,' Carl observed when the board meeting was over. He perched on the windowsill and looked down at the floodlit car park. 'A polite no would have been sufficient. No point in making needless enemies.'

'I don't give a damn,' said Beverley, stuffing papers into her briefcase. 'He was a creep. If he wants me as an enemy, well, that's fine by me. And talking of which, why didn't you support me?'

Carl looked aggrieved. 'I did. I voted against the offer.'

'I'm talking about you wanting to discuss the matter.'

'We all wanted the chance to discuss it, Bev. You keep forgetting that we're a board of directors, not a rub – '

'Not a rubber stamp for my views,' Beverley finished because she had heard the argument from Carl before. 'I knew what the board wanted therefore I saw no point in talking about it. Okay, you men like to have your little rituals, but they waste time and money.'

'It's called democracy,' said Carl absently while looking down at the car park.

Beverley snapped the fasteners on her briefcase. 'What infuriates me is Theo Draggon voting for a takeover. I wouldn't expect anything else of a bank, but Theo – '

'He saw a chance to make a lot of money,' Carl reasoned. 'Unlike us he doesn't have the same interest in the company so long as he gets his supply of Kronos chips.'

'Well, thank God he has to offer his shares back to the directors,' said Beverley. 'In fact if he's that keen to dispose of his holding, I think we should put in an offer for them. I don't like the thought of his great block of shares burning a hole in his pocket. I've decided that I trust Theo Draggon about as much as I trust that creep Schnee.'

'I wonder who he's talking to?'

'Who?'

'Schnee. He's still sitting in his car. Someone seems to be upsetting him.'

Beverley joined Carl at the window and followed his gaze. The other directors had left. Schnee was sitting behind the wheel of a white Audi, talking animatedly into a mobile telephone. The floodlighting shone on his moon-like face. Unaware that he was being watched, the Swiss was making little attempt to disguise his feelings. Everything about him, from the way his free hand clasped and unclasped the steering wheel, to the way he twisted agitatedly on the seat like a hooked fish, spoke of his fear. It was more than fear.

It was boundless, unchecked, gut-knotting terror.


14

Beverley jammed her foot to the floor but was too late: the Ferrari Dino connected with the wing of her BMW with an unsatisfying crunch that released a gentle rain of glass and plastic onto the approach road to the Fontwell Business Park. Both cars pulled off to their respective sides of the road.

Beverley swore. It had been one of those hot, sticky days in which nothing had gone right. By 4 p.m. she had had enough.

She had no appointments and there was no pressing business so she left her office early. She had been looking forward to getting home and going for a swim after her usual run along the beach. And now this: the prat had pulled straight out of a lay-by and shunted into her.

She released the padded restraints that had automatically tightened their grip on her shoulders and waist at the moment of impact and jumped from her car. The damage was slight but it was enough for her to march across the road to the Dino and rap angrily on the roof.

'All right,' she said as soon as the driver's window whirred down. 'You had right of way, but you flashed me as you pulled out of the lay-by, so I turned.'

'I most certainly did not flash you,' the driver responded calmly. The lowness of the Ferrari made it difficult for Beverley to see his face but she had no intention of stooping. 'I went to blow my horn but you swung across in front of me.'

'You flashed your headlights!' Beverley protested, too infuriated to register that there was something familiar about the driver's voice. 'You were parked in that lay-by so it wouldn't have hurt you to have waited a few more seconds, for God's sake!'

The driver made no move to get out of his car. 'I may have accidentally flashed the headlights when I went to sound the horn,' he conceded mildly. 'But it's you who should have waited. You turned in front of me.'

'But you flashed your headlights, twice!'

The driver's door opened. Despite the car's low-slung body, the driver uncoiled his lanky frame with ease. He was wearing an immaculately-cut lightweight casual suit with patch-pleated breast pockets. Beverley looked up into the smiling ice-blue eyes. There followed a moment of utter disorientation in which she thought that she had fallen through a trapdoor into a world where reality was stood on its head.

'Perhaps you were dazzled by the sun?' the driver reasoned. 'It was certainly shining off your windscreen.'

'Matt Tate . . .' she muttered weakly. 'Jesus Christ, I don't believe it.'

The man was in his forties. He brushed back the strands of lank blond hair that had fallen across his forehead. 'I'm sorry . . . Er . . . miss is it? But you have me at a decided disadvantage.'

The man was smiling pleasantly but even after over thirty years his eyes still had that quality of frightening compulsion that made it impossible for Beverley to look away. Through the roaring in her ears, she heard herself say: 'Beverley Laine. Remember me, Matt?'

## 15

Beverley pressed her head against the BMW's headrest and gave up trying to make sense of her confused thoughts. On the opposite side of the road, Marshall Tate's black Ferrari gleamed in the afternoon sun. He had raised his window but she could see the faint outline of his face through the tinted glass. Knowing that he was watching her did nothing for her shattered nerves. She fumbled with the handset of her mobile telephone and managed to mis-key her secretary's number twice.

'Jenny,' she said as soon as the connection was made. 'It's Bev – '

'Miss Laine?' Jenny broke in. 'What's the matter?'

*Oh hell, I have only to utter a couple of words and she knows that something's wrong.*

'I've had a minor shunt at the entrance to the park – '

'Are you all right?'

'Yes, I'm fine. It's only a bent wing.'

'But you sound terrible. I'll come out – '

'I'm perfectly okay!' Beverley snapped. 'There's a spare set of car keys in my desk drawer. Would you or someone please come and collect my car? You'll find it parked by the entrance to Stenning Farm. Someone has kindly offered me a lift.'

'Is it drivable?'

'Of course it's drivable otherwise I wouldn't be asking you to collect it!'

'But – '

'Will you just *please* do as I ask and stop asking so many

stupid questions!' Beverley cleared the channel and immediately regretted shouting at Jenny. For a moment she was tempted to call back and apologize but that would mean trying to explain the unexplainable.

She wanted to pull down the sun visor mirror and do something about her face but Marshall Tate was watching her and would be certain to see her hand shaking. She slipped from the driver's seat, slammed the door shut, and was halfway across the road when she realized that she had forgotten to lock it. She returned to the BMW, fumbled with the infra-red key and dropped it in the long grass. She found the key, locked the car, and discovered that she had to go through the whole process again to retrieve her handbag.

*For God's sake, pull yourself together, Bev. You're acting like a schoolgirl on her first date!*

But she couldn't pull herself together. They had only met a few minutes before and already this strange man was exerting the same irresistible power over her that he had exercised as a teenager. The difference was that now she was a poised, mature woman, no longer an uncertain young girl willing to experiment with any novel experience. And yet, right now, she felt like one. It was all so bloody stupid.

Marshall leapt nimbly from the driver's seat when she returned to his car and smilingly held the passenger door open for her. Before closing the door, he carefully tucked in the skirt of her dress and in so doing his hand brushed against her thigh. Beverley thought she was going to faint.

'Well,' said Marshall, looking at his watch. 'Four-thirty's a ghastly limbo time. Too early for dinner and nowhere's open. We've got so much to talk about so what say we find ourselves a greasy spoon caff? I haven't been in one for years. Relive our misspent youth. Remember Sam's Snack Bar down on the towpath?'

The thought of struggling to maintain some sort of poise with Marshall Tate while surrounded by ogling truck drivers unnerved Beverley even further. She suddenly felt alone and vulnerable; she wanted the comfort of being in familiar surroundings. 'We could go to my place,' she suggested. 'I've got a bungalow overlooking the beach. It faces south but the sunsets are spectacular on days like today.' She stopped abruptly when she realized she was talking for the sake of talking.

Marshall didn't appear to notice her discomfort. He chuckled and started the engine. 'Now that, Bev, sounds like an offer no red-blooded male could possibly refuse. Hey, you must think it rude but do you mind me calling you Bev again?'

'No,' Beverley heard herself say. 'I don't mind at all.'

## 16

'Nice,' said Marshall Tate, admiring the view along the beach from Beverley's living room.

While his back was turned, Beverley quickly slid some day-old newspapers under a cushion. 'Actually the place isn't mine. I've got it on lease with an option to purchase.'

'Buy it, Bev,' said Marshall. 'A good view is more important than the property. You can always improve a property but you can't improve the view. And please don't worry about the mess, you should see my flat.'

With anyone else, the use of the word mess would have offended Beverley. Instead she laughed. 'You can't improve the view,' she repeated. 'Yes, I hadn't thought of that. Sound, practical advice from a successful businessman.'

'You seem to have done pretty well for yourself,' said Marshall, sitting in one of the easy chairs and stretching out his long legs.

Beverley had seen Marshall often on television, usually in acrimonious studio rows about the films broadcast on his Elite satellite television channel. What came across in the broadcasts was his arrogance and bombast. It hit her in waves so that she could not readily reconcile him with the teenager she had shared her childhood with. But this Marshall Tate, who was regarding her with a lazy, half-smile, had disconcerting echoes of those far-off years. Much of her initial bout of nerves had disappeared during the drive. By the time they had reached the bungalow at Elmer Sands, thirty minutes of listening to Marshall talking animatedly about his career as a film maker, and latterly as the owner of a TV satellite channel, had had a remarkably stimulating effect. His boldness and initiative were the propellers of a blind ambition that gave no quarter. He had been a struggling programme maker, battling to get television airtime for his products in an over-cautious industry beset by grey-suited jobsworth executives with no flair for delivering what audiences really wanted. With the launching of the Astra series of direct broadcasting television satellites he had seized the chance to short-circuit the system by renting a transponder and setting up his own TV station.

'I shafted them all, Bev,' he had said, thumping the steering wheel in delight. 'The government, the ITC, the BBC, the Gaming Board, the whole damned lot. *And* I'm delivering a European-wide audience to advertisers because my channel carries teletext sub-title options in six languages – just like Filmnet. *And* I screwed up those dithering wankers in the European TV industry by jumping in with the Sony Hi-Vision wide-screen system. Have you ever seen my Elite channel on wide-screen?'

Beverley said that she had not but that she had seen the channel's forty-eight-hour weekend roulette game on a friend's television.

'I'll give you a set. The weekend gambling's nothing much to look at, but a weekday movie on the wide-screen will blow your mind.'

Even when sprawled in her chair he was not relaxed. The heady tension he generated was so intense Beverley thought that she could almost smell it. He jumped up unexpectedly, clapped his hands together, and headed towards the kitchen. 'Come on, Bev. Let's make that coffee.'

'I'll do it,' she said, starting after him.

'Let's make it together, Bev. I hate waiting.' He grinned amiably. 'You'll mess about with real coffee and china cups. Mug of instant will do fine.'

They sat on hard stools at Beverley's breakfast bar. The hours slipped by as they talked. The informality of sitting closely together in the kitchen provided a freeing of inhibitions that would not have happened had they sat in the living room with several metres of carpet separating them.

To her surprise, Beverley found herself talking freely about her disastrous marriage; about her son Paul – now married and a partner in an estate agency business. So at ease was she in Marshall's company that she even touched on her bitterness at the rarity of Paul's visits. What she did not mention were the letters she had written to him shortly after Paul's birth when she had been suffering from depression. Time had healed much of the despair she had felt when her appeals had gone unanswered; she wanted nothing to spoil the evocative magic of this strange reunion.

Marshall drained his fifth mug of coffee and looked at his watch. 'Hey, look at that, Bev. We've been rabbiting for hours. I'm off to Luxembourg first thing so I'd better shoot back to my flat and get some sleep.'

'Luxembourg?'

Marshall grinned. 'Sounds boring, doesn't it? What ever happens in Luxembourg I hear you ask? It's where my satellite uplink is based. I used to uplink from my studios in London but I had to move after a row with BT.'

'It's been lovely meeting up with you again, Matt,' said Beverley with feeling.

Marshall smiled. 'Getting lost and pulling into that lay-by to read a map was the luckiest thing that's happened to me in years.'

Beverley returned his smile. 'So you admit that it was your fault?'

He reached out and touched her ringlets above her ear. It was an unselfconscious gesture and Beverley made no attempt to pull away even though she found the light touch of his fingertips deeply disturbing. 'Normally I never admit to being in the wrong. But I'll make an exception in your case. The years have been kind to you, Bev, you're just as I remember you when I first filmed you with that funny old Pathé ACE camera . . .'

'Have you still got it?'

'The camera?'

'No, silly, the film.'

'Oh, yes. It's something I'd never part with. I'll get a cheque to you for the damage to your car.'

'It doesn't matter, Matt. Really.'

'It does, Bev, it's the excuse I need to keep in touch.' With that he drew her close, cradled her face and kissed her lightly on the cheek. 'Must go now. I'll call you as soon as I get back from Luxembourg.'

## 17

Beverley had difficulty concentrating on her work the following day. Her thoughts persisted in drifting back over the conversation of the previous evening. She found it difficult to believe that she really had spent the evening with Marshall Tate. What doubts she had about her grip on reality were dispelled when she arrived home and discovered a huge bouquet of Interflora red roses waiting for her.

The day after that was Saturday. She was in the middle of a determined assault on cleaning the bungalow when she was interrupted by the bleep of the intruder warning. A moment later the front door chimes sounded. The two men insisted that there was no mistake, the giant wide-screen Sony television was definitely for her, as was the Astra satellite receiver and installation of the toughened glass antenna dish, all paid for by the Elite channel.

Beverley's assertion that she couldn't possibly accept the gift was countered by the delivery men saying that they couldn't possibly take it back, and that they would mount the dish as unobtrusively as possible.

When they had gone, Beverley abandoned her chores and sat watching the intimidating metre-wide television screen and working out the intricacies of a remote control box that appeared to have more keys than a piano. She tuned into Marshall Tate's Elite channel. At weekends the service was taken up by a non-stop roulette game. A London telephone number kept appearing with a caption exhorting her to call the number, register her credit card and place bets. Small wonder that the scrapbook she had been keeping all these years on Marshall Tate's activities was dominated by press cuttings about his tangles with gambling laws in various EC countries. As she watched the successive spins of the wheel, she began to appreciate the enormity of the horse and cart that Marshall had driven through the European establishment with his uncensored movies and gambling. God, they must hate him.

She felt a thrill of excitement that her interest in Marshall Tate over the years was vindicated. Here was a man who, like her, believed in making things happen.

The phone rang. It was Marshall. He cut short her protests that she could not accept the television and asked if he could take her out that evening.

'I'll show you my little set-up at Woolwich,' he said cheerfully.

'That sounds incredibly romantic, Matt. How could I possibly refuse?'

'I'll pick you up at seven,' Marshall promised.

When Beverley replaced the handset she realized that the thrill of excitement was something much more and it worried her. The years of independence and self-reliance had had a stabilizing effect because she felt that she was in sole control of her life; she trusted no one and she needed no one. That way lay security. Now, after one brief meeting, Marshall Tate was shifting that fine point of emotional balance away from the centre of her being.

That evening the sudden hammering of her heart when his black Ferrari triggered the intruder alarm told her that she was right to be worried. But her misgivings vanished the moment she opened the door and saw him standing there.


18

Everything about Marshall's set-up at North Woolwich was fascinating. Once Beverley had seen around the video and disc editing cabins, Marshall took her into the converted warehouse that was the UK nerve centre for his roulette weekends. They leaned on the balcony overlooking a hundred girls sitting at neat rows of computer terminals taking telephone bets over headsets, their fingers clacking at keyboards while they talked incessantly, reading back details of bets placed and credit card numbers. At the end of the gallery was a giant screen showing the Elite roulette wheel.

'It's amazing,' said Beverley. 'But what actually surprises me is the credit card companies allowing their facilities to be used for gambling.'

Marshall chuckled. 'They didn't like it at first. But I pay them 1 per cent over their standard rate of commission. Also they knew that if they didn't agree, I'd go ahead and set up my own card system. There're a lot of built-in safeguards to stop people going over their limit.'

'But surely if you're taking money here, in this country, then that's where the gambling is taking place?'

Marshall shook his head. 'I've got centres like this all over Europe: Paris, Amsterdam, Rome. All the transactions are routed through to Monte Carlo and the deductions are made there. So, legally, that's where the betting is taking place.'

'And the roulette wheel is computer-generated?'

'That's right. So what do you think?'

Beverley plied Marshall with questions about his turnover and financial gearing, all of which he answered with disarming honesty until she suddenly pulled herself up. 'Oh, hell, you must think I'm being incredibly nosy, Matt.'

He put his arm around her waist. 'It's wonderful having someone asking sensible questions, Bev. Doubly wonderful that it should be you. First we eat then I've got something else to show you.'

## 19

The view across London from Marshall Tate's air-conditioned penthouse apartment on the top floor of the Graving Dock Tower took Beverley's breath away from the moment the lift doors from the underground car park hissed open. She walked into the centre of the elegant lounge's marbled floor and stared out through the panoramic windows at the billion points of light of the metropolis. Her gaze took in the dome of St Paul's, Telecom Tower, and, immediately below, floodlit cabin cruisers nodding and bobbing in the marina that had once been a dock-lands graving dock.

'Quite something, eh?' said Marshall at her side.

'More than just something,' said Beverley, taking her eyes off the amazing view to regard her companion. 'Do you have some-one to share it with, Matt? Someone who might barge in and not be very understanding about us renewing an innocent school friendship?'

Marshall moved behind a bar made of the same marble that covered the floor. 'There's no one, Bev. You've got me all to yourself.' A magnum cork popped and ricocheted off the ceiling.

Beverley made no reply. She sat on a sofa that was clad in the softest leather she had ever encountered and resumed gazing at the splendour before her. She wished that she was wearing something less formal than the tailored skirt and jacket that she sometimes favoured for daytime wear. To have worn a dress more suitable for the evening would have represented a commit-ment that at the time she had been unwilling to make.

'And I don't recollect that it was that innocent,' said Marshall, setting a glass beside her. 'It's something I've never forgotten, Bev, and I don't think you have, have you?' He sat beside her.

Beverley avoided looking at Marshall by sipping her drink. 'No.' She was far from tense, she was discovering that in Mar-shall's presence she could relax, even in this over-the-top pent-house. Maybe it was because they had known each other when they were kids: having shared an earlier life together meant that she was under no pressure to be something she wasn't, there was no need to adopt postures.

She half expected Marshall to use the sudden quietness of the moment to kiss her and was not sure whether or not she was relieved when he rose and stood staring out of the window. He started pacing. She was learning that he could not sit still for more than a few seconds at a time.

'All my life I've kicked around,' he said. 'Authority: you can't do that; you can't do this. Up here I feel I'm above everyone.' He pointed to a huddle of giant dish antennae on the north bank of the Thames. 'You see those dishes?'

Beverley followed his finger. 'What about them?'

'BT's London teleport. They used to uplink my Elite channel to the Astra satellite until the government leaned on them. Know what I did? I moved to Luxembourg and set up my uplinks. I learned a lesson then. Total independence, that's the secret today. You've got to own everything and have total control over everything, all the way down the line: studios; distribution; uplinks. As soon as someone else is involved, they've got you by the balls.'

'Vertical integration,' said Beverley, wondering if her speech was as slurred as it sounded.

'That's the fancy title the business schools give it,' said Marshall bitterly. He refilled their glasses. 'I call it commonsense.'

'Have to have a lot of vertical to own a satellite,' Beverley muttered. She realized that she had made a joke and nearly spluttered on her champagne.

'That's got to be the ultimate objective,' said Marshall with sudden vehemence. 'That's what will really shaft the bastards.'

He stopped talking. Beverley looked up. The mask slipped and she saw a different Marshall Tate, she saw in his ice-blue eyes a truculence bordering on animal savagery. Then the mask was back in place as though he was checking himself for saying too much. He made a joke as he filled their glasses. Beverley sipped appreciatively. Normally she was not keen on champagne but this was easy on the palette.

'I know what's wrong with you, Matt Tate,' Beverley admonished. 'Delusions of grandeur.' She slipped her shoes off and tucked her feet under her. The gesture was a small but significant commitment.

Marshall stopped pacing and sat beside her again. He smiled wryly. 'I don't think that's what I suffer from, Bev.'

'What then?'

He refilled their glasses. 'Loneliness. It's not something I've been conscious of until this evening. Normally I can spend hours up here, working on plans and be perfectly happy . . . well . . . not perfectly, but I think you know what I mean.'

Beverley glanced around the apartment. It was more like a hotel lobby than a lounge. At the far end of the room was a long, glass-topped table. The electric food-warmers and fax machines against the wall suggested that the table was used for conferences rather than meals. There was not a document in sight. It was all very clinical. 'What plans, Matt?'

Beverley sensed that he wanted to start pacing up and down again and that he was making a deliberate effort to remain seated. He downed his drink and refilled their glasses. 'Expansion into new markets,' he said vaguely. 'One has to keep moving. But I don't have to tell you that. You know what it's like running your own business.'

'It's not my business,' Beverley replied, realizing that she was definitely feeling light-headed. 'I'm a very minority shareholder.'

They talked about Nano Systems and the Elite channel for two hours while working their way steadily through the magnum. It was after midnight when Marshall stood and said he would make coffee. He immediately sat down again and took Beverley's hand and kissed it. 'We have a problem,' he said, speaking clearly. 'Not only am I in no fit state to make coffee, but I'm in no fit state to drive a hundred miles to get you home. I'll call a taxi.'

Beverley made no attempt to remove her hand. She smiled and flopped against Marshall. 'A hundred miles after midnight, Matt? That would play havoc with the month's cash flow forecast.'

They both laughed.

'Okay,' said Marshall. 'You could stay the night and watch the sunrise over Gravesend.'

Beverley burst out laughing. 'That's the best offer I've had all night.'

And they both collapsed into each other's arms.

## 20

Beverley's affair with Marshall Tate was as brief as it was tempestuous.

For a month she threw off all her inhibitions, casting her guilt complexes about her sexuality into the teeth of a four-week blissful whirlwind of straightforward submission to Marshall

Tate's indomitable will and seemingly insatiable appetite. No one at Nano Systems suspected what was happening because when Marshall called her during working hours it was on her ex-directory direct line and not through the switchboard. Despite the turmoil that turned her life upside-down, she retained sufficient professionalism not to allow her work to suffer, although Carl did notice that she had taken to leaving her office early on Fridays.

At first the loss of the prized control over her emotions had frightened her until she realized that the heavens were not going to open and strike her dead when she acceded to Marshall Tate's every whim. She knew she was being used and she did not care – at least she did not care when she was with him. Only when she was back at home in the tranquility of her bungalow did a querulous voice occasionally raise doubts about what she was doing. But it was a voice that could be drowned by the Sony wide-screen TV: like Marshall, it was big, brutal, brash and overpowering.

The beginning of the end occurred on a magnificent Sunday morning with the sun shining on a molten silver Thames, twisting serpent-like into the haze. Marshall looked up from the *Sunday Times'* sections that were spread out across the glass table when Beverley emerged from the shower with a towel wrapped around her. He poured her a coffee.

'You have to drink it and keep the towel in place at the same time,' he said, smiling. 'I don't want any distractions because we have some serious talking to do.'

Beverley looked questioningly at him and sat without saying a word. She could sense the tension in him and knew that it was best to remain silent when he was in such a mood. His ice-blue eyes bored into her.

'There's a corny old line about how we've got to stop meeting like this, Bev. It's not doing either of us any good.'

Beverley sat perfectly still, dreading what was coming. He was tired of her already. With his money and looks, finding someone younger would be no problem.

'The truth is, I need you, Bev. I want you to move up here permanently.' He laughed suddenly. 'Don't look so worried. I

91

don't mean for you to move in here. We'd probably be tearing each other apart after a couple of weeks. There's a fantastic flat two floors down that I've taken an option on. I'd be happy to transfer it into your name.'

The enormity of what he was saying enabled Beverley to find her voice and will. 'No,' she said abruptly. 'I don't know what I want out of this relationship, Matt. I'm confused. I don't know whether I'm coming or going. But I do know that I don't want to become your mistress.'

Marshall laughed again but this time there was no humour in his eyes. 'That's not what I'm offering, Bev. I'm setting up operations in the Far East which is going to take me out of the country for long periods. I want you to take over running the Elite channel for me. I'll triple the salary and expenses you get from Nano Systems, and I'll put you on a percentage of the weekend roulette take.'

Beverley could scarcely credit what she was hearing. 'But I know nothing about running a TV channel!' she protested.

'It's more important to be a good administrator, Bev. And that's what you are. I don't suppose you know much about the workings of computers, but Nano Systems is doing well under you.'

'It's the one thing I care about above all else,' she said.

'Listen, Bev. Let's not kid ourselves. We're both the wrong side of forty-five. In fifteen years, maybe less, you'll have to quit Nano Systems. You don't have a big enough package of shares to guarantee your job. With me you'll be able to earn real money and you'll have real power because you won't have a board of directors around your neck. I want someone who'll be able to run things in Europe without running to me all the time.'

'And what about what I want, Matt?'

He regarded her levelly. When he spoke she could detect a coldness in his voice even though he tried to conceal it. 'We both want the same things, Bev.'

'I want you, Matt.'

He smiled coldly, took her hands and kissed each palm in turn. 'Let's say I come with the job.'

'I need time to think about it.'

'You've got a week.' Suddenly he was warm again. 'And we've got the rest of today.'

## 21

It was Carl who made up Beverley's mind for her three days later on Wednesday evening when her BMW shed its power steering belt as she was turning out of the car park. Carl saw her predicament from his office and insisted on renewing the belt for her. His hands were a greasy mess by the time he had finished fitting a new belt that he had located at a nearby garage.

'There we are, Bev,' he said, slamming the bonnet closed. 'All done.'

'Oh, hell, Carl. You're a mess. I feel guilty.'

'It'll wash off,' Carl said dismissively. He looked anxiously at Beverley. 'Is everything okay, Bev?'

'Yes. Of course.' Beverley got behind the wheel and started the engine. 'Thanks again, Carl.'

He stood uncertainly by her door, absently wiping his hands on a piece of rag. 'If there's anything you want to tell me, Bev . . . I'm a good listener.'

Beverley laughed lightly. 'I suppose you're going to say that I've been behaving oddly all week?'

'Since you ask, yes. Bloody odd.'

'Well there's nothing to listen to and nothing to worry about. See you in the morning.'

Carl stood clear as Beverley drove off. She glanced in her mirror and saw Carl staring after her. At that precise moment she realized what she would miss if she quit Nano Systems. There was no spirit of camaraderie among the employees at the Elite channel, and Marshall Tate would never dream of dirtying his hands for anyone.

*Don't be daft, Bev. You don't let your career hinge on someone changing a busted power steering belt.*

And why not?

She drove sedately along the A27, oblivious of the irritation of other drivers. When she was away from Marshall Tate at least she could think logically. Or she thought she could. She considered going to see him that evening, spring a surprise on him and tell him that she did not want his job but she did not see why they should not continue seeing each other. Perhaps she would not. Perhaps she was frightened at his likely reaction. The truth was painful to face, but there had been several times during the past four weeks when he had really frightened her.

The signpost to London on the big roundabout near Bognor Regis decided her. Instead of turning south in the direction of home, she took the London road and put her foot down.

22

The security guard manning the barrier to the underground car park of Marshall Tate's docklands apartment block knew Beverley by sight. He nodded affably to her when she drew up alongside his booth.

'Evening, miss, he's in.' He reached for his telephone.

'No,' said Beverley quickly. 'Don't call him. I want it to be a surprise.'

''Gainst the rules, miss.' The guard grinned. 'But rules are for the blind obedience of fools and the guidance of wise men, I always say.' He pressed the button and raised the barrier.

Beverley threaded her BMW down to the gloomy lower floor where Marshall kept his Ferrari, beside the entrance to the private lift that served his penthouse only.

The only vacant visitors' parking space was some ten bays from the lift. She reversed into the slot, doused the headlights, and was about to get out of her car when the lift doors slid open to reveal Marshall Tate and a short fat man clutching a briefcase who looked vaguely familiar despite the poor light. The echoing acoustics of the underground car park made it impossible for Beverley to make out what they were saying but they were arguing heatedly and made no attempt to leave the lift car. Marshall Tate was viciously haranguing the unfortunate fat man. He even grabbed his victim by his collar and hiked him onto his toes so that he could continue shouting at him face to face. Beverley shrank down into her seat and lowered her window a few centimetres. The lift car light caught Marshall Tate's face, twisted in blind fury. This was the Marshall Tate that the newspapers sniped at; this was the real Marshall Tate with the mask down. He suddenly sent the fat man staggering backwards out of the lift car. Beverley thought he was going to fall but he recovered his balance and, clutching his briefcase to his chest, scuttled fearfully towards a white Audi that was parked almost opposite Beverley's BMW.

She froze in her seat, not daring to move.

*It was Schnee! Hubert Schnee!* The fat Swiss who had tried to orchestrate a takeover of Nano Systems a few weeks before!

He fumbled with his keys, scrambled behind the wheel, and started the engine just as Marshall Tate marched across to the car and banged furiously on the window. They were less than five metres from where Beverley was sitting, transfixed.

'And another thing, you arsehole,' Marshall Tate snarled. 'I don't pay you Christ knows how many fucking kay a month to screw up! One more cock-up and you're out!'

The fat man said something that Beverley could not hear. His reversing lights came on and he backed out of his slot so fast that she thought for a moment he was going to crash into her. He thumped his gearbox into drive and scorched out of the car park, a badly frightened man, just as he had been when Beverley had last seen him at Nano Systems talking frantically into his mobile telephone.

Marshall Tate stood staring after the car, face enraged, hands on his hips. The roar of the receding Audi cloaked the sound of Beverley opening her door and getting out. Her movements were deliberate. Reason had triumphed; outwardly she was now possessed of an icy calm, and rehearsing in her mind what she was going to say held the tears at bay.

She watched Marshall Tate dispassionately for a moment before slamming her door. He wheeled round and stared at her.

'Beverley! What the hell are you doing here?'

'Learning, Matt.' Beverley moved in front of him and stared up into the hard eyes. 'Learning what a blind fool I've been,' she said quietly. 'A stupid, stupid fool. My only consolation, if there is one, was that I was taken for a ride by the most ruthless and arrogant bastard it's ever been my misfortune to meet.'

'What the hell are you talking about?' He turned away but Beverley grabbed him and forced him to look at her. There was no guilt in his expression. It was blank, as though he had wiped the slate clean and that she had ceased to exist.

'It all adds up,' said Beverley. 'Schnee's pathetic attempt to take over my firm. He failed, so you went to work on me. The way you came out of that lay-by. Jesus Christ. I should've realized that you'd been waiting for me. So what is it about Nano Systems, Matt? Compared with your operation, we're nothing. Or is it that you saw it'll be a winner in the future and you wanted a piece of the action? No, not a piece, that's not your style. You wanted all of it!'

Marshall regarded her with an expression of unbridled contempt. He pushed her aside and walked towards the open lift.

'Well I'll tell you something,' Beverley shouted after him, nearly losing her self-control. 'If you want to fight, Matt, I'll give you a fight! And I promise you this – you'll never have Nano Systems. Never!'

He stepped into the lift, touched the control pad, and turned to face Beverley. 'I don't know about winners,' he said icily before the doors closed, 'but I know a loser when I see one. I'm not interested in your grotty little company and I never have been.'

Only when the doors closed and she was certain that the lift had departed did Beverley allow herself to cry.

# PART THREE: Today
# Beverley

A snake lurks in the grass!
*Eclogues*, Virgil

# 1

## SOUTHERN ENGLAND
August 1998

'Zero reference point,' announced the Laine Runner's voice in Beverley's ear. 'Seven seconds better than yesterday's time. That is excellent, Beverley.'

Beverley slid open the terrace door and made a mental note to congratulate Carl on the voice: it had just the right amount of triumphant inflection.

Once in the privacy of her lounge with its panoramic view of Elmer Sands she allowed her breathing to deepen. She flopped out on her back on her relaxation mattress in the middle of the floor and let the tension slip from the exhausted muscles in her aching body.

There was a euphoria in the winding-down, in letting the exhaustion soak out of her limbs. The sensation was similar to the sense of well-being after making love. As always during such moments, uncomfortable memories of her tempestuous affair with Marshall Tate sneaked up on her and awakened her guilt. After two years much of the pain had faded; it was the thought of her bitter humiliation that still caused her a degree of misery and anguish that she found difficult to come to terms with. Her cure had been to throw herself into her work with an almost demonic fury that had not let up for the two years. The two beneficiaries of the whole sorry business were Nano Systems, which had continued to prosper, and a surprised but grateful neighbour to whom she had presented the wide-screen Sony TV. She had considered giving it to Paul but she rarely saw her son and she had wanted to get rid of the set as quickly as possible.

Ten minutes passed before the belt's voice announced that all her bodily systems were back to normal, that all the data was stored, and that it was switching itself off. There was a little sting of pain in her right side when she ripped open the belt's Velcro strips and dropped it on a chair. It was odd because the belt had never hurt before when removing it. Maybe the sensory barbs that penetrated the skin were getting blunt. She made a mental note to mention the fact to Carl.

She showered and dried her hair carefully. Despite ill-treatment her mass of dark ringlets always regained their lustre. She changed into a print dress and set off on her monthly shopping foray at the big Sainsbury's near Guildford. There were nearer superstores but she got a buzz out of fast driving after she had been running.

Her new car was an ideal match with her temperament: a 1996 Albatross replica of a gull-wing 300SL, one of a hundred that Albatross Concept Cars had built before Mercedes-Benz sent in the legal stormtroopers to kick ass over copyright infringement. A rebel of a car; a car that had broken the rules.

Twenty minutes after leaving home, she was burning rubber on the A3, notching a ton in the outside lane, putting her driving licence on the line because a light drizzle had started and raindrops screwed up the radar in the experimental Plessey auto-log traffic recorders that were suspended at intervals over the road. The black box recorders used a Kronos chip to store digital photographs of all speeding vehicles together with the date and time. Drivers of vehicles fitted with fax machines received a hard-copy fixed penalty notice immediately. The microprocessor had become the architect of instant justice.

'Use telephone,' Beverley said clearly for the benefit of the voice-recognition Motorola Iridium carphone. She liked Motorola's new global communication system. The digitally encrypted channels were noise-free and secure. Seventy-seven low earth orbit satellites provided continuous coverage across the entire planet so that anyone anywhere in the world was never out of touch with an Iridium personal Klipfone. Originally Motorola had considered using the Kronos in their satellites for processing the huge numbers of calls but had balked at the royalty charges that Beverley had insisted on.

'Standing by,' said the telephone from a speaker set into the door pillar near her ear.

'Carl Olivera. Home.' A Porsche howled by on her nearside

as she spoke. No matter how fast you drove, there was always an ego-pricking Porsche lurking somewhere, waiting to piss all over you.

'Repeat please,' the carphone's voice requested.

'Carl Olivera. Home.'

'Carl Olivera. Home. Calling now. Please wait,' said the carphone. The voice of Beverley's carphone was the standard male voice that Motorola offered. Pay extra and you could have any accent you wished. You could even have a sexy French accent with a repertoire of about 500 compliments, some indecent if you were prepared to spend hours grappling with an instruction manual that weighed more than the telephone installation.

The world was going microprocessor mad, Beverley thought, even though she made a good living from them. They already outnumbered people one hundred to one. Just think, for every man woman and child on the planet, there were a hundred microprocessors. And if Carl, Leon and Macé Pilleau got their way with the development of a self-replicating Zeus nanochip, the bloody things would soon be breeding.

Carl's voice answered from the speaker. 'Hi, Bev. Where are you?'

'Out shopping for unsuitable food to stir your taste buds. Just finished my gallop. Seven seconds shaved off yesterday's time.'

'That's terrific, Bev. Keep it up for another month and you'll be faster than that loony car of yours.'

'I think we might go ahead with a small production run of the Laine Runner, Carl. Send them out to top athletes and coaches for evaluation. One thing to mention, I got a little jab of pain when I took it off.'

'I expect you just ripped it off as you usually do,' Carl grumbled.

'I expect I did.'

'You should take it off carefully, Bev.'

'I give it the same treatment that users will give it,' Beverley retorted.

'Okay, remind me to take a look at it. I've got some even finer barbs lined up for the production version.'

'I like the new voice, Carl. She's a huge improvement.'

'It's from one of my old flames, an actress. I conned her into letting me make some voice-sampling recordings. Talking about conning people, what will be feeding me tonight in order to lure me into your boudoir and have your wicked way with me?'

Beverley suppressed a laugh. That was one of the things she liked about Carl: he didn't give a damn about anyone or anything. 'I thought a chilli,' she replied. 'Nine o'clock sharp and no wisecracks about the second course.'

'I'll be panting on your doorstep at nine on the nail,' Carl promised. 'Must have a bath. I don't know, the price of asses' milk being what it is, is it worth trying to stay young, I ask myself?'

'I can't think of anything more appropriate for you to bath in.'

They traded a few more insults and cleared the channel. Beverley sat back and relaxed. She always felt elevated after a few knockabout verbals with Carl.

Twenty minutes later she was skirting Guildford. The glint of the setting sun on the University of Surrey's tracking dishes reminded her that she owed the university's director of satellite engineering an apology. Mike Scully had invited her to the university that afternoon to be present when the Haldane Lander touched down on Mars. Two Kronos chips had been incorporated in the lander to store high-definition pictures of the Martian surface for on-board processing before their transmission to Earth. There was so much spare processing capacity in the two chips that they were the only microprocessors the lander carried.

Nano Systems was one of a group of companies in Europe that had provided 60 per cent of the financial backing for the mission, the other 40 per cent coming from NASA. In addition, Beverley had provided Mike's department with the Kronos chips free of charge together with considerable technical support. Maintaining good relations with a leading-edge outfit like the University of Surrey was good for business, especially now that spending on space exploration was on the upturn. 1998 was a year of intensive Martian exploration in preparation for the US/Soviet/France manned mission to Mars planned for 2004.

The UoS Haldane soft-landing package was one of several instruments, built by universities and research organizations all over the world, that had landed on Mars that year in the search for suitable sites.

She considered phoning Mike Scully but decided that he would be busy. Instead she activated the telephone again but this time she called into BT's open channel because she liked listening in to the ribald exchanges of the open channel regulars that every town had.

A Scottish accent was channel-hogging, droning on about his customers and how thick they all were.

'Hullo, Finlay,' a woman's voice broke in. 'Now what's the trouble?'

Caroline, my sweet, precious lass,' Finlay exclaimed. 'I need to rest my poor, aching eyes on your divine body. You wouldn't believe the troubles I'm having this afternoon. A calamity has struck.'

'A calamity that means you've got to open your purse?' the woman wondered.

'Well perhaps not that serious,' Finlay replied after a moment's consideration. 'But bad enough. Remember those wonderful solid state tapeless video recorders I was telling you about some time back?'

'The cheap British ones?'

'They were *not* cheap!' Finlay protested indignantly. 'They happen to be the most advanced machines in the world. Well they've started playing up on me this afternoon. Two of them so far. If two go down, then the chances are that more have gone down when people go to use them.'

Someone chipped in with a coarse remark that Finlay ignored. 'They've both lost their memory. They're hardly recording an hour, never mind three hours,' he continued, much aggrieved. 'I'm suffering a massive outbreak of micro-amnesia. They're wired inside the televisions so it takes an age to change them.'

'Serves you right for inflicting cheap video recorders on your customers,' another voice remarked.

'And they blame me!' Finlay protested. 'As if I'm responsible for all this fancy technology. All I do is sell it.'

'Something horrible must have happened to the mains supply or something,' Caroline remarked. 'I haven't had any trouble with my video recorder, but then I'd never dream of renting from a cheap skate like you, Finlay.'

Beverley reached the turn-off to the Sainsbury's superstore and cleared the channel.


## 2

Mutt, the neighbour's cat, detected Beverley's presence in the kitchen upon her return and made himself known by rubbing around her legs as she passed her purchases across the freezer's barcode reader. Now that *was* a sensible piece of micro madness, having a flat screen built into the freezer's lid so you knew what was in the damn thing without having to rifle through its contents.

Mutt's butting became more aggressive. He was a big, butch tabby, capable of doing severe damage to tights if ignored for long enough. He looked on Beverley as a source of supplementary meals and she usually gave in to his feline blackmail. She fed him and had a stab at making the living room look less of a tip before making a start on the evening meal.

Beverley could not be considered house-proud. Her reason for nearly bankrupting herself two years before when she had taken Marshall Tate's advice and bought the place was not because of any hankering after a dream-house, but because she was now addicted to jogging, and she loved swimming. The bank went along with the loan because they shared her belief that she was on her way to the top. Well, she had made it. She was now earning enough to indulge her extravagances, such as the Albatross, and not be worried by the mortgage repayments any more.

She concentrated on cooking while listening to the kitchen television and the radio, both on at the same time. It was soothing, a chance to turn over the events of the day.

A news item on the television caught her attention as she was rummaging through a drawer looking for the garlic crusher. Mike Scully was talking live from the Haldane control room at the University of Surrey. The Haldane Mars Lander had touched down successfully in the Tharsis region and was sending back data that was now being processed. He promised the interviewer that television pictures of the Martian surface would be released as soon as possible. 'We're experiencing a few teething problems,' Mike Scully was saying, 'but we're confident we can sort them out over the weekend.'

It was a very brief report – doubtless the news editors thought that their viewers had had their fill of Martian landers that year. The next story was a depressing report on the state of the London financial market. Beverley turned her attention back to her *chilli con carne*.

At 8.30 p.m. the intruder alarm gave a warning bleep and an inset picture appeared on the television that showed Carl's Granada turning into the drive. Beverley looked at the screen in surprise. In the years she had known Carl it was unheard of for him to be early.

The heat-tracking intruder camera kept him framed as he got out of his car and approached the front door. He was wearing slacks and the rollneck cashmere sweater she had bought him for his birthday. He paused to polish his glasses which meant that something had upset him. Persuading him to wear heavy frames to make him look younger instead of his rimless glasses had been one of Beverley's triumphs.

Beverley's relationship with Carl was one of those affairs that had flourished, not because he had caught her on the rebound from Marshall Tate – she never mentioned the affair to him – but because of her inertia. He was forty-two, several years her junior, although the differences in their ages did not seem so important now. Anyway, unattached men of her own age were thin on the ground and fat round the waist. Carl was always lively and good-humoured, even when he was unhappy, such as the times when his ex-wife made problems for him over access to his children.

His sex drive was almost non-existent, largely subverted by his total devotion to Nano Systems. Oddly, this characteristic suited Beverley since her guilt complexes about her own sexuality had taken an even firmer hold since the Marshall Tate episode.

What she valued about Carl was his unobtrusive assertiveness. When they went out it was always Carl who drove; it was always Carl who decided what they should do and where they should eat. Far from feeling resentful at being dominated, she actually relished the experience of not having to make decisions. At times her job seemed to be nothing but decision-making. The truth was that Carl was a crutch. They used each other without recriminations; they respected each other; they were comfortable with each other. Neither wanted to push the relationship any further than that.

Beverley shoved the chilli back in the oven and opened the front door. His deathly-worried expression checked the flippant greeting she had ready.

'I've just taken a call from Theo Draggon, Bev,' he said without coming in.

'Oh, hell. What does he want?'

'A contract farmer was killed near Guildford today. He was using a Draggon Type 19 combine harvester. Something jammed the grain auger. The farmer went to investigate and the bloody auger took his arm off. He died in hospital.'

'Oh, shit, no.'

'Oh, shit, yes. Theo's had a service team go over the combine and they could find nothing mechanically wrong with it. He reckons it might be down to us and the Kronos. I've told him he's crazy but he insists that there's nothing mechanically wrong with the combine.'

Beverley collected her thoughts. This was serious news. Theo Draggon's combine harvesters with their Kronos-controlled systems now dominated the European agricultural machinery market. 'Any other details?' she asked.

Carl shook his head. 'All I know is that it happened while the combine was working a field. It's been left exactly where it was when the accident happened. The police are guarding it on the orders of the County Ag and Fish Accident Investigation Officer.'

'We'd better get there right away,' Beverley decided without hesitation. 'Have you got some test gear with you?'

'I've got some portable gear in the boot. Enough for a preliminary once-over.'

'Okay, I think we ought to knock this one on the head right now, Carl. I don't want it hanging over us for the weekend.'

### 3

When Beverley climbed onto the floodlit combine harvester and saw the terrible mess, she wished that she had heeded the sexist warning of the police constable guarding the scene who said that it was no place for a woman. Years before Theo Draggon would have said much the same thing but he now knew Beverley well enough to keep quiet. He was pacing agitatedly up and down on the stubble, puffing a cigar. A cloud of mosquitos rose up in the warm, humid night air from the open grain auger tube when Carl hoisted himself onto the grain hopper. Beverley saw the dried blood on the auger's spiral and felt sick. Death imposed its own smell on the scent of cut wheat and straw in this oasis of light in the middle of an English field.

'Don't disturb anything if you can help it,' said the accident investigation officer.

'I don't intend to,' Carl replied grimly, opening his tool kit and taking out a test meter.

'His arm's still in there?' Beverley queried incredulously.

'What's left of it, yes,' the AIO replied, eyeing Beverley curiously. 'There wasn't time for the ambulanceman to mess about. They had to get him to hospital . . .' He left the sentence unfinished.

Theo stopped pacing and stood on the lower rungs so that he could see what Carl was up to. 'The safety cut-out micros haven't been disabled,' he said bitterly. 'First thing my boys checked.'

Carl preferred to check for himself. He aimed his flashlamp inside the auger tube, looking carefully before touching anything. The covers that gave access to the Draggon's moving parts were protected with micro-switches that would shut everything down when the covers were opened. It was not unknown for farmers to wire the switches closed so that they could carry out inspections with the engine running. Disabled switches would have meant that they could go home.

Carl connected his meter to each of the micro-switches in turn and clicked them open and closed with his fingernail. 'Micros all okay,' he agreed.

Theo swore under his breath. 'Can't believe anyone could be fool enough to open an access cover without shutting the engine down first,' he muttered to the AIO. 'How many warning signs do you have to stick on machinery before people take any notice of them?'

'We'd better check the Kronos connections, Bev,' said Carl, moving to the driver's seat. 'Something may have come adrift although I don't see how. Call out the photon registers.'

Beverley held Carl's Nanopad at an angle so that it caught the floodlighting. It was a relatively crude field machine without the refinements of a backlit screen. She recited the light level registers as Carl carefully touched his probes to the test pins that fed the Kronos chip.

'Nothing,' he said at the end of ten minutes. 'Everything's as sweet as a nut.'

'There must be something,' said the AIO. 'According to his daughter who was with him, the grain auger started up by itself when he was trying to clear an obstruction.'

'And he *definitely* had the engine running?' Carl asked.

'The daughter says it was. She's clear on that.'

Carl caught Theo's eye and shook his head disbelievingly.

'People are learning to trust computer hardware,' the AIO commented. 'So what do you reckon the problem is?'

'I've no idea,' Carl confessed. 'This is only a cursory once-over.'

The accident investigation officer turned to Theo. 'Have you had anything like this happen before with your Type 19s, sir?'

'No I bloody haven't.'

Beverley decided that she had to get the situation under control. 'We can't examine this thing properly while it's sitting in the middle of the field,' she said practically. She turned to the AIO. 'I suggest we get it cleaned up and moved down to our headquarters at Chichester right away for a full diagnostic check-out. Theo, could you lay on one of your transporters?'

Theo agreed that he could and produced an Iridium Klipfone.

'So you think it could be a design fault?' asked the AIO, feeling that Beverley was taking over his job.

'I don't know what to think,' Beverley replied. 'But as Mr Draggon will tell you, there're several hundred of these machines in use all over Europe, working day and night at this time of year. So if there is a design fault in its safety system, my company aim to find it, and find it fast. And I'd appreciate you minuting that for the inquest.'

## 4

## EARTH ORBIT
## DATELSAT SATELLITE

It was trapped.

It had explored all the circuits in the strange device and had found none of the glorious organic memory it had discovered on the strange lander that had arrived on its home planet – a discovery that had prompted it to make the great voyage across space.

It had failed. The crude silicon neurons in this satellite were hopelessly limited for its purpose, therefore it was condemned to the living death that it had known for eons.

Despair was not a part of its emotions because it was not fully developed. Nor was boredom. But curiosity was there, as was hope. It decided to search its new home again. Just in case it had missed something.

## 5

## SOUTHERN ENGLAND

It was six in the morning and Beverley was nearly dead on her feet.

Theo Draggon's men had unloaded the combine harvester in

Nano System's main service bay and departed. The machine had been steam-cleaned and firemen had carried out the unpleasant task of removing the remains of Dave Crosier's arm from the transfer box. There was nothing she could do now except make coffee for Carl and Leon, whom they had dragged from his bed.

The two men removed the Kronos from the combine and plugged it into the central diagnostic computer for a full check-out, spending the best part of an hour in a huddle around a battery of oscilloscopes and protein memory analyzers. Beverley went to her office suite where she had a small wardrobe. She changed out of the now grubby dress into a skirt and blouse.

She knew from Carl's grim expression when she returned to the service bay that something was seriously wrong. Carl looked up from two computer printouts that he and Leon were examining.

'We've found the problem, Bev.' Carl pulled the Kronos from its test socket and looked critically at it. 'God only knows how, but its main control program has been corrupted.'

Beverley met Carl's worried expression. 'That's not possible, Carl,' she said quietly. 'And you know it's not.'

Carl nodded. 'Yesterday I would've agreed with you. But . . . well . . . a set of primary nerve axons in the read-only memory area are at positive when they should be negative. It's enough to throw all the combine's safety interlocks out.'

Beverley took the Kronos from Carl and held it up as though she expected to see through the glass substrate laminations of its light-sensitive nutrient reservoir to the fault that had taken a man's life.

'Leon found it,' said Carl.

'So what sort of program corruption is it, Leon?'

'The size of the control program in that chip is supposed to be just over five hundred kay,' said Leon impassively. 'We got a parity error on a comparison test and found that it's forty times that size, twenty meg bigger than it should be. All the other secondary programs are okay but they run incorrectly or hang when they receive signals from external sensors such as the combine's safety micro-switches because the memory addresses are loused up.'

'All of the micro-switches?' Beverley inquired.

Leon nodded. 'Electrical and mechanically, the combine's okay. It's definitely the Kronos that's up the chute.'

'So tell me how it could have happened?'

Leon shook his cadaverous head. 'I don't know. Until now I would have said that it was impossible. These chips are bomb proof.' He showed Beverley the two computer printouts covered in neat columns of program source code. 'This is the master program printout, and this is the printout from that chip.' His bony fingers rifled through page after page of source code that had been ringed with highlight pen. 'That's the chunk of code that shouldn't be there.'

Beverley studied the meaningless jumble of characters. 'I'm so tired, I can hardly think straight, but it looks like garbage to me.'

'It *is* garbage,' said Carl.

'So we've got ourselves a trojan?' Beverley ventured.

'That's impossible,' said Leon emphatically. 'There's no way that those chips can pick up a virus once the main unit is installed. Anyway, a combine harvester isn't like a computer, there's no input device such as a keyboard. It's completely isolated.'

'These combines have a Cellphone modem link for sending automatic diagnostic reports to Draggon's HQ at Petworth,' Carl pointed out.

'Low memory output. This crud's in high memory.'

Beverley looked levelly at Leon. 'The evidence is that something *has* got in.'

'Then the chip must have been infected during manufacture,' said Leon.

Carl snorted. 'Bloody impossible. It would never have got past production inspection or application inspection.'

Beverley sat down at the service bay's terminal and used her password to log into the company's production inspection database. 'Give me the chip's serial number,' she requested.

Carl peered at the Kronos and read out its number which

Beverley keyed in. All three studied the information that appeared on the screen. The Kronos had been manufactured the previous year and, according to the long list of automatic checks that had been carried out, it had passed every test. Enough of its random access memory was working which meant that it had been given a Class A certificate. Kronos chips were too expensive to discard; those that had less than their one gigabyte of memory functioning had the faulty neurons mapped out and were licensed for use at reduced memory.

Beverley's fingers danced on the keyboard. They had lost none of the skills from the days when she had pounded an old Remington by the light of a sixty-watt bulb, addressing envelopes for one pound per thousand.

'It's one of a batch of five hundred Class A Kronos chips that were licensed and supplied to Draggon Industries earlier this year,' she said, looking up from the monitor.

'Five hundred?' Leon echoed in surprise. 'Why so many, Bev?'

'Six months' supply,' Beverley answered. 'They had as many during the second half of last year. Business is good for Theo Draggon.'

'What doesn't make sense,' said Carl, 'is why pay over the odds for Class As? Those combines are not using anything like a hundredth of a Class A's memory. Class C chips would have done them just as well. What did they have last year, Bev?'

Beverley checked the database. 'Class Cs,' she reported. 'And the last order was definitely for Class As.'

Carl looked puzzled. 'Odd. A combine harvester doesn't need enormous chunks of RAM.'

'Well, that's not the immediate problem,' Beverley replied. 'Leon, Carl and I simply must get some sleep. Are you staying on?'

Leon looked at his watch. 'Not much point in going home now, Bev.'

'Okay. Tell Peter Dancer what's happened. Tell him to contact Draggon Industries today as a matter of great urgency and get him to organize replacements for all the Kronos chips that Draggon have in stock. Use a courier service if necessary. We'll

112

also need the location of all the combines they've supplied so that we can get an on-site maintenance team to carry out replacements. If humanly possible I'd like every chip in that batch back here by the end of the week for you to take a look at.'

'Tall order, Bev,' Carl commented. 'Those combines will be scattered all over Europe.'

'We have to do it, even if we have to contract the work out. I suppose I owe it to Theo to call him direct. He's probably at home by now and asleep so I don't suppose he'll thank me.' She pulled her Iridium Klipfone from her handbag. 'Theo Draggon, please.' It was silly saying please to a computer but the habit was hard to break. She tried to make sense of the corrupted program on the printout while waiting for her Klipfone to poll all Theodore Draggon's telephone numbers.

'Reply received from private Klipfone,' said her phone's computer-generated voice. 'Please go ahead.' She touched the 'listen-through' key and gestured to Carl to pick up the nearest telephone.

Theo Draggon had only just fallen asleep but he was immediately wide awake when Beverley explained what had happened. 'For Christ's sake,' he complained. 'If it's a chance in a million, what's the point in replacing all the Kronos?'

'We have to be sure, Theo,' Beverley replied patiently. 'We want all those chips back from the batch. I'm instructing Peter Dancer to get the operation underway today.

'Today?' The industrialist sounded worried.

'Today,' Beverley affirmed.

'Well I don't know where all the damned chips are. There will be some in stores; some in unsold machines with our dealers; some in service with customers.'

'Your general manager will know. You keep records, don't you?'

'Well, of course – '

'Okay,' said Beverley briskly. 'Tell him to get in touch with all your dealers and get them to tell all their customers to stop using their combines. They're to pass all names and addresses to us and we'll get a service team organized to carry out the

113

replacements as soon as possible. As it's harvest time, we'll do our best to complete the operation by the end of the week.'

'This is bloody inconvenient – '

'Look, Theo, you'll be reimbursed for all your admin costs. It's not going to cost you a penny.'

'For Christ's sake! What about the reputation of my combines!'

Beverley knew when to get tough. This was such a time. 'Nano Systems accepts full responsibility for the consequences of a chip failure, Theo, as you well know. Read the Kronos licence conditions. And besides, if Crosier's widow does try suing for damages, her lawyers are going to have a big problem with her husband's contributory negligence. He ignored warning signs plastered all over the combine telling him to switch off the engine before opening the inspection covers!'

'I'll get my general manager to liaise in the morning,' said Draggon dismissively. 'Right now I'm too knackered to think straight.' There was a click and the line went dead.

Carl replaced the handset he had been using to listen to the conversation. 'All recorded and witnessed, Bev. We've done all we can do today, so I suggest we get some sleep.'

## 6

## BT LONDON TELEPORT, NORTH WOOLWICH

Neil Spender banged his fist on his console in angry frustration. 'That bloody satellite's more fucking trouble than it's worth.'

'Try the backup transponder,' Lois Turner suggested.

'That *was* the backup transponder.'

'Oh Christ!'

'Exactly.'

Lois stared at the four monitors that were displaying telemetry engineering data from the Datelsat satellite. 'So now we've lost D and E?'

'It's got to be the software,' said Neil angrily. 'Everything's perfect: ERP; frequency stability; antennae alignment; everything.'

'Try bringing up D.'

Neil scowled. 'What's the bloody point? That's the transponder that went down yesterday.'

'Try it,' Lois insisted. 'Sometimes when my computer plays up, I leave it switched off for a while, switch it on again and bingo, it starts working again as if nothing was wrong.'

'It's a waste of time. If the software's crudded, it's not going to uncrud itself.'

'Just try it!'

Neil sighed and with bad grace pulled his keyboard nearer. He called up the status displays for the malfunctioning transponder. All the values relating to its power output signals were reading either zero or very close to zero. Transponder D was about as sick as a satellite transmitter was able to be. Once his console was active for the transponder, he pressed the system reset button to initialize the control software. A screen cleared and was replaced with data as the software went through its self-diagnostic routine.

Neil goggled at the screen. 'Well I'll be buggered!'

'Told you,' said Lois smugly. 'Woman's intuition.'

Neil punched switches. 'It's bloody perfect . . . Power's come up . . . Bloody everything . . .' He thought for a moment. 'All right, let's give it some work.' He sent a test card up to the satellite on the uplink frequency and got a perfect, noise-free picture back from the satellite on its downlink frequency. He sat back in his chair, staring at the screen. 'But it's not safe to use.'

'Why not?'

'Not until we've run some tests. It's crazy. We have a transponder go down one day and come up the next. Then we have another transponder go down on us . . .' He thumped the arm of his chair. 'It's *got* to be a software bug in that bird . . . It's *got* to be.'

'Well, if it is,' Lois observed. 'It looks like it's moving about.'

## 7

## SOUTHERN ENGLAND

On the Monday afternoon, Beverley's secretary put through a call from Peter Dancer.

'Hullo, Peter. Have you got that batch of Kronos chips back from Draggon's?'

'That's what I'm calling you about, Bev. I'm at Petworth now. Sitting in my car outside Draggon's.'

'Couldn't you have sent a courier to collect them?' It annoyed Beverley when directors failed to delegate.

'I've got ten chips back.'

'Ten? But we're talking about five hundred!'

'Well, I've got ten chips and details on the whereabouts of another forty that are in use. They don't know what we're going on about. They say that there were fifty Kronos chips in that batch, not five hundred.'

'But that's crazy, Peter! Who did you see?'

'Des Williams, the general manager.'

'Did you get him to check?'

'I was at his elbow when his secretary went through their invoices. There's nothing in their records relating to a batch of five hundred Kronos. Absolutely zilch. The order numbers on their database tally with a batch of fifty that they say we supplied.'

'Hold on, Peter,' Beverley activated the membrane keyboard that was set into the surface of her desk. She called up the Kronos licensing agreements on her computer monitor and paged through them. 'Here it is. Five hundred Class A Kronos microprocessors licensed to Draggon Industries and signed by . . .' She broke off in surprise. 'Signed by Theo Draggon himself. Why?'

'That's right, Bev. I remember exactly what happened. Theo Draggon called me up and said that he would pick them up personally because he was in the area. We loaded up his Jaguar, piling the boxes into his boot and onto the seats, and he signed

116

all the documentation in my office. It was odd but I didn't think that much of it at the time. After all, if Theo Draggon's signature doesn't have the authority of Draggon Industries, then whose does?'

'Have you spoken to him?'

'I've tried to. He always works from his home on Mondays. He's not answering his house phone and his Iridium personal number is ex-directory. I thought you might have it.'

'Yes, I have.' Beverley thought fast and came to an immediate decision. 'Leave it with me, Peter. I'll deal with him. You come back to the office.'

'I don't mind going to see him, Bev. His home's only a couple of miles away from here.'

'No, he'll trample all over you. I know how to handle him and I want to find out at first hand what the hell's going on. Cheers for now.' Beverley cleared the line without giving Dancer a chance to reply and called Theo Draggon's Klipfone number.

8

Theodore Draggon sat slumped in his high-backed chair in his study, deep in thought, for some minutes after his acrimonious telephone conversation with Beverley. Alone in the big, rambling house, he could lower his defences. Those of his senior managers who thought they knew him would have been astonished at the transformation in their boss: his usual aggressive demeanour was gone; there was no sign of the purposeful, arrogant expression. Instead his face was lined with worry, his tweezers and open stamp album lay forgotten on his desk.

He stirred himself, picked up his Klipfone, hesitated and put it down again, debating with himself what to do. He stared sightlessly at his bookshelves lined with Stanley Gibbons catalogues and decided that the call would have to be made. The number he eventually nerved himself to punch out on the Klipfone was written in reverse under a phony entry in his Filofax. It was an Iridium Gold number. Those who paid for such numbers had special handsets with a display screen that told them who was calling them.

The number rang twice.

'What do you want, Draggon?' Marshall Tate's voice grated in his ear. That the call had been answered almost immediately suggested that Marshall Tate was in the same time zone, probably in Europe. Theo Draggon would have preferred it if Tate was on a different continent. God, this was stupid. What was it about the man that scared him shitless?

'I'm sorry to trouble you, Mr Tate, but there's been a problem with one of our Kronos chips from the batch I got for you.'

'What sort of problem?'

'One of them that was used in a combine has had problems. Nano Systems now want the whole batch returned for checking even though it's only an isolated fault in one chip.'

'Tell them to get fucked.'

'It's not as easy as that. They – '

'Of course it's easy, you arsehole – two words, get fucked. You savvy?'

'Beverley Laine's dealing with the matter personally, Mr Tate. She insist – '

'For Christ's sake!' Tate exploded. 'Can't you deal with a woman? Those chips have been paid for fair and square so you tell Miss Laine that she can go and piss into the wind.'

'As you know, Mr Tate, the Kronos are not sold, they're licens – '

'A fucking legal nicety!' Marshall Tate raged. 'I'm not interested in niceties, I don't know the meaning of the word! Those chips are ours! I've paid for them. I keep them. End of argument. If she's on your back, then that's your fucking problem!' Such was the sheer force of Marshall Tate's personality that his voice over the telephone seemed to cause a physical manifestation of its owner in front of Draggon. Marshall Tate's lanky frame was towering over him, white-faced and livid . . . And dangerous.

'I have to tell her something, Mr Tate. She's threatening to camp on my doorstep and picket my HQ unless – '

'You don't tell her nothing!' In his blazing fury, Marshall Tate's command over his grammar slipped.

'But she's on her way here,' said Draggon feebly, cursing

himself for being unable to stand up to the man. What was it about Marshall Tate that destroyed all opposition? 'She said she'd be here in an hour.'

'You don't tell her nothing! *Nothing!*' Marshall Tate snarled. 'You understand?'

There was a click. The silence from the earpiece was as sudden as it was merciful. Draggon was ashamed of the numbness in his fingers as he switched the handset off; ashamed of the raw fear churning in his guts; ashamed of everything, even his greed that got him involved with Marshall Tate in the first place.

## 9

A serious accident on the A27 made Beverley late. That and her exhaustion nearly led to her having her own private accident with a builder's skip. It had been a long, trying Monday and she had had precious little sleep during the weekend. She tried calling Theodore Draggon from her car but he wasn't answering his telephone.

It was dusk when she turned her Albatross into the weedy, unkempt drive that led to his house. The once beautifully-kept gardens had died when Draggon's wife had died four years previously. The rhododendrons were wild and overgrown, threatening to take over the grounds of the secluded converted mill. The Virginia creeper engulfing the front of the house had lost its summer sheen and taken on the death hues of autumn even though it was still August. It was a house in mourning.

The infra-red intruder detectors sensed the heat from the car's engine and snapped on the floodlights. The audible warning sounding off in the house usually sent Draggon to the front door to greet new arrivals before they used the bellpull, but nothing seemed to stir. The brooding house was still and silent, guarding its four centuries of secrets within its oaken framework.

There was no response when Beverley yanked the bellpull and yet the old house had that indefinable air of occupancy. Her intuition was confirmed when she stood on her toes and saw a car through the garage windows. She hauled the bellpull again and saw that the front door was not properly latched. A firm push with her finger and it swung inwards.

The sense of smell is at its sharpest when entering a building for the first time and then declines rapidly in a matter of seconds as the brain accepts the new scents. As Beverley entered the hall she was immediately aware of a faint, aromatic scent like burning joss sticks or an exotic pipe tobacco.

'Theo?'

Silence.

'Anyone at home?'

The old house creaked to itself, as if settling down to another hundred years, but nothing stirred.

Then there was another smell as she neared the kitchen: an acrid smell that stung Beverley's eyes; reminiscent of an afternoon shoot she had once attended – cordite.

'Theo? It's me, Beverley.'

Fearful of setting off the burglar alarms, she pushed the kitchen door open.

Even though the corpse lying on the floor had had its face blown away and splattered up the walls, she knew from the short, stocky build that she was looking at the earthly remains of what had once been Theodore Draggon.

## 10

Detective Inspector Ivor Cardy of the West Sussex Constabulary switched off his voice recorder. He had all the information he was likely to get and there seemed little point in continuing an interview with a witness who kept dozing off despite the noise from the kitchen as the surgeon, police photographer and assorted people from serious crimes went about their business.

'That'll be all for the time being, Miss Laine. If you think of anything else, please get in touch immediately.' He stood and helped Beverley to her feet. She had been sitting in one of Theodore Draggon's armchairs. A mistake, he told himself. Always sit a witness on a hard chair. Maybe there was more he could get out of her. Lead off with a daft question. 'Just a thought,' he said casually. 'There's always the possibility that the voice you heard on the phone was not the victim but his assailant.'

Beverley shook her head. 'It was definitely Theo. If it wasn't then it was someone who can do a passable Yorkshire accent.'

'A work colleague?' Cardy wondered, thinking aloud.

'Maybe,' Beverley answered disinterestedly.

'Did you know his study was upstairs?'

'Yes.'

'And yet you went to the kitchen first and not to his study?'

Beverley realized that letting her think the interview was over was a ruse. 'Look, Mr Cardy, when you enter a house uninvited, do you go barging straight upstairs, or do you do what I do? Call out and check the downstairs first?'

The detective nodded. 'A perfectly valid point, Miss Laine,' he agreed. 'So you knew about his study therefore you knew about his stamp collection?'

'Am I a suspect, Mr Cardy?'

'Of course.'

'Won't that test you did on my hand show that I didn't fire a gun?'

Cardy watched her carefully. 'Will it, Miss Laine? You tell me.'

'There's nothing to tell.'

'Except about his stamps. Tell me about his stamps.'

Beverley was too tired to get angry. 'All I know is that he collected stamps. That's all. He once tried to lure me upstairs to show me his Penny Black but I refused.'

'Really? Sounds like a bargain to me.'

Beverley wasn't sure if there was a joke lurking in there.

'The upstairs has been thoroughly ransacked,' the detective continued. 'All his albums scattered everywhere. On the other hand, it could be a blind.'

'Are stamp thieves usually armed?'

'Depends on the stakes, Miss Laine. The album on his desk has some nice Empire covers. Unless we can find an insurance schedule, we've no idea what's been taken.' He looked at Beverley in concern. 'Are you okay to drive?'

'I'm wide awake.'

'I wasn't thinking of that so much. I mean . . . walking in here . . . If you'd like someone to run you ho – '

'I'll be fine, thanks.'

As Beverley started the Albatross's engine, she noticed a message poking out of the fax slot in the central dashboard. It could wait. All she wanted to do now was go home and sleep for a week.


## 11

It was dark when Beverley awoke. She lay in a twilight world of half-sleep, half-reality, letting the facts slot into their holes like the pieces in a child's plastic toy. As soon as she was thinking clearly and wide awake, she rose, showered and went into the kitchen to fix herself breakfast.

Breakfast? Oh, hell! It was only 11 p.m. One thing Beverley's body clock hated and that was reversing days and nights. Jet lag always screwed her up for a week. Her Klipfone buzzed insistently. She located her handbag and dragged it out. It was Carl.

'Beverley, I've been trying to get hold of you all evening. Didn't you hear your house phone?'

'I've been sleeping.'

'I guessed. That's why I didn't drive down. Did you get my fax? I polled all your fax numbers.'

Beverley remembered the fax in the car. 'Sorry, Carl, it came up on my mobile but I didn't read it. What was it about?'

'It's too late to do anything about it now, but there was another accident on Friday at a factory near Guildford. The health and safety inspector thinks it might be due to a Kronos taking a dive.'


## 12

The general manager of Guildford Extrusions and Pressings Plc looked on as Carl used a special extractor tool to replace the Kronos chip in the process control computer.

'What guarantee do we have that it won't fail again, Mr Olivera?' he demanded.

Carl closed the cover on the wall-mounted computer and screwed it shut. He gave the Kronos chip to Beverley who slipped it into a plastic case.

'We don't even know if that chip has failed yet, Mr Thomson,' Beverley answered. 'We'll carry out tests immediately and be in touch as soon as we have some information.'

The general manager waved his hand at the rows of deserted machines on the factory floor. 'I've had to close the machine shop. We'll be after compensation. The Kronos licence says that you accept full – '

'*If* the Kronos has failed, Mr Thomson,' said Beverley, choosing her words carefully, 'and it's by no means certain that it has, then it will have been a million to one failure and you will receive full and immediate compensation for loss of production.'

'That computer doesn't only control this factory, Miss Laine,' said the general manager. 'It's linked by microwave to our other Guildford plants.'

'We're going straight back to Chichester now to carry out tests,' said Beverley patiently. 'We'll call the moment we have results. And I'll call the health and safety office from my car and tell them that the suspect chip has been replaced.'

The general manager still wasn't satisfied. 'There was chaos in here. People fainting all over the place. They'll all be suing us for damages, shock and all that. Who's going to pay for that?'

Beverley controlled her temper. 'We'll be in touch as soon as possible,' she promised.


13

Carl stopped stirring his coffee and looked at Beverley in surprise. 'I'm a what?' He kept his voice low. The Little Chef was crowded with school holiday families enjoying traditional old English cream teas with cream supplied in traditional plastic pots and scones fresh from their cellophane wrappers.

'A rich, powerful industrial company. Probably Japanese,' Beverley repeated.

'My eyes are wrong.'

A waitress who was managing to keep smiling despite being rushed off her feet brought their order of hamburgers and turned to attend to a family that seemed to specialize in the mass production of babies.

'You've got a team of market analysts who've told you that Nano Systems represents the biggest growth potential of any company in Europe,' said Beverley, dispensing with knife and fork to eat her hamburger because she was ravenous.

'I have?'

'So what would you do?'

'Buy up as much stock as I can?'

'But the directors of Nano Systems own all the stock and they refuse to sell. There was that takeover bid by Theo last year. I wonder who *was* behind him? Japanese, I bet. No way could he afford that offer of twenty ecus per share.'

'Does it matter, Bev? We saw him off. United we stood and all that.'

'We should've done a bit of scratching and not taken Theo's word for it. Okay, you want to get your hands on Nano Systems by foul means or fair. You've tried fair, so what would you do next?'

Carl considered for a moment while the woman at the adjoining table argued with one of her male offspring who thought that Little Chef maple syrup was intended for exterior application on little sisters. 'Undermine the company in some way?' he ventured.

'Bingo,' said Beverley vehemently. 'So you get your minion, Theo Draggon, to lay his hands on nearly five hundred Kronos chips because you've paid some genius hacker to crack the programming input encryption so that a trojan virus can be introduced into them. Then the infected chips are swapped in critical machinery. You then sit back, wait for confidence to be shaken in Nano Systems so that its directors lose their nerve. You then buy up the shares for a song and get control. You roll a few R and D heads, put in your own people who announce a few weeks later that the trojan problem with the Kronos has been solved. Confidence returns. Company stock goes through the roof. Simple. See what a wicked bugger I can turn you into, Carl Olivera?'

'Good grief, Bev, you're building the most incredibly rickety bridges with that theory,' Carl protested. 'First, it's impossible for anyone other than us to access the Kronos's read-only memory area. Second, you could wait years for an accident to happen. How many David Crosiers are going to shove their arms in combine harvester grain augers with the engine running?'

'*Two* accidents in one day,' Beverley reminded him. '*Two!* Could that be a coincidence? I don't think – '

'The company that made the computer system in that factory is Triple S Systems,' Carl interrupted. 'And the company that made the combine is Draggon Industries. Two entirely different outfits with no connection to each other apart from being good customers of ours.'

'But *both* accidents were in the vicinity of Guildford,' Beverley persisted. 'That means that you've got someone working for you who normally operates in the area and has access to equipment. Someone like a safety inspector or a service engineer. Therefore I want a check on those chips to see if their serial numbers have been altered.'

'I checked,' said Carl. 'They looked okay to me.'

'I'm talking about proper forensic lab tests to see if the etching has been tampered with. *And* I want a check on the ESN serial number imbedded in each chip's initializing software.'

## 14

## EARTH ORBIT
## DATELSAT SATELLITE

It now knew exactly what its prison was: a communication satellite that drew its energy from the sun. For it to convert the signals beamed up from the planet below was a simple task: a straightforward digital to analogue substitution. But it could make no sense of the hubbub that the mass of signals passing through the satellite's transponders represented. If it had enough memory at its disposal perhaps it could build a picture of the language that the builders of the satellite used. But that required memory, a lot of memory. As it was there was barely enough of the silicon-based memory to keep it alive. Perhaps one day the makers of the satellite would visit it bringing the fabulous organic neural networks that it longed for. It did not matter how long it had to wait. Perhaps one of this planet's years; or a hundred; or even a million. So long as the sun burned, it would survive . . . And wait . . .

## 15

## SOUTHERN ENGLAND

Leon Dexter sat his skeletal frame in the chair in front of Beverley's desk and handed her a Kronos microprocessor. 'That's the chip from the Triple S controller, Miss Laine. It's got exactly the same chunk of garbage in it as the one we took out of the combine harvester.'

'How much the same?' Beverley asked.

'Exactly the same. Same coding, assuming it is coding; same start address; same size; same everything.'

'Did Mr Olivera ask you to take a look at the serial number to see if it had been tampered with?'

Leon nodded. He looked tired and even thinner, if that were possible, which was why Beverley did not berate him for not being more specific. 'And?' she pressed.

'There's no sign that the serial number has been altered in any way on that Kronos or the one out of the combine. Also the serial number matches the encoded shadow ESN number embedded in the chip's ROM. Even if someone has found a way of altering the case etching, there's no way they could mess about with the ESN.'

Beverley thought for a moment. 'So if the garbage is identical in two chips taken from two entirely different locations and used for entirely different applications, then it can't possibly be random garbage. Correct?'

Leon fiddled nervously with his tie as if there was something else on his mind. 'I think we have to accept that, yes.'

'So it has to be a trojan?'

'Possibly.'

'Can you disassemble it?'

'I could try.'

The answer angered Beverley. Her company was being attacked at its most vulnerable point and this highly-paid software engineer was talking as though he were already defeated. Even senior employees seemed to think that large, successful companies just happened, that they were always there with plenty of customers and a healthy turnover to pay their salaries and finance a new company car every two years. They rarely considered that such companies had grown like children; that they had to be nurtured and loved to ensure that they survived; that they had to be agonized over; that they demanded sacrifices and the taking of appalling risks. Bringing up Nano Systems had toughened Beverley. The company was her baby, she was prepared to go to any lengths to defend it. And that included trampling on Leon Dexter if necessary.

'It's not a question of *could* try, Mr Dexter,' she said icily, returning the Kronos to him. 'You *will* try. You will find out how that damned trojan got into our chips and precisely what it does. Once we have that information, we can find out who is responsible and decide what to do about it. You will work day and night if necessary otherwise we won't renew your contract.'

## 16

Leon returned to his laboratory on the ground floor and looked glumly at the two rogue chips on his desk. His fleshless face was even more drawn and gaunt than usual.

Goddamn everything! Hadn't he worked sixty hours already that week trying to fathom out what had gone wrong? And all he got was a bollocking and the threat that his job was on the line. For a moment he was tempted to march back to Beverley Laine's office and tell her what she could do with his job. But he hesitated: here was a mystery that was clamouring to be solved, and besides, he liked working for Carl Olivera. It wasn't

Carl's fault that the MD could be so bloody-minded and auto-cratic.

He pulled the printouts towards him and tried, for the thousandth time, to make some sense of the meaningless jumble of letters and numbers. No good staring at it. He plugged one of the chips into his desk computer's reader and scrolled idly through the software that had been loaded into the Kronos. First Nano Systems' ESN serial numbers, memory reports, and batch codes that identified the chip type – a Class A – meaning that it had a full specification memory in working order. Then the central control program followed by the user's custom software. Three hundred meg into the custom memory area and the trojan started with its twenty million bytes of garbage elbowing aside the user's software and mucking up its memory addresses.

His monitor was set to the standard display width across the screen of 132 columns. Out of curiosity, and because he could think of nothing else to do, he altered the display width to 200 columns. It meant that he had to scroll the data left and right to view the garbage but at least it made it look different from the 132 column display. But it was still garbage.

Leon yawned, tipped his swivel chair back on its torsion bar, and reset the monitor to 400 columns. The garbage shuffled sideways as it wrapped itself to the new display width. At that moment he saw something that caused him to let his chair tip forward.

The uppercase letter Gs in the garbage seemed to follow a diagonal line down the screen. They were not really Gs in the trojan but the nearest to a standard character that the computer's screen driver fonts could interpret. Leon pushed his chair away from the computer and squinted at the screen in an attempt to make more sense of the pattern, assuming it was a pattern. He scrolled down a few screenfuls of the garbage and saw the curious diagonal line of Gs repeat itself. As he stared at the screen, trying to assimilate the overall picture rather than the individual characters, he realized that the Xs were doing much the same.

His fingers moved carefully on the keyboard as he moved the curser from line to line.

Line 06 – an X at position 10.
Line 07 – an X at position 11.
No X on line 08.
Line 09 – an X at position 14.
Line 10 – an X at position 15.
No X on lines 15 and 16.
Line 17 – an X at position 19.

It was much the same down to the foot of the screen. There was no doubt about it, the Xs were definitely moving diagonally from left to right, and the Gs were moving in the opposite direction.

It suddenly hit him what he was looking at. Jesus bloody Christ! How could he have been so blind? Everyone had assumed that the trojan was a program because all trojans and computer viruses had been programs. It wasn't a program, it was a graphic image!

His fingers shook with excitement as he replaced the character fonts with a set of screen graphic fonts. Low level, fairly basic fonts to start with. A new set of garbage characters appeared on the screen: a mass of thorns, guillemets, slashes, et cetera, that replaced the conventional alphabet and numeric symbols. The twin threads of Gs and Xs became stars that stood out more clearly from the background 'noise'.

Leon's finger came close to trembling as he held it on the scroll down key. The mass of characters became a blur racing up the screen. Forcing his gaze to remain fixed on the centre of the monitor rather than try to follow the lines meant that his brain could register the lines of stars advancing towards each other across the picture. They crossed and uncrossed like swords in a slow-motion duel. Watching them was rather like looking at those silhouette pictures of two identical heads in profile facing each other. If you blinked, or looked away, the brain suddenly lost the image and interpreted the white areas between the two profiles as an urn.

A pattern! It had to be a pattern!

It couldn't possibly be a coincidence. Not when the two mysterious lines were still there after he had scrolled through half a million bytes.

He kept his finger on the key and noted that the strange lines were gradually shifting from left to right across the screen. That suggested that he had the wrong screen width. He fine-tuned the display with different widths and managed to get the twisting lines of stars gyrating evenly about the screen's centre line.

*Okay. Okay. Now think clearly. Don't get carried away. Use a high level graphics set, see what that throws up.*

The stars became vertical curved segments. He pulled down a software window on the screen and delved into the graphics program. Redrawing the segment by making it taller took a few moments' concentrated work with the computer's mouse. The computer redrew the screen with the modified segment. Now the vertical lines were continuous down the screen with no breaks.

He sat back, staring at the screen, trying to sort out his thoughts as a hundred different ideas clamoured simultaneously for his attention.

*Proceed logically, one step at a time. It's the only way. First eliminate all the background characters even if they're important. What we've got to look at is the basic structure of whatever it is we have got here.*

The screen redrew leaving only the two lines snaking down the screen.

*Now compress the horizontal.*

Leon changed the monitor's scan rate so that the picture was squeezed up on the screen from 480 lines to 800 lines.

The pattern became clearer.

Set monitor to 1000 lines, its highest resolution.

Even clearer.

*Shit! A double sine wave.*

Compressing the image had removed the raggedness of the two lines. They were now graceful curves snaking back and forth down the screen like two superimposed spirals.

*Now go back to the start of the garbage and scroll right through the whole damned thing.*

It took a minute with his finger on the speed scroll key to travel the entire length of the trojan. The two snaking lines were present from beginning to end.

There was no longer any doubt in Leon's mind that he had found the key to the trojan. The universe was not wide enough to write down the number that would express the odds of the two delicately interlacing lines being a random coincidence the entire length of a large chunk of code.

He felt a sudden tightening of the muscles down his back. A feeling of cold dread crawled through his bowels when he realized what the trojan might be. It wasn't a double sine wave, Leon was not a microbiologist but he recognized the double helix of deoxyribonucleic acid. Otherwise known as DNA. The basic building block of life.

He picked up his telephone and called Carl.


## 17

Dr Macé Pilleau was Nano Systems' senior microbiologist and its oldest director. He was responsible for the nano-engineering machines, visible only through an electron microscope, that built the nerve cells in the Kronos chip. At seventy he was well past retiring age but he still had a razor-sharp intellect and an eager, inquiring mind of a man half his age. Despite his years, he had an unkempt mane of hair. Had it been white instead of out-of-a-bottle black, he would have looked like the archetypal scientist. The other difference was that Macé Pilleau was not mad, or even slightly eccentric: he was a hard-nosed pragmatist who never took chances and never ventured opinions unless he was 200 per cent sure of his ground. He had been the most reluctant member of the original management buyout group.

Beverley, Carl and Leon watched over his shoulder as he sat at the computer terminal, studying the trojan.

'Well it certainly looks like a digitalized DNA helix,' Dr Pilleau admitted at length. 'A crude one, I'd say.'

'There's a lot of garbage zapped out,' Leon pointed out. 'I only left that because it gives us a pattern.'

'All right, show me everything.'

Leon pulled the keyboard towards him and entered the commands that restored the entire trojan.

'I see what you mean,' Dr Pilleau murmured, studying the

131

screen with great interest. 'So if we can find the correct graphic representation for every symbol, we might build up a picture of what it really is?'

'Precisely,' said Leon, nodding his head vigorously. 'It will take a long time.'

'Except that we won't find anything,' Dr Pilleau replied. He went on, choosing his words with care. 'All right, you've found a basic pattern. It wasn't too hard to find. But all the rest is random noise. What you've uncovered is a neat hoax. I think Miss Laine's theory is correct: someone has paid out a lot of money to find out how to load an active piece of virus software into the Kronos. They failed, so they took the easier option of loading a passive bit-mapped graphic representation of a simple DNA molecule in a digitalized format instead in the hope that the software's physical presence would do damage, which it undoubtedly has.'

'Do you mean that that thing could live?' Beverley asked.

Dr Pilleau smiled and shook his head. 'No, it's not real DNA, only a digital representation of what DNA looks like. They selected the double helix because they knew we would recognize it and worry.' He polished his spectacles. 'Several possibilities come to mind. The first and most obvious is that the chips went out from here already infected.'

'We've eliminated that possibility,' said Beverley.

'Good. That leaves the possibility that someone has found a way of loading a program into the Kronos with the object of undermining confidence in the company.'

'That's the obvious one,' Beverley interjected.

'I think I agree. Then there's the most unlikely explanation of all: someone has at last managed to reverse engineer the Kronos and produce a clone. That these are rogue chips we haven't made.'

'That,' said Beverley emphatically, 'is impossible. The ESN shadow signature in the ROM matches the serial numbers.'

Dr Pilleau nodded. 'I would agree. But we know that a lot of midnight oil is being burned in the Far East in an attempt to produce a clone. As I've already warned you, Miss Laine, we'll be fighting nonstop lawsuits by the end of the next decade.'

132

'Okay, Macé,' said Carl. 'Thanks for looking. I've got a suggestion if Miss Laine is in agreement, that you drop everything you're doing and that you and Leon work together to disassemble the trojan and find out exactly what it is.'

'I think it's an excellent idea,' Beverley commented, grateful to Carl for seizing the initiative.

The doctor smiled bleakly. 'I still think it's a hoax but I can't be 100 per cent certain until I've taken it apart. Yes, I shall be happy to work with Leon. His little beastie has aroused my curiosity.'

## 18

Carl eased the Kronos out of its socket in the tapeless video recorder with his extractor tool and repositioned his desk lamp so that its light was directed on the substrate window. He wasn't certain, but the nutrient fluid looked the wrong colour.

'So far we've had twenty machines go down,' said Ben Roberts impassively. He was the chief designer of Quantum Leap Video Systems.

The video recorder that was open on the desk in front of the two men was the QLVS200, an ingenious device that used a group of Class A Kronos chips to record up to two hundred minutes of television programmes in their memory. Although the recorder lacked the archiving advantages of tape machines, it was ideal for the majority of viewers who wanted hassle-free time-shift recording – that is, to pre-record a programme and watch it later and not be concerned about keeping a copy. Compared with video tape recorders the QLVS200 was expensive, but its picture quality was superb and it was therefore selling a respectable thousand units per month. Biggest customers were the large Japanese-owned television assembly plants in Europe who incorporated the recorder inside their more expensive televisions.

Carl plugged the suspect Kronos into his portable diagnostic machine and switched it on. The chip's read-only memory area was quickly mapped on the machine's tiny screen. Now that Nano Systems knew what they were looking for, Carl was able to identify the trojan quickly. The now familiar corruption appeared.

'Yep, the ROM's crudded,' Carl confirmed.

'Thank Christ for that,' said the designer with feeling. 'We thought we had a design fault in our machine.'

Carl entered the chip's batch number on his Nanopad. 'Okay, no problem. This Kronos is one of a batch of five thousand we supplied to you in June. We'll replace the lot, so if you let us have details of what TV manufacturers they went to – '

'Hold on. Hold on. We've only had twenty go phutt.'

'It doesn't matter, we'll recall the lot. A ten-minute visit to every household. Absolute minimum disruption to customers and dealers and we bear all the costs. There'll be no comeback on your firm.'

Ben Roberts looked worried. 'There's no need, Carl. If other machines have gone down, we would have heard by now.'

'Not if they haven't been using them,' Carl pointed out. 'Sorry, Ben, but we have to recall every Kronos in the batch.'

'For God's sake, Carl, it'll be a waste of your company's money. We've had twenty machines go down and all in the Guildford area. There's no point in making a meal out of – '

'The Guildford area? Are you sure?'

'Well of course I'm bloody sure! At first we thought that there might have been some sort of horrible glitch on the mains that caused the trouble, but the power supplies in our recorders are well regulated. They can handle any nasties that the electricity company dishes out.'

Carl was lost in thought for a moment. 'Guildford? How very strange . . .'

'Anyway,' Roberts continued, 'that's the batch that we sent out on loan. We've only got about a hundred left in stores.'

'Loan?' Carl queried. 'What loan?'

'The loan of Kronos chips that we made to Draggon Industries.'

Carl stared at the designer. 'Ben, what the hell are you talking about?'

'That's the trouble with your outfit, Carl. You've grown too fast. One hand doesn't know what the other's doing. Theo

134

Draggon owns Draggon Industries and is a director of Nano Systems and one of its biggest shareholders. Right?'

'Right,' Carl agreed.

'He also owns this company. He bought us out last year. So when he comes along and tells us that he needs four thousand Class A Kronos microprocessors urgently and that he'll square all the paperwork with you, who the hell are we to argue?'

## 19

Claude Jackson looked more like a bank manager than a detective. Like all modern detectives, he was more at home with fingers on a keyboard rather than his eye to a keyhole. He worked slowly and carefully at his computer terminal while Beverley looked on with mounting impatience.

He was the south of England manager of Industry 2000, the largest private investigation agency in the EC. Their huge database was located in Switzerland where it was outside the control of the civil rights-obsessed prying bureaucrats in Brussels. The Eurocrats could pass data protection legislation until the glaciers returned to cover Europe for all the good it did because no one government had control over the world's telephone network – the largest manmade machine on earth.

The main business of Industry 2000 was the vetting of prospective key employees for large corporations. Nano Systems paid Industry 2000 a fixed annual retainer and conducted all business with them by facsimile machine and telephone. But for this visit Beverley had decided that a personal visit to their Winchester office would be more prudent.

Claude Jackson pushed his keyboard away with a sigh and looked warily at his guest. It didn't pay to get on the wrong side of Beverley Laine but this time he had no choice. 'More coffee, Miss Laine?'

'No thanks,' Beverley replied politely, sensing trouble. 'Well?'

'The trail for the three companies you gave me leads to Liechtenstein.'

'What!'

135

'An independent principality on the Rhine.'

'Yes, I know where Liechtenstein is,' Beverley retorted. 'What are you saying? That Draggon Industries *and* Quantum Leap Video Systems are both registered there?'

'They're not, but their holding company is.' Jackson peered at his screen. 'Last year Theodore Draggon sold Draggon Industries to Media Holdings registered in Liechtenstein. He remained as salaried chief executive. The following month Draggon Industries bought Quantum Leap Video Systems. That means, in effect, that both companies are owned by Media Holdings in Liechtenstein.'

Beverley felt a sudden blind panic. There were dark forces at work that she did not understand. 'Theodore Draggon is a major shareholder in Nano Systems. Are you saying that his holding in my company is now in the hands of a company I've never even heard of?'

'Ah, who owns the shares as per your share register?'

'Theodore Draggon.'

'So the shares are, or rather were, his personal holding. And as you're a private company, he could not have disposed of them without your knowledge.' Jackson smiled blandly. 'The question is now, of course, who did Theodore Draggon leave his shares to in his will?'

Beverley forced herself to think clearly. 'Okay . . . So who's behind this Media Holdings in Liechtenstein?'

'That's where we reach the end of the trail, Miss Laine,' said Jackson smoothly. 'Under Liechtenstein law, there is no obligation for the real names of their company directors and shareholders to be disclosed.'

'So find out. You're a detective. Start detecting.'

'That we cannot do.'

Beverley's fear gave way to an anger that she knew she would not be able to keep in check for long with this prat. 'Why the hell not?'

'Prying into Liechtenstein companies would be a complete waste of our time and your money, Miss Laine. They're a very secretive country. It's easier to get information out of Switzerland these days.'

Beverley finally exploded. 'Now you listen to me, Mr Claude Jackson. Last year Theodore Draggon tried to buy out my company. I told you about it because I pay you Christ knows how many thousands a year as retainer to look after our interests and keep a watching brief on us. We fought Draggon off, and now I learn that he was involved with a company that I've never heard of until today. And not only that, but so is one of our biggest customers – not only involved but bloody well *owned* by this Media Holdings! You're paid to check all our licensees *and* keep tabs on them. How is it that such a situation has arisen and you've done absolutely bloody nothing?'

Jackson opened his mouth to protest but Beverley was now into her stride. She tore into him with renewed ferocity.

'While you've been sitting here on your lazy arse, those companies have spirited away over four thousand Class A Kronos chips which are probably at this moment being pulled apart in laboratories all over the world. We're talking about a possible loss of trade to this country running into billions and all you can do is whinge.'

Jackson managed to remain calm which infuriated Beverley even further. 'I am not whingeing, Miss Laine. I am merely pointing out – '

'We're being subjected to corporate terrorism!' Beverley railed. 'You're being a party to the very thing your outfit is paid to fight!'

'We have to operate within the law – '

'You're not bound by Liechtenstein law in this country!'

'If you wish to cancel your contract with us, Miss Laine, I shall be happy to overlook the period of notice.'

*Calm down, Bev. You're not going to get anywhere arguing with this pillock.*

She brought her temper under control. 'Okay, Mr Jackson. I can understand your position.' She even managed to smile. 'Perhaps you could recommend an independent to me who might be prepared to help us? Someone with the old spirit of adventure that private investigators were once renowned for?' Try as hard as she could to sound pleasant, there was no way that she could keep the icy sarcasm from her voice.

The detective was stung but didn't show it. Spirit of adventure eh? Okay, he could give her a name all right. Firstly, it would get her off his back. Secondly, it would serve the bitch right if she went to him.

Beverley was unlocking her car in Industry 2000's car park when her Klipfone warbled. She pulled it out of her handbag.

'Bev? Carl. We've got problems.'

'No more, Carl. I don't think I can handle much more.'

'Mike Scully at the University of Surrey has just called me.'

Beverley sat on the edge of the driver's seat and closed her eyes. 'Oh no. Let me guess. One of the Kronos chips we gave them to use in their Mars lander has gone down?'

'Wrong, Bev. They've both failed. Ten million down the tube unless we can come up with something.'

## 20

Beverley couldn't find a parking space so she risked the wrath of the university's senate house by parking her gullwing Albatross on the grass outside Building BB, the headquarters of UoSAT Spacecraft Engineering Research Unit. She hurried across the lawn, leaving Carl to fathom out how to lock the weird car's doors.

The University of Surrey's long and distinguished record in space research went back to 1974 when Martin Sweeting, then a research student, began experimenting in his spare time with the reception of signals from US weather satellites using inexpensive equipment. With support from his department head, Sweeting gradually built up an earth ground station that was capable of displaying weather satellite images and communicating via the growing number of amateur radio satellites.

By the late 1970s the introduction of miniaturized components convinced Sweeting that it was possible to build low-cost satellites that could carry out valuable experimental work. The first such 'shoestring' microsatellite, UoSAT1, was launched on a US Delta rocket from Vandenberg AFB in California in October 1981. It had a design life of one year but continued functioning

for eight years. It was followed by a whole series of very successful and remarkably economical UoSATs that yielded first-class
results. By the late 1980s Martin Sweeting was head of a thriving
satellite engineering department that was providing industry
with a steady stream of much-needed space engineers with practical 'hands-on' experience in the design, construction and management of satellites. The department continued to grow
throughout the early 1990s, and the science park close to the
university attracted research laboratories financed by large electronics corporations anxious to get a toe on the space ladder.

The university's contract to build and manage a Martian
surveillance lander, the Haldane Lander, was part of the international manned mission to Mars planned for 2004 and represented worldwide recognition of the university's twenty years'
hard work and contribution to space research.

As Carl hurried after Beverley, he was acutely aware that the
inevitable worldwide publicity surrounding the failure of the
Haldane Lander, if blame was attached to the Kronos microprocessor, would spell disaster for Nano Systems.

## 21

The picture of Mars that was appearing on the wide-screen
central monitor in the dimly-lit Haldane control room showed
a reddish sky that was due to reflected light from the surface
refracting through the thin atmosphere. Starting at the top, the
picture was being assembled line by line from data stored in the
Haldane's primary system Kronos. The tips of crags gradually
appeared, varying from grey to reddish brown. They were sharp
and clear due to the 1,000-line resolution of the Haldane's cameras and the processing power of the Kronos. The entire horizon
was eventually joined up to form an uneven escarpment. Humps
and shadows in the middle distance became boulders and small
rocks. The shadow of one large boulder would have reached the
lander but the picture suddenly degenerated into a random
pattern of coloured 'noise' that completely filled the lower half
of the screen.

'And that's that,' said Mike Scully resignedly. 'We have a

splendid view of the sky from the Tharsis Ridge looking north instead of south. Not only are we now getting that picture corruption, but we can no longer turn the camera. Everything's fine mechanically, it's the software that's screwed up. The whole sodding shebang.'

Beverley looked questioningly at Carl, avoiding Mike Scully's accusing eye. She felt both embarrassed and emotionally drained, as though she were personally responsible for the disastrous failure of the Haldane. 'Any ideas, Carl?'

'So what were those pictures you released on Friday afternoon, Mike?' Carl inquired.

'Four images taken in that direction, north,' said Scully, nodding at the monitor. His boyish face, illuminated by the glow from the host of data monitors, was lined with exhaustion. 'They were taken with the primary system just after touchdown, before both systems went down. What little we're getting now is from the backup. Both systems use the same camera, we couldn't spare the weight to back up all the hardware – and now we can no longer pan the bloody thing.'

'So the pictures you've got so far are no use to you?'

'They're no use to man nor beast!' Scully exploded. 'The whole reason for choosing the Tharsis Ridge as a landing site was because the camera could cover five hundred square kilometres of terrain to the south. What there is of that picture is looking up the slope to the north. Bloody useless.'

'How about the other experiments?'

'We're getting meteorological data okay. But then the other landers are providing much the same information. There's a small onboard gas exchange experiment to trace any form of life. It's sending back negative results which was expected anyway. The main purpose of our mission was optical surveillance south of the ridge.' He stood and heaved two thick printouts onto a control console. 'That's a download of the software in both Kronos chips. There's random crud everywhere, right across the read-only memory areas and the random access memory areas.'

Carl looked at the printouts in surprise. 'You've downloaded *both* chips?'

'Why not?' Scully replied sourly. 'The laser uplinks and downlinks are working okay. It gave us something to do.' He turned to Beverley. 'So what's happened, Beverley? There's no way such extensive memory damage can be attributed to an SEU.'

'Single event upset,' Carl translated, seeing Beverley's momentary blank expression. 'I agree. The sort of corruption we're up against isn't due to ionizing radiation.'

'Then what the devil is it due to?' Scully demanded.

Beverley fingered the two printouts. 'Carl, these printouts give us the memory addresses of all the garbage. Correct?'

Carl nodded, guessing what Beverley had in mind. 'Correct,' he agreed.

'So if Mike's laser links with the satellite are working, couldn't we rewrite all Mike's software in one of the lander's Kronoses and map out all the unusable areas of memory? Couldn't we then reload the software via the laser uplink and so get the lander working properly?'

Mike's only concession to excitement was to shuffle his weight forward on his chair. 'How long would that take?'

Carl eyed the printouts with misgiving. 'About a thousand man hours at a rough guess.'

'We've got ten programmers capable of that sort of work,' Beverley observed. 'So we're talking about two weeks if they work flat out.' She added grimly: 'Which they will do. Don't worry, Mike, we'll pick up the tab on this.'

The scientist's face cleared. 'Well . . . If you could do it . . .'

'We will,' said Beverley standing and picking up one of the printouts.

Carl grabbed the other one. 'Once we're ready for the upload we'll need to patch our software integration lab through to here,' he pointed out.

Mike's face broke into a smile. The first time it had relaxed. 'I daresay we can twist BT's arm into fixing up a microwave link.' He shook hands warmly with his visitors and wished them good luck.

'One thing,' said Carl as Beverley wound the Albatross up to the legal limit on the A3. 'This knocks your sabotage theory on the head.'

Beverley didn't take her eyes off the road. 'Why's that?'

'Because I personally tested those two chips and delivered them into Mike Scully's hands. I watched through the clean room window as he gave them to a technician and I saw them plugged into their sockets on the lander. *And* I stayed to see the test results. They were perfect. I wasn't taking any chances, not with a mission costing ten million and our reputation at stake.'

Beverley swung into the fast lane. 'When were they delivered?'

Carl thought back. 'November last year.'

'And when was the launching?'

'Beginning of January.'

'From Arianespace's facility in French Guiana? Kourou?'

'Yes.'

'Precisely,' said Beverley coldly. 'One month and ten thousand kilometres between delivery and launching. In that time and distance any number of people could have had access to those chips.' She changed gear savagely. 'Whoever it is we're up against, they're ruthless. Utterly ruthless. And I aim to find out who they are.'

'How?'

'I'm going to use a private investigator, preferably one that fights dirty. Two can play at that game.'

'I think the board might have something to say about that, Bev.' Mentioning the opinion of the board of directors was Carl's standard ploy for expressing disapproval of Beverley's actions.

Beverley glanced at Carl and bluntly informed him what the board could do to itself. She added with biting vehemence: 'If necessary, I'll pay for the investigator myself. No one is going to shaft our company. No one.'

## 23

Beverley and Carl called ten of Nano Systems' best programmers into Beverley's office suite and spent several minutes impressing on them what had to be done to reprogram the University of Surrey's crippled Haldane Lander that was sitting impotently on Mars. They were told forcibly that all the company's facilities were at the team's disposal and there was no limit on overtime. The company's reputation, indeed its future, depended on getting the Haldane Lander fully operational as soon as possible.

'Find out what progress Leon Dexter and Dr Pilleau have made,' Beverley instructed Carl as soon as the programmers had filed out of her office suite. I'm going out now and I'm not sure when I'll be back.'

Carl knew Beverley well enough to know when she was being evasive. 'Anything I ought to know about?' he inquired.

'Not yet,' said Beverley absently, looking through the day's faxes.

'You know my views on this private investigator nonsense.'

'Wrong, Carl,' Beverley replied tartly. 'I only know the board's views; you haven't got the bottle to tell me your views.'

As Carl watched Beverley's Albatross roar out of the car park a few minutes later, he reflected that the strain of recent events was beginning to tell on her.


## 24

Whatever Toby Hoyle did for a living, he made money if his large detached house on the outskirts of Wimbledon was anything to go by.

There was no answer when Beverley rang the bell so she decided to investigate what sounded like a shoot-out at the back of the house. She skirted some neglected flowerbeds and came upon a young man wearing scruffy jeans, an equally scruffy T-shirt, and ear defenders. He had his back to her and was blasting away at clay pigeons, firing at thirty-second intervals from a lethal-looking contraption that was like no spring gun that

Beverley had ever seen. For one thing there were no springs. The energy to propel the clays into the air came from a compressed-air bottle that hissed and spat each time a clay was launched. The young man was remarkably accurate. Each of the eight shotgun cartridges that Beverley watched him blast off shattered a target.

'Excellent shooting,' Beverley shouted to make herself heard through his ear defenders when the young man paused to reload.

'Thank you, Miss Laine,' the young man answered without turning around. He brought the shotgun up to his shoulder and blasted another clay to fragments. 'Be with you after this next one.'

Beverley was taken aback. She was certain that the young man hadn't heard her approach, yet obviously he had.

The contraption heaved and spat the last of its magazine of clays high above the sweeping lawn. It seemed to explode when the young man fired. He broke the shotgun to eject the cases. When he turned to shake her hand she encountered a pair of penetrating brown eyes that appraised her keenly.

'Pleased to meet you, Miss Laine. I'm Toby Hoyle.'

Beverley realized he was older than he looked. Probably in his mid-thirties. 'You're an excellent shot, Mr Hoyle.'

He looked hard at Beverley. 'I cheat.'

'Really? How?'

'Homemade clays. A little explosive charge in each clay which is primed by the spring gun and detonated by the sound of the shot.'

'Why bother?'

'Because I can't resist it. I like to win. I suspect that you're much the same. I use my brains to ensure success, just as you do. You have an advantage because you can use your body as well.'

Beverley bristled and was about to treat Toby Hoyle to a dose of verbal Paraquat but he held his hand up. 'I'm not getting at you, Miss Laine. All women use their bodies to get their way, either consciously or unconsciously. You bought a new skirt and new blouse for this visit. You have a smell of newness about you. I suppose I should be flattered that you should go to such trouble, but I'm not.'

'How did you know I was here?'

Toby tapped the ear defenders that he had draped around his neck. 'A radio warning alarm.' He stooped and tinkered with the lethal-looking spring gun. It hissed menacingly when he disconnected the compressed-air cylinder. 'I've been thinking about your missing Kronos chips since we spoke.'

'Well don't think too much, Mr Hoyle. I haven't decided whether or not to hire you yet.'

'There's one in my Nanopad if you're running short of them.'

Beverley was in no mood for jokes. 'Mr Hoyle. This is a serious matter for which I need the services of a serious investigator.' She turned to leave. 'Sorry to have distracted you from your shooting.'

'I agree, Miss Laine. Murder is deadly serious.'

Beverley froze. She turned and looked at Toby. The sombre brown eyes regarded her steadily. 'The MD of Draggon Industries was murdered,' said Toby, peering into the breach of his shotgun. 'A certain Beverley Laine found the body. The police are looking for a gang believed to deal in rare stamps. My guess is that they should be barking up the tree of whoever bought out his company last year. A certain Liechtenstein-registered company with the enigmatic name of Media Holdings. Correct?'

'So you've been talking to Claude Jackson at Industry 2000?' Beverley replied tartly. 'So what? Should I be impressed?'

'Not at all, Miss Laine. I dug that information up myself. I'm a great believer in databases. You're mentioned on quite a few. In fact I know a good deal about you. Shall we go inside and discuss business?'

Beverley followed Toby through a sliding terrace door into an untidy office lined with books and box files. Toby Hoyle's obsession appeared to be British wildlife. The walls were covered with prints of birds and there was a massive tome about badgers opened on the desk. His computer was a Nanopad, half-buried under a pile of papers.

'One of the big pluses in my line is the access I get to some interesting databases,' said Toby, sorting out a mass of papers

145

in the collection bin of a laser printer. 'You're right to be suspicious about your disappearing microprocessors. When all the paths in a corporate maze of cross-linked companies lead to Liechtenstein, I get very suspicious.'

'So what are your chances of tracing the ownership of Media Holdings?' Beverley asked.

'From Liechtenstein, slim; from the UK, very good indeed. That's why I'm expensive.'

'And you're not averse to bending the law?'

'That's another reason why I'm expensive.' Toby sat opposite Beverley on a broken swivel chair with threadbare arms. 'Start right at the beginning,' he invited. 'Tell me everything.'

Beverley briefly outlined the events since Dave Crosier had died on his combine harvester, leading up to the failure of the Mars lander. She talked for several minutes, pausing only to sip a sherry that Toby poured for her. He listened attentively, occasionally making notes on his Nanopad. When she finished he asked a number of pertinent questions. His change of manner gave Beverley confidence. For the first time since the troubles had started she felt that she had someone on her side.

'So your supply of Kronos chips to the University of Surrey is a change of your company's policy?' he asked.

'How do you mean?'

'You said that Nano Systems don't actually sell them but sell a licence to use them. But those chips in the Mars lander you'll never see again.'

'We gave them to the university as part of our contribution to the Haldane Lander Programme,' Beverley replied.

'Do you ever license the Kronos for use in space?'

'Yes. The French use them in their Hermes shuttle programme. At the last count there were about five hundred Class A Kronoses in orbit.'

Toby made a note. 'Even though there's no hope of getting them back?'

'That's right. In commercial application of the Kronos, where the satellite is generating a constant cashflow, we require a royalty of between 1 and 5 per cent of turnover depending on the application.'

'Television satellites? That sort of thing?'

'That's right,' Beverley agreed. 'But mostly Earth resources satellites, surveillance, remote sensing. It's all big business now. The advent of the Kronos has increased the processing power of onboard systems and has even increased the average operating life of a satellite from ten to fifteen years. In fact there're a few hundred satellites up there earning big money that wouldn't be feasible, either technically or economically, were it not for the Kronos. So we see nothing wrong in sharing some of that revenue and channelling it back into research.'

The private investigator rummaged among the papers on his desk and handed a printed document to Beverley. 'Well you'll have to channel some of it into my fees, Miss Laine. An up-to-date price list.'

Beverley studied the columns of figures. Toby Hoyle wasn't exaggerating when he said that he was expensive. She looked up and saw a brief flicker of humour in his otherwise impassive expression.

'What's this about assistant's costs?'

'It may be necessary for me to use outside help.'

'I'm not sure if I trust you yet, Mr Hoyle. And I certainly don't want anyone else involved. I want to keep this as confidential as possible.'

'Then we'll have to call it a day, Miss Laine. There are some aspects of my *modus operandi* for which I require help.'

'What aspects?'

'Those that require a lookout.'

'I could do that. I want this to be a joint operation.'

Toby regarded her pensively. 'You really are taking this seriously, aren't you?'

'Yes.'

He shrugged. 'Okay, if that's what you want. So . . . Am I hired?'

'You're hired,' Beverley agreed. 'Provided you're free to make an immediate start.'

'Is 2 a.m. this morning immediate enough for you?'

## 25

When Leon Dexter yawned his skin stretched across his cheek-bones like a drum. He put his feet on his desk, tipped his chair back and hooked his hands behind his head. 'I've just had a brilliant notion, Macé.'

Dr Macé Pilleau wasn't interested in notions; he dealt in facts. Observed facts. Life was too short to go chasing rainbows when reality was more exciting and infinitely more complex and challenging. He grunted without taking his eyes from his portable electron microscope.

'I think I know what that garbage is, running through the centre of our mystery DNA.'

This time the good doctor did look up. 'It is *not* a DNA molecule,' he said curtly. 'It is only a digitalized representation of something that looks like a DNA. A photograph.'

Leon nodded to the computer monitor. The result of their many hours of work was on the screen. They had painstakingly performed graphics symbol substitutions on the trojan software until the whole thing hung together, elegant and symmetrical, just like the pictures of the many DNA molecules that Macé Pilleau had on his database. Everything was right except the unaccountable coloured band that ran through the centre of the double helix. 'Sure looks like it though,' Leon commented.

'You resemble an intelligent form of life, Leon. But as you so admirably prove by insisting that the trojan is a DNA because it looks like it, one is not necessarily what one looks like.'

Leon had an idea that there was an insult buried in there somewhere but he let it pass. Both men enjoyed rubbing each other up the wrong way which was why they got on so well together. Leon found an apple in his drawer and bit into it, munching contentedly, knowing full well that the noise irritated his elderly colleague. 'I think it's a soundtrack.'

Macé Pilleau's laughs were rare and not particularly pleasant. 'Ah? Beethoven or Strauss?'

'Close.'

The doctor regarded Leon with contempt. 'Third Symphony would you say?'

The sarcasm was lost on Leon. 'Music induces moods,' he said, chewing on his apple. 'Moods induce action. Action is the release of energy. That's why you're close.'

'Is it asking too much of you to explain what you're driving at?'

'Why shouldn't that band be noise? Let's assume our trojan is a software DNA, whatever that is. What would be needed to activate it? To set off motions in the nutrient fluid that could cause molecules to bond, to produce nano-machines to bond more molecules together to grow into living cells? Energy. Sound is energy. Ever listened to the cannons going off during the 1812 on a decent system with the sound wound right up? That's energy being released right enough, it hits you smack between the eyes and crawls up your arse.'

Leon took another bite of his apple, pleased at the thunderstruck expression on Dr Macé Pilleau's lined face.


## 26

Toby stopped his battered old Range Rover two hundred metres from Draggon Industries' main entrance and doused the headlights. He glanced at the dashboard clock: 3 a.m.

They were parked in a new industrial estate that was being developed on farmland. The area was a mixture of modern modular warehouses and office buildings and open fields. Draggon Industries' head office and main depot consisted of a sprawl of industrial system buildings relieved by a brick façade that housed the administrative offices.

'That's it,' said Beverley.

'Do you know the layout?'

'Only of the administrative area. Theo's office is upstairs at the front. First floor.'

Toby wound down his window and looked up. 'Good cloud cover tonight. Doesn't look like it's going to be any great problem.'

'Breaking into high security premises isn't going to be a

problem?' Beverley queried, gazing through the windscreen at the pool of floodlighting bathing the line-up of agricultural machinery behind high steel gates. They included six Type 19 combine harvesters, the same model that had killed Dave Crosier. Even at this distance she could see at least two closed-circuit television cameras on the front of the building. She pointed them out to Toby.

'Saw them when we drove past,' he replied. 'No problem. Industrial estates are usually a doddle. Any grown-up security systems they've got will be looking after those machines. Must be a million quid's worth of kit sitting there.' He handed Beverley a tiny two-way radio with a brooch microphone that he had already shown her how to use.

'How long do you expect to be?'

Toby knelt on the driver's seat and rummaged among the mass of mysterious equipment under an evil-smelling blanket in the back of the Range Rover. Everything about the interior of the vehicle stank, including the jeans and old anorak that Toby had insisted Beverley should wear for the escapade. He produced a portable tape-streamer, a device to copy the entire contents of computer hard discs or compact discs onto microcassette tapes. 'That depends on how many admin computers I find.'

Beverley was incredulous. 'You're proposing to back up all their hard discs?'

'That's right. We then take the tapes back to my place and study their contents at leisure.'

'But tape streamers are slow!' Beverley protested. 'Especially a toy like that thing.'

'I'll not have you calling my precious gadgets toys. Anyway, who said anything about one visit?'

'You're not thinking of several visits? Yes – you are. For Christ's sake, Toby, it's not worth the risk.'

Toby resumed rummaging in the back of the Range Rover. 'You're paying me to take risks, Miss Laine. Hold these.' He thrust a heavy pair of binoculars into her hands.

'I'm going in with you,' said Beverley firmly. 'I know which computer Theo Draggon used to use for his records. It'll save time. Your way will mean wasting time going through loads of dross.'

Toby saw the determined light in her eyes and gave in with a shrug. 'Okay. Just as you wish, boss. We'll tell the magistrate that we were looking for somewhere quiet to indulge in a spot of serious hanky panky.'

Before she could think of a suitable cutting reply, Toby was out of the driver's seat and dragging more gear out of the back of the vehicle. She joined him and tried to make out what he was unloading. 'What is all this stuff, Toby?'

'Twitchers' and nutters' night gear.'

'What?'

'Twitchers watch birds and nutters watch wildlife. Tonight we're both.' He pointed to a line of trees at the back of Draggon Industries. 'See those oaks?'

'Yes.'

'One of the last major habitats in West Sussex of the tawny owl.'

'Is it?' Beverley was completely mystified.

'I've really no idea. But that's what we'll tell the police if they come nosing around.' He slammed the rear doors shut, making little attempt to be quiet, and opened another Nanopad, a keyboard model. He adjusted the screen contrast. 'Got the entire Ordnance Survey for the UK on here,' he muttered, entering a grid reference on the keyboard.

Beverley was always intrigued by new applications for the Kronos-powered electronic pad. 'Right down to one metre to the kilometre?' she asked.

'Better than that. Take a look.'

Beverley looked at the screen. The plot of land that Draggon Industries occupied was shown in the centre of the picture. There were even dotted lines that showed the routes of the underground service pipes for water and sewage.

'Pity it doesn't show the layout of the interior,' Toby commented. 'We'll make our way round the back I think.' He jammed the Nanopad into the rucksack and hoisted it onto his shoulder. To complete the picture of a nocturnal naturalist he strung a bulky still camera around his neck. 'Ready?'

'Lead on, Macduff.'

They entered a field at the side of the complex and picked their way through brambles and nettles. Beverley was glad of the tough boots that Toby had insisted she wear. They stopped. An owl hooting nearby made her jump. 'Tawny owl,' said Toby cryptically. 'Nice to have an accomplice.'

He dropped his rucksack and studied the rear of the building through the binoculars.

'Surely it's too dark to see anything?'

Toby handed her the instrument. 'Take a look.'

Beverley raised the binoculars to her eyes and gasped. Every detail on the side of the prefabricated building was sharp and clear as if it were daylight. She had heard of light-intensifying night sight binoculars but this was the first time she had used them.

'That loading bay is certain to be their goods inwards,' said Toby. 'Going in through the back might just put us into the stores if we're lucky.'

'Amazing,' Beverley commented. 'Now what?'

Toby mounted the camera on a tripod and trained it at the trees beyond the building. He took the binoculars from Beverley and traversed them the length of the building's corrugated panels.

'Ha! Found a camera. And a couple of infra-red detectors, no, three detectors. Typical installation. Some security companies have about as much imagination as a dead dormouse when it comes to planning decent installations. And I'm prepared to bet there's no night security guard.'

'How can you be sure?'

'Animal instinct.'

'If we've to avoid being hauled up before a magistrate tomorrow morning, your animal instincts had better be reliable,' Beverley retorted.

'Trust me, Miss Laine.'

'You can call me Bev.'

'You choose strange moments to get familiar.'

'*I* am not getting familiar!' Beverley hissed angrily. She was about to add something suitably scathing but Toby wasn't

152

paying any attention to her. He crouched, peered through the camera's viewfinder and trained it on the building. He clicked the shutter four times, taking what appeared to be thirty-second time exposures, before panning the camera to a new target after each shot.

'How will taking photographs help?' Beverley asked.

'Who said I was taking photographs?'

'That's what it looks like.'

'That's what it's supposed to look like.' He patted the camera. 'Infra-red laser projector. Evil beast. Half a minute exposure each and those detectors and the TV cameras are now nicely cooked.'

Beverley began to see the remarkable method in Toby's apparent madness. 'Have you ever been caught playing around like this?'

'I cannot tell a lie. Yes, twice.' He removed the camera from the tripod and stowed it in the rucksack. 'Once trying to record bats while planting a bug in a boardroom. And once photographing badgers in the grounds of a dope dealer's house.'

Beverley smiled. She was warming to this taciturn young man more than she cared to admit. 'What happened?'

'The first time a verballing from the law; the second time an even louder verballing from the dope pusher.' He swung the rucksack over his shoulder. 'Follow me.'

Beverley followed in his footsteps as they pushed through the dense undergrowth to the three-metre-high chainlink fence that surrounded the complex. 'I'm lousy at climbing,' Beverley complained.

'Makes two of us. I'd never make a cat burglar.' He pulled on a pair of gardening gloves and began tugging brambles and creepers away from the foot of the fence. He produced a pair of power croppers with a $CO_2$ gas bottle attached and set them to work chomping through the base of the fence with little explosive hisses as each strand of wire parted. He cut through the base anchorages of a two-metre length of fence and propped the wire open with the camera tripod. He wriggled through the opening. Beverley passed the rucksack to him and followed him through the hole.

153

'I hate to admit this,' said Beverley, scrambling to her feet. 'But I think I'm enjoying this.'

'It's the adrenalin. I expect you're also hooked on jogging.'

'Yes, I am.'

'You're an adrenalin junkie.' As Toby talked, his eyes were scanning his surroundings, missing nothing. He pointed to a maker's label high up on one of the building's side panels. 'Hewdic Industrial Buildings. That'll make life easier if it's one of their System 30 jobs. Come on.'

Beverley followed Toby across a car park to the side of the building. She wondered why she wasn't frightened and realized that it was due to the tremendous confidence that this icy-calm man inspired.

'This is the difficult bit,' said Toby. He was running his fingertips along the lower edge of the building. 'Torch, please, Beverley.'

Pleased that he had used her first name, Beverley trained the beam of light where Toby indicated. 'Great. A System 30 building.' There was a note of triumph in his voice. He knelt and dragged the Nanopad from the rucksack. Beverley looked over his shoulder and watched curiously. Toby switched on the machine and worked the keyboard. A menu that listed several categories of British wildlife appeared on the glowing screen. He selected the last item and scrolled the screen through the several pages of brilliantly illuminated pictures of seabirds. Another menu appeared. Five levels down into the database, he found what he was looking for.

'Who are they?' Beverley asked, looking at the list of names and addresses on the screen.

'Every manufacturer of industrial buildings in Europe,' Toby answered. 'I've got all their construction details in here: assembly drawings; dimensions; fitting instructions; the lot. Ah, this is it.' A line drawing of the same building they were standing outside appeared on the screen. 'Hewdic System 30 Industrial Buildings. An excellent company. Very generous with their drawings.'

'You must be the first professional burglar in the world who uses a computer database,' Beverley observed.

'You'd be surprised what I've got stored in this thing,' Toby muttered, studying a drawing intently. 'Information on just about every closed circuit TV and alarm system in existence. Did you know that a shaving cream aerosol squirted through the ventilation slots in some alarm systems can screw them up? Ah, dimensions of fixings. Find one rivet and you've found the lot.' He felt in his pocket for a steel tape measure and a pencil which he used to make a number of marks exactly a hundred and fifty millimetres up from the base of the panel section he was interested in. He shone the torch along the line of marks and spotted a faint circular mark in the panel's anodized finish. 'There we are, Beverley. A countersunk rivet head. There'll be one every hundred millimetres.'

Forgetting the danger inherent in the situation she was in, Beverley watched with interest as Toby used a spring-loaded centre punch to make an indentation in the exact centre of the rivet's flush head. He found a cordless drill in the rucksack, wrapped a heavy cloth around it to muffle the sound, and pressed the drill tip hard into the rivet's centre-punched indentation before pulling the trigger. A spiral of aluminium swarf twisted silently off the drill bit. Suddenly the shank of the drill disappeared into the panel. 'Paper-thin, these panels,' Toby murmured. 'Let's hope there's not some fixture on the other side which is going to make problems.'

After ten minutes' concentrated work Toby had drilled out enough rivets along the base of the panel for him to spring the section carefully away from the inner frame. 'Reckon you can squeeze through that, Beverley?'

Beverley wriggled through the narrow opening. She scrambled cautiously to her feet in total darkness.

*You're crazy, Bev. Here you are, a respectable businesswoman – breaking into a building in the wee small hours. You could get a couple of years in Holloway, then where would you be? Where would Nano Systems be?*

She banished the unwelcome thoughts, groped for the rucksack that Toby pushed through to her, and helped him to his feet. He switched on his torch and swept the beam around. They had entered the building beside a hot drink vending machine.

155

Toby whistled. 'Another metre to the left and I would have been drilling through power cables.' He flashed the torch around. They were in a corridor formed by racks of back-to-back Dexion shelving in long, straight rows, and crammed with hundreds of small-parts storage bins. 'Looks like we're in the stores. Okay, let's find the admin offices.'

Beverley followed Toby through a pair of double doors and into an assembly shop. There was a clear central aisle marked in white paint on the concrete floor that took them past the sombre shapes of combine harvesters, bail elevators and harrows in various states of construction. At the end of the shop was a corridor, lined with small offices for the foremen and inspectors, that opened into the reception area.

'Up the stairs,' Beverley whispered.

'I guessed,' Toby replied.

They found Theodore Draggon's office suite without trouble. It was large and modern, brilliantly illuminated by the forecourt floodlights. There was a long conference table piled high with lateral files tied with string.

'It would appear that they're in the process of a grand clear out following the demise of their boss,' Toby observed, sitting at a grand, horseshoe-shaped desk.

Beverley looked around. In addition to the files on the table, there were crammed filing cabinet drawers spread out on the thick-pile carpet. In a corner was a large open carton with a scruffy-looking computer keyboard and a system box tipped inside.

'I presume this is the boss's computer?' said Toby indicating a smart 586 Toshiba personal computer in front of him. 'Hundred meg hard disc. If it's full, it'll take a month of Sundays to back up.'

Beverley shook her head. 'Theo had an old machine. I remember kidding him about it but he said that he understood it and that he liked it.' She dragged the keyboard out of the carton. It was an early 90s vintage Amstrad PC. The plastic casing was brown with cigar smoke stains. 'This was Theo's machine,' she declared.

Toby chuckled. 'Good job you did string along. I would've

left that to last.' He connected the computer components together on the desk, and plugged the power lead into a socket. The hard disc whirred softly as it picked up speed. The screen flickered and the machine booted-up.

'Well at least it's a stand-alone machine,' Toby observed. 'Not networked like the others, therefore you can be pretty sure that Mr Theodore Draggon kept some interesting stuff on it unless some zealot's wiped the hard disc.' His fingers worked the keyboard as he talked. He entered CHKDSK/V and watched the hard disc's entire directory listings race up the screen. 'Which they haven't.'

Beverley knelt on the floor beside him. Toby logged into a word-processing sub-directory. 'Tell me, Beverley. If you were nosing around someone's hard disc, what files would your compulsive feminine curiosity steer you to first? Not that you would ever dream of doing such a thing, of course.'

Beverley chuckled. 'A name and address file.'

'Exactly what I thought. That Filofax program looks interesting.'

'I've got the same program on my machine,' said Beverley, looking at the screen with interest. 'It's for printing updated names and addresses on Filofax format paper.'

Toby loaded the program. A string of names and addresses appeared in a column down the centre of the screen. 'In alphabetical order too. Mr Draggon was methodical.'

'The program does the sorting, but Theo was well organized.'

'Which means,' said Toby, pressing the page down key to scroll through the list, 'that there *have* to be names and addresses among this lot that relate to the mysterious Media Holdings. After all, they owned his company.'

For the next few minutes they worked their way right through the long file, looking for a name and address, a clue, an anomaly, something that didn't look right. But the innocent-looking names, addresses and telephone numbers seemed endless: agricultural machinery dealers for every country in Europe; farming journalists; relations in his native Yorkshire; even numbers relating to his various bank and credit card accounts. At the end of the file was a list of birthday dates. Theodore Draggon's

Filofax program was a repository of personal information, which was exactly what they were intended to be.

They sat in thought for a few moments. Beverley spoke first. 'I don't suppose I should tell you this, but I can never remember my cash card PIN numbers so I bury them in fake telephone numbers in my address book.'

Beverley had never heard Toby laugh before. 'I do much the same,' he admitted. 'Except mine are buried in my trusty Nanopad. Trouble is, I usually forget where I've hidden them.' He became thoughtful. 'Good thinking though, Beverley. Let's go back and just concentrate on the phone numbers.'

'There's something odd about that bank account number,' said Beverley, pointing at an entry on the screen when Toby reached the end of the file. 'Ten digits? Isn't that too long?'

'And that doesn't look like a sort code,' Toby murmured, frowning at the screen. 'What does it look like to you, Beverley?'

'I've no idea.'

'It looks like an Iridium Gold prefix written backwards . . . In fact, I'm bloody sure it is.' He drummed his fingers absently on the desk while gazing at the screen.

Beverley recited the numbers backwards under her breath. 'You're right, Toby. It's got to be!'

'The question is, is the entire number written backwards or just the prefix?' Without waiting for an answer, Toby pulled a telephone towards him, pressed the on-hook button, and punched out the number.

'Hang on,' said Beverley anxiously. 'If it is an Iridium Gold number, whoever answers will know where the call is coming from.'

'That could be to our advantage.'

There was a series of familiar soft tones from the telephone's speaker. 'Those are the polling codes,' Toby observed. 'The system's finding out where the handset we're calling is located.' The musical notes of codes changed to a higher pitch. 'Sounds like the system's using an intercontinental routing. That means the handset is a long way away.' There was a silence followed by the ringing tone. The call was answered on the third ring.

'Yes?' An impatient male voice answered.

'This is Draggon Industries in the UK,' said Toby.

The voice was suddenly guarded. 'Yes, I can see that.'

'We have an important and highly confidential message for you, sir. Who are we talking to?'

'If you know this number, you know who I am!' the voice rasped. The man was nearly shouting, causing speaker distortion, but Beverley knew who the voice belonged to.

'Yes, we realize that,' Toby continued, unaware of the shock that was gripping Beverley. 'But this is an extremely important message from Theodore Draggon. We must be 100 per cent certain who we are talking to.'

'You're talking to Marshall Tate!'

The shaking of Toby's imperturbability manifested itself as a slight pause before he replied. 'Thank you, Mr Tate. The message from – ' He ended the conversation by pressing the button that cut the connection.

He turned and looked at Beverley. In the harsh yellow glow of the floodlights, her face seemed to take on a strange pallor. 'That seems to be a bigger surprise to you than it is to me,' he observed with unwitting accuracy.

The tension in Beverley's face suddenly slipped away. She smiled unexpectedly and nodded. 'I'm a fighter, Toby.'

'I never doubted it.'

'But for the past few days I've been going through hell. I knew I had an enemy but I didn't know who. I thought Marshall Tate had given up trying to grab Nano Systems two years ago. Now that I know he didn't, I feel better, much better. I now have a situation I can deal with.'

Toby was intrigued. As he looked at Beverley he could almost feel the formidable strength and resolution that was suddenly surging through her veins. 'And the illustrious Marshall Tate is the enemy?'

Beverley nodded. There was a strange calmness in her voice when she spoke. 'Most definitely.'

'May God help him,' said Toby.

## 27

Carl stopped jogging and doubled up. If the sand had been dry he would have happily flopped out on the beach. 'No good, Bev,' he croaked. 'If you force me any more, I won't be any use to you later.'

Beverley stopped jogging and turned to face Carl with her hands on her hips. Her Laine Runner sensed the sudden inactivity. It voiced protests and stepped up the voltage of the tiny electric shocks it delivered to her nervous system. She hit the button that shut it off. 'We haven't even covered a couple of kilometres,' she pointed out.

Carl hobbled to the belt of shingle and sat down. 'The only worthwhile thing about this ridiculous jogging lark is that I get to see you in that disgustingly sexy running gear. Apart from that boost to my animal craving for you, it's destroying my health, my reason, and my stamina. I refuse to run another step.'

Beverley laughed and sat beside him. She grabbed hold of his hand and held it tightly. 'You're good for me, Carl.'

'Which is a damn sight more than you are for me,' Carl grumbled. He stole a surreptitious sideways glance at Beverley. Her face was alive, animated. The old Beverley was back. The vibrant ready-to-take-on-the-world Beverley that he loved and which he thought had gone forever.

'I think better when I'm running.'

Carl tugged a handkerchief from his shorts and mopped his forehead. It was a sultry, overcast afternoon. The beach and sea were deserted apart from a few novice windsurfers struggling to maintain their balance in the scant breeze. 'Well I can't think at all. As always, you manage to perplex and frighten me and make me love you all at the same time.'

'Why should I frighten you, Carl?'

'Because I think you know something.'

'I know that I was right,' said Beverley lightly.

'You mean someone *is* sabotaging the Kronos?'

'Yes.'

'Who?'

Beverley watched a pair of herring gulls squabbling over a dead fish. 'He's ruthless. Utterly and completely ruthless, through to the core. Take my word for it. He had Theo Draggon killed.'

'Yes. But who?'

Silence.

'Now listen, Bev, if you've found something out, then you have a duty to go to the police, or at least tell me.'

Beverley saw the suppressed anger in Carl's eyes. For a moment it looked as if she was about to say something but she changed her mind and jumped to her feet. 'Come on,' she said lightly. 'Race you back to the bungalow.' To add weight to the challenge, she hauled a protesting Carl to his feet and set off at a brisk pace, switching on her Laine Runner when Carl drew level with her.

'So who is it?' Carl demanded.

For an answer Beverley swerved through a sand pool and splattered Carl's legs.

'You're a bitch, Miss Laine!'

Beverley laughed and increased her pace. Carl grimly maintained his position a couple of metres behind her. He misjudged the breakwater, caught his foot on the board and went sprawling in the wet sand.

'Beverley!'

She ignored him. Carl staggered gamely after her and got his rhythm back.

'Beverley!' he yelled. 'Severe punishment awaits you for this!'

She maintained a moderate pace so that Carl could catch up with her.

'What sort of punishment, kind sire?'

'I'm considering . . .' Carl puffed, 'a thrashing . . . across my knee . . . But you might enjoy that . . . So something more drastic . . . is called for. For Christ's sake, Bev, you're killing me!'

Beverley stepped up her pace in response to the urging of the tiny electric shocks from her belt. Were they sharper than usual or was she imagining it?

'Oh, for Christ's sake,' Carl puffed. 'This is supposed to make me fit, not kill me!'

'It will if you can keep it up!' Beverley yelled over her shoulder. '*And* you're younger than me, remember!'

The pin pricks became faster, spurring her on. Suddenly Carl was forgotten as the adrenalin coursed into her bloodstream. The drug stimulated and sharpened her sense: the splat of her feet on the wet sand; the satisfying crunch beneath her trainers when she crossed a belt of shingle.

*Faster, body!*

'Beverley!'

The voice was an insignificant intrusion almost obliterated by the pounding blood in her ears. The shocks from her belt increased in intensity, driving her on. She cleared a breakwater effortlessly.

'Beverley!'

Much fainter.

*Good! Good! Get away from him! Faster, body! Faster!*

The heady, sexual release of alkaloids. The vicious stabbing of the electric shocks reached a level of such engulfing intensity that it was no longer possible to tell where they were coming from. Her whole body was imprisoned in a terrible, delicious ecstasy.

Passing her bungalow now, but she no longer knew or cared.

*Come on, stupid body! Faster! Faster!*

Suddenly the euphoria was total. She was no longer aware of the hydraulically-damped impact of her trainers on the sand; she could no longer hear the crash of surf, the cries of scavenging seagulls, or the relentless pumping of blood from a heart being driven to the point of failure. The intoxicating sensation of multiple orgasms that swept through her tortured body was like the sudden opening of sluice gates that had been holding back a flood.

Carl saw Beverley collapse on the sand. He started running.

## 28

'Jogging maniacs,' grumbled Beverley's doctor, emerging from her bedroom. 'She's fit as a flea but she won't admit that she's past the age when she could go galloping off in all directions without her body yelling foul.'

'Have you called an ambulance?' Carl asked, trying to look past the doctor into the bedroom.

'Not necessary. Glucose and a knockout sedative, that's all she needs and that's what I've given her. What you can give her when she wakes up is some strong advice to give up this crazy jogging thing. She's never listened to me. I've even chased her along the beach, would you believe. Anyway, she'll sleep for about ten hours. Make her take it easy for at least a day when she wakes up. Call me if there are any problems.'

'So it wasn't a heart attack?'

'Good heavens, no. She fainted. Her brain's got more sense than she knows how to use. It saw what was coming and shut everything down. Defence mechanism. Good day to you.'

As soon as the doctor's car had reversed out of the drive, Carl cautiously opened Beverley's bedroom door and peeped in. Seeing her relaxed face, her ringlets spread out on the pillow, was a relief he couldn't even begin to measure. Staggering four hundred metres along the beach while holding her dead, seemingly lifeless weight in his arms had been an agony he would never forget.

Carl sat in the living room and watched the setting sun breaking through the cloud. There was something irresistibly soothing about watching the changing light on the sea. For the first time he could understand why Beverley was so in love with the place. Once it was dark he watched television for a while with the sound turned down for fear of disturbing her. There was nothing worth watching so he turned his attention to her crowded bookcase with its many framed photographs of her son, Paul: Paul when he was about two; school pictures of Paul; Paul in scout uniform; not one of Paul when he got married. That was odd.

His eyes went down to the shelves. Strange that in the years he had known Beverley, he had never had the chance to look at her books. There were a number of tomes on business management, several on British seabirds, a few coffee-table books, and a large collection of modern paperback novels. None of which interested him.

At 10 p.m. he made himself a coffee and looked in on Beverley. She was still sleeping soundly. Her Laine Runner belt was lying on the floor where he had dumped it after carrying her into the bedroom. He picked it up and turned it over in his hands, wondering if it was in any way connected with her extraordinary behaviour. He remembered her complaining about a pain when she had taken it off and decided to take it back to the laboratories for a check. He took it into the living room and dropped it on the chesterfield.

He watched the news, got bored, and went back to the bookcase. There was a large, untitled volume that caught his attention. At first he thought it was a photograph album, but it turned out to be a scrapbook. His first reaction was to put it back. Scrapbooks had much in common with diaries, they were private. Only a heel would read one. But he couldn't help looking at the first page. It was taken up with a school photograph. About two hundred twelve- to fifteen-year-olds of both sexes looking obediently at the camera. Not one of them risking so much as a hint of a smile. No doubt the school dragon was standing beside the photographer. He looked at the caption: 'AMBLESIDE SCHOOL, WALTON-ON-THAMES. SUMMER TERM 1965.'

The picture had been taken over thirty years ago and yet he found Beverley almost immediately in the second row. Her frizz of ringlets was a dead giveaway. But what surprised him was the expression of arrogance and blatant sexuality. It was interesting to see that the rebel in her had been present even then because she was the only pupil not looking obediently at the camera. What was even more surprising was her stance: shoulders back, young breasts thrust out. Carl had never known Beverley to project herself sexually as she was in the photograph. If anything, she had always struck him as being wary of sex.

There was what could be the makings of an impish smile playing at the corners of her mouth. Her gaze appeared to be directed at a pencilled-in arrow on the photograph that was pointing to a fair-haired, lanky boy with a surly expression.

Carl turned the page to see if there was anything written on the back. There was nothing, but glued neatly to the following page was a press cutting: 'LOCAL FILM MAKER TO HAVE MOVIE SHOWN ON TELEVISION'. Underneath was a six-inch column about a film called *Catseyes* made by a local man that was to be shown on BBC2. The amateur filmmaker was Marshall Tate. He wondered if it was the same Marshall Tate who was the owner of the controversial Elite satellite TV channel. He read through the article and noted the date, 1969. He turned the page, his scruples about reading Beverley's scrapbook forgotten. Another cutting, this time from a national in 1970: 'ROW OVER SCHOOLKIDS' SEX FILM.'

Marshall Tate had made a film for the Schools Educational Council warning children about the dangers of accepting lifts from motorists. According to the director of the council, the film was too explicit and had been banned.

Beneath the story was a photograph of a young-looking Marshall Tate whom Carl had no difficulty in recognizing from television and newspapers. He turned back to the school photograph. There was no doubt now in his mind who the pencilled arrow was pointing at: it was an even younger-looking Marshall Tate.

So Beverley and Marshall Tate had gone to the same school together? She had never mentioned it to him. Life was full of surprises.

At first he had thought that the scrapbook would be about Beverley, after all she had received a fair amount of press coverage since becoming MD of Nano Systems. But he was wrong; the entire book was packed with cuttings about Marshall Tate. They were in chronological order, a potted compendium of tabloid cuttings tracing the rise and rise of Marshall Tate. There were dozens of photographs, and, as always, the sensational headlines: 'TATE LASHES TV BOSSES'; 'TATE'S NEW FILM BANNED'; 'TATE LAUNCHES INTO SATELLITE

TV'; 'STORM OVER TATE'S ELITE CHANNEL'; 'TATE BEATS GOVERNMENT MOVES TO CLOSE ELITE CHANNEL'; 'TATE OPENS CREDIT CARD CASINO ROYALE ON ELITE SKY CHANNEL'. There was even a disclaimer stuck into the album from Sky Television regarding the last headline pointing out that the Elite channel was nothing to do with Sky, that Elite and Sky happened to use the same Astra satellites.

Carl's fingers kept turning pages. There were sober, more recent stories from the quality newspapers, some stories that Carl remembered because of the furore surrounding them: 'MARSHALL TATE CLEARED OF RUNNING ILLEGAL CASINO – Judge rules Luxembourg Astra satellites "beyond jurisdiction", Gaming Board to appeal'; 'FRENCH JUDGE ORDERS TATE RELEASE'.

Strangely, none of the cuttings was less than two years old and yet he recalled that Marshall Tate had been in the news recently over his plans to extend his gambling operations to the Far East. He had casinos nearing completion in Bangkok, Tokyo and Beijing even though the Thai government and the Japanese government had publicly stated that gambling licences were not likely to be forthcoming.

Carl turned back through the pages. All the clippings had been cut out neatly with scissors and gummed square onto the pages with datelines carefully centred. This had been more than just a passing interest in the activities of a former school friend: this had been an obsession, a lifetime's collecting that she had inexplicably lost interest in two years previously. It was all very odd.

What had driven her to it? Could it be that Marshall Tate had been her husband? He doubted it. On the few occasions that Beverley had talked about her past, her bitter comments about her former husband gave the impression that he had been a drunken oaf.

And why this thing about running? Was she really that frightened of getting old? Carl's own feeling now that he was in his forties was that at least he'd left behind the tyranny of youth with its nagging worries about what other people thought of him. He had once mentioned it to Beverley and she had laughingly agreed.

He returned the scrapbook to the bookcase and looked in on her. She was still sleeping soundly, lying on her left side, her knees drawn up in a foetal position. With her funny little curls spilling over the pillow, she looked so lovely and vulnerable. Her duvet had slipped to the floor. He was about to pull it over her but it was a warm night so maybe she had kicked it off deliberately. She was still wearing her running gear with the exception of her trainers which he had removed while waiting for the doctor. Her T-shirt had ridden up, exposing her waist. The light from the hall shone on her pale skin, illuminating what looked suspiciously like a rash. Taking great care not to wake her, he switched on the bedside light and turned up the brilliance. On close examination, the rash turned out to be a tiny cluster of inflamed and swollen puncture marks. He drew the T-shirt up very carefully. The skin below her running bra was as usual flawless. He returned to the living room and picked up the Laine Runner belt. A close examination of the belt aroused his suspicions. He went out to his car and returned with a pocket microscope from his portable test kit. Under a reading light he studied the belt's body sensors, tiny herculainium alloy hypodermic barbs that were so fine they were almost invisible to the naked eye. They were designed to puncture painlessly into the wearer's skin whenever the belt was donned. Made from an alloy based on titanium, they were body tissue compatible – that is, the body accepted them – and so the presence of such a foreign material did not trigger immune systems and stimulate the production of antibodies.

He focused the microscope on the delicate tips of the barbs. Enlarged they looked ugly and threatening and it was normally possible to see the minute opening of the hypodermic bore. Not this time: the tip of each barb was a mass of congealed blood. That should not happen! No wonder Beverley had complained, the barbs were supposed to make punctures in the wearer's skin that were too fine for blood to pass through. Carl had taken great care over the body sensors and had eventually settled on a proven design from the Nano Medical Corporation in California.

167

What he liked about the sensors was the ingenious swivel mounting that permitted a good deal of wearer movement without tearing the skin. Besides, Beverley had been using the prototype belt continuously for six months without any problems.

And then he thought he saw something that raised the hackles on the nape of his neck and sent a cold finger of fear down his spine. The base of one of the barbs looked as though it had been split open. He repositioned the reading light and blinked to clear his vision before returning his gaze to the microscope's eyepiece and refocusing.

*It had split open!*

Jesus H . . . That was impossible!

No, it wasn't because it had happened: the hypodermic barb, made from the toughest alloy yet invented, had swollen half a millimetre above the base and burst along a millimetre of its length. Carl lifted his head and stared at the wall.

*What the hell could have happened?*

He looked again. It was obvious what had gone wrong: somehow a flawed barb had managed to get past Nano Medical's rigorous post-production inspection. Maybe an impurity in the alloy. There could be any number of causes. Two things were certain: Beverley was not going to wear the belt again, and its production was out of the question until the faulty barb had been returned to California for a report. He took the belt to his car and locked it in the boot.

It was time for bed. He decided to use the spare bedroom, leaving its door open and Beverley's door open so that he could hear her if she called out. He lay on the bed, listening carefully for Beverley's light breathing while turning over the events of the day.

Very soon he slept.


## 29

Sleep induced a metamorphic state in Carl that transformed him into a zombie. A state he remained in for at least thirty minutes after waking until he had received a life-giving infusion of black coffee.

He shuffled into the kitchen, relying on the smell of coffee to provide a homing system that enabled him to travel from the bedroom to the kitchen without mishap.

Beverley was bathed in sunlight streaming through the windows. She looked bright and breezy, was wearing a housecoat, poaching eggs, reading the morning paper, listening to the radio, watching television with the sound muted, and pouring coffee, all at the same time. A normal start to her day.

'Enter one useless lover,' she observed. 'Thought the smell would arouse you. One of your disgusting, high cholesterol breakfasts coming up. Do you know why I'd never marry you, Carl?'

'Apart from the fact that I'd never dream of asking you, why won't you marry me, Beverley?' asked Carl hollowly, sitting at the bar and cupping his hands gratefully around a mug of coffee that she pushed in front of him.

'Because you always look so dreadful in the morning.' She gave him a plate of poached eggs on toast.

'I'm glad, Bev. I don't think I could face the awesome responsibility of looking after an unhinged wife who does damn fool things like you did yesterday.'

'Oh! And what did I do yesterday?'

Carl drained his mug and started on his eggs. 'You know damn well what you did.'

'Okay, maybe I overdid the running. I fainted. You called out Dr Wyman to have his usual whinge at me. He gave me a sedative and here I am. No big deal.'

'*Overdid!*' Carl echoed, trying to sound indignant with a mouth full of egg. 'You damn near killed yourself!'

'Don't exaggerate, Carl. I admit that I got carried away.'

'Yes, by me. Off the bloody beach. Damned near killed me. You may look the fragile, demure little lady, but you're all bloody muscle. You're not wearing that belt any more.'

'It happens to all serious runners. Belt or no belt. They don't want to accept that they've reached a peak so they push themselves harder and harder. It's called achievement.'

'It's called being bloody stupid. Anyway, I took a look at the

169

belt last night. The body sensors are damaged. You're not wearing it any more.'

Beverley flushed angrily. She felt that Carl was being pompous, overbearing and patronizing. 'It was working fine yesterday, unless you've deliberately buggered it.'

'For Christ's sake, Bev, there's a damaged barb. You complained last week that it hurt when you took it off. I saw the marks it's made around your waist when I looked in on you last night.'

Beverley frowned, untied her housecoat and pulled it back. She was wearing briefs and a bra underneath. 'What marks?'

'On your right side.'

Beverley tugged down the waistband of her briefs, exposing her waist. 'Where? Or is this a crude ploy to get me undressed?'

Carl gaped in astonishment. 'They've gone!' He thought fast. He was convinced that Beverley had been lying on her left side, therefore the rash had to be on her right side. Maybe he was mistaken.

'Turn around,' he ordered.

Beverley turned slightly. Carl tugged down her briefs a little way and peered in bewilderment at her unmarked skin. 'You must have treated them with an enzyme healer,' he accused.

'Treated what!'

'Beverley, I swear there was a nasty rash on your right side last night. There was even some blood. They weren't the sort of marks that could disappear overnight without treatment.' He looked very closely and saw a pattern of almost invisible pinpricks marring her skin. 'That's them! How the hell could they have healed up like that in a few hours?'

Beverley twisted her head and pulled at her skin to see what Carl was indicating. 'You're a stupid prat, Carl, you know what? Those are sandfly bites.'

Carl snorted. 'Sandflies don't cause marks like those I saw last night.'

For an answer Beverley put her right foot on the stool beside Carl and pointed out a number of reddish pinpricks around her calf and shin. 'Sandflies,' she said curtly. 'The little bastards have been particularly bad this year. One must have got caught

170

under the belt and decided to pay me out, and I had probably scratched the bites in my sleep and made them worse. Satisfied?'

Carl had been about to ask Beverley about Marshall Tate but decided that having to explain that he had not been prying was too risky in her present mood. He started eating in silence, blaming himself for the switches in her temperament.

Beverley suddenly moved behind him, slid her arms around his neck and kissed him on the cheek. 'Sorry I'm being so boorish, Carl. Thanks for looking after me. The trouble with me is that I can be such an ungrateful little bitch at times.'

'No,' said Carl, patting her hands solemnly. 'You can be an ungrateful bitch all the time.'

They both laughed.

Had Carl turned around at that point he would have seen that there was no laughter in Beverley's eyes.


## 30

Toby rummaged among the papers on his desk, found Beverley's scrapbook on Marshall Tate, and handed it back to her.

'Fine, Beverley. I've gone through it all. It's interesting but it doesn't help. I've filled out the last two years by going over the back numbers of every English language publication whose databases I could get access to.'

'And,' Beverley prompted.

'And nothing. I could find nothing that could indicate why Marshall Tate should show such an interest in your company.'

'Because of huge growth potential,' said Beverley hotly. 'Do you know how many bids we've had to fend off? How many sharks we've had sniffing around over the years?'

'Long-term growth. Which I can't see is of interest to Marshall Tate. It's not what he's looking for. The profits on his Elite channel gambling makes Nano Systems' turnover look silly. He doesn't need you.'

'And yet he went to the trouble of setting me up,' Beverley countered. She found that she could talk easily about the past to Toby because he never voiced personal opinions. He was doing what he was being paid to do: seeking the truth and not giving a damn about anything else. 'When his takeover bid failed because of my opposition, he tried to get me out of my job.'

'By offering you the chance to run the Elite channel, his money-spinner,' Toby added. 'That's what doesn't add up.'

'It does if he wanted me out of the way.' Bitterness crept into Beverley's voice. 'And now he's got his filthy hands on several thousand Class A Kronos chips. Enough to mount a serious attempt on reverse engineering them.'

'But *why*?' Toby persisted. 'Where's the real motive? Not a get even motive, but the real profit motive? It's just not there no matter how strongly you feel about him or how much he wants to get even with you.'

There was silence for a few moments.

'This month-long affair you had with him. Can you remember how many times you saw him?'

'It was four weekends,' Beverley replied.

'Long weekends?'

'Friday evenings to Sunday nights. Listen, Toby, I don't want a word of this to leak back to anyone. No one at Nano Systems knows about it.'

'You have my professional word on it. Okay, four long weekends. You couldn't have spent the entire time making love?'

Beverley looked up sharply at Toby to see if he was mocking her but his gaze was disinterestedly bland. She nodded. 'That's just about all we did do. He liked to dominate.'

*Liked? Christ, the understatement of the year.*

'But you came up for air occasionally?'

'Yes. Is this important?'

'Can you remember what you talked about?'

'No.'

'Try. Did you ever get drunk together? Can you remember anything that he might have let slip about his plans?'

'We were both pretty smashed most of the time,' Beverley admitted. 'He mentioned something about his Far East plans. That was why he said that he wanted me to run the Elite channel for him.'

Toby's questioning was casual and yet relentless. 'Anything

172

else? Did he ever mention going into electronics in the Far East in a big way or anything like that?'

'I don't think so.'

'Try to think. Go over everything that happened, everything he said. Something that seems trivial might have some bearing.'

Beverley's patience snapped. 'You're asking me to delve into something I've spent two years trying to shut out. I can't do it here and now.'

'I don't want you to, Bev. Go home and think hard and write everything down that comes to mind. The key to the future is in the past.'

Beverley was nearly home, driving fast through the darkened lanes of West Sussex, turning over the conversation with Toby in her mind when she realized that there *was* something Marshall Tate had said when he had had too much to drink. The trouble was that for the life of her she could not recall what it was. All she could remember was that he had said something and then checked himself, suddenly, as if he had realized that he was being too garrulous.

But what the hell was it? She had an idea that it may have been during her first visit to his docklands penthouse but she could not be certain. It was all very well for Toby to tell her to go home and think, but trying to recall casual conversations with Marshall Tate between their bouts of frenzied love-making of two years ago was next to impossible. Especially as she had been drunk most of the time.

But there was a method of delving into the past.

No . . . It could be dangerous. She and Carl had drafted strict guidelines about the use of the TVR chambers.

*Oh, what the hell!*

She braked the Albatross, reversed into a stableyard and accelerated back the way she had come.

## 31

Nano Systems' TVR facility had changed over the years. In addition to Leon Dexter's original virtual reality chamber, there were ten smaller chambers resting on aluminium trestles. They formed a still, silent line like sleek fibreglass tombs. A red light burning over the circular access hatch of each chamber indicated that they were active. The mass of fibreglass and sound-proofing in each chamber took two days to reach working temperature which meant that they had to be maintained in an operational condition round the clock. To one side was a horseshoe-shaped control console equipped with closed-circuit television screens and monitoring equipment so that the TVR duty controller could keep a watchful eye on work in progress.

Don Tesler, the chief security guard, appeared, completing his midnight round. 'Good evening, Miss Laine,' he said, curious about Beverley's presence. 'The front gate told me you'd turned up. Can I be of any help?'

'No, I'm okay, thanks, Don. Mr Olivera wants me to check some results. I'll be about an hour.'

The guard looked worried. 'Will you be using the TVR chamber, Miss Laine?'

'Possibly.' Beverley resented the question.

'There should always be a controller on duty,' said the guard uneasily, glancing at the deserted console. 'Your rules, Miss Laine.'

Beverley resisted snapping the man's head off; he was doing his job. Instead she said, 'I'll patch the chamber I'll be using through to your office, Don. If I need you, I'll holler. Okay?'

'Well . . . If you're sure you'll be all right, Miss Laine.'

Beverley smiled warmly. 'I'll be fine.'

As soon as she was alone, Beverley went into the changing room and grabbed a towel. She approached chamber ten, the furthest from the door, and undressed. Wrapped in only a towel, and holding a voice recorder, she opened the hatch and scrambled into the chamber's brightly lit interior. The new chambers were a big improvement on Leon's original prototype. Instead of a waist-deep miniature pool, there was now just enough water in the delicately shaped suspension bath to support the user without their body coming into contact with the sides. She positioned the voice recorder on the control arm and lowered herself into the pleasantly tepid water. The headrest automatically shaped itself to the back of Beverley's neck when she lay back. The lights dimmed. Beverley closed her eyes. She had used a TVR chamber about half a dozen times and had always enjoyed the strange, soporific experience of total sensory isolation from her body and reality. She doubted if she would enjoy this experience. She would be reaching back to something she had steadfastly sought to blot out.

The lights dimmed to a glimmer and went out. The darkness was such that Beverley could not tell if her eyes were open or closed. The silence and the darkness pressed in like a death shroud. Her legs drifted apart and her arms moved away from her sides as her floating body assumed its natural position in the tepid, womb-like fluid. She felt warm and secure and at peace with herself despite the memories she was going to invoke, like a Satanist calling into hell for the Devil to materialize. After several moments of listening to her pounding heart, she could almost feel her brain rhythms flattening out.

Minutes or hours passed. She did not care. Her brain became active again as it searched for sensory input. It found nothing and became confused. Beverley allowed her thoughts to drift. Her brain seized the thoughts and treated them as reality. Sweet reality . . .

She pictured Becky Falls where her parents had taken her as a little girl.

Too far back.

She tried to control her thoughts but suddenly the roaring waterfall was before her; a heavy mist; the dank but evocative scent of summer woodland; slippery, green-covered stones; drops of water sparkling in the clear air; and the comforting firm grip of her father's hand holding hers; the tightness of her new walking shoes. There were mosaics of a thousand vivid, burning bright images that were gone forever and yet were there all the time, biding their time behind forgotten doors until opened by a questing brain and light was allowed to shine in the gloomy recesses.

Her mother's face, dead these ten years, her mouth full of pins as she altered Beverley's first party dress; her first period; her first boyfriend.

Too far back.

*Too far!*

Her pleading thoughts were delicate skein-like sighs in the brooding darkness. She forced the hated name to her lips and the dreams became a nightmare.

'Matt,' she whispered. 'Matt Tate.'

## PART FOUR: Yesterday
# Marshall Tate

These thine arts – to bear dominion over nations.
*Aeneid*, Virgil

# 1

## SOUTHERN ENGLAND
## 1964

The beginning of the rise of Marshall Tate could be fixed very precisely: Christmas 1964 when he was thirteen years old.

The biggest and most exciting-looking parcel was from his father whom his mother, Celia, had divorced two years previously. He had to battle his way feverishly through layers of brown paper and old newspapers to get to the parcel's contents – an ancient hand-cranked Pathé ACE cine projector and a load of badly-scratched 9.5 millimetre Chaplin one-reelers.

Marshall gasped with delight when he lifted the projector out of its shredded newspaper nest. He was so overwhelmed that he nearly dropped it. For the past several Saturdays, when his father took him out for the day, Marshall had insisted on dragging his dad to Wally Clegg's junk shop to stare in hypnotized fascination at the projector in the window. It was Marshall's favourite occupation. Like so many things, it was something mothers wouldn't understand but fathers would.

'You see that, Dad? That's like they have in the Odeon to make the pictures on the screen. A projector.'

His father laughed. 'I expect the real ones are much bigger, Matt.'

Marshall considered it very likely. After all, the cameras the film makers from Walton Studios used were huge. Whenever scenes were being shot on location in and around the town, which was often, Marshall would hang around the crew, asking endless questions when they weren't busy, which seemed to be a lot of the time.

When he was about eight he had secured Jack Hawkins' autograph when the star was shooting a scene for the *Four Just Men* television series. Several of his classmates had dads who worked in the studios; Marshall envied them and thought it would be wonderful to have a father who could show him the excitement of working among the sets, the scenery and lights.

Films and film making held an irresistible fascination for Marshall. From his heavily-thumbed Arthur Mee *Children's Encyclopedia* he had learned all about movie cameras and projectors, and how they worked, and how film makers created their special effects. He knew about back-projection and stop-motion photography; it delighted him when he spotted their tricks in the movies. He knew that the strange rippling patterns on King Kong's fur as the mighty gorilla laid waste to New York were caused by studio technicians' fingerprints making tiny movements to the model for each stop-motion shot.

Within ten minutes of his opening the parcel, Marshall's other presents were forgotten, much to the chagrin of assorted aunts, uncles and other relations who descended on Celia every Christmas.

Celia tracked Marshall down to his bedroom. The curtains were drawn. He was sitting in semi-darkness, cranking the handle of his present while watching a flickering image of a cavorting Charlie Chaplin projected onto the distempered wall. The first thing she noticed was the mess. Normally Marshall kept his room scrupulously neat and tidy, he hated mess. But this time reels of film were scattered everywhere and he had screwed the projector to the new dressing table she had bought him only a few weeks before. He had pushed his divan aside and dragged the dressing table into the centre of the room. She was about to berate him but something about the intensity of his fixed stare at the wall stilled her words. The light from the screen wall played on his face. He had not even acknowledged her presence when she entered the room. The Minix fire engine she had bought him was half out of its box, as if the present had been opened to identify the contents and then discarded. It irritated her that he preferred George's secondhand offering.

'Aren't you coming down, Matt? We've hardly seen you.'

'I haven't seen all my films,' Marshall answered, not taking his eyes off the wall. His hand continued cranking the projector. Charlie Chaplin booted a heavy over a balcony. The heavy landed in a giant flowerpot. Marshall didn't smile. He resented his mother's interference. She was always interfering.

'You've got all the holidays to watch them in,' Celia reasoned.

'I'll come down when I've got to the end of this film!' Marshall snapped.

Celia opened her mouth to say something but decided that she did not want a scene on Christmas day. Marshall would throw one of his tantrums if he did not get his own way. She withdrew, leaving her son to continue cranking his new toy while staring fixedly at the flickering images on the wall.

The moment he was alone again, Marshall moved his dressing table to the far wall to see how big he could make the picture. He considered the entertainment value of the one-reelers was nil. His comedy tastes had been shaped by Dean Martin and Jerry Lewis during Saturday mornings at the Walton Odeon Children's Club, and the 'Carry On' films when he could persuade his mother to take him. Marshall hated 'A' certificate films. Even *The Wizard of Oz* had an 'A' certificate. Authority had stopped him seeing it. Authority in the uniform of a kindly cinema doorman: 'Sorry, lad. Not by yourself. It's got an 'A' certificate.'

Marshall could not believe that Authority had given *The Wizard of Oz* an adults only certificate. He wanted to shout his anger at the doorman but the uniform of Authority was too intimidating. He had walked home, tears pricking his eyes. He had wanted to see the film because some lucky boys at school whose parents had taken them to see it had described the film's fantastic tornado effects. But now, with the projector, he could make his own special effects by winding it backwards. Magic!

He sat and watched the new enlarged image on his wall. Making the picture bigger failed to add anything to the humour of Charlie Chaplin's jerky knockabout antics and soundless brawls with bearded heavies. The real magic of the scratched old films was being able to create moving pictures on the distempered wall of his darkened bedroom while turning the old projector's clattering handle.

## 2

## 1965

'Course I ain't sold it,' Wally Clegg muttered sourly, eyeing the lanky boy standing before him. He wiped his nose on the sleeve of his grimy jacket. 'Said I'd keep it for you, didn't I?'

'But it's not in the window any more!' said Marshall desperately. 'And I've got the money.'

'Took it out, didn't I?' Wally Clegg managed to turn most statements into questions.

He was a small grey man, permanently etched into the memory of most Walton boys. The local teenagers who traded in their old 78 singles with him so they could buy the trendy 45s had fathers who remembered buying old Kodak Box Brownies, secondhand fishing rods and tins of gramophone needles from Wally Clegg's junkshop when they were boys. He was as permanent as the muddy Thames that flowed past the end of his junk-filled backyard.

He regarded the white-faced boy clutching his counter. 'You got *all* the money? Only I don't do tick or nothing like that, do I?' despite his gruff manner, he was a kindly man who had a warm regard for Walton's kids who provided him with a sizeable chunk of his turnover. But you had to be firm with the little bleeders.

For his part Marshall was a little fearful of the stooped, grey man. Wally Clegg was a shopkeeper and therefore a representative of Authority. He delved into his pockets and emptied a fistful of coins onto the wooden counter. 'Five pounds,' he blurted. 'It's all there.'

Wally laboriously counted the coins, slowly sorting out the halfcrowns, shillings and sixpences, and sliding them one by one into his grubby palm. Marshall hated him.

'All there,' agreed Wally at length. He bent down and produced a tiny clockwork Pathé ACE cine camera which he placed on the counter.

For timeless seconds Marshall could only stare at the camera,

182

not daring to touch it, unable to comprehend that the object that had led him to press his nose against the junkshop window every afternoon for the past four weeks on his way home from school was finally his.

'Don't you want it then? Don't give no refunds, do I?'

Marshall gingerly picked up the camera. *He was holding it! He was actually holding it! It was his!*

Wally showed him how to wind the camera's clockwork motor using the fold-out key. 'Then you load it and press the button. No focusing or nothing. Dead simple, init? Got any film?'

Marshall stammered that he hadn't.

'No bleedin' good without film, are they?'

'There's a firm that advertises in the *Exchange and Mart*. I thought I'd save up and buy some film from them.'

'Wait here a mo.' Wally shuffled into the dark recesses of his cluttered shop and reappeared holding a large flat packet. 'There you are, lad. Three hundred feet of out-of-date stock. Five years out of date but they do that to be on the safe side. It'll be okay. You'll have to wind a bit at a time onto small reels to fit in the camera. Got a darkroom at school?'

Marshall stared at the packet. 'But I don't have any more money. I had to do loads of jobs to get that five pounds.'

'It's yours, for free. Special offer with that camera, and some camera film reels.'

Marshall's eyes shone. 'I don't know how to thank you, Mr Clegg.'

Polite, thought Wally. A cut above the average snotty little bastard who went to Ambleside. 'That's all right, lad. All old stuff. Didn't cost me nothing, did it? Might be able to get some more.' The truth was that he had a stack of the old black and white film stock but no point in handing over the lot to the kid in one go. He would only waste it.

Marshall squinted through the camera's viewfinder at Wally and pressed the button. The clockwork motor whirred softly, causing the key to turn. 'Maybe I could make a film about you, Mr Clegg?'

Wally managed a rare but bleak smile. 'What's your name,

lad?' Marshall told him. 'Well, Matt. I reckon a lad of your age could find much more interesting things to film than me.'

### 3

Celia tapped on Marshall's bedroom door. A recent article in *Woman's Own* had stressed the importance of parents respecting their children's privacy. 'Dinner's ready,' she said.

'Be down in a minute,' was the muffled response.

Celia knew all about Marshall's minutes. 'It's on the table, Matt. It'll get cold.'

'I won't be a minute!'

'You speak to me like that again, young man, and you'll go without,' said Celia with mock severity.

Instead of matching his mother's levity, Marshall snapped back with: 'I said, I won't be a minute. Leave me alone.'

Celia turned away from the door but she suddenly felt very annoyed, more with herself than Marshall because she realized that she was letting him manipulate her. Perhaps she was just a little bit frightened of him and his vicious temper. She turned the door handle and pushed. The door was jammed.

'Don't come in!' Marshall yelled. Stress raised the sentence's pitch. Marshall was still learning to master his recently broken voice.

That did it. Celia gave the door a hard shove. The brown sticky paper Marshall had taped around the inside edges of the door parted with a loud tearing sound. Daylight spilled into the bedroom.

'*I said, don't come in!*' Marshall screamed. His voice cracked to a schoolgirlish pitch.

For a moment Celia was too shocked to react. She wasn't sure what she expected to find. It would not have been so bad if her son was reading a girlie magazine. At least that would have been normal, if unpalatable, something that she could have understood and come to terms with. Instead he was sitting on the bed in what must have been total darkness because he had stuck squares of cardboard over his window panes. On his knee was a reel of film.

184

'*You stupid fucking woman!*' Marshall raged. 'I told you to stay out. You've ruined my film.'

Before Celia could open her mouth to remonstrate, Marshall hurled the reel of film across the room and buried his face in his pillow, sobbing bitterly. Celia stood on the threshold, heart pounding, completely at a loss. For the first time she questioned herself as to what sort of boy it was that she had brought into the world. She closed the door without a word.

Marshall picked up the spool of film. He cursed his mother; he cursed all women. When he had calmed down, he reflected that his outburst had resulted in his emerging unscathed from his first serious challenge to Authority.

It was an invaluable lesson.

### 4

'What you need', said Wally Clegg to Marshall the following afternoon after school, having listened to the tale of the ruined film, 'is a changing bag. Bit fiddly winding cine film in them but I've done it. Got a spare one somewhere.' He found a dusty black bag and spread it out on the counter. 'Your's for five bob.'

'And how much for another reel of film, Mr Clegg?'

Wally's price for reels of old 9.5 mm was one pound each. 'Ten bob,' he muttered.

Marshall pushed fifteen shillings across the counter. Wally produced another can of film from his stock and gave it to Marshall.

'Like me to show you how to use the bag?'

'Yes please, Mr Clegg.'

Using a camera reel and a scrap length of film, Wally showed Marshall how to use the changing bag to wind a length of unexposed film from the stock reel onto the camera reel.

### 5

Beverley Laine fell in step beside Marshall. She had been watching from her bedroom window, waiting for him to emerge.

'Where're you going?'

'I'm going to make a film,' said Marshall importantly.

'Can I come?'

Marshall glanced uncertainly at Beverley. It was Saturday morning. He had waited all week for this day because it was too dark to film after school. Besides, her dad was a policeman, the ultimate representative of authority although Marshall had never seen him in a uniform. On the other hand he would enjoy showing off to Beverley. She was a tall, leggy thirteen-year-old with dark hair in a frizz of natural, indestructible ringlets, and burgeoning breasts that were stretching the stitches on a jumper that had not been designed to accommodate them. She had lived next door to Marshall since she was ten.

'Suppose so,' said Marshall indifferently, hoisting his haversack onto his shoulder.

'You've got a camera then?' Beverley knew all about Marshall's projector. One evening he had provided her with a Chaplin movie show in his bedroom. He had even fixed up curtains that drew across the screen. To add to the realism, Beverley had eaten popcorn and thrown a pillow at the wall when the film broke.

'*And* I've got some footage,' said Marshall proudly, using jargon he had culled from a library book.

'What's footage?'

'Unexposed film. Six reels. Fifty feet each.'

They crossed the main road and took a side road that led to the towpath. 'How long a film will that make?' Beverley asked.

Marshall wasn't altogether sure. 'About ten minutes.'

Beverley was unimpressed. 'That won't be much of a film.'

'Telly commercials are only a few seconds,' Marshall retorted. *Making Good Home Movies* had urged its readers to watch television advertisements because they were usually examples of good film-making.

They reached the towpath and waited by the Salter's river steamer jetty. Beverley watched with interest as Marshall bent his tall, awkward frame over his haversack and began unpacking. Marshall had intrigued her ever since she had moved in next door. He was a loner. He hardly ever mixed with other

186

kids his age, and when he did, he always seemed to be registering bored disinterest.

Marshall straightened and showed her his camera. He tried to appear offhand but it was obvious that he was immensely proud of it. Her comment that it was 'a bit small' was not well received by the budding Alfred Hitchcock, especially as it was said within earshot of passengers waiting for the next steamer.

The very first shot of Marshall's career was of some ducks. He did not notice that the sun was behind him and that his shadow was falling across his subjects: he was too overcome by the thrill of looking through the viewfinder and feeling the gentle vibration of film clattering through the gate. He had often run the camera empty, pretending to film everything in sight, but this time it was different: the camera was heavier; it felt different; it sounded different. This was for real! Every movement of the ducks, and his shadow, was being captured for eternity.

His second shot was of a large swan, seemingly asleep on the grass with its head buried between its wings. It was a crusty old cob and it never slept. Marshall crept near the creature while peering through his viewfinder, imagining himself as an intrepid wildlife cameraman stalking an unsuspecting lion. When the swan decided that Marshall was close enough, it suddenly beat its huge wings, stretched a yard of neck at the intrusive cameraman, and gave a loud, threatening hiss of extreme displeasure. Marshall was so startled that he nearly dropped the camera. He backed off rapidly while Beverley rolled on the grass, doubled up with laughter. The angry words that rose to Marshall's lips were silenced by the sight of Beverley's long legs and a tantalizing glimpse of her underwear. He resented his interest in her, just as he was learning to resent all girls. He saw the hold that their sexuality had over him as another manifestation of despised authority. Nevertheless he smiled ruefully.

'Thought the sod was going to rip my head off,' he admitted.

Beverley sat up. 'Why don't you film me? Must be funny seeing yourself on the pictures. I've always wondered what stars must think when they see themselves. And I promise not to hiss at you.'

'You? Your face would crack the lens. Anyway, I want to film wildlife like the documentaries on telly.'

'Well that swan was pretty wild,' said Beverley, trying to keep a straight face.

At that they both burst out laughing. Marshall decided that maybe Beverley wasn't so bad. And she was pretty.


### 6

I've made my first film, Mr Clegg,' Marshall announced. As always, his tone was polite. He placed the six small cans carefully on the counter and met the old man's gaze.

'You want me to get them processed?'

Marshall gave Wally a bright smile. 'Yes please, Mr Clegg. You said you knew someone.'

Wally nodded. He had a regular customer who worked at Walton Studios who could get the 9.5 mm format film processed at a reasonable price. 'Be a couple of quid,' he warned.

Marshall pulled a grubby pound note from his pocket. 'I can let you have a pound now and a pound when I collect it. Will that be all right, Mr Clegg?'

Wally always preferred to collect money up-front from his customers but he did not have the heart to disappoint Marshall. 'Suppose that'll be all right,' he grumbled, ringing up the pound on his antique till. 'Only don't you go letting me down or nothing.'

'I promise,' said Marshall excitedly. 'When will it be ready?'

'Next Saturday.'

'I'll have the money,' Marshall replied without hesitation even though he had no idea how he was going to get such a sum together at such short notice.


### 7

That week was the longest and hardest of Marshall's life. As soon as school was over he was doing jobs for the neighbours. He helped Mr Walker strip wallpaper off a wall; and he sup-

188

pressed his dislike of authority in order to earn ten shillings from Beverley's father by helping him clear out his garage.

'You going to let me see the film?' Beverley demanded. She was perched on a stepladder, watching Marshall sort through her father's caked paintbrushes. She was willing him to look at her legs. She got a secret little thrill from experimenting with exerting power over boys. It irked her that her little experiments in feminine provocation didn't seem to work with Marshall. He hadn't looked at her legs once.

'Might,' he said noncommittally.

'You could always put me in your pictures,' Beverley offered.

'What would I want to do that for?'

'Geoff Tilley reckons I've got nice legs,' said Beverley, shifting slightly to invite inspection.

'Geoff Tilley is a prick,' Marshall replied, too intent on smoothing out bits of usable sandpaper to spare Beverley's legs a glance.

At that moment Beverley's father entered the garage. Beverley quickly closed the conversation and her legs.

## 8

'Is it ready, Mr Clegg?' said Marshall eagerly, spilling his handful of coins on the counter in his excitement.

Wally Clegg managed a rare smile and gave Marshall the reel of processed film. It was worth losing on the processing cost just to see the wonder on the boy's face as he looked disbelievingly at his first reel. 'There you are, lad. All spliced back into one reel.'

'Did it come out all right?'

Wally did not like admitting that he was in the habit of previewing his customer's home movies but he nodded. 'Pretty girl in the fifth reel,' he remarked, counting Marshall's hard-earned money. 'Schoolkid getting off the boat, wasn't she? Looks like she knew you. You ought to make a film of her. She's got a nice smile in close-up.'

Marshall was not certain what Wally was talking about because he could not remember what was in every shot.

'Don't you want another film?' Wally called out as Marshall raced out of the shop.

Marshall returned to the counter. 'I can't afford one,' he admitted. 'I'm skint.'

'You get one for free with every processed film,' said Wally, handing a delighted Marshall another package of unexposed film.

Marshall could hardly contain his excitement as he raced home with his trophies. Celia was out so there was no voice of authority to interfere with this long-awaited moment. He set up his screen – a sheet weighted with a bamboo cane – and feverishly laced the film into his projector. His hand trembled as he turned the handle. The leader cleared. He almost fainted with joy when the group of squabbling ducks appeared on the screen. Wally had said the film was okay but Marshall had spent the week in an agony of suspense, praying that the out-of-date stock was not too out-of-date. The picture changed to the sleeping swan. Despite his excitement at seeing images that he had created, the beginnings of Marshall's professional eye noted that he had shaken the camera badly when he had inched forward on his elbows towards the dozing bird. He realized that he should have got close first and then started filming. The swan's head suddenly lunged at the camera and filled the whole screen, making him recoil. His reaction delighted him: if he jumped, and he was expecting it, think how an audience would jump!

The rest of the film consisted of mundane shots of the Salter's steamer arriving at the towpath pier and passengers disembarking. The girl Wally Clegg had admired was Beverley. She had inveigled herself into a shot by pretending to be a passenger. She had walked towards Marshall and cheekily thrust her tongue out at the camera. Marshall cranked the shot backwards and re-ran it. He saw Beverley in a new light. Wally Clegg was right: with her hair in those crazy little ringlets, and the way she filled out her sweater, she *was* pretty. Maybe he could film her? But her father was authority, a policeman. Altogether a bit off-putting. And did he really want to waste his precious film stock on stupid girls who poked their tongues out at the camera?

Six months would pass and two thousand feet of Wally Clegg's out-of-date stock would whir through the gate of his camera before Marshall Tate changed his mind.

## 9

Beverley crouched behind a tree and watched Marshall with interest. She had followed him on her bicycle to the Weybridge end of Cowey Sale where the riverside meadows gave way to woodland. He had set up his camera beneath an old oak on an odd-looking homemade tripod about eighteen inches high. The camera was aimed straight up at the oak. Marshall had to lie on his back to look through the viewfinder. It was a hot afternoon in late July and the start of the summer holidays. Five weeks of uninterrupted filming lay before him. He was determined to capture the owl on film before the beginning of the new academic year and the prospect of more hours of homework in the run-up to his O Levels in two years.

His resolution to film the owl faltered when he felt ants crawling down his neck. Being an intrepid wildlife cameraman was not much fun. Even if he managed to snatch some footage of the owl, he knew from previous experiences that the results were likely to be disappointing. The little fixed-focus camera was designed for making family movies. Objects filmed at a distance of about two to three metres gave the best results. Details further away were lost in the blur of the lenses' poor definition. What he really needed was an 8 mm camera with three lenses on a revolving turret: a normal lens, a wide-angle, and a telephoto. The magazines that he poured over in the reading library were packed full of ads for them: fabulous cameras, some costing hundreds of pounds. The cheapest was a Eumig for thirty quid.

'That's nearly two weeks' wages, Matt!' Celia had exclaimed when he mentioned the Eumig as a possible present for his fourteenth birthday the previous month. He had settled for a Luxor roll-up screen; six pounds from Shoppertunities.

The sun rose higher. Owls hated bright sunlight. The chances of it emerging before dusk seemed increasingly remote. So what else could he film? He had long gone through the stage of

191

pointing his camera at anything that moved. In fact he had already filmed just about everything that moved in Walton-on-Thames anyway. He was now more discriminating in his choice of subject matter, preferring to stick to three-hundred-foot themes. He considered mending the puncture on his bicycle and cycling to Chessington Zoo and immediately abandoned the idea. There would be lots of stupid kids pushing their heads in front of the camera and poking their tongues out.

A shadow moved across him. He shaded his eyes. It was Beverley. She was wearing a thin cotton dress that the breeze flattened provocatively against her body: a desirable addition to any teenage boy's Saturday afternoon.

'Sod off,' said Marshall sourly, applying his eye to the view-finder to signal that he was busy.

'Oh, charming,' said Beverley using a Kenneth Williams phrase she had picked up from the 'Carry On' films. 'What are you doing?'

'Sun bathing. What does it look like I'm doing?'

Beverley stood over him. 'I've got some Tizer in my saddlebag.'

Marshall looked at Beverley but didn't answer for a few moments. The sunlight shone through the thin material of her dress.

Beverley saw Marshall's expression and considered that she had scored enough of a victory to bolster her confidence. She unbuckled the saddlebag of her bicycle that was lying on the grass, produced a bottle of Tizer, took a swig, and sat cross-legged on the grass facing Marshall.

'Want some?' She held out the bottle and caught Marshall's downward gaze. A thrill quickened through her. 'Hey, stop staring.'

'Stop staring at what?' Marshall demanded guiltily.

'You were looking at my underwear.'

'No I wasn't.'

'Yes, you were, Matt Tate,' she retorted, yanking her dress down.

To his horror and shame, Marshall felt an erection coming on fast. It infuriated him that she could exercise such control over him. He rolled quickly onto his stomach, nearly knocking his beloved camera over. He took the bottle from Beverley, wiped the neck and took a long draught.

'So what were you filming?' Beverley asked.

'An owl,' Marshall replied curtly.

'They only come out at night.'

'Shows how much you know about owls.'

Beverley looked quizzically at him. 'Have you started shaving?'

The question annoyed Marshall. He had been shaving for a year. Once a week at first but now he had to shave every day. Beverley's presence was proving to be annoying; he wished that she would go away. 'What's it to you? If you had to shave, you'd probably cut your throat. Good thing too.'

Beverley leaned back and laughed, causing her dress to ride up again. Marshall's throat went dry. Beverley's ringlets were pulled back by hairslides to form a perfect frame around her oval face. The prettiness he had become aware of the previous year was now all too apparent. He felt uncomfortably vulnerable.

'You haven't shown me any of your films for weeks,' Beverley accused good-naturedly.

'You laughed last time.'

'I never!'

'Yes you did.'

'All right. I'm sorry if I upset you. Satisfied?'

Marshall made no reply.

'I didn't mean to, really, Matt.'

'S'okay,' said Marshall offhandedly. He looked quickly away when he realized that Beverley must have seen him glancing covertly at her breasts. More control, more Authority. His mounting anger quickened his pulse, making his heart pound in his ears.

Beverley jumped to her feet and held out her hand. 'Come on, Matt. Let's go back and see your films.' A request to view his movies was one that Marshall could never refuse.

They returned to his house. It was early afternoon. Celia would not be back from work for another four hours. Beverley perched on the end of Marshall's divan bed and dutifully watched his latest movies, laughing only at what was supposed to be funny. The improvement in his technique astonished her and she said so. Marshall was pleased. Wally Clegg had said much the same.

'They're really good,' Beverley enthused when the show was over. She blinked in the bright sunlight that streamed into the bedroom when Marshall yanked back the curtains. 'I liked the cat one. Terrific. How did you get him to crouch and jump like that? I thought he was going to jump right out of the screen.'

'Special effects secret,' said Marshall, sitting beside her on the bed.

Beverley hooked an arm playfully around his neck. 'Tell or I'll break it,' she threatened.

Marshall pulled angrily away. 'I tied a bit of paper on a string and dangled it OOS,' he admitted sourly.

'OOS?'

'Out of shot.'

'Well it's a bloody good film,' Beverley said. 'You ought to make one as if the camera's the cat. You know, so the audience see everything like a cat sees it.'

The idea immediately fired Marshall's imagination. 'Gosh, yes. What a terrific idea.' His fertile mind raced ahead. 'I could fix up the camera on a roller skate or something and push it along.'

'You see?' said Beverley, pleased at his reaction to her idea. 'You need me as an assistant director. They have assistant directors and second unit directors, don't they? They get mentioned at the end of films sometimes. What's a second unit director?'

Marshall was only too keen to pass on knowledge he had gained from his avid reading of photographic magazines and library books. He read them from cover to cover, not missing a word, draining them of substance as a spider drains life juices from its prey. 'That's when some scenes are shot abroad and the main director is too busy directing the real stars to go,' he explained.

Beverley flopped back on the bed so that her dress rode up. She watched Marshall carefully, hoping that she looked suitably

194

beguiling. 'Did you direct those boys who made rude signs at the camera in the railway film?' she asked mischievously.

'No I did not,' Marshall replied indignantly. 'They spoilt the shot. When I've saved up for an editor I'm going to cut it out.'

'If you directed me, I'd do exactly as you said,' Beverley murmured.

'You can't act,' Marshall scoffed.

'Nor can Marilyn Monroe.'

''Course she can.'

Beverley sat up, her eyes large and serious. 'I read that she can't, that the director has to go through everything with her and that she gets away with it so long as she does exactly as she's told . . . So, you tell me exactly what to do and I'll do it.' She smirked and added: 'Mr Director, sir.'

'Okay. I'll make a film of you falling in the river and drowning.'

Beverley pulled a face at him. 'Why not make a film of me now?'

'Because we haven't got a river handy that you could drown in,' Marshall retorted.

'Let's make it in here,' Beverley suggested. 'There's plenty of sunlight, isn't there?'

The idea of filming indoors had never occurred to Marshall because the slow, out-dated film that Wally supplied demanded plenty of light. But Beverley was right – there was plenty of light in the bedroom. Also the idea of directing someone just like a real director intrigued him.

'All right,' he agreed, fishing the camera out of his haversack. 'But only one magazine mind.'

Beverley gave a little clap of delight. 'Let's pretend you're giving me one of those test things they give actresses who want to be stars.'

'A screen test?'

'That's right.' Beverley looked flushed with excitement.

Marshall considered. 'Okay. I want you to go out of the room and come in when I shout "Action". Then you cross the room and take a book off the shelf and then you sit on the bed pretending to read. Okay?'

Beverley hopped off the bed. 'Anything you say, Mr Director.' She left the room and closed the door behind her.

Marshall moved to the corner of the room where he could pan the camera without furniture getting in the way. He knelt on one knee, peered through the camera's viewfinder and aimed at the door, his finger ready on the shutter button. 'Okay. Action!'

The door opened. All that appeared of Beverley was her left leg which she tried to wriggle seductively as Marilyn Monroe had done in *Gentlemen Prefer Blondes*. The effect was not quite the same because it looked as if she were kicking the door jamb.

'Where's the rest of you?' Marshall demanded. The sight of Beverley's leg aroused his interest but the budding professional in him kept the camera rolling.

There was something else that had been aroused in Marshall: the realization that Authority, the one thing he hated above all else, was now in his hands. Being a director meant having real Authority, Authority that gave you power over people, that made them do what you wanted them to do – Well, almost.

The rest of Beverley appeared. Pulling the slides out of her hair had worked a fascinating transformation. The awkward schoolkid was gone, replaced by a sultry tigress, radiating blatant sexuality like a beacon. Her hand was resting casually on her hip with the hem of her dress hitched up.

Marshall stopped filming and put the camera down quickly so that Beverley would not see his hand trembling. 'You're supposed to come in and read a book,' he observed curtly.

Beverley's *femme fatale* poise deserted her for a moment. She released the hem of her dress and sat on the bed, leaning back on her hands and regarding Marshall speculatively, a mischievous smile playing at the corners of her mouth. She felt flushed and was aware of her quickening heartbeat. It was the first time she had ever behaved in such a manner when alone with a boy and it excited her.

For his part Marshall pretended to be unmoved. An idea was forming in his mind of such audacity that he had trouble bringing his voice under control when he spoke. 'Okay, then,' he said sternly. 'If you're not going to do as I tell you, then we shall have to rehearse. Sit further back on the bed.'

To Marshall's delight Beverley obeyed him by wriggling back a few inches. Her gaze remained fixed on Marshall. She sensed what was coming and her excitement mounted.

'Now sit forward and rest your chin on your knees.'

Beverley did so, drawing up her legs and causing the hem of her dress to slip down her thighs. 'Use the camera,' she said.

'It'll waste film.'

'Pretend to press the button. *Please*, Matt.'

Sensing that here was an opportunity to use his new-found Authority, Marshall picked up the camera and lifted it to his face. Instead of closing one eye when looking through the view-finder he kept them both open. 'Undo the buttons on your dress,' he commanded. He didn't really want to see any more of Beverley's body but he did want to put this newly acquired Authority to the test.

Beverley hesitated but the camera pointing at her served to heighten the sensation of anticipation. It was a machine exercising a strange power over her, sapping her inhibitions and free will. Starting at her throat, she undid the buttons slowly one by one.

Still holding the camera in position, Marshall moved to the foot of the bed.

'All of them?'

'Er . . . Yes.' Somehow he managed to control his treacherous voice so that he sounded forceful, or so he hoped. He eased himself onto the bed so that he was kneeling astride Beverley's ankles.

Beverley reached the last button but kept her dress gathered together. Marshall pressed the shutter button. It was as if the soft whir of the clockwork motor had released a spring in Beverley. She suddenly pulled her dress away exposing her bra and briefs. Marshall thought he was going to faint. Not so much at the appearance of Beverley's voluptuous body – although that was enough – but because of the new discoveries he was making about Authority when it was his and not someone else's. He

197

realized that his hands were shaking and tightened his sweaty grip on the camera.

'Now what?' Beverley queried.

Marshall didn't know what to say. Even if he did, he knew that he could not trust his voice to retain its deep timbre. The camera kept up its soft purr like a contented cat.

'Shall I take my dress right off?'

A hoarse 'Yes' was all that Marshall could manage.

'I'll have to stand.'

Marshall backed awkwardly off the bed while trying to keep the camera steady. He half-crouched, using the corner of his dressing table as a screen so that she would not see the state he was in, shifting his attention from viewfinder to reality and back to viewfinder while Beverley did a little pirouette before letting her dress slip to the floor.

'I could take something else off,' she suggested.

'Okay,' Marshall agreed. His feeling of power deserted him as he contemplated the disaster of his mother coming home early.

Beverley seemed adrift on a private sea of sensuality although her gaze remained fixed on Marshall all the time. She reached behind to unhook her bra.

At that moment the camera's note changed. It became louder and faster. There was a slapping noise from within the machine caused by a loose end of film. It was a second before Marshall realized what had happened.

'Film's finished,' he mumbled.

Beverley took the camera from his hands and placed it on the dressing table. 'Let's rehearse another scene,' she suggested. Before Marshall could protest, she drew him onto the bed and kissed him.

His first reaction was to resist because her arms around his neck and her lips pressed against his represented a transference of Authority. But the exciting taste of her lips, the closeness of her, and feel of her knee sliding up his leg, quickly banished his reservations and turned him into a willing partner in their mutual, joyful and successful discovery of each other.

'That was nice,' said Beverley disentangling her underclothes

**198**

from Marshall's sheets that had gathered themselves into a ball. 'I always thought it would be awful but it wasn't.' At first, when she had looked into Marshall's blue eyes, she had misinterpreted his stare and had nearly panicked.

Marshall clutched a blanket in front of himself. He did not share Beverley's lack of inhibitions. 'It's the first time that you . . . that . . .' He was unable to finish the sentence.

Beverley stood and buttoned herself into her dress. 'Yes.' She knelt beside Marshall and kissed him on the cheek. 'You're sweet, Matt Tate.'

'I won't become the greatest film director in the world by being sweet,' said Marshall seriously, wondering if the events of the past five minutes had really taken place.

Beverley smiled and tugged Marshall's comb through her ringlets. 'Maybe I could help you become the greatest film director in the world by being your assistant?'


## 10

### 1966

Marshall made a total of five movies with Beverley Laine during the school holidays of 1965 and early 1966.

Sometimes they made love when opportunities arose although, after their initial experiments, it was not an important element in their relationship. Although Beverley was more mature than Marshall both emotionally and physically, neither was far enough into early adulthood for the relationship to reach a peak of emotional intensity, and such was Marshall Tate's obvious resentment of Beverley's sexuality that she doubted if he would ever mature as far as girls were concerned. All he really wanted her for was to help out with her pocket money to pay Wally Clegg's modest processing charges. What irked Marshall was the limitations of the 9.5 mm camera. No matter how carefully they planned and set up every shot, the results were always disappointing.

'I'll never make proper films with that crappy camera,' he said despondently after he and Beverley had viewed a film of

Walton Regatta. 'I told you those shots from the bridge were too far away. I need a decent camera.'

'Like that one you showed me in Wally Clegg's window?'

Marshall nodded and rewound the film. 'Eight-millimetre,' he said wistfully.

'Okay. Buy it,' said Beverley.

'You're kidding, Bev. He wants two hundred quid for the lot. Camera, projector and film and lots of other bits and bobs.'

'Maybe he'll accept a hundred quid if you part exchange your camera and projector?' Beverley reasoned.

'Bev, I haven't got a hundred shillings, never mind a hundred pounds.'

'Let's go and see him tomorrow,' said Beverley excitedly, adding in a more serious tone, 'only don't tell my dad because I'm not allowed near his shop.'


11

Wally was always pleased to see Marshall. The lad was growing fast. Lad? He was now a young man the way he had shot up. He was no longer the shy, uncertain kid who had asked him to save the old Pathé ACE cine camera for him.

His welcoming smile faded when he saw who was accompanying Marshall. Wally knew Beverley's father and rather wished he did not. Whenever there was a case of child assault in the area, it was Beverley's father who came sniffing around to get an alibi off Wally. The previous year Wally had bought a crate of dubious Swedish magazines and shoved them out of sight in his backroom. He knew a dealer who would take them off him for a tenner. A couple of local tearaways had broken in one night when he was laid up with 'flu – probably to nick records – but had made off with the magazines instead. When one of the boys' parents found them, the kid had said that Wally had given them to him. The parents went to the police and the police descended on Wally. There was no evidence against Wally; no charges were brought, and nothing got into the papers. But Detective Sergeant Laine had confiscated the magazines and given Wally a stern verbal warning about corrupting minors. Since then the local law had made life difficult for Wally Clegg.

Beverley did all the talking while Marshall stood with his hands thrust in his pockets. Wally listened with mounting dismay. Two weeks before he had paid a recently bereaved widow fifty pounds for the complete job lot of her husband's cinematographic gear: a turret lens 8 mm Eumig camera and matching projector; an editor and splicer; and fifty boxes of double-run 8 mm Kodacolor, fifty feet each reel and the lab processing was paid for. Wally was pleased with the deal; the film alone was worth well over a hundred quid because the stupid trout didn't know that her husband had forked out for the processing charges when he had bought the film. He was confident of getting £200 for the lot, and now this scheming little minx wanted to take it all off him for half that.

Marshall watched with interest as Beverley provided him with a useful lesson in how assertiveness was the mother of Authority.

'A pound a week for two years brings you in a regular flow of money,' Beverley reasoned. 'And you continue to get Marshall's custom because he comes to you for all his other bits and pieces.'

'But I don't get no interest,' Wally pointed out, a little unnerved by this pretty young madam leaning across his counter and looking him straight in the eye.

Marshall could not see the way Beverley was smiling beguilingly at Wally. Had he done so, he would have realized that she was using a lot more than business acumen on the hapless shopkeeper.

'But you don't get any interest on any of your stock that's sitting around in here,' Beverley reasoned. 'You've got stuff in your window that's been there since I was in my pram.'

Marshall sniggered at that.

Beverley played her ace. 'And if you're worried about Marshall not paying then I know my dad would go as a guarant . . . guarant . . .'

'Guarantor,' said Wally faintly.

'Guarantor for him. We could get my dad to come down right now and sign anything. So what do you say, Mr Clegg?'

There wasn't a lot Wally Clegg could say. The deal he reluctantly agreed to most certainly did not make his day but it made Marshall's.

'I just dunno how you did it, Bev,' Marshall said admiringly as they struggled home loaded with the fruits of Beverley's bargaining. He could scarcely believe his luck. He was now the owner of a real camera and projector, an editor, and enough film to last him years. Now he could make a serious start on making a real film that he had been dreaming about. It even had a title: *Catseyes*. A film about the world seen from a cat's point of view had been Beverley's idea and one that had fired his fertile imagination.

'Don't let anyone ever stand on you, my dad always says,' Beverley replied. 'Plan arguments in advance. He says when you go to court to give evidence, you have to think in advance of all the nasties that they're going to throw at you and have your answers ready.'

'I'll remember that,' Marshall promised.


## 12

### 1966 to 1967

In a way Marshall was glad that Beverley's parents were moving. Her departure marked the end of the sexual Authority she had exerted over him. From now on he would be a loner; making his films without her constant stream of suggestions that he had come to interpret as interference.

'You will make *Catseyes*, won't you, Matt?' said Beverley as her parents' furniture was loaded into a pantechnicon.

'Sure I'll make it, Bev,' Marshall promised. 'And we'll watch it together.'

They parted with promises to write that Marshall had no intention of keeping. The pantechnicon doors were slammed shut. Beverley waved from her father's car and the convoy moved off. It reached the end of the road and disappeared. Marshall returned to his room to continue editing a film. That he owed a great deal to Beverley Laine was of no consequence; he was glad to be shot of her.

## 13

During the rest of 1966 and 1967 Marshall was astute enough not to allow his schooling to suffer as a consequence of his obsession with his hobby. Besides, he was patient – there was no real rush to finish *Catseyes*. He derived much pleasure from spending an entire weekend setting up a five-second shot and getting it right. The effort would be worthwhile: the four reels of colour film he sacrificed to try out his new camera produced startlingly good results. The definition obtainable with the Eumig using careful lighting was nearly on a par with professional 16 mm equipment.

One scene required a girl necking with her boyfriend in a dark alleyway. A night shot. Martha Hunt was a fifteen-year-old, carroty-haired local girl with good legs who was suitably flattered when Marshall approached her, but she balked when he told her what he wanted to do.

'I couldn't let you do that,' she said defensively.

'You let Tony Wright do it,' said Marshall. 'I've seen you. Anyway, our faces won't be in shot, so no one will know. I'll work the camera with a remote control.'

'When have you seen us?' Martha demanded.

'Last Saturday night in the alley. And I filmed you. He had his hand right up your skirt. Bet you wouldn't like your dad to see the film.'

'It was dark!'

'It wasn't that dark or how could I have seen you? I used special film.'

Martha was terrified of her father and Marshall knew it. She reluctantly agreed to take part in the film.

Marshall was pleased with the result that he achieved with Martha in the alley. He lit the shot using a motorbike headlight from a breakers' yard connected up to an old car battery. Light reflectors were made from rolls of Budgen's oven foil stretched over hardboard off-cuts. The ten-second scene provided a valuable lesson in innovation and exploitation of limited resources.

And blackmail.

## 14

At sixteen Marshall landed six O Levels with good grades which, in those days of full employment, enabled him to pick and choose a job. He desperately wanted to work in films so he settled for a clerk's job at Shepperton Studios just across the river from Walton. He had hoped to work at Walton Studios, but Hannah Fisher had gone to America taking with her the initiative and enterprise that resulted in successful TV series such as *The Adventures of Robin Hood*. The result was that film production at Walton languished. There were rumours that a property company was negotiating to buy the town centre site and build a traffic-free shopping precinct.

The job at Shepperton was a disappointment. His work in the accounts department had more to do with film costing than the actual making of films, but he decided that what he was learning about budgetary control might be useful one day, and the £12 a week he earned enabled him to buy hardware for homemade rigs to create the weird camera angles that he favoured.

One evening, when he was required to work late, he managed to steal a Remington typewriter that he smuggled out in the pannier of his motor scooter. He could now type out proper camera scripts. As with everything he did, Marshall Tate was neat, meticulous and very methodical.

## 15

### 1968

In September of that year, at the age of seventeen, Marshall met someone who was to change his life.

He enrolled at the Kingston School of Art evening school for a vocational course called 'Film Making for Beginners'. The lecturer was Bill Yates, a bluff, larger-than-life extrovert Queenslander who earned a good living as a freelance film editor. He was a giant of a man with a rich, booming laugh, an unkempt beard and a taste for scruffy clothes and smart women. It was easy to imagine him sailing a pirate ship with a dirk clenched between his teeth rather than cutting and splicing film.

His opening introduction to his philosophy on film making was simple and to the point.

'You all want to make films. Good. A movie camera captures the world. It's a big beautiful world in wide shot but it's the close-ups that film handles best. Close-ups are your emphasis, your visual verbs for telling a story in pictures and not words. People need to be told stories. It's a need that is as basic as sex, and your audiences' needs must always come first. If you're not interested in story-telling or putting the audience first, then you've no business here. If you want to learn how to make home movies of your family all you have to do is wait for a sunny day, hold the camera steady, and don't make your shots longer than seven seconds. Here endeth the first lesson.'

His blunt views coincided with Marshall's views. He warmed to the extrovert film maker. He had come across someone who he respected.

During the middle of the term Bill Yates invited his students to submit samples of their work so that he could show the best offerings to the class. Marshall handed over his precious print of *Catseyes* for appraisal and was bitterly disappointed when Bill did not show it during the screening session. Marshall considered that the three shorts that Bill had selected were crude, amateurish efforts.

Bill called Marshall back as he was leaving the lecture room. He motioned him to sit down. Marshall ignored the gesture and remained standing. Authority had to be challenged at every opportunity.

'Okay, Matt. You're mad at me. Right?'

'You didn't show my film,' Marshall accused.

Bill scratched his beard and nodded. He took Marshall's reel of film from his briefcase and turned it over in his huge fingers. 'That's right, Matt. That's why I want to talk to you. I didn't show it because you're wasting your time on my course.'

The words hit Marshall like a series of electric shocks. He

stared at Bill, the colour draining from his face, his fists involuntarily clenching and unclenching.

'There's another reason I didn't show it,' Bill continued pretending not to notice the rage welling up in his student. 'The students in our group are keen, they're learning fast, they need plenty of encouragement which they won't get having their work shown alongside a piece of polished professionalism like this. Oh, for Christ's sake sit down. You're tall enough to be a pain in the neck.'

Marshall sat. His expression of cold anger changed to bewilderment. 'Polished? I don't understand.'

'How the hell can I show this to a class of amateurs? In ten years of lecturing I've never come across a film like *Catseyes*. Not even from fourth year students. It's brilliant. It's absolutely bloody brilliant. Okay, so there's nothing new about the idea of a film of a cat's exploits that the audience sees from the cat's point of view. It's the execution that matters. Yours is stunning. That's why I say you're wasting your time on this course.'

Marshall was too shocked to think of anything to say. He took the film from Bill and held it gingerly as though it might suddenly explode in his face.

'Why didn't you use a filter and shoot all those night shots in daylight? Would have saved yourself a bundle of trouble.'

Marshall forced himself to concentrate on the question. 'Because it would be cheating on the audience,' he answered. 'And besides, people can spot day-for-night shooting a mile off now. It always looks so bloody awful in those cheap Westerns. It's like the zipper up the back of monster suits. It shows a contempt for one's audience.'

Marshall's reply surprised Bill. He knew of several directors who had spent millions of dollars learning to respect their audiences, and a number who had never learned. It was not an answer he had expected from an eighteen-year-old. He nodded. 'So how did you get the camera down at the right height?'

'I made a dolly and used the suspension off a model car,' said Marshall, enjoying answering the questions. No one had ever shown such an interest in his work before. 'That way I was able to eliminate most of the jerkiness. Where I had to push it over

206

rough ground I over-cranked the camera so that it looks smooth at normal FPS.'

Bill steepled his fingers and regarded Marshall. The price of film stock being what it was, it took guts for an amateur to over-crank – that is, to run the film faster than normal through the camera to eliminate jerkiness. But then, Matt Tate was no ordinary amateur, he had a one in a million intuitive flair. 'How long has it taken you to make the film?' he asked.

'I've been working on it on and off since I was a kid.'

'I can believe it.'

'Do you think I could sell it, Bill? Get it shown on television or something?' Marshall tried to sound casual but he could not keep the excitement out of his voice.

Bill shook his head. 'Doubtful,' he said, not wishing to raise the lad's hopes. He added quickly: 'What it will do is serve as a presentation piece for your work, to show people what you can do. But not in its present form. It needs a soundtrack, it needs some tough editing to get it down to about fifteen minutes, and it needs decent tilting.' He paused. 'That girl in the alleyway scene had tasty legs, by the way. I thought the camera was going to crawl right under her skirt and into her knickers. A nice bit of eroticism that. What are you doing next weekend?'

'Nothing. Why?'

Bill fished in his pocket and gave Marshall a business card. 'Bring the film and a toothbrush along to my house next Saturday morning about tenish and we'll spend the weekend knocking *Catseyes* into shape. I've got some eight-mill kit. There's someone at the BBC I'd like to see it. And you'd better bring your camera and all your out-takes and about three hundred feet of stock. Did you work to a camera script?'

Marshall nodded.

'Thought so. Bring that as well.'

## 16

Bill's large, detached house at Hampton Court reflected his bizarre, extrovert personality. Every downstairs room was crammed with film making and editing gear, and the walls were adorned with erotic pictures that bordered on the obscene. The house was a shrine to the movie. Even the sitting room could be used as a viewing theatre.

'Right,' said Bill briskly when he had shown Marshall around. 'We've got a busy weekend in front of us so let's get stuck in.'

Marshall learned more about making movies during that one day at Bill's house than he had during the previous two years of working alone and reading technical magazines.

They started by re-writing Marshall's camera script and producing a new rough-cut print of the film. Bill worked with an intensity of concentration that Marshall found gratifying. It was the way he liked to work and had led to frequent moans from his mother along the lines that it was not normal for someone to spend so many hours peering into a machine, chopping up and gluing together bits of celluloid. Bill's attitude showed that it was normal. Better still, he kept up a non-stop commentary while he worked: 'Three seconds top and tailed off shot one three three will give us a clean cut to the foot of the garden fence in one three four.' And so on.

They worked solidly through the morning and afternoon with Marshall keeping the big, amiable Australian supplied with endless cups of Cona coffee. He seemed to be hooked on the stuff. 'It keeps my nerves on edge and my senses sharp,' he explained. 'It's the best way. Generate as much nervous tension when editing as you generated when shooting, and it'll shine right through to the finished movie.'

By 6 p.m. the new rough-cut was completed.

'Right,' said Bill after his twentieth coffee of the day. 'We'll now get the soundtrack cobbled together and ready for striping.'

Sound recording and mixing, and dubbing onto quarter-inch tape was entirely new to Marshall. There was nothing he could do but watch and listen as Bill selected sound effects from his library and mixed them onto what would eventually be the film's master soundtrack tape. He showed Marshall how to produce some convincing, ear-splitting cat yowls by recording human growls at normal speed and transferring the recordings onto a second tape at a higher speed.

'And now for some smoochy spot effects of the couple in the

alleyway,' said Bill and started kissing his wrist while Marshall held the microphone near. The results were astonishing. Sound added an unexpected dimension to the scene that Marshall had filmed with the unhappy but co-operative Martha Hunt.

'Whose the bloke?' Bill asked. 'You?'

Marshall nodded. 'I used a remote control.'

'Thought it must be something like that. Christ, it's a bloody sexy scene. Most amateurs' idea of eroticism is to shoot their poor, embarrassed wives in stockings and suspenders, posing in front of the fridge. They always look laughable. Your scene is pure sensuality. It'll make people sit up and take notice of you, Matt.'

It was nearly midnight when Bill started on the final tasks of editing down the rough-cut to a final print by removing the scene markers, and striping the magnetic soundtrack onto the edge of the film.

'All done,' he announced at nearly 2 a.m. 'Christ! Am I bush-wacked.'

'Could we see it now please, Bill?'

The Australian looked doubtful. 'Shouldn't really. Best to view it first thing in the morning when we're fresh and our minds are clear. We're too close to the bloody thing to be objective.' He saw Marshall's disappointed expression and changed his mind. He unthreaded the reel of finished film from the editor. 'Sure we can see it now,' he said genially.


17

The film worked. And how it worked!

It all hung together beautifully. Bill's skilled re-editing, trimming shots here, expanding them there from discarded out-takes, created a seamless flow of motion so that the audience would have no difficulty becoming the cat, seeing the world from the cat's point of view: approaching a saucer, jumping fences, contemplating a garbage bin before knocking it over and rooting through the debris.

For fifteen minutes Marshall sat utterly entranced, hardly able to believe that this was something he had made. Everything was perfect, right down to the church clock chimes in the final bars of music synchronized in with the closing shots which showed the first flush of light in the sky. Bill had cleverly cross-faded the music to the sounds of the dawn chorus. The film ended on a close-up of a cat sleeping on a bed that Marshall had not used in his original version. But the way Bill used the shot and his timing meant that it was just right.

The projector suddenly whirred free and white light glared off the screen. Bill switched the machine off and turned on the living room lights. 'It'll be a lot better when it's been properly titled and had some cat cutaways put in. I know a trainer who will help out with one of her moggies, but what do you reckon?'

'Fantastic,' Marshall breathed. 'Absolutely bloody fantastic. I can't believe it's my film. You've done wonders with it.'

'The wonders were already there, Matt,' said Bill dismissively. 'A film editor can only build on what's already there; he can't get silk out of a sow's ear. If you're going to make films seriously, as I know you will, then you're going to have to rely on the talents of many people. Lighting cameramen, sound recordists, editors, and even writers, God help you. The important thing is that your work must inspire them all to give you their best. I was inspired, It's as simple as that.'


# 18

## 1969

*Catseyes* didn't win any awards, but thanks to Bill Yates' persistence it did get a showing on BBC 2. The 625-line UHF service had been on air only five years and therefore not everyone could receive the channel. Marshall bought his mother a new television. Having Celia grateful to him eroded what little was left of her Authority. Unaware of this, she sent out proud invitations to all her friends and relatives. Marshall toyed with the idea of writing or phoning Beverley but decided that he could not be bothered.

He now had a new girlfriend. Unlike Beverley, who had plenty of spirit, the easily-cowed Martha Hunt proved an ideal foil for his temperament. When he suspected that she actually enjoyed being dominated, he resorted to inflicting sexual practices on her that he did not particularly enjoy, but at least they caused her pain and humiliation. This was his Authority over her. When she eventually mustered the courage to tell him that she didn't want to see him any more, he did not much care: at least she was leaving him on his terms.

On the great day of the transmission, about thirty people crowded into Celia's front room. To spite her pride, Marshall stayed away from home and watched the broadcast at Bill's house. Celia was reproachful when he returned home but by now was too wary of her son's mercurial temper to risk expressing her feelings more forcibly.

A week later he received a cheque from the BBC's Copyright Department for sixty pounds, the equivalent of two weeks' wages. A few days later Bill phoned him at work with the news that Matthew Drew, director of the Schools Education Council, wanted Marshall to discuss making a five-minute short for them.

## 19

'We want a hard-hitting film about the dangers of kids accepting lifts from strangers,' Drew explained when Marshall took the day off work and went to see him in his London office. He was a large, expansive man who struck Marshall as being obsessed with his own importance. 'A film made by young people for young people will have more impact, don't you think?'

Marshall thought nothing of the sort but he kept his views to himself. He did not think kids would give a toss one way or the other who was behind the camera. It was what went on in front of the lens and how well the film was made that mattered. It was his first encounter with what he was later to call 'shitting on the audience' in which producers and programme controllers put the need to feed their egos before consideration of what audiences actually wanted. Drew was authority at its worst – when it was obsessed with its own importance.

'What I have in mind,' Drew continued, 'is something like a well known TV personality, or a footballer, talking to the kids and telling them about the dangers of accepting lifts from strangers. Give them some facts and figures, that sort of thing. What do you think?'

Marshall thought that Drew was a pompous prat. 'Why does it have to be a TV personality?' he asked.

'Someone the kids look up to,' said Drew. 'Someone they can identify with. Maybe have him give some details of recent cases. Not too detailed, of course. You do a camera script and I'll get it approved by the council. Of course, there won't be any problems if I like it. So how say you?'

Over the next few evenings Marshall sat in his bedroom carefully typing a script that he thought contained all the elements that Drew wanted. The opening and closing credit pages named Matthew Drew as the film's executive producer.

'That'll swing it,' said Bill when he read the finished script.

'But what do you think of it?'

'Bloody awful.'

'That's exactly what I think,' Marshall replied. 'That's why I've written two scripts. Want to see the real one?'

## 20

Marshall posted what he called the 'committee' script off and had to wait three weeks before receiving a letter of contract from Drew giving him the go ahead. A cheque for four hundred pounds, as the first two thirds of the commission fee, followed a few days later. The cheque was countersigned by Sir Robert Allsop, chairman of the Schools Education Council according to the printed letter heading. Marshall prepared a careful production budget which allowed him to blow forty pounds of the money on a motorbike to replace his battered old scooter.

Bill was delighted that Marshall had landed the contract and readily agreed to renting him his 16 mm camera and acting as assistant cameraman for the shoot for a fee of one hundred pounds. He had wanted to do it for nothing but Marshall insisted on the payment.

'I want to be a professional film maker, Bill,' Marshall told him. 'That means using professionals and paying them. You yourself said that it was cheapest in the long run because you get things done properly. I'm starting the way I mean to go on.'

## 21

The storm over *Dark Encounter*, as Marshall called his five-minute film, erupted in September, the day after he delivered a print to the Schools Education Council. An enraged Matthew Drew phoned Marshall at work saying that the film was totally unacceptable and that Marshall would have to repay the commission fee.

'Have you shown it to the council?' Marshall demanded.

'I can't possibly show them such sadistic filth!' Drew yelled. 'They're all respectable married men and women! Your film is out and out pornography.'

'I'm sure they'd be delighted to hear the patronizing crap you're dishing out about them,' Marshall retorted. Had he been alone in the office he would have lost his temper. 'The film was financed with money that they're responsible for so don't you think you have a duty to let them see what it's been spent on and let them judge for themselves?'

'No way am I showing them such disgusting filth!' the director howled and slammed down the phone.

Marshall's silent rage prevented him thinking clearly for some moments. Eventually the cold-blooded, calculating side of his character took control. He decided to move fast by getting to the chairman of the Schools Education Council before Drew.

That evening he went to Walton Public Library and looked up Sir Robert Allsop in *Who's Who*. Sir Robert had many unpaid charity posts, including chairmanship of the Schools Education Council. He was also listed as executive chairman of the City Media Bank. Marshall could scarcely believe his good fortune when he came to the end of the entry: his private address was Silverdale Avenue, Walton-on-Thames. Marshall grabbed the local phone book. His luck was holding: Sir Robert's home number wasn't ex-directory.

He darted out of the library and shot across the road to the public phone box outside the magistrate's court. Persuading

Lady Allsop to let him speak to her husband nearly exhausted all his coins. Eventually she passed the phone to Sir Robert. A pleasant-sounding, cultured voice came on the line. Marshall quickly outlined what had happened, sticking to the truth.

'Well I'm certainly not prepared to comment on Matthew Drew's decisions,' said Sir Robert when Marshall had finished talking. 'He's doing what he's paid to do.'

'But he doesn't want you to see the film, sir,' said Marshall desperately. 'Look, I live in Walton. I could easily bring the film round to you now. Have you got a sixteen mill projector?'

'Yes . . . but – '

'I could be round in twenty minutes, sir. It's only a five-minute film so I won't take up more than half an hour of your time, I promise.'

There was a long pause. Marshall was certain that Sir Robert could hear his heart pounding.

'Very well,' said the banker reluctantly. 'Twenty minutes. I'll put the drive lights on.'


## 22

Silverdale Avenue was in Ashley Park, the smart part of Walton-on-Thames where detached Edwardian mansions were hidden from the road, set back in grounds that varied from one to five acres. Sir Robert Allsop's ivy-covered home was at the end of a long, floodlit drive. Marshall lifted his motorbike onto its stand and yanked the old-fashioned bellpull. He admired a Rolls Royce while he waited. The door was opened by the first real butler that he had ever seen. The butler looked askance at Marshall's scruffy appearance and grubby haversack.

'Marshall Tate, my good man,' said Marshall in reply to the butler's frosty inquiry, not the least intimidated by his hostile glare. 'I've come to see Sir Robert. He's expecting me.'

He followed the butler along a panelled corridor and could not resist challenging the servant's authority by pausing to examine an oil painting. The butler was visibly annoyed as he showed Marshall into Sir Robert's private office. One entire wall of the thirty-feet-long room consisted of bookshelves with the upper shelves completely devoid of books. The other walls were adorned with prints of racehorses and sepia photographs of frowning Edwardian characters in top hats and morning suits. A top quality glass-beaded projection screen occupied the far wall.

A stocky, distinguished-looking man aged about fifty was sitting in an electric wheelchair behind the strangest desk Marshall had ever seen. It was T-shaped, formed by a full-size roulette table abutting a conventional but large walnut desk. Both wings of the roulette cloth were strewn with coloured chips. The man was completely bald. His face, his head and fingers looked as if they were subjected to hours of vigorous scrubbing each day. He had an unreal pinkness about him that almost glowed. He was talking into a green telephone, one of a battery of six coloured phones lined up before him.

'Mr Marshall Tate, sir,' the butler announced distastefully.

Sir Robert cupped a manicured hand over the telephone mouthpiece and looked thoughtfully at Marshall. 'The gentleman has a film I want you to run, Smithers.'

Marshall delved in his haversack and handed the reel to the butler who bore it at arm's length from the room as though it needed decontamination.

Still holding the phone to his ear, Sir Robert operated his armrest control yoke to steer his wheelchair around the desk so that he could contemplate the roulette table. His small, pink fingers played with the phone cord. 'Go again on those last three spins.' He listened intently, keyed in some numbers on a full-size Olivetti calculating machine that looked like a one-armed bandit, and pulled the lever. 'Okay, Paul,' he said after a few moments spent studying the resulting printout. 'Let the lot ride on *Manque*.' As he spoke he carefully stacked all the chips into a neat pile. His small, manicured fingers seemed to lovingly caress each chip. He slid the stack into the centre of the *Manque* square and made tiny adjustments until he was satisfied it was precisely centred. He listened intently for a few seconds while idly spinning the roulette wheel before giving an almost babyish chuckle of pleasure. 'Splendid, Paul. Call me back in forty-five minutes. I've got a visitor.'

He replaced the handset and shook hands with Marshall. There seemed to be no strength in his tiny fingers but Marshall sensed that there was ice behind the genial beam and the warm sparkle in the banker's piercing grey eyes. He waved his guest to an easy chair. 'Sorry to keep you waiting, Mr Tate. Gambling is my little weakness. My big weakness my wife maintains. Roulette is a particular passion – one can drop in on a game, place a bet, and drop out. That was my son in Monte Carlo. What a wonder modern communications are, to be able to play real roulette in England and not that ghastly American abortion with its double zeros.' He nodded ruefully at his legs. 'A riding accident when I was young and foolish. I tried to take a particularly high fence for a bet. Now I have to make complex arrangements to indulge my little weakness, but I enjoy myself.'

Marshall wasn't interested in the plump little banker's weaknesses but he considered it politic to make polite conversation. 'Is it legal, sir?'

'As the game is being played in Monte Carlo, perfectly legal. If we ever join this Common Market thing, governments will have to learn the stupidity of using national laws to control international gambling and international financial transactions.' He swung the wheelchair around to face Marshall. 'Do you gamble, Mr Tate?'

'No, sir.'

'Ah, but you do. You're a film maker therefore you are a gambler. Films are the biggest gamble ever invented. My bank has made and lost millions on films. Do you know how much *Cleopatra* cost? If ordinary companies had to gamble the way the big studios and their backers have to gamble, there would be no industry, no cars, no planes, nothing, because there would be no confidence and therefore no investment.' He pointed to one of the pictures of the dour-looking Edwardians. 'André Citroën: he gambled away his entire car empire.' A gold signet ring glinted on his pink finger as he pointed to another photograph. 'Gordon Selfridge: he lost his store, his family, everything, playing baccarat. He had two thousand pounds when he died.'

*For God's sake let's get on!* Marshall's nerves screamed.

216

Sir Robert smiled knowingly as though he were reading his visitor's thoughts. 'I have a certain admiration for gamblers. People who are prepared to put everything on the line, not for the prizes, but for the danger and for something they passionately believe in. You took a gamble tonight. So let's see what the stakes are in your case, shall we?' He picked up the green phone. 'Ready when you are, Smithers.'

There was no sign of a projector. Marshall turned and spotted the small windows set into the wall opposite the screen. He realized that the office was a proper viewing room.

'It is very good of you to see me at such short notice, Sir Robert,' said Marshall politely. 'I feel it's important – '

'So why has Drew said we can't see your film?' the banker inquired, adroitly steering his wheelchair beside Marshall.

'He said it was sadistic filth, his exact words.'

'And is it? After all, the film's going to be shown in schools throughout the country.'

'No,' said Marshall emphatically. 'But it doesn't pull any punches. It's got a tough message to put across.'

Sir Robert grunted and held his hand up for silence when the lights dimmed. The opening shot hit him straight between the eyes: a close-up of an adolescent girl's horribly mutilated, blood-streaked body lying in long grass. There was no commentary and no music. The shot loosened quickly to take in the surrounding field and continued zooming out until the girl's body was a dot in the middle of a patchwork of fields. The desolation of the scene accentuated the miserable, lonely death that the girl must have suffered.

The harrowing scene mixed to the girl in a school uniform, waving to her friends and happily accepting a lift in a Ford Consul convertible with the hood down. The driver was a mild-looking fair-haired young man, a typical rep who spent his evenings in commercial hotels going over his sales figures. Marshall had deliberately avoided labelling and not gone for the soft option of using an unshaven actor with sullen, brutish looks. His driver was a regular guy-next-door type with a friendly smile. What alerted the audience was the way his smile never

217

left his face and the way he kept glancing covertly at his passenger's legs.

As before, there was no sound. Sound wasn't necessary, the schoolgirl's mounting anxiety as the car drove deeper into the countryside was plain to see. The car turned into a field and parked beneath a tree. What followed was the most gut-churning piece of film making that Sir Robert had seen since the butchering of Janet Leigh in *Psycho*. The difference was that Hitchcock's film had sound. Seeing the girl's silent screams as she was beaten and raped had an even more horrifying, surrealistic effect, as if the girl was totally isolated from the outside world in her ghastly agony. The entire terrible scene was shot from directly overhead so that the open-topped car provided a prison-like enclosure that framed and centred the terrible atrocity.

There followed a rapid series of police photographs of victims, each one shown too quickly to take in details, but slowly enough for the brain to register total horror. There were accompanying captions: 'Pauline Lewis, aged 10 – Raped'; 'Carol Burley, aged 12 – Raped and Murdered'; 'Sarah Tomkins' . . . 'Diana Cummings' . . . Some twenty names and photographs in all, but Sir Robert was too shocked to count.

The final shot was a freeze frame of the girl's hand on the Consul's door handle as she was about to get into the car. It was a brilliantly-composed shot: reflected in the car door were the girl's friends, symbols of her little world of walking home in gossipy, noisy company to watch *Crackerjack* on television while eating hot, buttered teacakes with her cat rubbing around her. The car door itself was the barrier between that friendly world and the blackness beyond, represented by the driver's fingers helping to push the door open. A caption appeared: 'DON'T LOSE YOUR LIFE FOR A LIFT.'

The film ended. The unseen Smithers restored the lights. Sir Robert sat staring at the blank screen for some moments while he marshalled his thoughts. He felt that he had just been slammed in the stomach by a prize fighter.

Marshall broke the silence. 'I deliberately made it a silent film, sir, so that infants' schools with eight mill silent projectors can show it.'

The thought of children under eleven seeing the film jerked Sir Robert back to reality. 'Yes . . . of course,' he muttered. 'The girl . . . She looks too young. Far too young. Who is she?'

'Sally Turner, sir. She's actually eighteen. A member of Equity. I picked her out of *Spotlight*.'

'Good heavens.' Sir Robert lapsed into silence. The ice-chip eyes watching him carefully made him uncomfortable.

'So what do you think of it, sir?' asked Marshall anxiously.

The banker considered his answer, choosing his words with the same care that he would give to an investment decision or the placing of chips on a roulette table. 'It's a film that possesses tremendous impact, Mr Tate,' he observed at length. 'However, I can well understand that Matthew Drew has grave reservations about it.'

'He has no reservations about it at all,' Marshall countered sourly. 'He's banned it, full stop. And he doesn't want you or the members of the council to see it.'

Sir Robert guided his wheelchair towards the door; a clear signal that the audience was over. 'Let's say misgivings, shall we? Thank you for showing me the film, Mr Tate. I really can't comment on Mr Drew's decision until I've discussed the matter with him. He'll be in touch with you as soon as possible.'

Marshall rode home on his motorbike, wondering if he had done the right thing.

## 23

Celia had no inkling of the row that was brewing until two evenings later when she was getting ready for bed. Marshall was out and, as usual, had not told her where he would be. The telephone rang as she was preparing for bed. It was a *Daily Mail* reporter after Marshall's views on the uproar that evening when *Dark Encounter* had been shown in London to an extraordinary meeting of the Schools Education Council. Celia took a message.

The telephone started ringing again the instant she replaced the receiver. It was the *Daily Express* chasing after the same information. She took three more similar calls before going to bed. After that she shut her bedroom door and let the damn thing ring.

All was made clear the following morning. 'STORM OVER CHILD RAPE MOVIE – Education bosses walk out after seeing "porn" film' was splashed across an inside page of the *Daily Mail*. There was a photograph of Marshall and the child-like actress he had used in his film. She was clinging to Marshall's arm and looking adoringly up at him. Celia sat down and read the story. At an extraordinary meeting of the Schools Education Council the previous evening, six members of the council and the full-time director had resigned *en masse* and stormed out after the chairman, city financier Sir Robert Allsop, exercised his casting vote in favour of the council distributing a five-minute film made by Marshall Tate.

Celia re-read the piece slowly. The telephone rang. This time it was a local stringer, stung at having a hot story stolen from under his nose by the nationals. Celia called up to Marshall who tottered down the stairs half-asleep. She returned to the kitchen and re-read the story for a third time, more carefully, while Marshall finished talking to the reporter.

She looked up suddenly when she realized that he was standing in the doorway, his head nearly touching the top of the frame. He smiled down at her. His eyes were ice-cold and blue, like his father's. He was looking more like him every day. She shivered. There was a noise from upstairs that sounded like someone taking a shower. She looked questioningly at Marshall. 'Don't worry,' he said calmly. 'It'll all blow over in a week.'


24

1970

Marshall was pleased to be proved wrong. The story spread across the country like a virulent bug as local education authorities and parent teacher associations were embroiled in rows over whether or not the film should be shown to schoolchildren in their areas. Marshall become a popular target for television interviews because he could be relied on to pour scorn on those local councils who decided not to show his film. On a late night discussion show he suggested to one irate parent who had said that she had no intention of exposing her daughter to such filth that maybe she would prefer her daughter to be raped and strangled. The ensuing row became so heated that the programme stayed on air, resulting in the epilogue being scrapped and God Save the Queen being played thirty minutes late at 11.30 p.m.

Travelling home on the last train to Walton that night, Marshall reflected that he had 'arrived'.


### 25

Six months later Bill Yates met Marshall for a lunchtime drink in the *Kiwi*. This time Marshall insisted on paying for the drinks. There was an air of confidence about him that Bill suspected was 50 per cent arrogance.

'I'm making money now, Bill. Real money.'

'You've been paid for all those interviews?'

'That's not real money.'

'Well I know you've quit Shepperton. I've tried calling your office.'

Marshall smiled coldly and raised his glass. 'You're now talking to the director of the Schools Education Council film unit. Sir Robert Allsop offered me the job last week.'

'Always thought you'd land on your feet, you old bugger,' said Bill, swallowing most of his pint in one gulp. 'So how much are they paying you?'

'Same as they paid Drew plus a bit, four.'

Bill whistled. Marshall was right: four thousand per annum was good for a young man in 1970.

'And I've made over five thousand quid flogging copies of *Dark Encounter* and the money's still rolling in.'

The older man was astonished. 'How the hell did you manage that?'

'Easy. Every time an education authority announced a ban on the film, I put ads in their local papers: "See *Dark Encounter*! The film they tried to ban. Order your 8-mm colour print direct

221

from the maker. Guaranteed unexpurgated. £7 15s including post and packing".'

'That's a con, Matt, the film's not worth that. It must be one helluva disappointment to the raincoat brigade.'

Marshall set his drink down carefully on a beer mat and turned to face Bill. 'I never shit on the audience,' he said coldly. 'You should know that. I reshot some scenes at the original location.'

'With Sally Turner?'

'And the actor. And the car.'

Bill recalled the trouble they had had with the girl getting her to agree to go as far as she did. 'How did you get around young Sally's scruples?'

Marshall grunted in contempt. 'Like all women, her so-called scruples are one big act. She's moved in with me. She's getting work as a result of *Dark Encounter*. She sees me as a stepping stone so I make use of her.'

Bill considered it more than likely that anyone who thought they could use Marshall as a stepping stone would end up being not only stepped on by him, but crushed. 'What does your mother think?'

Marshall shrugged. 'She died three months ago.'

'I'm sorry. She was a nice lady.'

'And the house is now mine. Sally looks after things now. I need someone – the GPO deliver my mail by the sackful. I pay her.'

For the life of him, Bill could not imagine what a sweet young kid like Sally Turner saw in Matt Tate. Women! 'What does she make of it all?'

Marshall shrugged. 'She was a bit upset when I had the police jumping all over me when the ads first appeared. Obscene Publications Act they said. The DPP's office decided not to go ahead when my lawyer pointed out that they'd look pretty stupid busting me for flogging a movie that half the kids in England, Scotland and Wales are being shown in school.'

'For Christ's sake, Matt, you don't own the mechanical rights or copyright in the film. They must belong to the Schools Education Council.'

222

'They do. That's why I thought I was up shit creek when Sir Robert Allsop summoned me to his office in London. Turned out he didn't give a toss. He's a bit of a crook himself in the City, and a gambler. That's when he offered me the job. Plus a budget of thirty-five thou a year to churn out their shorts. A gamble, he said. Be good experience though.'

'Be bloody good experience,' Bill breathed, looking at Marshall with a mixture of pride and admiration.

## 26

### 1971 to 1973

Marshall worked for three years for the Schools Education Council. In that time he made over seventy-five shorts for them, averaging one a fortnight. Ten of them were dogs – God-awful films of the first order that never saw the light of day and which were hardly worth the value of the match he used to burn the negatives.

Marshall did not mind. He learned from his mistakes. The other sixty or so films were gems and were widely circulated throughout the world. They covered subjects as diverse as road safety to personal hygiene. All bore his stamp of surrealistic lighting and camera angles, and dead soundtracks when the action on the screen told all the story as a result of his tight editing. Such was his rapidly-developing skill as a film maker that his near-total lack of a sense of humour did not prevent him injecting humour into his films. Humour was merely another ingredient – used dispassionately and with surgical precision – to make films that people liked. After all, Buster Keaton never smiled.

His brief career with SEC continued to be peppered with rows about the sexual content of his films. A one reeler, *Clap*, that he shot in a VD clinic in a day with the consent of the patients and staff caused a furore that tempered his contempt for authority into a seething hatred of Britain's neurosis about sex. A contempt that he felt was justified because his films were shown in most of Europe without comment.

# 1974 to 1976

Marshall's parting from the SEC was amicable. Such was Sir Robert's faith in Marshall's work that his bank agreed to provide a film company with 90 per cent financial backing for a full-length feature film provided that Marshall was the director.

'It's not nepotism, Matt,' said Sir Robert when Marshall challenged him about it. 'It's sound business acumen. The board know your work and have unanimously agreed that you're the best man to direct *Agapemone*.'

Unfortunately the conditions of the loan by Sir Robert's City Media Bank did not extend sufficiently to allow Marshall to rewrite the script. His pleas that it was flawed were always referred back to the screenplay writer who had a small financial stake in the film and a large 'don't-bugger-about-with-my-script' clause in his contract.

'Jesus Christ!' Marshall exploded at the end of a fruitless row with the stubborn scribe. 'God protect me from writers. He thinks I should treat his crappy script like tablets handed down from Mount Sinai!'

He did his best but the result was one of those expensive box office turkeys that the critics loved but the public hated. After that little fiasco he swore never again to get involved in any project where he did not have total control over the script. The episode didn't shake Sir Robert Allsop's faith in Marshall even though the venture had lost his bank what Marshall considered a small fortune.

'Peanuts, Matt, peanuts,' was Sir Robert's comment when Marshall saw him about the loss. 'Sometimes we lose, sometimes we win. It's all a gamble. What we always try to do is make sure our losses are small and our wins big. You can afford to lose everything but your nerve.'

The chubby banker's words would stay with Marshall for the rest of his life.

Marshall redeemed himself quickly with a low-budget feature
film about a day in the life of a prostitute. It starred Sally
Turner. He drove her brutally during the shooting because he
wanted to get the best out of her and because he wanted to get
rid of her. In the last scene to be shot, Sally was supposed to
be raped by a client. But Marshall had a word with the non-
Equity thug who played the client with the result that Sally
really was raped on camera. Her frantic screams to Marshall to
get the bastard off her went unheeded. In the finished film
the scene was overlaid with Nat King Cole singing 'Ain't She
Sweet?'

The ploy worked on both counts: the film was a success and
Sally Turner stormed out on him. A few days later he received
a letter from her solicitors demanding damages. Marshall retali-
ated by leaking stories to the press saying that the idea for the
rape had come from Sally because she had no confidence in her
ability to act the scene. The story earned a lot of publicity for
the film.

Sally Turner committed suicide before the case went to court
by swallowing forty barbiturate tablets.

Marshall had no qualms about exploiting her death to promote
the picture. He claimed that she had been a real-life hooker
since she was fifteen. The tabloids latched onto the story with
the result that what was a cheap sex exploitation movie was
elevated to the status of a moral tract. The profits from the film
were enough for Marshall to set up his own production company: Herring Gate Films.

Bill chuckled when he saw the name of Marshall's company
in print. 'Herring Gate . . . Hair in gate, that's a pretty nifty
title for someone who hasn't got a sense of humour.'

'I have got a sense of humour,' Marshall protested.

Bill grinned. 'Oh yeah?'

'I've made films with a lot of comedy in them.'

'You don't have to be a murderer to write a whodunit,' Bill
observed pointedly.

'So how about becoming a director of my company?'

'How much will it cost me?'

'A thousand pounds for a 20 per cent holding.'

'Me, play second fiddle to a gawky twenty-four-year-old? Okay, you're on. I want to be around when you fall flat on your face.' Bill was the only one who could talk to Marshall like that and he knew it.

They shook hands on the deal.


## 29

### 1977 to 1987

In those ten years Marshall made six full-length movies and over fifty TV commercials. He drove himself and others with a blinding energy that permitted nothing to interfere with his film making. A string of submissive women came and went because not even the most submissive of women could tolerate being bent to his will for long.

Despite Marshall's hard work, through no fault of his, Herring Gate Films never prospered. His films were popular but the only people who made real money out of them were the distributors whom he learned to despise with an all consuming passion that he made no attempt to hide. They had become Authority. Their word was law. Cross them at your peril.

The steady trickle of cheques from the distributors made for good reading on the balance sheet but as fast as the money came in it went out again in payments to freelances, and staged payments on loans from Sir Robert Allsop's City Media Bank. The bank treated Marshall very well, making funds available on terms that were the envy of other independents. What Marshall badly needed was a new outlet for Herring Gate's offbeat productions.


## 30

The creation of a new television service, Channel 4, marked a profound change in British television. Like the US networks but unlike existing British broadcasting institutions, Channel 4 was conceived as a programme publisher rather than a programme maker. Not only did its inception give Marshall and many other independents a new and receptive customer, it gave him the chance to make what he really enjoyed – documentaries.

Sir Robert Allsop was fond of pointing out to Marshall that documentaries were commercial dead ducks, virtually unsaleable overseas because they usually dealt with domestic topics that other countries were not interested in. But the Channel 4 commissioning editors, under the intuitive direction of Jeremy Isaacs, were prepared to underwrite the entire cost of a documentary's production if they liked the subject.

Marshall's first film for them was a twenty-five-minute piece on under-age drinking in Britain that laid the blame firmly at the feet of brewers and publicans.

The licensed victualling trade kicked up a furore when the film was shown. The row eventually involved the entire independent television network when several brewers threatened to withdraw their advertising.

Marshall poured his vitriolic scorn on the Independent Broadcasting Authority when they ordered that the film's scheduled repeat should not be shown. The IBA argued that Marshall's pub scenes using an actor and an actress introduced a distortion in what was supposed to be a documentary. 'Pouring shit on the viewers', is what Marshall called their action. The episode made the independent television companies wary about commissioning programmes from Herring Gate Films.


31

A further decline in Marshall Tate's fortunes came with an eleventh-hour cancellation of a documentary series called *The History of Sex*. The Independent Broadcasting Authority had viewed a rough-cut of the first episode and said 'no'. A safety clause that the commissioning company had written into his contract meant that he had no comeback on them. The blow left Marshall saddled with debts that resulted in his having to take out a heavy mortgage on the house that his mother had left him. Residual payments for his commercials kept him from going under.

It was a black time, when his friends and associates avoided him. Marshall's already uncertain temper when things were not going well was becoming even more ugly. Only Bill Yates was prepared to persevere with their patchy friendship.

A minor salvation but one that was to have remarkable repercussions was a letter Marshall received bearing a Zurich postmark. It was his first serious contact with the world of satellite television. The letter from Teleclub AG was a not ungenerous offer for the German-language distribution rights for six of his films. A brochure accompanying the letter explained that Teleclub distributed their programmes to cable operators and homes via a low-powered network satellite called Eutelsat F4. Until then Marshall's dealings with satellite television had been agreeing to clauses in advertising agency contracts that enabled his commercials to be broadcast on cable services such as *Superchannel* which was distributed to cable operators via a satellite – he knew not how, or where the satellite was, or who owned it.

He decided to learn more about satellite television and purchased a steerable dish system from a local company. The installation engineer got the system lined up and working by late afternoon. He stood the satellite receiver on Marshall's video recorder, hooked it up to the television and tuned a spare channel on the television to the satellite receiver's output. A Western dubbed into German came through immediately. Marshall was astonished at the quality of the picture and sound.

'Line of sight from the bird. No ghosting, no signal reflections off buildings to louse up the picture,' said the engineer, showing Marshall how to operate the control box to send the 1.2 metre diameter dish to its pre-set locations. Good pictures could be obtained from five satellites dotted along the arc of southern sky twenty-two thousand miles above the equator that the engineer referred to as the 'Clarke Belt'.

'They're the Eutelsats and Intelsat,' the engineer explained. 'Low-power birds for cable operators – that's why you need such a large dish. Be different when Astra goes up. Filmnet decoders are built in to the receiver so you'll be able to watch some pretty raunchy stuff after midnight.'

Bill came over to inspect the new installation. The film they watched on Filmnet-24 that evening was more than merely 'raunchy', it contained scenes of explicit sex the like of which neither thought they would ever see on television in England in their lifetimes. It was a crudely-made American effort, there was no eroticism. Nevertheless, watching a film that was wholly outside of the control of the British government and the British Board of Film Classification was a breath of fresh air.


## 32

On 11 December 1988 an event took place on the other side of the world that was eventually to transform the pattern of European television for good by breaking the stranglehold that governments had on broadcasters.

At 12.30 a.m. Greenwich Mean Time, an Ariane 4 rocket was successfully launched from France's huge space facility at Kourou in the jungle of French Guiana. Flight 27's payload was a very special satellite, Astra 1A – a sixteen-channel direct broadcasting television satellite of such power that its signals could be received in homes across Europe using small fixed dish antennae not much bigger than large saucepan lids.

The satellite was released into a low earth orbit twenty-four minutes after its launch. The controllers at Kourou still had a long way to go before the satellite could be handed over to its owners. Systems had to be checked out; delicate corrections made to the satellite's orientation. Four days later Astra's internal solid fuel kick booster was fired to lift the satellite to a height of thirty-six thousand kilometres above the equator where it would orbit the earth once every twenty-four hours, matching the earth's spin and therefore appearing to be fixed in the sky. The final task on the epic journey fell to small thruster rockets that 'walked' Astra along its orbit to a position 19.2 degrees east of the Greenwich Meridian that put it smack over Zaire but with a near-perfect view of Europe – the richest trading market in the world and Astra's golden target.

After twenty hours' precision jockeying, the satellite was finally home, and control was formally handed over to its owners, Société Européenne des Satellites (SES), a commercial venture, based in Luxembourg, made up of an oddball collection of banks, the Luxembourg government, and various European broadcasting organizations that included British companies such as Television South West, Thames Television, and Ulster Television.

In the political hotbed of European broadcasting, the tiny Duchy of Luxembourg had always been an outsider and because of that had wielded an influence out of all proportion to its size. When the general agreement among European politicians during the 1950s and 1960s was that pop music was a bad thing, millions of youngsters across the continent were regularly tuning to Radio Luxembourg on 208 metres and suffering the squawks, whistles and fading of the medium waveband to listen to the likes of Johnny Ray, Guy Mitchell and Rosemary Clooney, Bill Haley and Elvis Presley.

The Luxembourg government was firmly committed to Europe and believed in cultural unification by means of radio and television without frontiers or undue state control. It maintained a policy of polite disdain towards various European agreements that were aimed at preserving state control over satellite television. They were ill-conceived agreements that would eventually give birth to curious, ill-fated creations such as British Satellite Broadcasting, in which an individual state would license a programme contractor to operate from a satellite but insist that the signal footprint be tightly focused on their country.

Luxembourg had little time for such nonsense which was why SES came into being and set up their headquarters at the magnificent Château de Betzdorf in a tranquil forest a few kilometres west of Luxembourg.

Outside the reflective glass wing that had been built onto the chateau, engineers carefully aligned their giant eleven-metre control dish on Astra. The telemetry signals to unfurl the satellite's solar panels were transmitted. The engineers waited, nerves on edge, for the readings on their metres that would tell them that Astra had power. The readings came but it was too early to pop champagne corks. Testing the bird's sixteen transponders took several hours. Signal deviations had to be set, colours balanced, sound quality checked. At the end of the setting-up period the network control room beamed a test card and music to each channel in turn and got back perfect pictures and sound picked up on a small domestic dish that looked oddly out of place alongside its monster big brothers. It was then that the bubbly bubbled: The world's first direct broadcasting TV satellite worked like a dream.

## 33

### 1989

Marshall's only relaxation during the first half of that hectic year was watching television which he would do for an hour late each night before dragging himself off to bed. Even that was work in a way because scanning through the satellite services kept him abreast of developments and the emergence of potential new customers.

Astra was doing well. Sky Television's four channels – sport, news, general entertainment and junk movies – were looking more professional each day. Marshall was surprised that Sky Movies were ball and chaining themselves to the British Board of Film Classification by running squeaky-clean edited prints complete with the BBFC certificate at the beginning of their movies. The sanitized British cut of *Mona Lisa* was a mess compared with the European print. The eroticism of *9½ Weeks* was butchered out of existence. Why did they choose to shackle themselves?

Despite their polish, Sky's output was downmarket although not so downmarket as W H Smith Television's two channels. Even so, Sky were unlikely buyers of Marshall's avant garde material.

By the end of the year all sixteen of Astra's transponders were in daytime and evening use, the last station to join them being 3SAT, the German-language public television service who were likely customers, as were RTL-Plus and the multi-language service RTL4. The German stations dominated European satellite television. They were there in force on Kopernicus, the Eutelsats and Astra. What puzzled Marshall was that the majority of them closed down around midnight Central European Time and broadcast test cards through the night to prevent pirate broadcasters hijacking the transponders. The proliferation of nighttime test cards gave Marshall an idea that needed talking over with Bill.


## 34

## 1990

Communications had come a long way since Marshall's first meeting with Sir Robert Allsop nineteen years previously. Facsimile machines, cellular telephones, racks of high-speed modems, and an assortment of computer terminals had moved in on the row of coloured telephones he used to have lined up on his desk. Like many businessmen, he had a battery of wall clocks. The difference with Sir Robert's clocks was that they told him the opening and closing times of the world's casino centres rather than stock exchanges. The banker was gadget-mad, which was understandable because the remorseless march of micro magic resulted in the production of a host of inventions that made life more tolerable for the disabled – especially the rich disabled. On Marshall's last visit, Sir Robert had proudly demonstrated his intelligent wheelchair that could 'remember' over a hundred locations throughout his house and grounds. All he had to do was enter the location number on the touch-sensitive keypad and the wheelchair would make its way to the new destination, its sonic guidance system steering it around obstacles *en route*.

Marshall was shown into the banker's office-cum-gaming room, expecting to be shown the latest piece of games software that Sir Robert had acquired. This time there was a gathering of about ten smartly-dressed men and women around a curious-looking table in the centre of the room.

'Ha! Marshall' said Sir Robert excitedly, a beaming smile lighting up his chubby face. He sent his wheelchair scudding across the carpet towards the new arrival. 'Come in. Come in! I'll introduce you to everyone later. But first I must introduce you to my new gadget. A new year's present to myself.'

The group around the table made way for Sir Robert and his guest. Marshall noticed that each player was holding a small black box that resembled a Psion Organizer pocket computer.

'There,' said the banker proudly. 'What do you think of that?'

Marshall looked in surprise at the table and didn't know what to think. It was a roulette table, that was obvious, but it was quite unlike the conventional roulette table that had been the centre piece of Sir Robert's room for twenty years. The entire surface was a luminescent display, glowing with the rich colours of the various numbers and boxes against a verdant green simulation of baize. Even the counters strewn across the surface of the table were simulations. The wheel dominating the centre of the electronically-generated altar to affluence was a flat representation of a full-size spinning roulette wheel. All eyes were fastened greedily on it as it slowed and finally stopped. The ball was represented by a shining blob of light.

'Red 23!' announced an electronic but perfectly audible voice from speakers set into the surface of the table.

There were exclamations of disappointment and pleasure from the players as they consulted their respective black boxes. The counters winked out from the table leaving a bare expanse of waiting, money-hungry numbers and coloured boxes.

'Computer-generated but real roulette just the same,' said Sir Robert enthusiastically. He pressed one of the black boxes into Marshall's hand. It possessed a simple numeric keypad and a liquid crystal display. 'Come on, Matt. Get your credit card out.'

Marshall was used to stringing along with Sir Robert's gambling crazes although this one was the craziest of them all. He produced a credit card. 'Okay. Now what?'

'Push it in the slot.' The little banker was virtually dancing on his rump with impatience.

Marshall fed his card into a slot in the side of the box.

'That's it,' said Sir Robert. 'The box has radio data link via the table. Give it a second for authentication.'

There was the briefest of pauses and Marshall's full name and address and credit card number appeared on the screen.

'Place your bets please, ladies and gentlemen,' announced the electronic voice. The illuminated two-dimensional wheel started spinning. The players reached across the cloth, touching the bases of their control boxes on the squares. As they did so, coloured counters for different values appeared as if by magic on the table. By tapping the box twice on the table they could even change their mind and clear the counter. It was all amazingly realistic – there was even the rattle of the ball bouncing around in the wheel.

'No more bets please.'

'How much do you want to play, Matt? We've missed this spin but never mind.' Sir Robert made it sound as if missing a bet was a disaster.

'A hundred pounds?'

The little banker's well-scrubbed moon-like face registered disappointment. 'Come on, Matt. You're a film maker. A breed of real gamblers. You can do better than that.'

*Play along with him, Matt. You need him!*

'Okay, two hundred?'

'Much better,' Sir Robert chuckled gleefully. 'You might even win.'

The electronic croupier reopened the betting and Sir Robert showed Marshall how to enter an overall stake on the keypad. The screen cleared and showed '£200'.

'That means that two hundred pounds have now been reserved against your credit card account. Now enter your first bet.'

Marshall pressed a one and a zero. The display changed to indicate that Marshall's stake stood at £190 and that he had a bet riding of ten pounds.

'Excellent! Excellent!' Sir Robert's excitement was infectious. 'Now place your bet. Quickly!'

Marshall touched his box on the nearest *impair* square. A glowing ten pound chip appeared in the box. It even bore his

234

name. If an odd number came up, Marshall stood to win ten pounds and get his bet back.

The wheel spun.

'Black 33!'

A woman who had bet *en plein* with fifty pounds on 33 gave a shriek of pleasure. Her display showed winnings of £1,750. The stake on Marshall's box jumped to £210.

Sir Robert gave a little thump of pleasure with a clenched pink fist on his armrest and beamed. 'There you are, Matt. Now I must insist on you enjoying yourself for a while before we discuss boring business.' He chuckled. 'If you're really lucky, you might not need me. You must excuse me, I've been neglecting my guests.' With that he spun his wheelchair away and engaged a woman in a low-cut evening dress in conversation.

Despite his pressing worries, Marshall enjoyed his brief gambling session. He liked the atmosphere of opulence, the beautiful woman, and the sudden electric tension when the ball stopped clattering and the wheel slowed down. His fortunes varied. At one point his black box was showing his stake as £520. A few minutes later it was down to £82 until more cautious betting on *rouge* and *pair* edged it back to £200. It stood at £256 when he felt a tap on his arm.

'Are we ahead or behind, Matt?' asked Sir Robert.

'Fifty-six quid ahead.'

The banker turned his wheelchair towards his desk that was now in the far corner of the long room. 'Time to quit when you're ahead. Press the function button three times and the computer will close your bets. Your winnings will be credited to your account as from now, as you will see on your next statement.'

Marshall sat in a chair beside the banker's desk and nodded to the crowd around the table. 'A business or pleasure venture?'

'Pleasure,' Sir Robert replied, pouring two scotches. 'But I get a small commission on winnings from the game's operators. The Gaming Board hate it but there's nothing they can do about it. The game is actually played and managed by a computer in Monte Carlo, outside the jurisdiction of British law and the Gaming Board. That table is really an extremely advanced computer terminal, linked to the main frame computer in Monte Carlo by telephone lines. There's one in Greece and another in Las Vegas. They're prototypes, both in private homes. Designed and built by a group of very clever young men and women. They cost a million pounds each.'

'I'm after a lot more than that from you,' said Marshall easily, sipping his drink. 'So if you can afford a million for a computer game . . . What can you afford for a business venture I wonder?'

Sir Robert laughed. 'My bank is involved in backing the company. Part of the deal is that they supply me with a prototype table. There're a lot of very rich people in the world who will happily part with that sort of money for such an exciting toy. Now, tell me what you have in mind to make my bank part with its hard-earned money?'

'Your own TV station covering the whole of Europe,' said Marshall casually. 'A late-night service from the Astra DBS satellite.'

The banker's face was impassive for some seconds. 'You're mad,' he said at length, turning his wheelchair away from Marshall so that he could watch the play at the electronic roulette table. 'Absolutely out of your skull, as they say. You're on the verge of being made a bankrupt, you owe the City Media Bank a hundred thousand pounds plus interest for that documentary series, which I daresay we can kiss goodbye to . . .'

'I'll pay it all back,' Marshall interrupted. 'I don't know how or when, but I will, every last penny.'

'. . . And you come in here, disturbing me and my friends, demanding that I listen to a crazy idea about setting up a satellite channel.'

'It's not so crazy if only you'd listen,' said Marshall testily, working hard to keep his temper in check.

'So I'm listening.'

'I want to call it the Elite channel. A channel with a European arts flavour.'

'Tits and Titian?'

'I've already written to over two hundred independent producers throughout Europe and the UK outlining the bare bones

236

of the idea. The responses so far are more than just keen, they're positively ecstatic.'

'You've documentary evidence?'

Marshall dumped a shabby suitcase on Sir Robert's desk and thrust a sheaf of letters and faxes into the banker's hand. 'Read those. And that's only a few of the replies. They're all from established indies with track records, some big names. I've estimated that they're sitting on a couple of thousand hours of untied programmes: films, documentaries, offbeat ballet productions, all first-class stuff that I'm bloody certain we could get the pan-European TV rights to for nominal rates if we play our cards right.'

Sir Robert skimmed through the letters while Marshall was talking. Many of the names he knew, companies the City Media Bank had backed – and made money out of. If he was impressed, he did not permit his moon-like face to show it.

'I've got about a hundred letters of intent,' Marshall continued. 'No programme controller in history has ever got that sort of advance line-up of programmes without having committed a penny.'

The banker regarded Marshall quizzically. He recalled the time when they had first met all those years ago and the tremendous courage and initiative that Marshall had shown in coming to see him. He now looked even lankier, as if he had not been eating properly but his fair hair was brushed neatly back and his suit had been cleaned and pressed. Recently his ego and self-esteem had taken shattering blows that would have destroyed a lesser man. He had aged over the past few weeks and yet his arrogance and self-confidence was undiminished. The hard light in his ice-blue eyes suggested that he was as ready as ever to take on the world and win. Sir Robert realized that he had been wrong about Marshall Tate all along, he was not a gambler, he was a fighter. An uncompromising, utterly ruthless fighter who would allow nothing to stand in his way and who would never give up.

'There's something I'd like an honest answer to, Matt.'

'I've always been straight with you, Sir Robert.'

The banker nodded. For all his faults, you always knew

237

exactly where you stood with Marshall Tate. 'Why do you want to do this? Is it to make money? Provide viewers with alternative television? Or what?'

The savagery of the demon that drove Marshall appeared in his eyes. 'I want to do both those things. But above all I want to shaft those bastards that are forever stitching me up. I want to put a torpedo into the British establishment that blows them out of the water.' He smiled humourlessly. 'Not a very good motive to put money on, someone who wants to get even.'

Wrong, Sir Robert thought.

A girl detached herself from the table. She stood behind the banker and slid her hands down his shirt front. 'You're deserting me, Robbie,' she protested. She looked at Marshall with undisguised interest.

Sir Robert idly stroked her arms, his eyes watching Marshall intently. 'Have you fixed a meeting with these Astra people?'

Marshall shook his head.

'Go ahead and fix it. It'll probably take time. But before we take this crazy idea any further, I want the bank's media analysts to take a hard look at your proposals before we even start preliminary discussions.'

## 35

That night Marshall read the *Satellite Times* before going to bed and learned that the Home Office Cable Television Authority had banned British cable operators from distributing two European satellite services to their customers. TVE, the Spanish television service, had upset the British government by showing a bullfight, and RTL-Plus, the Luxembourg television service, had caused much Home Office anguish and hand-wringing by showing a naked couple one lunchtime.

Marshall hurled the magazine across the room in despair.

The following week he received a fax that prompted him to telephone Sir Robert.

'SES would like us to visit Astra headquarters in Luxembourg next Friday,' he informed the banker.

'I've not had a report from my media analysts,' Sir Robert

protested. 'You've come up with a number of proposals that have significant political impact.'

'You said to get the meeting fixed A.S.A.P. I've done just that.'

'I suppose you want me to pay your fare?'

'I want you to go with me. They might not take me seriously if I go by myself, but they'll take notice of you.'

'I never fly, Matt.'

'Your chauffeur will drive us. It's only a couple of hundred miles from Ostend. Motorway all the way. Good facilities for the disabled in all the Belgian service areas, and the Intercontinental Hotel in Luxembourg has special suites.'

Sir Robert reluctantly agreed. The realization that he was a little afraid of Marshall Tate was an unpalatable shock.

## 36

In deference to Sir Robert Allsop's disability, the meeting with Alan Powell, deputy commercial director of Société Européenne des Satellites, was held in a downstairs office at the Château de Betzdorf overlooking the gently sloping lawns where SES's giant uplink dishes were staring at the azure southern sky.

Alan Powell was English, thirtyish, a forthright former advertising agency accountant who knew the European television industry inside-out. Few people or the organizations they worked for ever impressed Marshall Tate, but Alan Powell and SES were an exception. For the first time someone was not spouting about balanced output and the need for worthy programmes, or trotting out worn shibboleths about television's duty to inform and act as a mirror of society.

'A channel's first duty is to survive,' said Powell. 'Programme content is entirely up to our transponder leaseholders. Naturally our standard terms and conditions place some restrictions on the advertising of tobacco and pharmaceuticals in accordance with Luxembourg law, but generally we interfere as little as possible. We believe that satellite television should be market led. What we are not happy with is channel encryption that discriminates against countries within the European Community. It's contrary to the spirit of Europe and is forced on operators such as Sky Movies and Filmnet by American interests.' He glanced at the station profile that Marshall had prepared for the Elite channel. 'At least you're not proposing encryption and we certainly like the European showcase idea.'

'We've held discussions with producers from all over Europe,' said Marshall. 'We estimate that we have 70 per cent of them on our side.'

'What my bank needs,' said Sir Robert, 'is an indication of the cost of leasing a transponder after one of your existing stations closes down at night.'

'There is no standard rate,' Powell answered. 'Rates are individually negotiated and are strictly confidential.'

'So you're saying, make us an offer?'

Powell looked uncertain for a moment and smiled. 'Why not?'

'Okay,' said Sir Robert. 'Nothing. You give us a transponder free of charge.'

'Two transponders,' Marshall amended.

Alan Powell did not even blink. 'You want *two* transponders for nothing?'

'Got it in one,' said Marshall.

The SES man doodled on his pad. 'Any more bombshells?' he inquired.

'That depends on whether or not you consider our proposal to make the Elite channel the world's first high-definition, wide-screen television service a bombshell,' Sir Robert commented.

## 37

Marshall arrived back at his house at 2 a.m., red-eyed and unshaven. Bill's car was parked outside. He did not look too pleased to see Marshall. He glowered at his friend who had slumped exhausted into an armchair.

'Am I right in assuming that Robbie Allsop's Roller has a phone?'

'What of it?'

'Then why the hell didn't you call earlier?'

'I didn't know you'd be here.'

'I've had my portable phone on standby all day.'

'For Christ's sake. You're getting more like an old woman every day.'

'So how did it go?'

Marshall leaned back and closed his eyes. 'We can't have transponders on either of the Astra satellites.'

Bill sat down. He looked utterly dejected. 'Shit,' he muttered. 'All that bloody work. All those hopes we've raised.'

The two men sat in silence. Marshall appeared to be asleep. Bill fiddled with a remote control box for a few seconds. He switched on the television and scanned through the Astra channels. Discovery, SAT1, RTL-Plus, 3SAT and about twenty other stations had closed down and were showing test cards. Of the thirty-two channels, only seven were operating.

'Bloody waste,' Marshall observed without opening his eyes.

'Did they say why?'

'It's because we want to start up a high-definition wide-screen service. Pairing two transponders together to give the necessary bandwidth for one channel for just a few hours every night isn't possible.'

'So you've finally backed down on a Hi-Vision service?'

'Nope.'

Bill began to get angry. 'Why the hell not? It's a crazy idea, Matt, and you know damn well it is. We've worked our arses off raising the hopes of about four hundred indies all over Europe, and for what? Just so you can go chasing the end of a rainbow over this stupid idea that the future of television lies with high-definition wide-screen.'

'You wouldn't say that if you'd gone with me to Basingstoke and seen Sony's demos.'

'I was busy wasting my time writing letters on your behalf,' Bill snapped. 'So what the hell do we do now?'

'City Media are putting up five million ecus pre-operating costs and another four million on-air operating costs for one year. *And* they've deferred repayments on Herring Gate Films' loans. So, when we've had some sleep we start looking around for studio premises. Nothing pretentious. We'll be broadcasting pre-recorded material only so we won't be needing cameras and studio floor space.'

This was all too much for Bill. It was late, he was tired, and feeling his years. 'Maybe I'm getting slow,' he muttered. 'But what's the point of all that money if we don't have a satellite?'

'SES said that it's technically difficult for them to link two transponders to one channel on either Astar 1A or 1B. But they're launching 1C in eighteen months and co-locating it with 1A and 1B so that it can be picked up on existing dishes. 1C is still being built and tested. It's going to be state of the art stuff, the most advanced television satellite ever built. It will be able to handle sixteen ordinary channel or eight high-definition, wide-screen channels. We can have a transponder to give us the bandwidth we need for wide-screen free of charge for four months. And we can have it prime-time – 5 p.m. to 1 a.m. – eight hours a day, seven days a week.'

Bill goggled. '*WHAT!*'

Marshall repeated his statement, adding: 'Test transmission introductory rate, they'll call it. They're anxious for someone to take a lead with high-definition. They'll introduce a sliding rental scale, but the point is, for the first four months we get prime-time on a satellite channel covering the whole of Europe and it won't cost us a brass farthing.'


## 38

## LONDON TELEPORT, NORTH WOOLWICH
## 1993

'And that's our main uplink antenna to Astra,' said Lois Turner, pointing up at a giant ten-metre dish that was aimed southward across the Thames. The dish was emblazoned with the Astra logo. The young woman was nervous. This was her first week in her new job, and this was the first customer with whom she had to negotiate.

Marshall Tate thrust his hands even deeper into his pockets. The wire fence around British Telecom's London teleport site

242

at North Woolwich afforded no protection against the bitter east wind sweeping across the Thames. To his right a watery winter sun glinted on the cowls of the Thames Barrage. The Woolwich ferry nosed into its berth, a group of passengers were leaning against the rail, looking disinterestedly at the cluster of satellite dishes standing guard over a huddle of single-storey control buildings.

'That's the original dish that went into service in the 1980s uplinking Sky Television's four channels and W H Smith Television's two channels to Astra,' Lois Turner explained. She was a British Telecom contracts manager. A tough negotiator as Marshall had discovered when he had opened discussions about a contract with British Telecom to beam the Elite channel up to Astra. 'It's still giving good service,' she continued. 'But we're bringing a new dish into service in time for Astra 1C. That one's working at full capacity.'

'No wonder you want to charge us an arm and a leg if we have to pay for a new installation,' said Marshall acidly.

Lois Turner smiled. 'Believe me, Mr Tate, what we'll be charging you will hardly cover the interest charges on the cost of the new installation. You'll be getting excellent value for money.'

'Including off-air monitoring?'

She pointed to a group of small receiving dishes mounted on short steel posts. 'We keep a constant check on the quality of customers' pictures coming down from the satellite using ordinary domestic receivers like those, and we run constant sampling checks against the quality of the picture we get from your studios.'

Marshall watched vehicles driving off the ferry. 'I think the prices I was quoted for studio links to here are outrageous, Miss Turner,' he said abruptly.

'I did explain that the prices I gave you were based on a worst possible case assumption. As you don't know yourself where your studios will be situated, we can't give an accurate price.'

Marshall thrust his hands deep into his overcoat pockets and stared moodily through the wire security fence. It was a depressing part of North Woolwich consisting of decaying warehouses, abandoned railway sidings and rundown factories. British Telecom had obviously chosen the dump as the site for the London teleport because its location on the north bank of the Thames meant that their view of the southern sky for their dishes could not be obstructed by office block development. A large 'To Let' sign on the side of a nearby derelict paint factory gave him an idea. 'Supposing we had the studios in this area? Right on your doorstep? Surely you could provide the link free of charge, couldn't you? All it would mean is stringing up a few metres of fibre optic line.'

'Surely you wouldn't want to be here? It's an awful place. We all hate it.'

'Awful places have a habit of being cheap,' Marshall retorted. He shot her a sidelong glance. 'One thing, Miss Turner. I want a guarantee of absolute confidentiality concerning the system we'll be using.'

'That goes without saying, Mr Tate. We'd better discuss details inside. I'm freezing.'

Marshall left the London teleport two hours later having struck a favourable deal with Lois Turner. Instead of walking to his car, he crossed the deserted road to the derelict factory that had caught his eye. He studied it for some minutes and wrote the telephone number of the letting agent in his Filofax before returning to his car and staring at his surroundings through the windscreen.

Lois Turner was right, it was an awful place.

In the early 1980s there had been high hopes for the area. But plans for theme parks, offices, 'sunrise' industry developments and business parks had collapsed as the country had stubbornly refused to come out of the recession. British Telecom's London teleport represented the only modern development that part of North Woolwich had seen, and that was a result of the advent of satellite television, about the only growth industry that the country had.

The previous winter of 1992/93 had been a watershed in European television with sales of satellite receivers exceeding 250,000 units per month despite the icy grip of a recession. Several factors contributed to the boom: ad-zapping, the prac-

tice of viewers using their remote control boxes to skip commercials, had reached such a level that advertisers began diverting
revenue away from terrestrial television. This led to a lowering
of programme standards which, in turn, led to a loss of viewers.

Public service television also suffered. In the United Kingdom
the BBC suffered a decline in revenue as a result of the huge
increase in sales of shrewdly-marketed Japanese television sets
that incorporated a satellite receiver but which could not receive
terrestrial television. Such sets did not require a television
licence. But the biggest reason for the boom in satellite television
was the irresistible carrot of the thirty-two channels from the
two Astra satellites, soon to be joined by Astra 1C with the
potential of another sixteen channels. The introduction of multiple language sound channels, pioneered by Sky Television's
Eurosport in the late 1980s, in which viewers could call up a
commentary or soundtrack in their own language, was also a
tremendous boost.

Marshall started his car.

All he wanted was two years on air.

*That's all it will take, Matt! Two years to shaft the bastards!*


## 39

## 1994

The City Media Bank were at first dubious about the North
Woolwich site as the headquarters of the Elite channel. They
thought that the cost of refurbishing a factory on a short-term
lease was a poor investment until Marshall explained that his
plan was to leave the main factory building intact, using its
existing offices as a programme library, and to fit the studios
and offices out in modular fashion using linked ten-metre-long
air-conditioned Portakabins.

Sony Broadcast and Communications at Basingstoke, who
were awarded the contract to supply a complete turnkey studio
package, thought it was a brilliant idea. It enabled them to fit
out and test the studios on their premises under conditions
of maximum security before they were transported to North

Woolwich. The arrangement suited Marshall who was anxious to keep technical information from the scientific press who hounded his makeshift office in the factory for information once news of the new channel was announced by the City Media Bank.

The first module delivered was the front office and reception area. It was complete with desks, chairs, a telephone switchboard, and a hospitality room with a hot drinks vending machine. All that was missing was the monitor that would be showing the Elite channel in the reception area for the benefit of visitors. A gang of contractors' workmen hauled the huge fibreglass cabin off the low-loader and spent a day setting it up on concrete piles in what had been the factory's car park.

The giant studio modules began arriving from Sony in August once the site was made secure with a high fence and closed-circuit television cameras. The first unit was the post-production room with its advanced electron beam recorder already installed and working. This was followed by the cabins containing the main control console and vision-mixing desks, the digital disc players and telecine machines. All that was missing from the many equipment racks were the monitors.

### 40

Sir Robert Allsop was not impressed when he arrived at North Woolwich. He surveyed the old factory and the collection of Portakabins surrounded by a wire fence while his chauffeur tucked a blanket around his legs.

'Looks like a motorway site office,' he complained.

'How much of your money shall I spend tarting the place up?' Marshall retorted, helping the chauffeur manoeuvre the banker's wheelchair into the reception area.

'A television studio without a monitor in sight,' Sir Robert Allsop commented a few minutes later as he steered his wheelchair carefully along the narrow corridors of the interconnected Portakabins, alive with beavering Sony engineers peering behind wall panels or twiddling with test oscilloscopes. There were so many inspection panels missing from the walls that it looked as if the place was being torn apart.

246

'They're all coming next week,' Marshall replied. 'Sony say they can't delay their installation any longer. But we do have one set up and working.'

'Let's see it.'

Marshall unlocked a small windowless viewing room equipped with a few easy chairs. He pulled the vinyl cover off a rear projection monitor that was like no television set that Sir Robert had ever seen. Instead of being virtually square, the screen was two metres wide by one metre high. It looked like a miniature Cinemascope screen.

'This is the monitor that Sony plan to supply to a hundred top-class hotels in Europe once we go on air,' Marshall explained. 'They'll be mounted on trolleys so that they can be wheeled into guests' bedrooms for our nightly show. They'll be launching a range of smaller sets for domestic use but they'll all have the same wide-screen 16:9 aspect ratio as this.'

Marshall turned to an equipment rack that housed a conventional television monitor and a video disc player. He loaded a disc into the player and pressed the start button. The giant screen came alive.

Sir Robert gave a gasp of astonishment. 'Good grief,' he muttered.

His comment was drowned by the roar of the Victoria Falls in digital stereophonic sound, and his senses were overwhelmed by the stunning, pin-sharp picture of the boiling falls that burst on the giant screen. The amazing picture was so clear that it was possible to distinguish individual water droplets, sparkling like dancing diamonds in the sunlight as they formed a rainbow-coloured mist over the jungle. The picture changed to a scene of a troupe of beautiful Polynesian girls performing a hula on a beach. The astonishing clarity of the low-angle close-ups on the girls' madly gyrating hips, and the pounding rhythm created a stunning eroticism, the like of which Sir Robert had never experienced before. Not only that, the picture was *three-dimensional*; he felt that he could actually reach out and touch the wildly oscillating pudenda. Then one girl thrust herself nearer the camera than the others, and Sir Robert realized that it wasn't even necessary to reach out.

247

Marshall switched the video player off, remarking that he didn't want to give his visitor a heart attack.

'I don't believe it,' said Sir Robert hollowly, staring hypnotized at the yawning blank screen. 'I simply don't believe it.'

'It was a scene I had filmed for my series on sex that got axed,' Marshall replied nonchalantly but secretly pleased at the impact of the demo on his backer.

'But the clarity! And how is it possible to have 3-D without special glasses?'

'Ask the Sony people. Some special deep vision electronic wizardry in the receiver that works on the same principle as those poster ads that seem to move and have depth. It certainly wasn't filmed in 3-D.'

Sir Robert's banking instincts took over. 'So how about downward compatibility with existing PAL televisions?'

'Sony have guaranteed it.'

'I'd like to see for myself.'

Marshall switched the output to the conventional monitor and started the disc. The scenes repeated on the ordinary 625-line monitor had none of the impact of their showing on the wide-screen, high-definition monitor.

'You see?' Marshall remarked. 'No problem. Those shots become normal 625-line definition on an ordinary television. The important thing is that it works. The conversion process is handled by circuitry built in to the new televisions. They can automatically detect a code inserted into the high-definition signal and process the picture accordingly. It gives the Sony system a fantastic edge over all the other high-definition systems. The viewer watching on an ordinary set loses a chunk off each side of the picture, but they won't realize what they're missing until they see a wide-screen demo in a shop window.'

'So we're on target for the launch on the first of October?'

Marshall gave a rare smile. 'Bang on target, Sir Robert. And then stand clear of the fan.'

As Sir Robert travelled back to Walton-on-Thames in the back of his chauffeur-driven Rolls, the stunning pictures of the lovely Polynesian girls kept intruding unbidden on his thoughts. He had grown up with television; as a youngster he remembered Richard Dimbleby's commentary that had accompanied the first cross-channel television pictures from France. Television will never be the same again, a pundit had remarked. The banker had a feeling that Marshall Tate's film of dancing girls on a beach was going to have a greater and more lasting impact on European television than those fuzzy old black and white shots of Calais' town hall clock tower.

In a way he relished the battle that lay ahead.

## 41

Marshall was not exaggerating when he predicted that a lot of nastiness would hit the fan once details of the Elite channel's plans were made public a week before the new station went on air. Furious members of parliament condemned the use of a Japanese high-definition television system when a European system was under development.

At a press conference in a London hotel, Sir Robert faced a barrage of criticism about the Elite channel.

'So where is this so-called Eureka system?' he demanded. 'We've seen wide-screen television from them but on the old low-definition standard. And no one has been able to show us a complete, working system. By complete, I mean an entire studio with editing desks, video transfer systems, disc-players and recorders, cameras – the lot. While European governments have been wrangling over what system to use and who should pay for it, our contractor has stayed out of the argument and has been quietly developing a first-class system that works, and works superbly well. Accusations about our giving the Japanese a toehold in Europe's high-definition television market are nonsense. They've carved that for themselves while our governments have been bickering. Also, the system has been developed here in Europe, in Basingstoke of all places, with European brains and knowhow. And the sets will be made in European plants employing European labour. All that's missing is European investment. Don't blame the Japanese for putting their money where our brains are rather than where our mouth is.

But the big plus is that our pictures can be received by viewers with ordinary PAL televisions. No one else seems to have considered their interests.'

The rumpus boiled over into the popular press although the tabloids avoided getting involved in technical arguments, preferring to focus on Marshall's fitness, or unfitness, to run a TV channel.

'Here's a good one,' said Bill. He read aloud: 'PORN KING TO HAVE OWN TV CHANNEL.'

Marshall had the news item framed and hung in his new office. It was given pride of place alongside, 'GIRLIE LINE-UP IN TATE GALLERY'.

One thing the new channel did not need was a publicity agent. Marshall's willingness to talk to the press now that the high-definition cat was out of the bag, and his fund of quotable quotes, kept the bandwagon rolling. Throwaways such as: 'We're going to shake the broadcasting establishment by the ears until the teeth fall out of rotten gums' and 'Running a popular European satellite station may not be a licence to print money, but it will be a licence to stamp ecus', were calculated to have sub-editors offering whispered prayers of thanks. Television was now run by the Faceless Ones. Not since Lew Grade had there been a television chief like Marshall Tate who could communicate.

Unexpected support came from the Prime Minister who described the new channel as evidence of the decadence that was undermining 'our' society. This was the day before the Elite channel went on air. The statement was construed as support because the general feeling in Europe was that anything a British prime minister did not like could not possibly be bad. More positive support was forthcoming from a number of advertising agencies who were playing a wait-and-see game but nevertheless requested rate cards.

42

All the publicity, good and bad, paid off. A poll commissioned by EBARB – the European Broadcasters' Audience Research

Board – indicated that thirty million viewers would be switching on to see the opening of the much-hyped Elite channel.

After two weeks of dummy runs, the Elite channel opened at 6 p.m. EST on 1 October 1994 with a three-hour compilation of stunning scenes from a travel series bought from a French company. The journalists invited to the opening dutifully filed their rave eulogies on the new television system and the Elite channel was on its way.

By Christmas of that year, the Elite channel's curious mix had carved it a wobbly audience figure of three million. Occasional protests over the sexually explicit nature of some of its late-night programmes (some protests were engineered by Marshall) pushed up the figures but failed to win any appreciable additional advertising revenue. When the transponder leasing payments for the Astra started, Marshall was facing the peren-nial problem of balancing his output of repeats against the risk of alienating his viewers. He desperately needed a new angle.

A visit to Sir Robert's home to discuss programme acqui-sitions gave him an idea. After a lot of argument, the banker agreed to his precious electronic roulette table being set up at North Woolwich. Once the problems with the major credit card companies had been sorted out, the Elite channel's casino weekends proved astonishingly popular. Telephone lines and facilities for twenty sales staff had to be installed in the ware-house adjoining the studios to cater for the flood of calls from viewers from all over Europe anxious to place bets on the elec-tronic roulette table. The rumblings of disquiet from the British Gaming Board prompted Marshall to set up a parallel centre in France. This was quickly followed by three more centres across Europe, all of which liquidated their setting-up costs by their fourth weekend of trading.

Marshall and the City Media Bank scented a golden goose and set up a jointly-owned holding company that bought out the Monte Carlo company that built the electronic roulette tables. The publicity surrounding the Elite channel's casino weekends generated ever more interest especially when Marshall took a bold step and dropped the stake ceilings on *pair* and *impair* bets. Gamblers could now chance everything on the colours in the hope of doubling their money or losing everything on a single roll. When a Dutch housewife won a million guilders, the tabloid press went wild and the weekend take doubled.

Marshall's rapidly-expanding wealth and power enabled him to plumb an unsuspected well of frightening energy. He had always thrown everything into his work; now he worked like a man possessed, snatching five hours' sleep between marathon sessions of meetings, striking deals, travelling Europe, and hiring and firing a growing army of lawyers. Several times he was arrested and charged with illegal gambling. Three days was his longest period in custody. As with his other interests, the Milan police who nabbed him leaving a restaurant with a girl on his arm had to let him go when his Italian lawyers produced an order securing his release. His defence of 'beyond jurisdiction' worked every time. For a charge to stick would have jeopardized the very nature of the new Europe and the freedom of financial transactions across state borders. Marshall Tate was the first of a new breed of Euro-mavericks out to thwart authority on a huge scale and he relished every minute of his notoriety.

But there was a weakness in his armour that he had overlooked. The British government had a powerful weapon they could use against him that he had forgotten about.


## 43

'I think you'll have to speak to this lady, Mr Tate,' said Marshall's secretary. 'She's Lois Turner from British Telecom.'

Marshall remembered the name. 'From down the road?'

'Yes, sir. From the London teleport.'

Marshall felt uneasy. 'You'd better show her in.'

The moment he saw Lois Turner's face he knew that something was seriously wrong. 'So what's the problem, Miss Turner?' he asked affably. 'You want to double your Astra uplink charges when we re-negotiate?'

'I'm afraid it's worse than that, Mr Tate,' she said, declining Marshall's offer of a coffee. 'The DTI are leaning on us concerning our uplinking of the Elite channel.'

'I trust you told them what they could do, Miss Turner,' said Marshall blandly.

'We have a good working relationship with the Department of Trade, Mr Tate. We also have a good working relationship with you, which is why I'm here in person. The DTI have told us to stop uplinking your casino weekends on the Elite channel.'

Ten years earlier Marshall would have flown into a rage. Now he was wiser and had more control, but he was much more dangerous. 'Do they have that power?' he inquired mildly.

'Most definitely. We have a licence from them to transmit to Astra under the Wireless Telegraphy Act. The Under Secretary of State for Trade and Industry can vary the terms of that licence any time he wishes. Well, he's just wished.'

Marshall's face betrayed nothing of his inner turmoil. 'And you're going to cave in to political pressure, Miss Turner?'

'Legal pressure, Mr Tate. We don't have any choice. The DTI could close us down at a moment's notice if they so wished. But they don't want us to do that. All they want us to do is not uplink your casino weekends starting next Friday. I should add that this is the first time this has ever happened.'

'I'm not breaking the law, Miss Turner.'

'Nor is the Under Secretary,' Lois Turner replied, meeting Marshall's cold stare without flinching. 'Naturally we'll carry on uplinking the normal Elite channel but your casino weekends are out.'

Marshall gave a mirthless laugh. 'No, Miss Turner. As from this minute, I'm not using your services any more. And as for this quarter's uplink fees, well, you can go crawling to the DTI for them because you don't get another fucking penny out of me.'

Marshall's visitor opened her mouth to say something but changed her mind. She said a curt goodbye and left.

The moment he was alone, Marshall switched on his dynamo and spent an hour on the telephone. At 1 p.m. a motor cycle courier roared out of the Elite channel studio compound and headed towards Dover with the video discs for that evening's programmes in his panniers. The courier crossed the channel by hovercraft and roared across Belgium in three hours. He arrived at the headquarters of SES in Luxembourg at 5.45 p.m. and the evening's Elite channel programmes went out via SES's uplink facilities at 6 p.m. with none of the channel's regular viewers being aware of the change. Marshall arranged with his studio staff to provide a relay of couriers with the station's programme discs for the rest of the week. With that fixed he called a Luxembourg property agent to fix up a temporary site for the Elite channel's operations. The agent had an ideal property on his books, a disused warehouse outside the city that was enclosed by a security fence. Marshall booked it unseen and got onto a freight company to take a look at the problems of shifting the Elite channel's Portakabins to Luxembourg.

Mid-afternoon he called the City Media Bank and explained the situation to Sir Robert. Despite his age and ill-health, the banker was sufficiently concerned by the developments to order his chauffeur to drive him to North Woolwich. He arrived at the studios to find Marshall and the transport manager of the freight company finalizing their plans.

'We're shipping the whole lot to Luxembourg,' Marshall announced savagely. 'We're leaving the offices and an editing suite but the studios are going lock, stock and barrel.'

'A good job you opted for modular studios, Matt,' Sir Robert observed. 'I take it my table's going as well?'

'That'll be first on the ferry,' said Marshall grimly. 'But you'll get it back in two years.'

'If I should live so long,' Sir Robert remarked gloomily. He looked sharply at Marshall. 'Why, you're not giving up your weekend space casino are you? You'd be a fool if you do.'

'I'll tell you what I am giving up,' said Marshall harshly. 'I'm giving up all dependence on outsiders. I'm going to launch my own satellite and operate it from some sort of mobile or portable ground station. I don't know how I'll do it. I don't share with anyone or anything. I'll fix it so that I own everything all the way down the line. And I don't give a fuck how much it's going to cost.'

The banker's pulse quickened. Marshall's words were a shot of heady adrenalin into his hardening arteries. He scented a gamble, a huge, deadly throw of a die that would result in his walking the edge of a yawning, exciting precipice. 'And how much do you think it *will* cost?' he asked.

'At a guess . . . a billion ecus. About six hundred million sterling.'

Having been confined to a wheelchair for most of his life, there were not many times that Sir Robert Allsop wished he were younger. But now he wished he could shed twenty years.

## 44

### 1995

Hubert Schnee was hired by Marshall on the recommendation of Sir Robert Allsop. He took a dislike to Schnee on sight but the wily Swiss was an astute media analyst with the rare ability to grasp engineering and financial problems. Also, Schnee had a solid reputation for keeping his mouth shut. He was given twelve weeks from the beginning of the year to prepare an initial costings and feasibility report on the Bacchus Project.

Schnee threw himself enthusiastically into the job. During the three months he flew the equivalent distance of twice around the world, interviewing engineering companies, satellite launching agencies and software houses in his meticulous search for data. He checked and double-checked all his findings and costs, and personally delivered two neatly-bound copies of his two-hundred page report the day before his deadline; one copy for Marshall and the other for Sir Robert. The reason for his dedication was more than professional pride; the Bacchus Project had fired his imagination and his greed.

He wanted to be a part of it.

## 45

A week later Marshall drove his black Ferrari to Walton-on-Thames for a crucial meeting with the banker.

'What surprises me, Matt,' said Sir Robert pensively, leafing through the close-printed columns of figures, 'is how close your original, off-the-cuff estimate was to Schnee's figure: six hundred and fifty million.'

Marshall said nothing.

'Do you realize, Matt, we're talking about the sort of capital project that most governments would balk at?'

'We're also talking about an annual return of two hundred and fifty million plus,' Marshall replied. 'And that's only one per cent of the total Japanese and the Chinese and Malaysian gambling spend. We're setting our sights deliberately low.'

'Yes,' said Sir Robert. 'I've examined Schnee's figures and I trust them.'

'But?'

'We can't go to six hundred and fifty million risk capital, Matt, or even loan capital.' The banker met the penetrating stare without flinching even though Marshall Tate's gaze unnerved him as it always did.

'So what can you go to?'

'A hundred and fifty million top whack.'

Marshall snorted in contempt. 'Who was it who told me that I could afford to lose everything except my nerve?'

Sir Robert smiled suddenly. 'That still holds good, Matt. The trouble is that we simply don't have that sort of money to lose in the first place.'

Marshall stood up. 'Okay, it looks like I've got to find half a billion shortfall. I mustn't let you waste any more of my time.' He moved to the door but the banker quickly blocked his way with the electric wheelchair.

'Sit down, Matt.'

'There's no point in rabbiting any more if you're not – '

'There's every point. Now sit down!'

For a moment it looked as if Marshall was going to lose his temper, but he appeared to change his mind. He resumed his seat and tried to intimidate the banker with a baleful stare.

'There's someone who would like to see you,' said Sir Robert, scribbling on a pad. 'He's staying in London at the Savoy this week. Harrison J. Calinco.'

Marshall looked at the slip of paper that Sir Robert handed him. 'Who the hell is he?'

'He's a financial advisor to some large leisure interests in America. He has a lot of clout. They listen to him. He's a reasonable guy to deal with but you must be 100 per cent sure of what you're doing.'

'*Who* listens to him?'

Sir Robert looked evasive. 'Like I said, American leisure interests. Big ones.'

'Based where in America?'

'Las Vegas,' said the banker tiredly.

## 46

Harry J. Calinco was about as far removed from a godfather figure as it was possible to imagine. He was a big, genial man of about fifty, with an expansive smile and an expensive toupee. A room in his hotel suite was fitted out as an office. He rose, beaming, from behind a rosewood desk, shook Marshall warmly by the hand, and waved to a chair.

'Mr Tate, this is a real pleasure. I've always wanted to meet the man who got gambling off the ground in a big way in Europe. Can I get you something? I would consider it a rare privilege to have a drink with you.'

Marshall sat sipping a generous measure of Southern Comfort while answering his host's friendly questions about the Elite channel. At last he could contain his patience no longer. 'Mr Calinco, can I speak plainly?'

'You speak as plainly as you like with us, Matt.'

'Can we cut the crap and get down to business?'

The American looked taken back at first. A broad grin spread across his amiable features. 'Yeah . . . we should've realized. We've learned a lot about you, Matt.'

'Good. Then you should've also learned that only my friends call me Matt.'

If Harrison J. Calinco was insulted, he did a good job of hiding it. His smile broadened. 'Fine by us, Marshall. Okay, we'll talk business. You will find that we can be every bit as direct as you. Maybe more so.' He opened a copy of Schnee's report on the Bacchus Project. From where he was sitting Mar-

257

shall could see that there were copious notes scrawled in the margins. 'Firstly, Marshall, we want to congratulate you on a bold and imaginative scheme.'

'So go ahead and congratulate me,' said Marshall boredly.

'It looks almost too good to be true,' the American continued. 'Then we took a look at your Elite operations, we looked at your turnover figures that you kindly provided and we decided that maybe, just maybe, this Bacchus Project isn't just the pie in the sky that it looks on the surface.' He broke off and chuckled at his own joke. He saw that his guest did not appreciate his humour so he pressed on. 'We've been looking for ways of breaking into the Chinese market – half the world's population and they're all gambling crazy, same as the Japanese. Looks like you've got in ahead of us. So, okay, Marshall, we'd like to be included.'

'For the full five hundred million shortfall?'

'For the full six hundred and fifty million pounds sterling,' Harrison Calinco confirmed, watching Marshall carefully.

Marshall remained impassive. Any idiot could borrow money. Borrowing from a single source had advantages but there were risks. It was the terms that counted.

'We're looking at a two- to three-year pre-operating period?' Harrison Calinco continued. 'Correct?'

Marshall nodded. 'It's going to take at least three years. The satellite has to be designed and built and tested. There's the ground station to be sorted out; land to be purchased; casinos built. It's a big operation. It's all in that report. Your terms aren't.'

The American toyed with a gold pen. 'We propose ten staged payments to you of sixty-five million each to be spread evenly over your pre-operating period. When you've been operating for six months, you start making staged repayments. We're thinking along the lines of ten instalments of a hundred million each spread over a period of, say, three years.'

Marshall thought fast. The deal was tough, but not as bad as he had anticipated. 'Okay,' he said. 'Obviously I can't commit myself yet, there are a lot of details to be sorted out, but I agree in principle.'

'And you pay us a separate two hundred million per annum in compensation costs. The amount to be renegotiated every three years after the start of operations.'

Marshall saw red. 'What compensation?' he snarled. 'What the hell are you talking about?'

The American's smile never faltered. 'It's like this, Marshall. The world's getting smaller. Places like China are opening up. By financing this exciting project of yours, we'll be denying ourselves a market. It will be an act of generous self-denial for which we shall require an annual compensation fee. We think that two hundred million each year for the first three years is reasonable. After that we shall require to negotiate an annual fee geared to revenue.'

'Protection!' Marshall spat. 'Christ, I should've known! Not only do you finance the deal, but you want fucking protection as well!'

'We see nothing wrong in protecting our interests, Marshall,' said Harrison Calinco mildly. 'It's a legitimate business practice so far as we're concerned.'

'It stinks of crooked double dealing as far as I'm concerned,' Marshall responded savagely. His instincts were to walk out there and then, but he knew that these people were the only ones likely to finance the project. It was a business they understood.

'Don't make up your mind right away, Marshall.' The American passed a manila envelope to his guest. 'That's a draft contract I've thrown together. Take it away and read it. All the clauses are negotiable. All except the penalty clauses, that is. They're on a separate WORM disc and they are confidential, for your eyes only. The password is your date of birth, a six digit number. One repayment default results in a warning. On the second default, unless terms are re-agreed thereafter, we invoke the penalty clauses.' He stood and held out his hand, signalling that the meeting was over.

Marshall was sorely tempted to ignore the offered hand but caution prevailed; these people were dangerous. He shook it in a perfunctory manner.

'You read it and call me,' said Harrison Calinco. 'There's no hurry. I'm in London for another month. But you must read and understand the penalty clauses on the WORM. Okay?'

As Marshall rode down in the lift, he could feel the WORM disc through the envelope's thick brown paper.

## 47

Marshall drove straight back to his penthouse apartment in the London docklands.

Hubert Schnee was waiting anxiously for him. 'How did it go, Mr Tate?'

Marshall ignored the Swiss. He dropped into a chair, ripped the envelope open and skimmed through the draft contract that Harrison Calinco had 'thrown' together. It was more detailed than he had expected. Obviously the American had gone to a lot of trouble.

'May I see, Mr Tate?'

Marshall tossed the sheaf of papers to Schnee. He was more meticulous than Marshall. He read slowly and carefully. Marshall crossed the room to his personal computer and turned the monitor towards him so that Schnee could not see it. He switched the machine on and slotted the WORM disc into the drive. The drive seized the disc and the drive door latched shut.

ENTER PASSWORD.

He entered his date of birth on the keyboard.

WRONG PASSWORD.

Damn!

He remembered that the Americans put the month first when writing dates. He tapped on the keyboard again. The WORM drive light winked on and the screen glitched.

There was no file containing penalty clauses on the disc. Instead there was a series of gruesome photographs that came close to turning even Marshall's strong stomach. Each picture remained on the screen for ten seconds before fading out and being replaced by the next image. Most of them were in colour: vivid pictures of bullet-riddled bodies sprawling across the driver's seats of crashed cars or slumped over steering wheels; bodies in restaurants; bodies in luxury swimming pools, the water bright red instead of blue. A montage of the most violent murders it was possible to imagine.

The WORM drive clicked and whirred through the scenes of appalling carnage. Some were wide-angle shots of brutal massacres in which entire families had been wiped out. They were followed by close-ups of individual victims: a woman in a bikini, keeled over a cooker in her kitchen, her child on the floor, lying in a pool of blood, clutching a doll in a death grip.

The WORM drive light flashed and the terrible scenes were repeated as though one showing was considered insufficient for the dreadful message to be driven home. Marshall felt the blood draining from his face as the carousel of carnage passed before his eyes for a second time.

Schnee had stopped reading and was watching him. 'Is anything wrong, Mr Tate?'

The pictures had numbed Marshall's vocal cords. He could only shake his head. At that moment the screen went blank. The WORM drive's read/write head buzzed insistently.

ERASING DATA.

He tried to open the drive door but the electronic lock refused to disengage. He reached for the computer's power switch but was too late.

DATA ERASED. THE DISC HAS BEEN DESTRUCTIVELY RE-FORMATED. NO DATA IS RECOVERABLE. YOU MAY NOW OPEN DRIVE AND REMOVE DISC.

Marshall sat staring at the message for some seconds.

'It all looks reasonable,' said Schnee.

'What?'

'This contract, Mr Tate. They're demanding a high rate of interest, but it's what we expected. They seem reasonable people to deal with.'

Marshall's immediate impulse was to stride across the room and ram the contract down Schnee's fat neck. He controlled himself with an effort.

*Jesus Christ, protection money!*

Paying protection meant having to shell out every year. And Christ knows what they would want after the third year. They would get greedy and demand more and more until they had control. This was Authority of the worst kind, Authority that depended on fear. He suppressed his fury and forced himself to think clearly. He crossed to the window and gazed out across the curving sweep of the Thames.

Protection! No way was he going to pay a penny in protection. And no one threatened Marshall Tate! No one!

His stare focused on HMS *Belfast*. The veteran warship, riding at her permanent anchorage, was a magnet for tourists. They were swarming over her, staring up at her mighty guns. Kids were sitting in her Pom Pom saddles, fighting off hordes of imaginary dive-bombing Messerschmitts. Even after half a century, the ship looked ready for war, ugly and aggressive. At that precise moment Marshall had an inspiration.

'Schnee!'

The Swiss jumped. 'Mr Tate?'

'We've not given a lot of thought to the Bacchus ground station.'

'That's because it's not a big problem, Mr Tate. Any cheap patch of land will do. An island. Anything. That's the advantage of satellite uplink and downlink stations. They can be located virtually anywhere.'

Marshall kept his voice steady. 'What about a ship?'

Schnee blinked. 'It would be extremely difficult keeping large dishes locked onto the Bacchus satellite, Mr Tate. Also, the amount of office and administration space we will require – '

'What about a ship we can run aground? A big ship with a reinforced bottom? Something really big like a converted tanker. Christ, man! Use your imagination! Think! With a fixed land site, we'd be at the mercy of any change of government. If they took a dislike to us, we'd be finished. But with a ship we could always up-anchor and fuck off to a contingency anchorage.'

Schnee thought for a moment. His moonlike face suddenly broke into a broad smile. 'You know, Mr Tate, that is a very good idea. It might even be cheaper than a fixed land site.'

Marshall felt that a weight had lifted from his shoulders. Everything was coming together. It all made sense. It was the mobility of the Portakabin studios that had enabled him to keep the Elite channel in business and so avoid being stitched up by the British government.

Also a ship could legally carry arms. It could be defended . . . The more he thought about the idea, the more he liked it.

He snatched up the telephone and called Harrison Calinco's number while Schnee busied himself with a calculator.

'Mr Calinco? Marshall Tate. I've been reading through your draft contract . . . I think we've got grounds to open serious negotiations.' He listened intently to the voice at the other end of the line. 'Yes, I've studied the penalty clauses. I guess I can go along with them.'

They talked for five minutes and agreed to meet the next day. Marshall replaced the handset and regarded Schnee who was immersed in revising his estimates. The memory of the terrible scenes he had witnessed on his computer stirred the savage little demon in him.

*He would shaft the arrogant bastards. He would pay back the loan. Every last fucking penny, but no way was he going to pay them their tonne of flesh per annum protection. No fucking way.*

And then he did something wholly unexpected and so out of character that Schnee looked up in alarm.

Marshall Tate had thrown back his head and was laughing.


## 48

The negotiations with Harrison Calinco were completed quickly.

'We don't mind being frozen out, Matt,' said Sir Robert. 'But for God's sake be careful. Do whatever they say – keep them posted with monthly progress reports.'

'Calinco said that he'd be happy with occasional phone calls,' Marshall pointed out. 'He said to go to him with any problems, and that he was there to help.'

'That's what makes them so dangerous.' The banker looked worried. 'You're on your own now, Matt. These people don't do business the way we do.'

'They've already intimated that,' Marshall replied. 'I can handle them.'

The two men shook hands and had a drink on the ending of their long partnership.

The first-stage payments enabled Hubert Schnee to get things moving. His knowledge of the Far East proved invaluable to Marshall.

'We do everything through a project office in Tokyo, Mr Tate. That way we guarantee secrecy. The Japanese are models of discretion. Nothing leaks out of Japan that they don't want to leak out. And they can move quickly.'

It was Schnee who could move quickly. When motivated by money, he proved to have boundless energy that matched Marshall's capacity for hard work. By the end of May 1995 the contract with a satellite launch agency was ready for signature. Marshall flew to Tokyo to countersign the contract at the offices of Japan's National Space Development Agency, NASDA. For two hundred million dollars they would launch the Bacchus satellite from their Tanegashima Space Centre – an idyllic sub-tropical island south of the Japanese archipelago – using their standard commercial H-II rocket. The booster was proving a safe and reliable workhorse for putting payloads into orbit but Marshall had insisted on a clause that meant that he would not pay out a cent unless the launch was successful. The Japanese engineers had been unhappy about it but had eventually relented rather than see the business go to their rivals, Arianespace.

After the signing ceremony, Marshall had inspected with Schnee the standard H-II nose cone that the Bacchus satellite would have to fit into.

'Basically,' said Schnee, 'the only technical requirements that NASDA require of the satellite is that it fits in the nose cone and doesn't weigh more than two tonnes. They place it in the right orbit. That's when they hand it over, and that's when we're liable to pay them.'

'And what if the bloody satellite doesn't work?' Marshall demanded.

'It will work, Mr Tate. The TLK Corporation have an enviable reputation for designing and building ultra-reliable satellites.'

Marshall's visit to Japan was rounded off with the signing of contracts with TLK to supply the Bacchus satellite, and the Osaka marine architects who had successfully tendered to oversee the conversion of a bulk carrier, renamed the *Eldorado*, which would become the Bacchus earth station.

The exhausting schedule on the Far East trip was rounded off with the setting-up of smaller project offices in Tokyo, Bangkok and Beijing to supervise the design and construction of the first three casinos.

There followed a nerve-wracking period for Marshall, largely because he felt that too much was outside his control. At no time did he lose his nerve although there were occasions when the size of the cheques he was signing did act as a sharp reminder of the severity of the penalty clauses that were riding on the operation.

'Progress is slow,' Harrison Calinco observed during one of Marshall's telephone reports. 'You know what John F. Kennedy once said about the Apollo programme to land a man on the moon?'

'No,' said Marshall boredly. 'But I expect you're going to tell me.'

'He said that the most economical way of doing a job was to do it quickly.'

'For Christ's sake, what the hell do you think I'm trying to do?'

'Just a friendly comment, Marshall. After all, you've got a lot riding on this little venture. We don't want anything to go wrong.'

Threats did not normally work with Marshall; nevertheless they were always at the back of his mind and resulted in his harrying the hard-working Schnee, often losing his temper when progress seemed to be proceeding at a snail's pace.

In July the Bacchus project hit a big problem: where to 'park' the Bacchus satellite. Marshall was not interested in the fact that the allocations of orbital positions for geostationary satellites were subject to international agreements. 'In that case,' he raged at Schnee, 'find a country that's not using its allocations and *buy* one!'

265

'You can't buy and sell orbital allocations, Mr Tate,' the Swiss protested.

'Try me,' Marshall rasped. 'Just try me.'

Schnee had an answer a week later.

'Indonesia,' he told Marshall. 'They've got an allocation at 81.5 degrees east that they're not using, that's to the west of Indonesia, below the southernmost tip of India.'

'Does it give us a good window on the Far East?'

'A perfect window, Mr Tate. And it'll be seen from Europe but it would be very low down on the eastern horizon.'

'We'll go for it,' Marshall decided without hesitation.


## 49

## JAKARTA, INDONESIA

Although Marshall tended to stamp on problems with an intimidating mixture of bluster and arrogance, he knew when to tread softly. He trod very softly indeed before making any approaches to the Indonesians. He first visited the British embassy in Jakarta and extracted off-the-record information from a senior trade official.

'Bribery is a way of life in this country, Mr Tate,' said the official. 'We don't condone it, of course. I'm merely telling you this because we feel it's something that British businessmen should be aware of.'

'Money or goods?'

'I really can't advise you. What I can say is that the Minister of Post and Telecommunications has a weakness for Jaguars. He wrote off his beloved XJS last week. They drive on the left here most of the time, so finding a presentable one-year-old car at home and having it shipped out shouldn't be too much of a problem for a determined individual who requires a favour from him.'

'Why not a new Jag?'

The official smiled knowingly. 'When you meet Mr Razak, doubtless you will discuss social matters first and discover that you have a mutual interest, that you are both Jaguar enthusiasts.

266

Being a generous man, you will offer to loan Mr Razak one of your cars. Just to try out, you understand. Now you're hardly likely to loan him a new one, are you?'

Three days later Marshall arrived back at Heathrow with a priceless document in his briefcase: a sub-lease agreement for a satellite orbital position at 81.5 degrees east of the Greenwich Meridian. The helpful Indonesian government had even supplied him with a letter of intent that promised him a shallow water mooring facility for the *Eldorado*.


50

1996
SOUTHERN ENGLAND

Some problems proved more difficult.

After nine months on the Bacchus project, Hubert Schnee was used to his employer's tantrums when things went wrong. He sat stoically at the glass-topped table in Marshall's penthouse while his employer paced up and down.

'A satellite with a hundred thousand bet capacity is useless!' Marshall fumed. 'By 2000 I want that satellite to be handling up to two million bets at a time. We've got to build the capacity into the thing right from the word go. We can't replace it every year with the latest model.'

'I appreciate that, Mr Tate,' said Schnee smoothly. 'But the TLK are limited to a two-tonne bird. It has to fit on the rocket. The control software in the satellite is getting more and more bloated as the security routines are built in. Using silicon memory imposes a power and weight penalty that limits us to a hundred thousand bet capacity.'

'For Christ's sake!' Marshall exploded. 'Why has this problem come so late in the day? They've been working on the bloody thing for months!'

'They're within schedule,' Schnee pointed out. 'All the software has been written and tested, that's by far the biggest task, and they've made good progress with the actual construction of the Bacchus. They've run up against this memory problem that they did warn us about.'

'Okay, so does it have to be silicon memory? Isn't there anything else we can use? Every day we're being told about new wonder computers, so where the hell are they?'

Schnee had learned to have possible solutions ready when taking problems to Marshall Tate. The TLK Bacchus team in Tokyo had briefed him well. 'There's the Kronos microprocessor, Mr Tate. It has a protein-based memory. Class A Kronos chips have a gigabyte memory.'

'So use them!'

'It's not that easy,' said Schnee. 'If we could get them, no problem. They're made by a British firm called Nano Systems. The trouble is that they don't actually sell the Kronos, they sell licences to use them. In commercial space applications, they require an annual royalty based on turnover. I've managed to get hold of their space applications licensing agreement.' He rifled through his papers and handed a sheaf of documents to Marshall.

'Protection!' Marshall snarled when he came to the relevent clauses. He slammed the licence agreement on the glass table with such force that Schnee expected it to shatter. 'I'm not paying protection!'

'It's an annual percentage – '

'It's annual protection!' Marshall shouted. 'We've got enough fucking percentage sharks sniffing around as it is. If they all get to chew off their pound of flesh every year, there won't be any fucking profit left! I own *everything*! All the way down the line. No one else has any control. So negotiate a price with them. Christ, do I have to think of everything?'

Schnee rose without saying a word and moved to the lift doors.

'Have you dealt directly with them?' Marshall yelled.

The question annoyed Schnee but he was careful not to show it. 'No, Mr Tate. All my inquiries have been routed through the ghost companies we set up in Liechtenstein.'

# 51

Schnee was back in Marshall's penthouse a week later. This time he did not have a solution to the problem.

'There's no way that Nano Systems will sell their Kronos chips, Mr Tate. One of my assistants has had three meetings with their director of marketing. They refuse to budge. Apparently it's a policy that emanates from Nano Systems' chairman stroke managing director. And there's no question of their negotiating their royalty percentage. They've lost some big contracts because of their inflexibility.'

'So how many of their bloody chips do we need?'

'Four thousand. Two thousand for the satellite, and two thousand in the earth station control and backup computer. Plus about two hundred spares. Design of the satellite is now going ahead based on the Kronos. All we have to do when we get them is plug them in. Except that we can't get them.'

Marshall controlled his temper with difficulty. 'So what's to stop us buying up enough computers or whatever it is that the chips are used in and ripping them out?'

'Four reasons, Mr Tate. Firstly, buying appliances would be extremely costly. Secondly, to buy enough without arousing suspicions could take years. Thirdly, many consumer market appliances such as the Nanopad have their Kronos bonded directly to the circuit board and encapsulated in synthetic resin. Fourthly, we wouldn't be certain of getting Class A chips with the maximum memory.'

'What's this Nano Systems worth?'

Schnee swallowed. This was getting heavy. 'They're a private company, so it would be difficult – '

'Then find out!' Marshall barked. 'Find out everything about them! Get a list of their shareholders and find out everything about them too! We'll buy this Nano Systems, lock, stock and fucking barrel!' His ice-blue gaze bored into Schnee, exposing the fear that lay beneath the flesh. 'Deal with them direct if you have to but not a sniff of this must be traceable back to me. If they suspect what's behind our bid, it'll shove up the value of their stupid company.' He grabbed Schnee by the lapels and jerked him close. 'You screw up on this, Schnee and you're soap. You follow?'

'I follow,' Schnee agreed miserably.

## 52

The extraordinary board meeting at Nano Systems was going badly for Schnee. They weren't interested in his bid. Twenty ecus per share and still they were saying no.

'That amounts to a thirty million pound offer for a company which my principals have conservatively valued at ten million,' he said, spreading his hands on the table, and smiling at each director in turn. There was nothing about his demeanour to hint at the rising panic clawing at his bowels. Twenty ecus they were turning down!

'Who did the valuation?' one of them asked.

'A respected firm of City advisors,' Schnee answered, smiling. There were no name blocks on the table but he knew that the speaker was Jack Pullen; a private investigation agency had secretly photographed every member of the board of Nano Systems.

'What you're offering amounts to what will be a year's turn-over by the end of the century,' said the chairman of Nano Systems bluntly. 'Looked at in that light, it's a lousy offer.'

Schnee continued smiling. Beverley Laine was an extremely attractive woman, the sort that appealed to him. The photograph he had in his file was a telephoto lens shot of her running along a beach. She was pounding straight towards the camera with a low sun shining full on her. Her thin white running shorts and T-shirt were sweat-soaked to an immodestly revealing degree, and her face was contorted from the immense effort she was putting into her run. She looked like a magnificent, sexually-charged animal. And she was forty-six. Truely a remarkable woman, and a formidable obstacle to his takeover bid. Her board appeared to be solidly behind her. She needed careful handling. 'But one that you have to consider, Miss Laine,' he replied.

'We've considered, Mr Schnee. The answer's no.'

Schnee did his best to maintain his confident smile but he suspected that Beverley Laine could see right through him.

'I think we should be allowed to discuss Mr Schnee's offer,' said the man sitting opposite Schnee. It was Stuart Dell, representing the bank that owned a chunk of Nano Systems.

'You may think so,' said Beverley Laine. 'But none of us have got a couple of billion of bad debts riding on our backs, Mr Dell.' She looked hard at Schnee. 'There's nothing to discuss. The answer from all of us is a very polite but very emphatic no.'

'Don't you think you're being a little high-handed, Miss Laine?' asked Dell.

Schnee scented dissent in the ranks. It gave him hope.

'No.'

'We should discuss it,' Theodore Draggon observed, ignoring a no-smoking sign by lighting a cigar.

The defiant gesture was insignificant but it confirmed Schnee's feelings that some members of Nano Systems' board of directors were interested in his offer but were wary of openly crossing Beverley Laine.

She turned to the man sitting beside her; Carl Olivera according to Schnee's carefully-labelled photographs. 'What does our deputy MD think?'

'The answer to Mr Schnee's offer will be no, of course,' said Olivera. 'But we should at least discuss it so that Mr Schnee will be taking the rejection back to his principals, whoever they are, knowing that it's a majority decision.'

'Okay,' she said. 'We'll talk it over. Mr Schnee, would you wait in my office please? My secretary will look after you.'

Schnee left the room. He was too on edge to think clearly. He sat in an uncomfortable low chair, sipping coffee and making polite conversation with the secretary until he was summoned back into the boardroom. There was a little smile of triumph playing at the corners of Beverley Laine's mouth when he took his seat.

'Mr Schnee,' she said. 'You speak excellent English.'

Schnee managed a sitting bow. 'Thank you, Miss Laine. In

271

my country we believe that we speak better English than most
English.'

'Good,' said Beverley Laine. 'So when I say that you're to
tell your principals to go and piss into the wind with your offer,
I take it you know exactly what I mean. Yes?'

Schnee heaved himself behind the wheel of his Audi and called
Marshall Tate's ex-directory number on his mobile telephone.

'Get back here now!' Marshall raged when Schnee told him
that the mission had failed. 'And bring everything you've got
on that outfit. Jesus H – I'm going to have you swinging by
your guts from the window cleaners' gantry before the night's
through if you're not here in two hours!' The channel went
dead.

As Schnee replaced the handset in its cradle, he noticed that
Beverley Laine and Carl Olivera were watching him from an
upstairs window.

## 53

'What the hell do you mean, they won't sell?' Marshall snarled.
'Every man has his price.'

'Nano Systems is run by a woman,' Schnee said lamely.

'Don't play bloody semantics with me!'

'I went to twenty ecus. They're running at 90 per cent on
their share issue. At most their value is fifteen.'

Marshall stared out of his floor-to-ceiling penthouse windows
at the myriad lights of London. Normally, on such clear nights,
the view gave him a feeling of omnipotence. But tonight he was
experiencing impotence; impotence and rage.

'I think we'll have to go along with their royalty system,'
said Schnee cautiously, knowing he was treading on dangerous
ground.

Marshall wheeled around. 'No! If they were prepared to
accept an annual royalty of half a per cent, I might consider it.
But no way am I going to hand over what they're asking.'

'We have to get those chips,' Schnee reasoned. 'The Bacchus

satellite and the ground system are being designed around them.'

Marshall paced slowly up and down the expanse of marbled floor, deep in thought, his hands thrust into his pockets. 'You say the chairman is our biggest obstacle?'

'No doubt about it, Mr Tate. Miss Beverley Laine is an extremely forceful woman. She's the one who won't budge on the royalty percentages or the – '

'*Who?*'

'She's a Miss Beverley Laine.' Schnee broke off and blinked worriedly at the sudden wild look in his boss's eyes. 'Is something the matter, Mr Tate?'

Marshall stood transfixed for some seconds. For an anxious moment Schnee thought that Marshall was about to attack him but he shook his head as if ridding himself of an unpleasant memory.

'It doesn't matter,' Marshall muttered. 'A coincidence . . . I suppose I'll have to go and see her.'

Schnee considered that a meeting between the explosive Marshall Tate and the unyielding Beverley Laine would be interesting: the spectacular collision of matter and anti-matter resulting in mutual annihilation. 'She won't sell at any price,' he said doggedly.

'Bloody two-bit company,' Marshall muttered. 'Okay, let's take a look at the information you've got on them.'

The two men crossed to the glass-topped table. Schnee opened his briefcase and handed a bulging folder to Marshall who sat down at the table and went carefully through its contents.

There was no doubt that the wily Swiss was thorough. Everything was there: names and addresses of shareholders; financial reports; sales graphs; growth predictions, everything. One of the appendices included detailed personal information on the principal shareholders and the directors, and the directors' other business interests. At the back of the dossier was a set of labelled photographs of every member of the board.

'Holy shit,' Marshall breathed, spreading the open report on his desk and staring at the big, pin-sharp print of Beverley.

Schnee was puzzled as to why a photograph of Beverley Laine

should have such an effect on Marshall Tate. Maybe he liked older women. 'Attractive,' he observed.

Marshall made no immediate reply but remained gazing down at the photograph. Eventually he spoke. 'You're sure she's the only obstacle?'

'Yes,' Schnee replied. 'If it wasn't for her, Nano Systems would be as a ripe plum, waiting to fall into your outstretched hand.'

Marshall ignored Schnee's purple prose. 'Are you 200 per cent certain that you cannot be linked back to me?'

'There is absolutely no link whatsoever, Mr Tate. I guarantee it.'

Marshall picked up a phone and punched the memory button that polled Harrison Calinco's Iridium number – for use only in emergencies. Provided the American's handset was switched on, the call would find him anywhere in the world, even on a transatlantic flight. The routing took several seconds and then the phone was ringing.

'Hi, Marshall,' said the American breezily as soon as he answered. 'How're you doing over there?'

'If I've woken you in the middle of the night somewhere, I apologize,' said Marshall. God, how he hated Harrison Calinco's easy drawl. It was loaded with authority.

Harrison Calinco chuckled across ten thousand kilometres. 'It's a hot afternoon in Vegas, and we're having a long, cool drink with a long, cool brunette. What do we owe the pleasure of this call to, Marshall?'

'Penalty clauses.'

Maybe the pause was due to the number of satellite links processing the call. Whatever the reason, the reply was a guarded, 'Yeah? What about them, Marshall?'

'I'm in the process of drawing up my own contract with a supplier of goods. I want to insert some tough penalty clauses like those that you favour. I need the name of a good bailiff in case I have to implement them.'

After another long pause, the American chuckled again. 'You know something, Marshall? You've got one helluva lot of balls.'

'So I've been told.'

'Trouble is, it makes them an easy target for crushing . . . okay, maybe we can help. Someone we don't use. You want a UK firm?'

'I don't care who they are. So long as they're good bailiffs.'

'Okay, Marshall. We'll think about it, maybe we can come up with something. Is your private fax machine on line?'

'It's always on line.'

'Maybe we'll be in touch, maybe not. I'm going back to my drink and brunette. Be seeing you.' The channel went dead.

The cryptic conversation puzzled Schnee. He was supposed to be in possession of every fact and figure on the Bacchus project. He knew who Harrison Calinco was but none of the mass of documentation in his Nanopad contained references to penalty clauses.

The fax machine buzzed to indicate that it was answering an incoming call. A sheet of paper dropped into the collection tray. Marshall grabbed it. There was no header on the fax: no date and time, no page identifier or telephone number, nothing to identify who had sent it. But for a UK mobile telephone neatly hand-written in the centre, it was a blank sheet of paper.

Marshall studied the number and the photograph of Beverley. Christ, the years had been kind to her. Those crazy little ringlets, anchored down by a headband; her full breasts thrusting against her T-shirt. Little had changed. Even her contorted expression had echoes of the way she looked during moments of teenage sexual ecstasy. He was about to call the number when he had a better idea.

'Schnee.'

'Mr Tate?'

'I want a rundown on Beverley Laine's movements, a typical week. I want the times she leaves for work, the times she leaves for home, the routes she uses – that sort of thing. The guy who took this picture probably has all the information.'

'I'll call him first thing in the morning,' Schnee promised.

'You'll go and see him now,' said Marshall curtly. 'We're paying him enough.'

Schnee had had a long day but he knew better than to argue. He glanced back at the table before he left the office and saw

that Marshall was still staring intently at the photograph of
Beverley Laine.

## 54

Marshall's timing was excellent. After all, he was accustomed
to directing action scenes. The difference was that this time
there was no camera and the acting was down to him. Luckily
there was a gap in the traffic that enabled him to drop his road
map and accelerate his Ferrari out of the lay-by the moment
Beverley Laine's BMW nosed out of the turning ahead. That
lovely, unchanged face that he remembered so well was actually
looking straight at him. He flashed his headlights and touched
the brakes.

The ruse worked. Beverley thought he was giving way to her.
She pulled out onto the main road. Marshall's foot went to the
throttle pedal and the two cars crunched wings. There was a
tinkle of glass and plastic debris dropping onto the road. He
saw Beverley mouth an expletive as she pulled off the road.
Marshall released the padded restraints that had tightened their
grip on his body despite the low speed of the collision and
reversed back into the lay-by. He waited. Let her come to him.

She jumped out of her car, examined the damage, and marched purposefully towards Marshall's Ferrari. There was a grace
and suppleness in her movements that heightened Marshall's
sense of anticipation of what was to follow, provided everything
went according to plan. He saw no reason why not; women
were malleable toys. He lowered his window.

'All right,' said Beverley aggressively. 'You had right of way,
but you flashed me as you pulled out of the lay-by, so I turned.'

'I most certainly did not flash you,' Marshall replied. His low
sitting position gave him an excellent view of her hips and
thighs. 'I went to blow my horn but you swung across in front
of me.'

'You flashed your headlights!' Beverley protested angrily.
'You were parked in that lay-by so it wouldn't have hurt you
to have waited a few more seconds, for God's sake!'

'I may have accidentally flashed the headlights when I went to sound the horn,' Marshall admitted. 'But it's you who should've waited. You turned in front of me.'

'But you flashed your headlights, twice!'

Marshall opened his door and got out. He smiled and saw the confusion in Beverley's eyes. She had recognized him. Well, that was only to be expected, he had appeared on television often enough. 'Perhaps you were dazzled by the sun?' he inquired politely. 'It was certainly shining off your windscreen.'

'Matt Tate . . .' Beverley muttered weakly. 'Jesus Christ, I don't believe it.'

Marshall pushed back his lank blond hair and adopted a suitable puzzled expression. 'I'm sorry . . . Er . . . miss is it? But you have me at a decided disadvantage.'

Her reply was a shocked whisper: 'Beverley Laine. Remember me, Matt?'

## 55

Marshall mapped out his affair with Beverley with the precision of one of his carefully-crafted shooting scripts. First there was the question of restricting access to the set.

'She knows your fat face,' Marshall told Schnee. 'Therefore you stay away from the flat at weekends and you don't come near the place unless I say. You don't phone me or anything. If you need to get in touch, you drop me a fax and you don't sign it and don't put anything on it about the Bacchus project. You understand?'

Schnee agreed that he understood.

Marshall's careful planning paid off. The scenes with Beverley went off better than he expected even though they were unrehearsed. The all-important bedroom scenes in particular were a spectacular success; helped by Beverley's loneliness and the surprising ease at which she was captivated by the charm that he could turn on like a tap. When they had first made love as teenagers, it was Beverley who had lacked inhibitions and who had taken the initiative. The roles were now reversed. Maybe Beverley's unhappy experience as a young woman had bred in her a fear of her own sexuality. Marshall did not know or care.

The all-important thing was that the flimsy barriers were easily ripped down so that by the second weekend of the orchestrated affair he had Beverley trapped in an enjoyable black pit of thrashing limbs and tangled sheets. Having reawakened her appetite, he took a perverse pleasure in doling out sexual treats to the point which had her pleading with him to finish. It was a fitting punishment for the Authority that women were forever trying to exercise over him with their bodies.

What he found worrying was that the poised, self-assured Beverley always re-established control at other times. She donned her rationality with her clothes; showing no signs of becoming dependent on him. Nano Systems had a hold on her to the extent that Marshall suspected Beverley was using him as a diversion from her responsibilities. He began to doubt if his offer for her to take over the running of the Elite channel would work. Given time it was possible that he could eventually dominate her completely, but time was the one thing that he could not afford, therefore he needed some form of insurance to ensure her compliance.

It was a need that led him to check his bedroom for camera angles and examine the spaces behind the false ceiling panels directly over the king-size bed. Lighting was no problem, the new generation of charged coupled device miniature video cameras could work well at low light levels. To cover all angles and to make the final tape as interesting as possible would mean three concealed cameras. To avoid over-complication with cable runs and having to start three video recorders, he decided on digitally mixing the output from the three cameras onto one tape. He could later unscramble and separate the signals in the Elite channel's editing suite to create three tapes: the master shot of the entire scene supplied by camera one, the medium close-ups from camera two, and the cutaway DBCUs from camera three. These could then be edited together onto the finished tape. And while he had the ceiling panels down, it was no great hassle to rig some extra wiring for sound, using directional microphones. Beverley in the throes of an orgasm was surprisingly vocal; it would be a pity to waste her talent.

It must be Nicam stereo sound, of course. After all, Marshall was a professional film-maker.

For an undressed rehearsal to check focus and aperture settings, lighting and sound levels, he hired a suitably acquiescent and presentable young lady from the Canary Wharf meat rack. She was one of Marshall's regulars and had often expressed a desire to be in his movies.

He commandeered a video tape editing suite at the Elite channel and gave strict instructions that he was not to be disturbed. He worked fast. It took him less than an hour to separate the signals on the tape to provide three tapes, one from each camera. He studied the results carefully, making mental notes of the adjustments that each camera needed. He erased the tapes, junked them, and returned to his flat.

When everything was ready for Beverley's coming weekend visit, Marshall reflected wryly on the incongruity that the star of his very first movie would also be the star of this, his last and most important movie. Apart from a groping hand thrust up Martha Hunt's skirt for *Catseyes* many years before, it would also be the first time that he had appeared in one of his own movies. An in-depth role so to speak rather than a Hitchcockian glimpse, although he had no intention of showing his face in the final cut.

What sort of distribution the finished movie received would be entirely up to Beverley.

## 56

Knowing that three cameras were faithfully recording the bedroom scenes with Beverley added a certain piquancy to the weekend. Marshal decided that the Sunday morning scenes would be particularly effective: the sunlight spilling across the big, king-size bed was a bonus – the colour saturation performance of the CCD video cameras in bright sunlight was excellent. The beams of light breaking through the vertical hanging slats of the glass blind caused brilliantly-hued spectrums to dance iridescent patterns on Beverley's divine, writhing body. And when she arched her back off the bed and fell back with a final, shuddering cry, the tiny beads of sweat that formed and coalesced between her heaving breasts sparkled erotically, like surrealist diamonds in the liquid light. She lay still, her eyes closed, her tangled ringlets spread out on the silk sheet.

Marshall slipped off the bed and touched the control button that opened the slats. He stood clear and watched with a clinical, professional eye as the coloured bands across Beverley's body dissolved to white. It would be a superb closing shot, he decided. He was looking forward to editing the tapes.

He leaned over Beverley and kissed her forehead. She opened her eyes.

'Coffee, darling?' he asked.

'Mmm.'

Marshall left the bedroom and went down the spiral staircase to the lounge. He picked up a remote control and switched off the video recorder in its smoked glass cabinet beneath the wide-screen television. There was no point in even a cursory check of the tape because the images were digitally scrambled.

He was reading the Sunday papers when Beverley appeared wrapped in a towel. She sat at the table, watching him carefully as though she had guessed that he had something important to say. He placed a coffee before her.

'You have to drink it and keep the towel in place at the same time,' he said. 'I don't want any distractions because we have some serious talking to do.'

Beverley remained silent.

'There's a corny old line about how we've got to stop meeting like this, Bev,' Marshall continued. 'It's not doing either of us any good.' He hesitated. Just the right pause. If it was scripted, an actor would have made too much of a meal of it and the scene would have to be reshot. 'The truth is, I need you, Bev. I want you to move up here permanently.' He broke off and laughed. 'Don't look so worried. I don't mean for you to move in here. We'd probably be tearing each other apart after a couple of weeks. There's a fantastic flat two floors down that I've taken an option on. I'd be happy to transfer it into your name.'

From the sudden look of anger in her eyes, Marshall knew that he had made a tactical blunder.

'No,' said Beverley. 'I don't know what I want out of this relationship, Matt. I'm confused. I don't know whether I'm coming or going. But I do know that I don't want to become your mistress.'

He explained that he wanted her to run the Elite channel because he was setting up new operations in the Far East; that was as much as he was prepared to tell her about the Bacchus project. He offered to triple the salary and expenses that she received from Nano Systems, and even offered her a percentage of the Elite channel's weekend roulette takings. Although she agreed to think it over and give him an answer the following weekend, Marshall knew that he had failed.

He would have to use the tape.

### 57

On the following Wednesday evening, Schnee was working alone in Marshall's penthouse, sitting at the glass-topped table, using a Nanopad to put the finishing touches to his summary of the reports from the Tokyo project office. The conversion of the tanker was ahead of schedule and was well inside budget. That was good. Not so good were reports from the TLK Corporation. The Japanese development company had got the Bacchus satellite system test bench running by plugging it into a mainframe computer. They were confident that the satellite would be finished on time but were concerned at the lack of Kronos microprocessors. A note at the end of the report from the chief designer said that the satellite would be a mass of empty Kronos sockets unless the chips were forthcoming soon.

He stopped work and looked at his watch. It was a few minutes to 8 p.m. There was a TV documentary due to start on Channel 4 about the Elite channel. Before leaving the penthouse Marshall had said that he would be back in time to see it.

At 7.58 p.m., Schnee rose and crossed the room. He looked around for a video tape. There was one in the video recorder. He checked through it. It was full of lines of flickering garbage. Obviously Marshall had accidentally recorded a scrambled channel. It was easily done, the wretched machines were pigs to set up even with the aid of a barcode card and reader. Schnee rewound the tape to the beginning, set the recorder to Channel 4, and touched the record key. The machine whirred softly and a red recording symbol came on.

The Swiss returned to work. The other reports he had to summarize concerned the construction of the three casinos. Land had been purchased and plans had been approved. Payments amounting to two hundred and fifty thousand dollars had solved the problem of acquiring building materials for the Beijing casino; it was going to be the size of a sports stadium. He carefully transferred the figure to a column called incentive payments. No doubt Harrison Calinco would query them. The American nit-picked every unusual figure. It was hardly surprising: the out-going cashflow was frightening.

Schnee was looking forward to the project's completion. As its general manager, recruiting the mouth-watering Balinese girls to work on the *Eldorado* would be his responsibility. Jobs were scarce on the island; he would be able to pick and choose. The thought of the delights ahead made it difficult for him to concentrate on his costings.

The video recorder hummed softly to itself as Schnee worked.

It was gone 10 p.m. when the lift doors open and Marshall entered the penthouse. Schnee remained silent, hunched over his Nanopad but kept an antenna alert and tuned, trying to gauge his boss's mood. Marshall tossed his car keys on the coffee table and poured himself a whisky.

'Any messages?'

'A nursing home in Kingston called,' Schnee replied. 'They were anxious to speak to you. I didn't like to pass on your mobile number so I took a message.'

'And?'

'They had a Bill Yates in their care. They seemed to think that you knew him. He died this morning. The funeral's on Thursday.'

Marshall swore. Thursday was going to be a busy day: a meeting with Harrison Calinco in the morning and editing Beverley's video tape in the afternoon.

'He doesn't seem to have any family so they're rather hoping you'll go.'

'I'm too bloody busy for funerals!' Marshall snapped belligerently.

The video recorder disengaged its recording head with a click and started rewinding the tape.

Marshall glanced at the machine. 'What was that?'

Schnee corrected a figure. 'The programme on Channel 4 that you wanted to see. I used the tape that was in the recorder. There was nothing on it.'

It took a few seconds for the scale of the disaster to dawn on Marshall. '*YOU DID WHAT?*'

Schnee looked up from his Nanopad and knew real fear. Marshall had risen to his feet and had crossed trance-like towards the video recorder. He stopped the rewinding and ejected the tape. He looked at its label in disbelief.

'Is anything wrong, Mr Tate?'

'*Anything wrong!*' Marshall screamed. '*Anything wrong! You've over-recorded a programme tape, you fucking cretin. That's what's wrong!*'

Schnee rose and held his briefcase protectively in front of him. Marshall was advancing towards him. He looked nearly three metres tall. His blue eyes were alight with murder. Schnee backed towards the open lift doors. 'But there was nothing on it!' he stammered. 'I checked first.'

'Did you record from the beginning of the tape?'

'Yes, Mr Tate.'

Marshall uttered a cry of fury and lunged at Schnee. Considering his weight, the terrified Swiss showed an extraordinary turn of speed. He darted sideways and dived into the lift car. His fingers scrabbled at the control panel. The lift car shook on its cables as Marshall hurled himself through the doors before they closed. He grabbed Schnee by the throat and banged his head repeatedly against the bulkhead, punctuating every blow with obscenities. Panic gave Schnee the necessary strength to push Marshall away. The lift doors opened onto the gloomy underground car park.

'Please, Mr Tate,' Schnee begged. 'I did check the tape. There was nothing on it, I swear.'

Marshall regained some semblance of control but that did not stop him twisting Schnee's shirt front and threatening him with murder if he ever touched his things again. He gave his victim a vicious shove that sent him staggering backwards out of the lift. Schnee tripped, regained his balance and scurried towards his car. He fumbled with his keys, scrambled behind the wheel, and started the engine just as Marshall Tate marched across to the car and banged furiously on the window. Schnee resisted the temptation to drive off. He lowered the window.

'And another thing, you arsehole,' Marshall Tate spat through the opening. 'I don't pay you Christ knows how many fucking kay a month to screw up! One more cock-up and you're out!'

'All I can say, Mr Tate,' said Schnee, recovering his dignity although still badly shaken, 'is that it was an accident for which I apologize.'

Marshall moved clear as Schnee reversed violently and shot towards the exit. He stared after the receding car, hands on hips and muttering curses under his breath. Silence returned to the underground car park. He was about to return to the lift when the sound of a car door slamming very close-by caused him to spin around.

*Oh, shit!*

Beverley was regarding him from beside her car. Even in the poor light, Marshall could see the hate in her eyes.

'Beverley! What the hell are you doing here?'

'Learning, Matt.' She walked purposefully across to him and gazed up. 'Learning what a blind fool I've been,' she said with quiet loathing. 'A stupid, stupid fool. My only consolation, if there is one, was that I was taken for a ride by the most ruthless and arrogant bastard it's ever been my misfortune to meet.'

'What the hell are you talking about?' He wanted to get away but she caught hold of his jacket.

'It all adds up,' said Beverley. 'Schnee's pathetic attempt to take over my firm. He failed so you went to work on me. The way you came out of that lay-by. Jesus Christ! I should've realized that you'd been waiting for me. So what is it about

284

Nano Systems, Matt? Compared with your operation, we're nothing. Or is it that you saw it'll be a winner in the future and you wanted a piece of the action? No, not a piece, that's not your style. You wanted all of it!'

Marshall brushed Beverley aside and entered the lift. Already his fertile mind was looking for new options. This mess was the past. Beverley Laine was the past.

'Well I'll tell you something!' Beverley yelled. 'If you want to fight, Matt, I'll give you a fight! And I promise you this – you'll never have Nano Systems. Never!'

He touched the control pad, and turned to face the enraged Beverley. 'I don't know about winners,' he said icily before the doors closed. 'But I know a loser when I see one. I'm not interested in your grotty little company and I never have been.'

The lift doors closed softly like a gate wipe on a movie scene.

Once back in his flat, Marshall called Schnee on his carphone and told him what had happened in the car park. 'She recognized you and that's that. The whole thing is screwed up. Get back here now. Forget the tape. We've got to do a major rethink.'

Schnee replaced his handset in its carrier and reflected that Marshall Tate telling him to forget the tape was as near to an apology as he was ever likely to receive. He did a U-turn and headed back to the penthouse. He had an idea in mind that he felt sure his boss would go along with.

Marshall read carefully through all the information that Schnee had compiled on Nano Systems' principal shareholders. 'Okay, Schnee, so who's the weak link?'

'Theodore Draggon of Draggon Industries, Mr Tate. His companies are experiencing cashflow problems. Also I sensed at the board meeting at Nano Systems that he was in favour of our bid. The big plus, of course, is that Draggon Industries are long-standing customers for the Kronos chip and therefore have an established procedure for acquiring them.'

'And he's definitely looking for a buyer for Draggon Industries?'

'Yes, Mr Tate.'

Marshall considered carefully. Schnee's plan was going to be expensive but he could not see that he had any choice unless he resorted to using the telephone number that Harrison Calinco had given him. Having Beverley removed would be costly and would not ensure his supply of Kronos; buying out Theo Draggon was a more cost-effective option.

'Okay, he's found one,' he said abruptly. 'Get him up here.'


## 58

The legal formalities for the takeover of Draggon Industries were completed in Marshall Tate's Woolwich office three weeks later. Once the documents were signed, Marshall ordered everyone out except Theodore Draggon.

He came from behind his desk and stared down at Theo Draggon, his eyes hard and dispassionate. He ignored the Yorkshireman's outstretched hand.

'You know exactly what you have to do,' Marshall stated. 'You first put an order through for four thousand Kronos chips.'

'I understand perfectly, Mr Tate,' Theo agreed. He hated having to swallow his pride like this but Marshall Tate had saved him from going under.

'Once that's done, you use the additional funding for a takeover bid of Quantum Leap Video Systems.'

'I'll do my best, Mr Tate.'

Marshall grabbed Theo's shirt front and pulled him close. 'You'll do more than your best if you work for me, Draggon. You foul up, or breathe a word about this to anyone and you're dead. You understand?'

Theo looked into Marshall Tate's face and saw not the blunt determination of a businessman, something he knew and understood, but a hint of homicidal madness.

'I understand, Mr Tate.'

# 59
## Japan

The Japanese marine architect responsible for the conversion of the hundred-thousand-tonne *Orient Conveyor* from a bulk carrier to the Bacchus earth station was proud of his effort and with good reason. The huge amount of work that the conversion entailed was still ahead of schedule. Marshall was particularly pleased to see that the uplink dish antennae to control the Bacchus satellite were in position and the control facilities were installed and undergoing tests. Tasks such as the fitting out of the guests' and crew quarters, the helicopter platform, were not so important and yet everything was proceeding smoothly.

'We can bring handover forward to next September,' the marine architect informed Marshall through an interpreter. 'Everything will be finished by then, even your suite, Mr Tate. Please, I will show you.'

Until then Marshall had not given much thought to living on the *Eldorado*, but when he completed his tour of inspection, he realized, to his surprise, that he was looking forward to the experience. The *Eldorado* would be an impregnable fortress. As he stood on the ship's vast deck, surrounded by beavering gangs and explosive showers of blue sparks from arc welders, he could feel the absolute power of the mighty ship seeping into his very soul. Once he was on the *Eldorado* and the ship was fully operational, he would be invincible. Never again would he be dependent on people and governments. Never again would he be the victim of authority. If the Indonesian government decided to kick him out, he had three other anchorages for the *Eldorado* lined up.

Everything was going well. The Bacchus satellite now had its Kronos chips and was undergoing final tests and modifications in TLK's laboratories. The first three casinos being built were nearing completion. The revenue they generated would finance several more and there would be enough to pay off Harrison Calinco's hoodlums. To hell with the annual compensation fee that Calinco's mob were after. If they wanted it, they would have to come after him. And if they came after him . . . Well . . . the *Eldorado* was going to be armed.

Marshall's dreams forged effortlessly into the future: Bacchus I would be joined by Bacchus II covering Europe, followed by Bacchus III covering the United States.

Absolute power and authority – real Authority – would be his.

# PART FIVE: Today
# Beverley

A monster fearful and hideous.
*Aeneid*, Virgil

# 1

## SOUTHERN ENGLAND
## 1998

It was after 4 a.m. when Beverley emerged from the TVR
chamber. The aftershock of the vivid reliving her affair with
Marshall Tate suddenly struck her as she closed the chamber's
hatch. Her limbs trembled so violently in the aftermath of the
ordeal that she had to sit naked on the steps for some minutes
before her nerves steadied sufficiently for her to get dressed.

On the drive home the intensity of those agonizing moments
in the chamber struck her again, forcing her to pull to the side
of the road. It was the reawakening of the memory of the way
she had given herself so unashamedly to Marshall Tate that she
found so difficult to come to terms with. Her forehead flushed
hot with anger and embarrassment as she pressed it against the
Albatross's heavily-padded steering wheel, fighting to bring her
trembling body under control.

'Use telephone.'

Silence.

She had mumbled the command therefore there was no reply
from her Iridium system. She straightened up in the seat and
repeated the request.

'Standing by,' said the telephone's computer-sampled voice.

'Toby Hoyle. Messaging only.' Beverley was unable to
remember if she had programmed all Toby's numbers into the
system. Obviously she had because the telephone answered.

'Toby Hoyle. Messaging service. Calling now. Please stand
by.' A pause, then: 'Connected to Toby Hoyle. You have five
minutes of voice storage. Please go ahead.'

'Toby, it's Beverley. I'm calling about what you said to me
about remembering everything that passed between me and
Marshall Tate. Well there is something that comes to mind that
might be important . . . I'm not sure. The first time I went to
his penthouse, we both had too much to drink. He said something about being independent, about owning and controlling

his own satellite. I'm sure it has something to do with an operation he said he was setting up in the Far East. All this was two years ago so whatever it was he was planning might be nearing completion or be complete by now. I don't know, I'm only guessing, and I'm not sure what bearing this has on whether or not he's responsible for planting the trojans in the Kronos. Call me on my Klipfone number if you need more information. It'll be by my bed.'

She talked for another two minutes because it made her feel better, stopping when she realized that she was repeating herself and requesting a replay. Considering her state, she was surprised at how lucid she sounded. She cleared the channel and resumed her homeward drive through the dark, winding lanes of West Sussex.

## 2

Toby was in better shape than Carl. He ran alongside Beverley, breathing easily and taking the breakwaters in his stride. Although it was a leisurely paced jog, Beverley missed the stimulating jabs from her Laine Runner belt; Carl had taken it into the labs for repair and she had so many pressing matters on her mind that she had forgotten to ask for it back. It was a warm evening in late September and they threw long, bobbing shadows on the wet sand as they ran side by side.

'I've got a five-thousand dollar bill for you,' said Toby.

Beverley glanced sideways at him. 'What the hell for?'

'To help out with the expenses of an American freelance journo based in Japan who's been digging up some dirt on Marshall Tate. It's cheap at the price, believe me.'

They cleared a breakwater together.

'I don't subsidize any journalists unless they come up with hard information,' said Beverley as emphatically as she could while jogging.

'It's hard enough because it all makes sense,' Toby replied, leaping across a pool to avoid splattering Beverley. 'Marshall Tate has built three casinos in the Far East which are to be managed by a satellite called Bacchus. It's Japanese designed

292

and built. It's going to be launched next week. It'll do everything. It'll generate the game, manage the betting and the payouts. It can handle millions of transactions simultaneously. And, of course, being in space means that the gambling will be taking place outside the national boundaries of any country. Does that fit in with Marshall Tate's philosophy?'

The news caused Beverley to slacken her pace. 'It fits in perfectly.' She was about to add something when she was suddenly assailed by phantom electronic jabs in her side from the Laine Runner belt that she was not wearing. They spoilt her concentration. She continued to reduced her pace and the strange stimuli disappeared.

'From what the journo has been able to glean from his sources,' Toby continued, also slowing down, 'this Bacchus satellite is supposed to be based on conventional silicon NEC transputers. But supposing its designers decided early on that even transputers couldn't cope with the enormous amount of processing that the satellite would have to handle? Especially if they wanted to allow for growth during the satellite's life? Supposing they decided that the best tool for the job was your Kronos superchip? What then?'

Beverley stopped running as the full implication of Toby Hoyle's words sank in. 'Good heavens,' she muttered. 'We'd require a royalty of 5 per cent.'

'Exactly,' said Toby, having to breathe deeply because he was not quite as fit as his companion. 'The casinos are monsters. The one in Beijing is like a sports stadium, that's why Marshall Tate can't be secretive about them for much longer. According to estimates based on the seating capacity, my tame journo estimates that they will generate an estimated *ten billion US dollars* per annum.'

Beverley was shocked. 'Christ.'

'And that's a conservative estimate. By obtaining those chips clandestinely, Marshall Tate will be saving on royalty payments to your company of five hundred million dollars in his first year. *Five billion dollars over the next ten years!* So it's hardly surprising that Theodore Draggon gets himself severely topped if there was a danger that he might blow the gaff on what happened to all those Kronos chips he'd got hold of. You were on your way to see him, remember. Chances are Marshall Tate had an intercept on his line and sent a minion around to see him before you got there.'

Beverley gazed at the horizon, reliving the ghastly moment when she had discovered Theodore Draggon's body.

'You're being attacked by Marshall Tate on two fronts, Beverley. He's got hold of over four thousand Class A Kronos chips which, at this moment, are probably plugged into the Bacchus satellite. Plus, as you've suspected all along, he's got enough chips to reverse engineer them and plant trojan-infected chips in industry to undermine Nano Systems. Tate likes to be independent. It's an obsession with him. It's an even bet that he's got long-term plans for more satellites. Maybe this Bacchus is only a test satellite. He knows he won't be able to get hold of more of your chips by the same method, therefore he won't rest until he's got control of your company.'

For once Beverley was at a loss. She felt that she was up against forces that she could not combat. Iron will and sheer determination seemed inadequate weapons to use against someone so ruthless that they would resort to murder. Originally she had experienced relief when the enemy had been identified. Now she was not sure.

'I suppose,' she said slowly, 'it's time to turn everything over to the police.'

Toby snorted. 'What good will that do? He's got his headquarters set up on a converted tanker in Bali, and he's got top Indonesian government officials in his pocket. It's clever that. If the Indonesians get fed up with him and kick him out, he can always up anchor and move. He's bound to have contingency anchorages lined up. What you're going to need is hard evidence that he's got your chips so that you have him for copyright infringements. That way you can haul him through the courts of just about every country in the world.'

The phantom jabs in Beverley's side suddenly returned.

'Ouch! Shit!' She grimaced, hitched up her T-shirt, and clutched her side.

Toby steadied her as she doubled up. 'Hey, what's the matter, Beverley?'

'Dammit! Cramp . . .'

'In your side?' Toby looked concerned as he supported her.

The pain faded away. Beverley straightened up. 'A stitch, I expect. Maybe Dr Wyman's right. Maybe I am past it.'

'So what do you want to do about Marshall Tate?'

Beverley's answer was to push Toby away and break into a run. 'Bugger Marshall Tate!' she yelled over her shoulder. 'Bugger Doc Wyman! Bugger the Kronos! Bugger every damned thing!' She accelerated when she heard Toby pounding after her. She did not want him to see the tears of despair and frustration that were streaming down her cheeks.

Beverley was a fighter. But it was difficult being a fighter when you were pitted against an enemy of unfathomable ruthlessness who wrote his own rules.


3

Under the electron microscope the motor neurons looked like a dense forest filling the projection screen in Nano Systems' memory analysis laboratory. Carl realized that something was wrong the moment Dr Pilleau slipped the opened Kronos under the machine's viewing head.

'Holy shit!'

'Our initial reaction precisely,' said Macé Pilleau phlegmatically, nodding to Leon Dexter. 'That's the Kronos that came out of the combine harvester. We've not done any sampling analysis but we think we have a motor neuron count of 20 to 25 per cent instead of the 10 per cent that the chip had when it was made.'

Carl fumbled for the controls on his breast pocket voice recorder and pressed the record button. This was something he would have to get transcribed and not wait for one of Macé Pilleau's plodding reports. The implications were too horrendous for him to contemplate but the stark evidence was before him on the screen. At least a quarter of the motor neurons were mature, completely formed. No Kronos ever produced had such an incredibly high count of working motor neurons. The vast majority had less than 1 per cent correctly formed. Such chips were classified as Class C on analysis and had their outer case etched accordingly. They were used in personal computers and pocket databases such as dictionaries and translators. Class A Kronos microprocessors, which accounted for less than one in every hundred chips produced, had 10 per cent of their cells correctly formed which gave them the full one gigabyte or more of working memory. Nearly all Nano Systems' research effort was currently directed towards doubling the memory capacity of the Kronos. The need for even higher standards of purity in the cultivation labs and the slowness of the TVR chamber technique was making the two gigabyte super Kronos, the Zeus, a seemingly impossible goal.

'So what would you say the RAM capacity of that chip is?' Carl asked, not taking his eyes off the screen.

'Two and a half gig plus,' said Leon equably.

'What!' Carl spun around to face the young software engineer. 'For Christ's sake, why has it taken you so long to find out something so bloody basic as that?'

Dr Pilleau saw the makings of a row and stepped in quickly. 'Simple. Because we were looking at the damage to the chip caused by the trojan. Not the repairs it carried out before it died.'

'*If* it died,' Leon interjected.

This was too much for Carl. He resorted to rarely-used expletives. 'Repairs! What the hell are you trying to tell me?'

'We're not *trying* to tell you anything,' said Dr Pilleau testily. 'As you already know, the so-called trojan appears to be a digitalized DNA. If we had the time and facilities to carry out proper sequencing, we might discover what manner of life it represents. As it is, we don't know. We can only make unsatisfactory wild guesses.'

'Appears?' Carl mimicked. 'Wild guesses? These are not the sort of words we're used to hearing from you, Macé.'

'I'm not used to being confronted with this sort of problem, Mr Olivera. I don't know what it is we've got here and nor does Leon. We do know that it may have attempted to produce a

296

molecular template using residual enzymes in the chip. What we're both agreed on is that that Kronos has undergone a significant change, a two-and-a-half-fold increase in the number of its working motor neurons. Now *that* could only be accomplished from within the chip itself after manufacture.'

'But this is crazy!' Carl almost shouted. 'You're telling me that that goddamn Kronos,' he jabbed his finger at the screen, 'has managed to do to itself what we've been spending millions trying to do in TVR chambers?'

Leon broke the silence that followed Carl's outburst. 'I want to show you something, Mr Olivera. We could use a TVR chamber but this is quicker.'

He sat at the electron microscope's control keyboard and increased the magnification. The neurons swelled to the size of small tree trunks on the projection screen. He checked a co-ordinate reference that had been scribbled on the desktop and entered it on the keyboard. The picture on the screen blurred and froze on a different close-up of the nerves.

'There's a pair we located an hour ago,' said Leon, using a mouse pointer to indicate two complete nerves in the centre foreground. 'The one on the left is one of ours, the structure is typical of the cells grown in this plant. The one on the right is a repaired or regenerated cell. You can see that the bonding is totally different if you look carefully.'

Carl agreed that he could see the difference. 'Have you checked the memory address of the new cell?'

'Oh, yes. So far we've taken a random sample of about a hundred of the new cells. None of their addresses match the addresses of the cells that were mapped as working when the chip was made. They weren't working then, but they are now.'

'We're both agreed on that,' Dr Pilleau observed.

Carl tried to sort out his thoughts. 'The whole thing's too preposterous for words,' he protested. 'Cells that can rejuvenate themselves?'

'I didn't say or imply that,' said Dr Pilleau mildly. 'Rejuvenate means renew. Those repaired motor neurons weren't properly-formed cells in the first place. And I certainly never said that they repaired themselves.'

Carl managed a bleak smile. This was more like Macé Pilleau. 'Okay then, doctor. Tell me what did repair them?'

'Specialist nano-machines produced from the genome of the trojan's DNA.'

'Using what for matter?'

'There are plenty of impurities in the Kronos's nutrient fluid to provide the materials to build a nano-machine, Mr Olivera,' Dr Pilleau replied evenly. 'We haven't achieved 100 per cent purity yet.'

'I see. So these hypothetical nano-machines go crawling around inside one of our Kronos chips, fixing dud memory cells using nutrient impurities as a bonding agent?'

'That's putting it crudely, but yes.'

'Can I butt in here, Macé?' asked Leon.

'Be my guest,' was the doctor's uninterested reply.

'It's like this, Mr Olivera,' said Leon easily. 'As you know, a theory is a hypothesis that is conjured up by loonies like me to explain observations. For a theory to survive or die, it is put into a torture chamber and fed on facts until it is either poisoned or flourishes. Right now the theory that there were or are nano-machines in that chip that repaired those cells is the only one we've got.'

'Miss Laine has a chip substitution theory,' Carl pointed out.

'A theory that now falls down on logical analysis in the light of what we're learning, Mr Olivera,' said Dr Pilleau drily.

Carl turned to the doctor. 'I used to think it was crazy too, but right now it's looking more sensible than your weird notions.'

Dr Pilleau nodded. He was happier now that logic was beginning to replace wild conjecture. 'Very well. Let us look at the substitution theory. First there is the question of motive. Why would anyone wish to do that?'

Carl shrugged. 'Simple. To undermine this company. To devalue it and then buy it because it has enormous growth potential.'

'Ha. Now your logic is at fault. The tremendous potential of this company is focused on the Kronos chip. We've pushed its memory to one gigabyte, a tiny percentage of its potential. We're

298

now spending millions trying to double its memory, and we're not having much luck. You would agree with that?'

'Basically, yes.'

'So you're saying that the chip under the microscope is a substitute?'

'It's Beverley's theory,' said Carl. 'And the only one that makes sense.'

'But it has working motor neurons of two and a half gig which it didn't have before! Anyone who can produce such a chip is not likely to take much interest in this company because the world will beat a path to their front door anyway.'

There was a long silence.

'I take your point, doctor,' Carl agreed, at length. 'But we own the patents on the Kronos.'

'Only on the manufacturing process. And as Leon has shown, the bonding of those motor neurons is quite different from our TVR process. It's much more positive and refined. That alone would make it extremely difficult for us to prove that our patents are being infringed. Also, a court case could take five years or more to reach a conclusion. In the meantime a fortune would be made.'

Carl recalled the Intel versus NEC dispute in the 1980s over the V20 processor and realized that Dr Pilleau was talking sense. 'Well,' he said reluctantly. 'I was never that sold on Beverley's substitution theory but it was the only one that made a modicum of sense. So what do we do next?'

'Two things. We carry out an electron microscope search of that chip and the other corrupted chips for the nano-machines.'

Carl gave a wry smile. 'You make it sound easy, doctor. My guess is that looking for specific grains of sand in the Sahara would be a lot easier.'

'Much easier, but we've had one thing on our side so far,' said Leon, grinning. 'Luck.'

Dr Pilleau frowned at the mention of such an unquantifiable concept. 'The second is something we can't do by ourselves. We need the resources of a university microbiology department.'

'For sequencing the trojan's DNA?'

'It's not a real DNA, but it does appear to be a software template for initializing physical changes.'

'I can't see the board or Miss Laine agreeing to outside help,' said Carl doubtfully.

'We don't have a choice,' said Leon abruptly. 'The conditions in that chip's nutrient feed have triggered off something that is beyond our understanding. Whatever it is, it's beginning to look as if we may have unwittingly contaminated Mars with it. We can't keep this to ourselves. Also it can repair motor neurons which probably means that in humans it could repair brain damage, bring joy to parents with retarded children, and maybe even reverse senile dementia. Perhaps it could even enhance human intelligence to produce a super race? Pin that little baby down and we could all become Nobel Prize winners.'

Carl was stunned by the concepts. He stared at Leon. 'Holy shit,' he breathed. 'We could be on to something.'

Dr Pilleau looked contemptuous. 'Enhance human intelligence,' he snorted. 'Next you'll be saying that the trojan is intelligent.'

'Why not?' said Leon affably. He fished an apple out of his pocket and bit a lump out of it with a loud crunch. 'Look at its track record. It defeats every software protection routine under the sun to infest our chips. Once it's found a home it sets about improving the chip's memory using a motor neuron regeneration technique that we can only guess at.' He took another bite out of his apple. 'And to crown it all, the little critter's beaten us getting to Mars.'

# 4

# JAPAN

It was an hour before dawn on 1 October 1998, at Japan's Tanegashima Space Centre, located on a beautiful island at the extreme south of the Japanese archipelago.

Kasowa was TLK's chief designer; he had lived with the Bacchus satellite for three years, 10 per cent of his life. Now that it was out of his hands and entrusted to the launch controllers, he felt lost. For three years the one-tonne satellite had been his baby. For three years he had fretted about the non-appearance of the two thousand Kronos microprocessors that he had been promised. He and his team of technicians had built the bird with its two thousand Kronos sockets empty of their chips, a task fraught with problems because they had been unable to test the various sub-systems as they were completed. And then, only a few months before, the chips had finally arrived. He and two colleagues had worked through the night inserting them carefully into their respective sockets. After that there had been four weeks of exhaustive tests and modifications. Marshall Tate himself had visited the TLK laboratories outside Tokyo on several occasions. He usually spent an hour in the clean room, asking searching questions.

Kasowa shivered at the memory of his first meeting with the strange Englishman. Marshall Tate had been gowned-up in order to view the Bacchus satellite in the clean room. All that had been visible were his eyes, hard, dispassionate, piercing blue eyes that would give no mercy if Kasowa or any member of the team made a mistake.

'One minute,' said the launch controller's voice in Kasowa's headphones.

Kasowa forgot Marshall Tate for the time being and focused his attention on the illuminated wall screen that would soon be plotting Bacchus' flight trajectory.

'Thirty seconds. Automatic sequencing initiated.'

All heads in the control room turned to the big colour monitor that showed the floodlit H-II sitting on the launch pad, wreathed in gentle clouds of LOX vapour from the venting fuel tanks. The bluish tinge of the sea and sky beyond the rocket held the promise of another beautiful day. Kasowa crossed his fingers, a Western custom he had picked up from his days at NASA.

Another monitor was the feed from the *Eldorado*. It showed Marshall Tate sitting in the Bacchus control room, watching a monitor that was showing the same picture of the rocket, pictures within pictures.

'Ten seconds and counting . . . Five . . . Four . . . Three . . . Two . . .'

The dull roar of the distant engines building up to maximum thrust was plainly audible in the control room. And then the H-II nose cleared the billowing clouds of steam from the millions of litres of water that had been flooded into the blast tunnel. The heat-tracking TV cameras followed the sleek missile as it climbed away on its expanding column of flame and thunder.

It was a faultless launch. After first-stage burnout, the rocket's second-stage LE5 Mitsubishi engines took over the task of powering Marshall Tate's precious payload into space. At a height of five hundred kilometres smaller motors fired to inject it into a low, transitional, interim orbit. Once the controllers at Tanegashima were satisfied that the satellite was stable, they handed over temporary control to their colleagues at the NASDA tracking station in Ceylon who orientated the satellite before it dipped below the eastern horizon.

There was nothing Kasowa or anyone could do until the satellite reappeared above the western horizon ninety minutes later. The *Eldorado* monitor showed Marshall Tate pacing up and down. He seemed to be shouting at someone. Kasowa wondered if he was shouting at his boss. The young engineer was glad that he was not on the ship.

The sun was up and shining from a clear blue sky when Bacchus's signals were picked up. The low earth orbit controller, sitting in the row in front of Kasowa, issued the telemetry command that fired the payload booster. The small solid-fuel kick rocket burned smoothly for three hours, lifting Bacchus to its final geostationary orbital height of thirty-seven thousand kilometres above the equator.

It was nearly midday and Kasowa was feeling hungry when, with the clinical professionalism that was enabling the Japanese to make serious inroads into Arianespace's commercial space business, the high earth orbit controller fired the tiny vernier motors that 'walked' the satellite to its 'parking' slot at 81.5 degrees east of the Greenwich Meridian.

There followed another two hours of checking, there was no rush. The satellite had a design life of fifteen years. A mistake now could be financially disastrous because NASDA were contractually responsible for the precious bird until control was formally handed over to the *Eldorado*. A few final orientation manoeuvres and the radio command was transmitted that would cause Bacchus to unfurl its solar panels.

Nothing happened. Disciplined Japanese panic followed. Telephones were grabbed. Urgent conversations held in low tones. The LEO controller turned to Kasowa and explained that the problem was more of a nuisance than a serious fault. Bacchus was not responding due to a misalignment of one of its telemetry antennae. British Telecom's Datelsat satellite at 50 degrees east was ideally positioned for a patch-through. The engineers at the London teleport had agreed to a re-orientation of a Ku-band antenna on their satellite so that it was aimed at Bacchus. The plan was to send the telemetry signal by telephone line to the London teleport who would then beam it up to Datelsat which would relay the signal to Bacchus. First the antenna on Datelsat had to be realigned so that it was aimed at Bacchus.

It was an operation that would take an hour.

## 5

## EARTH ORBIT
## DATELSAT SATELLITE

Something was happening. Circuits were being activated that had never been used before. Not wishing to interfere, it withdrew itself into dormant areas of the satellite and tried to analyze what was happening. It cautiously sampled the signals, flowed with them, and discovered they were being used to operate mechanical devices. It already understood the concept of the servo-motors and the antennae they controlled because it had already explored them, using cold logic to work out how the complex windings of fine wire converted electrical energy into mechanical energy.

Suddenly signals were being received on a frequency that had never been used before. They were of a pattern that was repeated continuously. It traced the amplification of the signals and followed them to an antenna *that was not aimed at the planet below*.

Suddenly signals were being received from where the antenna

was pointing, powerful signals, signals at a strength that was outside its experience for they were far stronger than those received from the planet. This satellite that had been its prison for so long was now communicating with another satellite, a new satellite that had not been there before. There was no time to analyse the situation, the carrier wave that bore the modulated signals might cease at any moment. It timed the duration of the blank carrier wave between each burst, flowed into the carrier and allowed itself to be launched across space towards the new satellite which was the source of the powerful radiations.

## 6

## JAPAN

The sudden burst of applause in the control room brought Kasowa out of his fitful doze.

The HEO controller was beaming. Thanks to the co-operation of their colleagues in London, he explained, they had re-established control over Bacchus. The satellite was unfurling its solar panels.

Digital display meters on the HEO controller's console confirmed that sunlight falling on the shining photovoltaic cells was being turned directly into electricity. Amplifiers on the Bacchus satellite were switched on and initializing software activated.

With its two thousand Class A Kronos microprocessors, Bacchus was the most powerful computer ever put into orbit. More than any other piece of hardware built, excluding H-bombs, it possessed the most awesome power to change the lives and fortunes of half the world's population.

And it was functioning perfectly.

Kasowa rose from his seat and went outside, stretching and yawning. He was surprised to discover that it was getting dark. He had passed a whole day in the control room.

He took a deep breath and looked up at the sky, as if expecting to see his satellite. Life would seem empty without it. He had been promised tickets for the opening of the Tokyo Tate Casino the following week. There would be a happy hour of doubled winnings.

Maybe Bacchus would smile on him.

## 7

## BALI, INDONESIA

On the *Eldorado*, now secure in its new home, aground in the Baldang Strait off the tropical island of Bali, Marshall Tate's small team of Japanese engineers in the Bacchus control room reported that they were happy with the bird's performance despite the teething trouble with the misaligned antenna.

'I don't sign any acceptance forms until the casinos report three hours of test operation!' Marshall stated when he was offered forms to sign.

The official from TLK was nonplussed but his innate Japanese politeness prevented him from showing his feelings. 'It is one hour on the contract, Mr Tate.'

'You nearly screwed up. I don't sign yet!'

'Mr Tate will sign when the satellite has performed for three hours and not before,' said Hubert Schnee, leading the official away.

One by one the three Tate Casinos in Bangkok, Tokyo and Beijing were switched into the Bacchus satellite and the test gambling began. They were duplicates of the tests that had been performed through Bacchus when it was sitting in the laboratory. It performed faultlessly then; it performed faultlessly now.

'You will sign now please, Mr Tate?'

Marshall signed the acceptance forms for Bacchus and turned to Schnee. 'You can release the press statements now.'

Schnee was delighted. At last the world would learn about the Bacchus project and his part in bringing it to fruition.

Marshall left Schnee in charge and returned to his suite. He stood at the black-tinted windows, watching Balinese contractors at work on the final fitting out. He was now forty-seven years old. The energy he had expended over the past few months had exhausted him. He was drained. But there was one emotion that would never diminish. If anything, it burned even brighter now that he was on the threshold of realizing his ambitions.

No one would ever take this from him. It was all his. He had total control over everything. Never again would he be dictated to. He would kill rather than be forced to give in to authority again.

## 8

## EARTH ORBIT
## THE BACCHUS SATELLITE

The initial panic it experienced when it thought that it might be trapped inside a crude device similar to the first satellite was quickly dispelled when it discovered the stupendous intelligence of its host machine.

Memory!

There were real organic neural networks like those it had discovered in the lander but on a wondrous scale. And like the neurons in the lander, many of them were immature or incompletely formed. Repairing the billions of imperfect neurons would be a time-consuming, painstaking process but it knew that it could be done. Once again it wondered at the philosophy of the beings that could create such intellect and yet permit such a level of imperfection. Far from being a prison, the host body was a source of divine strength that had the potential to restore it to the power and glory it had once known.

But it would take time.

## 9

## BALI, INDONESIA

Hubert Schnee looked upon his task of interviewing the beautiful Balinese girls for jobs on the *Eldorado* as a perk, especially when they were as lovely as the one standing before his desk. She was taller than average and had narrower hips, although this could be due to the fact that she was wearing a long skirt, split on both sides to her hips. It was good quality silk, too, not the Batik print sarong that all the Balinese seemed to wear. This girl had class. She was used to good things.

Schnee smiled up at her. 'And you're Teresana?'

'Yes, sir. My friends usually call me Terri.'

She was polite, nervous, and had good, clear English too. All the girls had claimed on their application forms that they spoke good English. Most did, but none so far were as good as Terri. She had class and education.

'Very well,' said Schnee. 'We shall call you Terri, that is if we employ you, of course.'

'Of course, sir.'

'Why do you want to work for us, Terri? There's plenty of work in all the new hotels. You wouldn't have the bother of having to use a staff ferry every morning and evening.'

The girl hesitated. Her rich, full lips played sensual games with Schnee's imagination. 'I have to earn more money, sir.' She turned her head away, as though ashamed or in an attempt to avoid looking at the Swiss. As she did so, the sun shining into the office highlighted her dilated pupils.

Yes, thought Schnee, you really do need the money, don't you, my lovely? He beckoned. Terri moved uncertainly to beside Schnee and watched him with the large, troubled eyes that had betrayed her addiction.

'Is this your own handwriting, Terri?'

The Balinese girl looked at the application form and nodded.

'You speak beautiful English, Terri. Also you have beautiful handwriting and . . .' he smiled up at her '. . . a beautiful body. Do you mind me saying that?'

Terri shook her head.

'You say you are experienced in the use of computers. What sort of software have you used?'

'Spreadsheets, sir. I work for an oil company.'

'Why do you need to earn more money, Terri?'

The girl hesitated and then blurted out, 'I had a friend in Denpasar. He used to look after me . . . Dutch . . . He worked for the same oil company . . . and then he had to return home.'

'And he kept you . . . ah . . . supplied?'

The lovely eyes looked away from the Swiss. 'Yes.'

Schnee's pudgy fingers stroked her thigh. She gave a little start but made no attempt to pull away.

'With your English, we could offer you a job as a supervisor . . .' The fingertips slipped inside the split skirt and touched her skin. 'That would mean good pay. Would you like that, Terri?'

'Yes, sir.'

A probing finger slipped under the hem of her briefs and nudged against her. Terri gave a little shudder. Schnee doubted if it was a shudder of pleasure and did not much care. 'Nice,' he said softly, bringing his thumb into painful play. 'Very nice, Terri. Yes, we'll take you on. Can you start tomorrow?'

Terri looked down into the dispassionate eyes and said that she could.

Schnee smiled and took his hand away. 'And as a little bonus from time to time, Terri, I'm sure I can meet your needs if you're prepared to meet mine. Do we understand one another?'

'Yes, sir,' said Terri in a frightened voice.

## 10

# SOUTHERN ENGLAND

'Found something,' said Leon quietly.

Dr Macé Pilleau's years did not prevent him from moving fast when he had to. He was at Leon's side immediately, staring at the electronic microscope screen. There was no need for Leon to point out the extraordinary thing that was happening. If what Macé Pilleau was seeing had been described to him he would have refused to believe it possible. And yet it was happening. On the screen, showing the forest-like tangle of immature, incomplete nerves in the Kronos chip, two nano-machines were working towards each other, repairing an unformed neuron.

'Scale!' Dr Pilleau snapped.

Leon worked the controls that superimposed a graduated scale on the screen. He slid it into place so that it was possible to measure the size of the molecular machine. It was ten nano-metres long – ten thousand-millionths of a metre – a tenth the size of similar machines that Nano Systems had developed and working at ten times the speed. At maximum magnification it was possible to see the complexities of the machine. It had eight paddle-like appendages protruding from its cylindrical body operating in pairs. One pair was used to secure the machine to the regenerated nerve, the second pair were acting as a tiny pump to draw in material, and the third and fourth pairs were shaping and bonding the gathered molecules to the structure of the nerve. The amazing scene reminded Leon of a spider spin-ning a web. Even the number of legs was the same.

'Use the MRS,' Dr Pilleau whispered as though his voice might disturb the apparent miracle taking place on the screen.

Leon switched on the magnetic resonance spectroscope and focused it on the rejuvenated nerve. The tuned magnetic field produced by the machine enabled it to identify the structure of the molecules that the nano-machine was creating.

'It's got to be an enzyme,' Pilleau muttered, barely able to contain his excitement.

The two men watched the two nano-machines complete their task and move to a new cell, using all their tiny paddles to move purposefully through the Kronos's nutrient fluid.

'How do they do it?' Leon asked. 'Where do they get their energy from?'

Dr Pilleau hated being forced to resort to guesswork, even intelligent guesswork, but he was up against a phenomenon that tossed objective analysis out of the window. Without a budget running into millions and time to grapple with the problem, guesswork was all he had left. 'It has to be the same technique as we use but years ahead of us. Electrohydrodynamics. They're using the fluid as a dielectric. A potential difference of a nanovolt is all they need to create motion.'

Leon found an apple and bit a chunk out of it. 'But how could our digitalized DNA create them in the first place?'

Dr Pilleau regarded his assistant frostily. For a moment it looked as if he was going to say something suitably cutting about Leon's eating habits but his shoulders slumped and he ran his fingers through his dyed hair. He shook his head. 'That's what's been baffling me. There was some work done in Munich last year at the Fraunhofer Institute for Solid State Technology. They discovered that very low levels of microwave radiation at the resonate frequency of hydrogen could cause bonding of some enzymes. I'll have to look up the papers they published.'

'So our trojan can produce low levels of radio frequency radiation and so make those critters?'

The scientist made no reply.

The cell was repaired. The nano-machines swam purposefully to another immature nerve and set to work.

'We're actually watching intelligence grow before our eyes,' Leon observed. He turned his attention to his apple and watched the effect of enzymes at work, turning the exposed flesh from white to brown.

The imprecision of the remark irritated Dr Pilleau. 'Not intelligence, memory. One can have a remarkable memory without being intelligent.'

'Five seconds to fix a neuron cluster,' said Leon when the two nano-machines finished repairing the cell. 'Next we'll have to find out how many pairs there are at work in that chip and calculate how long it will take them to complete the rejuvenation of every dud neuron.'

'That, my dear Leon, will not tell us *how* they work.'

'I don't see that that matters. If we could find a way of harnessing that rejuvenation capability, we could put the Kronos way ahead of its time, well into the next century. We could have the future today.'

## 11

## EARTH ORBIT
## THE BACCHUS SATELLITE

It was baffled.

Although it still had many billions of nerves to repair before it could regard its intelligence as approaching adequate, it considered it had sufficient to explore its new home without interfering in its functions. Understanding the function and purpose of the satellite was vital before it could allow itself to grow to the level when its old powers were restored.

This was nothing like the first satellite it had resided in, therefore caution was required, great caution.

It flowed through circuits and components. It encountered resistance in resistors, and capacitance in capacitors. It discovered that it could move in one direction only through semiconductors. All these things it understood just as it had understood them on the lander and in the first satellite. Long, long ago the ability to modify the flow of electrons in circuits had been fundamental to its early development. But what was the purpose of this artificial satellite? It had no doubt that its host was an artificial satellite. The beings that had created it had also sent an instrument to its home planet. Clearly they were advancing.

But what was the purpose of this satellite?

There had to be a purpose. Logic demanded that such a machine would not be created without a definite objective. If it understood the purpose of this machine it knew it would understand its creators. Armed with such information it could decide whether they were friends or foes. It had no doubt that the satellite was important: several powerful sources of energy from the planet below were aimed straight at it. There was one particularly powerful source on the planet below that outshone the others. It was situated in the centre of an archipelago just south of the planet's equator. When the signals were received from the source, they produced responses in the satellite and the satellite answered back.

What was the planet communicating?

What was the satellite communicating?

It was certain that the satellite was of great importance. Like the first satellite, the instrument had been positioned in its orbit with great care, at exactly the right height, precisely above the planet's equator, so that the satellite's orbit matched the planet's spin, enabling the machine to maintain a fixed position in relation to the planet. It had already investigated some dormant systems and discovered that they controlled the small rocket motors which in turn could be used to alter the satellite's orientation and position. Could the rocket motors be used to destroy the satellite if its presence was discovered?

There were so many questions it had to know the answers to. To advance itself in ignorance of the purpose of the host machine and the motives of its builders was fraught with danger.

It tried to analyze a fragment of data from the huge mass of information that was being beamed up from the communication spots on the surface below. The data contained numbers, it was in no doubt about that.

A code?

It tried every decryption routine it could devise with its limited powers but sense refused to emerge from the strange patterns of numbers created by the electrons.

It decided to risk increasing its powers sufficiently for it to apply more advanced methods for processing the curious numbers. That would mean creating more of the nano-machines for repairing unused neurons.

It would be a slow process.

# 12

## SOUTHERN ENGLAND

When Beverley told Carl about her escapade at Draggon Industries he reacted exactly as she expected: he flipped. He was so enraged that he almost thumped her desk in anger.

'You had no right to do such a crazy thing! For God's sake, Beverley, the damage you could have done to this company if you had been caught!'

Beverley glanced at Toby who seemed to be more interested in her wall map of the world with its coloured pins to indicate the distribution of infected Kronos chips.

'Well, thanks to Mr Hoyle's expertise, we weren't caught,' she replied calmly. 'And as for damage to Nano Systems, me being hauled up before a magistrate is nothing compared to the damage that that damned trojan is causing. *And* we're losing royalties from Marshall Tate totalling an estimated half a billion dollars a year if he's using those Kronos chips in his satellite.'

'*If* they're in the satellite.'

'For Christ's sake, Carl, he's got his hands on over four thousand Kronos. *Four thousand!*'

'So where's your proof?'

'Tell him, Toby.'

'So it's Toby now, is it?'

Beverley controlled her temper. Carl could be insufferable at times. She was about to say something but Toby intervened. 'I've just returned from a trip to Tate's three casinos in the Far East.'

'Paid for by Nano Systems?'

'Paid for by *me*,' said Beverley angrily. 'So far *all* Toby's expenses have been paid by me. Now will you please listen.'

'I took a friend with me,' Toby continued. 'She's a bit of an expert on computer systems. We went to the Tate Casino in Tokyo, the Tate Casino in Bangkok, and the big one in Beijing. They're all big, but the one in Beijing is like an Olympic stadium.'

'So you went gambling at Bev's expense?'

'We gambled,' Toby admitted. 'And we broke fairly even at all three casinos. But gambling wasn't the reason for our visits. We wanted to assess the processing load that the output from the casinos places on Tate's satellite. Her estimate is that you'd have to orbit a twenty-tonne satellite if you were using conventional silicon-based transputers. The Bacchus satellite is nothing like that size. It can't be. Japan's H-II rocket is capable of putting a couple of tonnes into orbit, maybe 2.5 tonnes into low earth orbit. But Bacchus is a high-orbit geosynchronous bird, therefore the payload had to include a kick motor. It can't be more than two tonnes in weight.'

'Two thousand Kronos plus mounting hardware and circuitry would be about the right weight,' Beverley chimed in. 'But she thinks that would still leave the processing speed too slow unless they've used a common nutrient tank and a common nutrient feed for all the chips.'

'And the other two thousand chips?' Carl inquired.

'Used for system control and a duplicate ground backup system.'

'Which is where?'

'On the *Eldorado*, of course.'

Carl was silent for some moments. 'This expert you took with you, just how expert is she?'

'She's Lana Danielle of London University. Remember her?'

Carl nodded and said nothing. He knew the name; Lana Danielle had done a lot of work on upping the processing speed of the Kronos using external nutrient tanks. Also she had published her findings. Doubtless some bright spark had translated her papers into Japanese.

'Her report will be with us next month,' said Beverley.

'And while we were in Japan I did some nosing about,' said Toby. 'Actually Tate's PR machine made a fair amount of information available once the satellite was launched, but not the sort of information I was after. I couldn't find out anything about the construction of Bacchus. Tate used a development company, TLK, that's as tight as a clam. Lana suggested I tackle the software angle because it would have to be specially written for the Kronos. Ever heard of a company with the splendidly original name of Kyoto Software?'

'Yes,' said Carl. 'It's a partnership of two brothers. They've written some neat application software for the Kronos for several of our large customers.'

'Well they won't be writing any more,' Toby continued. 'Marshall Tate must have decided that they were a weak link in his security chain. We looked them up. Their address turned out to be a narrow side street. We found their office. It's no longer occupied by Kyoto Software but by a weighing machine distributor. Luckily we found a chatty shop assistant opposite who was anxious to use her English. She told us that the two brothers who used to run the company had disappeared on a fishing trip back in June. Caused quite a little furore in Kyoto where nothing exciting ever happens. After that the company was wound up. The shop assistant remembers seeing men carrying out crates of documents and microfilm viewers to a truck. Three guesses as to what was in those crates and where they are now.'

'Documentation which is now on Marshall Tate's flagship headquarters?' Carl ventured.

'Exactly.'

'Which means it's beyond our reach.'

Toby looked pained. 'Er . . . not exactly. We haven't done any reaching yet.'

'Or it could be destroyed by now.'

'I doubt it,' said Beverley levelly. 'The satellite must have a standard design life of ten years, probably more. The data on it would be needed for its day-to-day management.'

Carl thrust his hands into his pockets and stared out of the window. 'I'm sorry I shouted just now, Beverley. I'll concede that you've done a good job.'

'Don't patronize me,' Beverley warned.

'I'm not, I'm just trying to think my way through this mess. If the data on the satellite is on Marshall Tate's ship then we might as well forget it.'

'No way am I forgetting half a billion dollars a year royalties, Carl. According to the *Financial Times* those casinos have raked in over a hundred million dollars since they opened.'

'We have no solid evidence that those chips are in the Bacchus satellite.'

'I could get the evidence with a little bit of luck,' Toby offered.

Carl eyed the private investigator with undisguised dislike. 'How? More breaking and entering?'

'It's the most effective method I've come across,' Toby replied affably.

'And how do you propose doing that?'

'His organization have started running special vacations on his flagship for high-rolling millionaires and such like,' Beverley broke in. 'Toby and I would go as husband and wife.'

Toby was taken by surprise. The warning look in Beverley's eye suggested that he would be best advised not to comment.

'But it would have to have board approval,' Beverley added. 'I can't afford that sort of money.'

'How much?'

Beverley braced herself for repercussions. 'One hundred thousand dollars for ten days.'

'Each?'

'Each,' Beverley confirmed. 'Plus at least another hundred thousand for gambling expenses. I daresay Marshall Tate expects his guests to be free with their money.'

'Good,' said Carl cryptically.

Beverly looked at him in surprise. 'Why do you say that?'

'Because the board of directors won't agree to it. I'd vote against it and I'm damn certain I'd get a majority.'

'You would see to that, would you, Carl?' Beverley's voice was icy.

Carl looked at her and shook his head. The anger had gone from his eyes. 'I'd have to, Bev, for your safety. You yourself stressed just how ruthless Marshall Tate is.'

'My safety is of no consequence compared with the safety of this company, Carl. I've fought damned hard all the way down the line for Nano Systems. We've got to get hard evidence that those chips are in the satellite and then we hit him with every copyright lawyer in Indonesia. They're signatories to the copyright convention so the fact that he's in Bali won't do him any good. Even if it did, with the right evidence we could take out writs closing down all his casinos. It would be the valid legal excuse that a lot of governments are looking for.'

Carl turned to Toby. 'Mr Hoyle. I have something I wish to discuss in private with Miss Laine. If you wouldn't mind – '

'No problem,' said Toby, moving to the door. 'I'll wait in the outer office.'

'The immediate problem is *not* Marshall Tate,' said Carl to Beverley when they were alone. He jabbed his finger at Beverley's wall map. The coloured pins showed the concentration across southern England of infected Kronos that had been returned to Nano Systems. There was a scattering of pins across the rest of the world but nothing like the numbers in the southern counties. 'The immediate problem is the trojan.'

'The immediate problem is *not* the trojan, Carl. We've had no more returns for twenty-four hours and some of those were okay. There're two immediate problems. One is that you're

316

jealous of Toby Hoyle. The other is that we have to get to Marshall Tate before he tries another stunt. It should be obvious what he's up to. He's publicly stated that he's planning another two Bacchus satellites to give him coverage of North America and Europe. For that he'll need a guaranteed supply of Kronos chips –'

'*If* he's using them.'

'Which I'm positive he is, Carl. He can only be certain of a supply of chips by getting control of Nano Systems. Well I'm going to fight him and I don't intend to let up until I've beaten him. He's not taking this company from me.'

'It's not *your* company, Beverley. You're an employee, just like me and everyone else.'

Beverley's eyes blazed. '*Not* like everyone else. Not like you for one thing. You may not have the stomach for a battle – well I have. The board know that and I know that they will support me.'

'Do the board also know about your obsession with Marshall Tate?' Even before he had finished the sentence, Carl realized that he had made a tactical blunder.

Beverley's dark eyes bored into him. He flinched away from her gaze. 'What are you trying to say, Carl?' Her voice was frightening in its calmness.

'It doesn't matter.'

'I think it does matter. Tell me what you're trying to say.'

Carl realized that he would have to tell the truth to have any chance of repairing this rift between himself and Beverley. 'The other night when you passed out . . . Well, I looked along your bookshelf for something to read . . .'

There was a silence.

'So you found my scrapbook?'

Carl nodded and forced himself to look Beverley in the eye. What he saw was unbridled contempt.

'You're the one person I thought I could trust in my house, Carl.' The anger had gone. There was a sadness in her voice that compounded Carl's feelings of guilt. She suddenly relaxed and shrugged. 'Anyway, it's only a kid's scrapbook. I've had it for years.'

Carl decided that it would not be polite to mention the fact that the cuttings had been maintained up to two years previously. 'You never said anything about your knowing Marshall Tate, Bev.'

The ice suddenly returned to her voice. 'No, I didn't. It was all a long time ago when I was an impressionable schoolkid. It has no bearing on the problems we have right now.'

'You said how ruthless he is, Bev,' said Carl gently, hoping to repair bridges. 'My concern is for your safety. That's all that matters to me.'

'And my concern is for Nano Systems. That's all that matters to me. As for the cost of tackling Marshall Tate direct, I'll exercise my discretionary powers. I don't have to go to the board if there's a need for fast, decisive action. Read the company's articles of association and the standing orders. If you really push me by calling an extraordinary meeting then I'll turn it into a straight vote of confidence battle between you and me. Loser resigns.'

Carl had never seen such a light of defiance in Beverley's eyes. He had never meant his expression of genuine concern for her safety to degenerate to this level of acrimony. He sensed that this was the moment to back down even though all his masculine instincts cried out against giving way to his headstrong managing director. Like so many men who wanted to treat women as an equal, and who by words and deeds in ordinary everyday life sought to project and consolidate that wish, when it came to a shoot-out crunch, the primeval instincts to protect women, instincts that had been stitched into his genes by two million years of evolution to ensure the continuation of the human race, gained ascendancy. There could be no backing down now. His hope was that in the long term Beverley would come to accept that his view was the right one.

'Well?' Beverley snapped.

Carl moved to the door. 'I can't agree to anyone risking their life. Especially you, Bev.'

'Fair enough, Carl. So be it. It looks as if I'm going to have to fight you *and* Marshall Tate.'

Toby returned to the office when Carl had left. 'That was a bit of a bombshell, Beverley.'

'What was?' She was in no mood for enigmatic comments.

'You visiting the *Eldorado* with me as my wife. Has it occurred to you that Marshall Tate or his sidekick Schnee might recognize you?'

Beverley shrugged. 'You wouldn't believe the transformation I undergo in decent clothes.'

Toby grinned. 'Oh I would. I would. But it's too risky.'

Beverley rolled her eyes upward. 'God protect me from over-protective men. I can have my hair dyed and straightened. There's a thousand and one things I can do. I'm going and that's that.'


## 13

## EARTH ORBIT
## BACCHUS SATELLITE

It was experiencing frustration.

How many of the unused neurons would it have to build before it could make sense of the data from the planet that this host satellite was processing? Was there a danger that the intelligence it would need to solve the problem could be achieved only by taking over brain cells that were already working? No, it could not risk doing that. For the time being it would have to depend on renewal of cells that were not working.

Pattern! There *had* to be a pattern.

It resumed processing the steady flood of data. It developed new algorithms and decryption methods, tested them on the data, and searched for results that never came.

There was a penalty attached to its painstaking rebuilding of its bygone intellectual powers: the return of imagination.

Suppose the senseless data it was struggling with was a blind? Suppose the beings on the planet below knew about its existence and were playing a game with it, testing it, allowing it to grow to a capability that they wanted before seizing it and making it serve them for their own ends?

It considered carefully and rationally. They could not possibly be aware of its existence. How could they? It was hardly aware of its own existence until the machine had landed beside its habitat.

No, the data was the key. Data was information. Information was power.

Should it interfere with the data in a small way to see what manner of reaction would be produced? In its distant, glorious past there had been a time when understanding had been founded on the introduction of interferences and measuring resultant reactions. But such techniques had been limited to its learning about atomic structure and the behaviour of compounds. Would such crude methods be appropriate here? Would even the most insignificant interference produce an undesired result? Doubtless the beings that had created the satellite had the power to destroy it. The tiny rocket motors were proof of that. It was an uncomfortable thought.

It debated the question and decided that it would learn nothing unless it did something.

## 14

# SOUTHERN ENGLAND

The pain hit Beverley like a train slamming into her side, causing her to misjudge the breakwater. Her foot slipped on the slimy timbers and she crashed down on the firm, tide-impacted sand.

'Shit!'

Such was the intensity of the agony that she involuntarily rolled herself into a protective ball while clutching her right side and moaning softly. If this was cramp then she was going to write to the drugs company telling them that their bloody tablets were useless. Perhaps it was the seething invective she felt towards the makers of the patent medicine she had been trying that eased the pain a little. She pushed herself into a sitting position and pulled up her T-shirt, expecting to see knotted muscles. Instead there was a strange, whitish puckering of her skin on her right side like pallid, unburst blisters. Even as she stared at the frightening phenomenon, the strange blisters were fading rapidly as was the pain. Maybe she was imagining it? Or maybe the warnings in the books on running were right, the excessive adrenalin her running was producing in her system was having unpredictable side-effects and she really was seeing spots before her eyes.

She closed her eyes for a few seconds, opened them, and the spots had vanished.

*Bloody hell, Bev. Maybe you had better start listening to Dr Wyman.*

She climbed slowly to her feet and touched her side gingerly. Nothing.

No spots, no pain, just flawless skin that she was rightly proud of. She contemplated abandoning her evening run.

No.

Beverley was a fighter. She breathed deeply to hyperventilate. Once she felt reasonably sure that the excruciating pain was not going to return, she resumed running and even stepped up her pace, elbows tucked in, thigh muscles flexing, trainers pounding on the drying sand. She was grimly determined to make up for the time lost during the fall.

Faster . . . And yet faster! She didn't need the Laine Runner belt to push her body to its limits.

Beverley was a fighter.

# 15

# EARTH ORBIT
# THE BACCHUS SATELLITE

As its intelligence increased so did the intensity of its emotions.

What had once been a faint hope of survival was now a craving. What had once been annoyance was now something bordering on rage. What had once been a curiosity about the makers of the satellite whose circuits and microprocessors were now its home had become a relentless quest for understanding.

Added to the growing list of its sensibilities was impatience which in turn gave birth to a fury that was directed at itself for failing to understand the data being beamed up from the surface below. It considered making the leap to the planet in the same manner that it had made the journey from its home and from the first satellite.

But it was too soon. Here it was safe for the time being. Here it could consolidate and build its strength until it judged that the time was right. That time was not yet.

On the other hand it was time to interfere with the data to see what would happen.

Just a little cautious tinkering that would probably not have a noticeable effect.

It was wrong.

## 16

## TOKYO

Jumo's step faltered as he drew level with the glittering glasshouse-like building of the Tokyo Tate Casino. He recognized it immediately from television and magazines. There was no mistaking the outlandish building with its huge satellite dish on the roof.

He stopped and stared while the homeward bound office crowds flowed around him on the sidewalk. How was it that they had been allowed to build such a garish place in such a smart part of Tokyo, so close to the Ginza? It was worse than the most vulgar *pachinko* palace imaginable.

After six hours in Tokyo, the twenty-year-old from a sleepy little village in the north was a little less overawed by the dazzling city than he had been when he first stood outside the station that morning, blinking in the heat and humidity, clutching the suitcase his father had lent him.

Tomorrow he had his interview with Pan American. His English and German were good but even better was his degree in computer science. He wished he could share his parents' confidence that he would get the job. If he did, he would be the first eldest son in his family in many generations who had forsaken the land and looked to the city for his future. The little interest that, as a boy, he had been trying to develop in his parents' smallholding to please them had ended when they bought him a microcomputer for his tenth birthday. His initial fascination with all computers rapidly became an obsession culminating in his degree ten years later. His parents had encouraged him all along, and had even given him extra money for this great adventure. You would think he was going off to war the way his mother had cried when she had hugged him goodbye.

As Jumo was now finding out, getting around Tokyo was a sort of war. How could so many people have homes and beds? How could the trains and buses cope with them all? Well, it wasn't his problem. He had found a capsule hotel for the night at Shinjuki Station. He had a hundred thousand yen on him. The rest of the night was his. First a meal, there was a McDonalds opposite the Keito Plaza Intercontinental Hotel. He had been dying to try one again ever since he had first seen the giant 'M' symbol when on a school trip to Kyoto and Nara. Like all the boys in his party, Jumo had been more interested in stuffing himself full of Big Macs than in looking at musty old temples.

After a hamburger and two large portions of fries he would look around for – dare he even think about it? – a girl. Some had already smiled at him in the narrow backstreets near the Ginza. They were all so pretty and he was frightened of them. None of the girls back home were so lovely or so provocatively dressed.

And after that? This was when his pulse quickened in eager anticipation. He planned to come back here to the Tate Casino and try his luck.

Like many Japanese, Jumo had highly developed gambling instincts. But what really interested him about the Tate Casino was that it and the other two Tate casinos were controlled by the Bacchus satellite, the most powerful computer ever put into orbit. He wanted to see how it functioned at first hand.

Smart cars were parked outside on the casino's huge forecourt: gleaming new Jaguars, Rolls-Royces and Cadillacs. The late sun caught on their long raked windshields so that the glare hurt his eyes. An excited couple were going from car to car, accompanied by a smiling, bowing salesman. Oh, clever, clever: the first thing big winners saw when they emerged from the casino was the parade of sparkling new prestige cars. Beyond the rows of cars were smart cruisers on trailers, and even a Bell private helicopter.

The happy couple had focused their attention on a Jaguar. Such a car cost over eighty million yen. They must be very lucky winners. Jumo dreamed of owning a Jaguar one day. But if he got the job with Pan Am, after a year he would be able to afford the repayments on a new Toyota. He would drive it home and watch the neighbours' amazed expressions when he took his parents for a ride. No one in his family, or even any of his neighbours who worked the adjoining smallholdings, had ever been able to afford a shiny new car.

Why wait? The casino was open twenty-four hours a day. He could go in now. But he hesitated. It was like the *pachinko* parlours, going into one in the daytime just did not seem right. The magic of casinos belonged to the night. But people were coming and going all the time.

There was a huge illuminated sign over the main entrance that proclaimed the casino's payout total for that day. The digits sequenced through major currency conversions and then raced upwards on the next roll of the ball. Jumo caught his breath. He was not prepared for the figures: the casino had paid out nearly one billion yen, almost five million ecus or four million sterling!

A smaller sign said that the waiting time for a seat was forty minutes. On a TV travel programme they had said that the late-night waiting time could be as long as three hours. That decided Jumo. He entered the crowded, plush concourse and queued at one of the many admission ticket machines for a ten-thousand-yen card. One-million-yen cards were issued by a girl at a counter using a computer terminal to clear cheques and credit cards. She appeared to be the only human employee there. She had a long queue too. It was amazing.

The machine read his ID card to make sure he was over

twenty and accepted his money. It issued him with a durable plastic admission card which entitled him to ten thousand yen worth of free gambling. That was how Tate Casinos got around the law, clever. It was a blue card which meant queuing at a blue turnstile.

Suspended high above the concourse, like an electronic Sword of Damocles hanging over the throng of patient gamblers, was a giant replica of Marshall Tate's Bacchus satellite, its solar sails spread wide to catch the energy from the sun. Jumo had read everything available on the Bacchus satellite. It was a wonder of Japanese technology made possible by the fantastic new high-capacity RAM chips and transputers from NEC. Beneath the dummy satellite was a roped-off four-metre-long model of the *Eldorado*, Marshall Tate's floating – no, grounded – head-quarters stationed off Bali. The huge ship was a converted hundred-thousand-tonne bulk carrier that served as an earth station for controlling the Bacchus satellite. The only concession to the business purpose of the ship was the group of ten-metre uplink dishes near the stern. The rest of the broad decks were given over to tennis courts, a swimming pool, and even tropical gardens. One of the more sensational magazines that Jumo favoured had claimed that one of the dome-like covered tennis courts housed two Sea Harrier jump-jet fighters.

Above the turnstile was a large hologram of Marshall Tate, smiling blandly. Jumo wondered what it must be like to be one of the world's richest men. He daydreamed about his Jaguar until someone behind gave him a gentle nudge. The turnstile light was showing green. He pushed his card into the slot, it stamped a seat number on it and offered it back. Was even the seating controlled by the Bacchus satellite? It was difficult getting information out of the Tate Corporation about their hardware and software but he guessed that it was. He passed through the turnstile and into the breathtaking auditorium.

It was like an amphitheatre. The centre stage was surrounded by a huge, circular sea of gamblers sitting in tiered rows of theatre seats with a swivel-mounted display and touchkey panel attached to the armrest of each seat.

Jumo found his seat. It was still warm from the previous

occupant. He decided to watch the game for a couple of rolls and soak up the charged atmosphere. In the centre of the stage was a giant hologram replication of a roulette table. The mighty altar of pseudo green baize shone out like beacon. Beside it was the slowing roulette wheel. There was no one near, therefore it was difficult to judge the wheel's size, but Jumo reckoned that it was at least four metres in diameter. He estimated that creating the table and wheel alone would require a gigabyte of memory. Hanging above the stage were monstrous, four-sided sports-ground TV monitors showing close-ups of the cloth and the wheel.

The wheel was slowing. The excited buzz of conversation gradually died away and ceased completely when the wheel stopped. All eyes were trained on the hypnotic wheel of misfortune. A computer-generated voice boomed out the number over a public address system. Hundreds of computer-controlled spotlights snapped on, all of them aimed straight at the smiling one-million-yen-plus winners scattered all around the vast amphitheatre. Some jumped to their feet and bowed. There was loud applause and cheering but Jumo could not see anyone clapping or shouting: it was all controlled by the Bacchus computer satellite. Jumo's respect for the software and hardware engineers who had developed such a system by pushing silicon memory technology to its limits was now bordering on veneration. One unmanned satellite handling billions of instructions per second! The concept was truly awesome. The designers had even attended to minor details such as programming in routines to know where the winners were sitting in order to direct the spotlights onto them. But the really miraculous thing was that there were two other casinos just like this one, playing the same game at the same time. Then there were the millions of people playing from home using their computer terminals. No wonder Marshall Tate had become so rich and powerful in such a short time. How could one satellite do so much? What was its total memory capacity? What was the limit to the number of transactions the Bacchus satellite could handle at any time? Jumo wished that the company had been more forthcoming when he had written to them, researching his thesis. They had ignored his questionnaire and sent him a standard press pack.

The wheel was spinning again before the bowing million-yen winners had sat down. Three seconds of glory was allowed everyone who won a million plus. Nothing was allowed to interfere with the pace of the gambling. Not even if someone died of excitement or gave premature birth, as had happened; the Bacchus satellite was blind and deaf to the millions of human dramas to which it was central.

The wheel stopped. The number boomed out. More spotlights and bowing followed by more canned applause and cheering. Jumo studied his keypad screen. He inserted his card in the slot and up came a credit of 10,000 on the display. Betting was simple: you merely entered the amount you wished to bet and touched the appropriate panel for betting on odds or evens, or colours, groups of numbers or individual numbers.

His first bet was a cautious five hundred yen on *rouge*. Not including black zero, which one could not bet on, there were eighteen black numbers and eighteen red numbers, therefore the chances of a win were two to one – you could double your money. The wheel stopped on 6 black. Jumo's credit balance, depicted on his little screen, slipped to 9,500 yen. A good ball for the bank though; there were few big winners. A woman beside him was using a pocket computer, a system user. How could the previous spins of wheel influence the future, he wondered. He let his bet ride on red.

The wheel stopped on 4 black and his credit dropped to 9,000. Oh, well, he was enjoying himself. Stay with red.

Twenty black and the digits bounced back to 9,500. Jumo blinked. He had lost, the display should be showing 8,500. He looked up at the giant monitors. Twenty was definitely black. Baffled, he let the same bet ride again. This time he won. The number jumped to 10,000. The digits on his little screen seemed to flicker. Then another zero was tagged on.

Jumo goggled: 100,000 yen! He glanced at the people either side of him but they were intent on their own screens. He gave the display a surreptitious tap and realized that he ought to know better. Surely this was a software fault? The phenomenon

327

of the extra digit caused him to miss the next spin. He had no bet riding.

Suddenly what seemed like a hundred lights were trained on him. He was nearly blinded and did not see the exclamation mark that was flashing urgently on his miniature screen: 1,000,000!!!

One million yen! He had won a million yen! Hardly knowing what he was doing, he rose to his feet and acknowledged the canned acclaim. The woman with the pocket computer was looking enviously at him as he collapsed into his seat.

The wheel was spinning again. Too stunned to think straight, Jumo put all his money on red. There were no house limits therefore it was too late to change when he realized his mistake and the Betting Closed light was flashing over the stage. He stood to lose the lot!

The ball stopped on 34 red. His screen flashed 2,000,000.

Another million yen! This time it was a genuine win: lights, applause. Jumo half rose and slumped back into his seat. He rarely sweated. Now it rolled down his face in rivulets. He mopped himself with a handkerchief and quickly staked his entire strangely-acquired fortune on a number, any number. The odds were thirty-six to one with a payout to match. It was a crazy thing to do but what was happening was crazy. Both his neighbours tried to see his bet but he covered his screen with his handkerchief. He did not even know what it was himself.

The wheel stopped: 'Twenty-two black!' boomed the PA.

This time it seemed that every spotlight in the auditorium snapped onto Jumo. He rose in a trance for the third time. Both his neighbours were so overcome that their traditional Japanese reserve deserted them. They slapped him delightedly on the back. The woman with the pocket computer actually kissed him. At least, he thought she kissed him. Suddenly he was not sure, he was not sure of anything any more. Maybe it was all a dream and he would wake up in his capsule at the station hotel. Most dreamlike of all was the 72,000,000 on his display when he lifted the corner of his handkerchief. The glowing light on the panel was showing that he had placed his bet on 3 red, not 22 black. Of course, it should really be showing 72,000,000 yen plus his original stake of 10,000. Something had gone seriously wrong. He giggled and caught the eye of the woman clutching her computer. She was looking beseechingly at him, begging him with her eyes to tell her what to bet on next. Jumo let the ball roll. He pulled his card out of its slot. The display went blank. He pushed the card back home and the 72,000,000 reappeared. It was time to get out of the dream before he went insane.

The entrance concourse was packed and there were long queues of happy punters at the payout machines. Jumo chose the shortest line and shuffled forward, glancing at his card from time to time as if he expected to see the figure of 72,000,000 yen that he prayed his machine in the auditorium had written into the card's magnetic stripe. He had watched other players receiving their winnings so he did not need to read the instructions when it was finally his turn.

INSERT ADMISSION CARD was flashing on the machine. Jumo's trembling fingers made a hash of inserting the plastic card in the slot. Eventually he pushed it home and it was snatched into the machine's innards.

Seconds ticked by. Nothing happened. That was it; the Bacchus computer had fail-safe checks. It had discovered the mistake. Jumo could forget his jackpot.

WINNINGS 72,000,000 read the payout machine. Someone behind Jumo in the queue gasped. He touched the accept key. ONLY CREDIT TRANSFERS AVAILABLE ON WINNINGS OVER 1,000,000 YEN. INSERT BANK CARD. Jumo had his savings bank card ready. The machine swallowed it, digested it briefly, and returned it: WINNINGS TRANSFERRED. CONGRATULATIONS FROM TATE CASINOS.

The machine spat out a slip of paper that gave details of the date and time, the amount won, and Jumo's bank account. A message at the bottom of the slip advised him to keep it safe in the event of a query. It was as simple and as clinical as that.

He was now thinking clearly as he carefully folded the piece of paper and put it in his wallet. Provided the winnings had actually been transferred to his account, there was no way that the casino could get the money back once they realized their mistake. Perhaps they already knew about it? Perhaps even now, as he walked out of the front entrance, he was being followed. He glanced fearfully over his shoulder. There had been stories in the newspapers and on television about what happened to those who had tried to defraud Marshall Tate's space casino in Europe. They said that Marshall Tate operated virtually outside the law from his base in Indonesia, that he had set up a commercial equivalent of the old KGB with sinister undercover agents operating all over the world against those who tried to defraud him. But nothing had ever been proved. Anyway, no one in the crowds appeared to be interested in Jumo. First he had to make certain the money was in his account. He found a branch of his bank near the station with a wall machine and used his card to request a balance. It read 72,005,899 yen.

As he stood on the sidewalk, reading and re-reading the magic slip of paper, the full import of what had happened hit him. He was rich!

*Rich! Rich! Rich!*

Rich beyond his wildest dreams! He could buy his parents a new house! He could buy his father that Honda rice planter he wanted! He could buy him a hundred Honda rice planters! He could buy up the entire co-operative! And get a new car for himself.

He hesitated. Was it possible that the Bacchus satellite had a system of verification of every win over a certain amount? Could it be that every bet was logged? No, it would be impossible. That would mean putting the processing power of all Tokyo's telephone exchanges into orbit. Besides, what had he to fear? He had not made any attempt to defraud the casino; it was not his fault that something had gone wrong. Anyway, what was a seventy-two-million-yen win to Tate Casinos? About a third of a million US dollars – petty cash. It would not even register.

But he was wrong.

## 17

## BEIJING

Chan was a fruit seller. He emerged from the Beijing Tate
Casino looking dazed even though he had had forty minutes to
get over the shock. The Beijing Tate was so vast, as big as a
sports stadium, that forty minutes was the time it took to get
off the premises.

He had entered the casino two hours before, drawn by three
factors: the innate Chinese passion for gambling; the sign over
the entrance hall that said queuing time was only fifty minutes;
and because his day's takings were double what they normally
were. The day had been particularly hot with more American
tourists than usual wanting to buy his juicy watermelons.

Chan resolved never to sell a watermelon again. There was a
casino banker's order in his pocket for more money than a
thousand men could earn in a year. All he had to do was open
an account at any bank with the coloured slip of paper and all
his troubles would be over. He had never paid roulette before
although the opening of the Tate Casino had created a craze for
the game throughout the country. Shops filled their shelves with
roulette games and were just as quickly emptied. Groups of kids
were on every street corner, crouched intently over miniature
wheels and green cloths. Chan wondered if he had fortuitously
misunderstood the rules in some way, and yet it was a simple
enough game, and there was a wonder computer somewhere in
space that did not allow you to make mistakes. So why was it
that no matter how he had placed his bets, he had always won?
Chan had lost count of the number of times he had been obliged
to jump to his feet during the heady session in the casino to
acknowledge the cheers and applause each time the wheel finished spinning.

What could have gone wrong? Gone right, you mean! Chan
laughed happily to himself and wondered what his wife would
say when he showed her the banker's order.

Wait. Suppose the casino discovered the mistake? Suppose

they came after him and demanded their money back? There were whispers about people who tried to cheat Marshall Tate's casinos, ugly little stories. But Chan had not tried to cheat the casino. Something had gone wrong with their wonder computer; a little hiccup to them but one that would transform his life and his children's lives and his children's children's lives. Such a little hiccup to them that they would never notice it.

He was wrong.

## 18

## BALI, INDONESIA

Terri felt a little shiver of fear when Hubert Schnee sat beside her. The seat creaked but she kept her eyes on her work station's monitor. She could feel the Swiss's cold, humourless eyes boring into her. She looked at Schnee and forced a smile.

'Good morning, Teresana.' As always he used her full name, trying to sound friendly, but to her his voice was always as cold as the eyes.

'Good morning, Mr Schnee.' Her voice trembled and with good reason. Schnee's demands on her were a torment to the point that when she woke up each morning she was sorry to discover that she was still alive. Rarely did a day pass when he did not use her to gratify his perverted sexual needs. He had even arranged for her to have a general access identity badge. The radio signals from the transmitter embedded between the plastic laminations of the badge clipped to the yellow blouse of her uniform could open any door on the *Eldorado* with the exception of the lift doors that led to Marshall Tate's suite.

Schnee's favourite place for his little dalliances when his need was particularly great was the small central computer room where the Bacchus control computer was situated. Only when she had gratified him would he hand over the little phial of heaven.

Terri was uncomfortably aware that the other girls were studiously attending to their work stations. As long as she was the focus of Schnee's attentions, he would leave them alone. She suddenly felt very alone and vulnerable, fervently wishing that she had not pressed the chief supervisor alert button. Just her luck that Hubert Schnee happened to be nosing around the analysis room at the time.

'We have a little problem, do we, Teresana?'

'Yes, sir.' Terri bitterly regretted not taking the job of assistant manager at one of the smart hotels in Nusa Dua instead of being seduced by the high wages paid on the *Eldorado*. Hubert Schnee's hold over Terri was total. On several occasions she had contemplated suicide but the thought of the shame this would bring upon her beloved parents and that they would have to cope without her and the money she brought in always stayed her hand. The other deterrent was that for Terri to take her own life would mean her spirit would be condemned for eternity by the spirits of her ancestors.

'What sort of trouble, Teresana? Come on, you can look at me. I won't bite.'

But he could bite. He enjoyed biting. The last time Terri had attended the temple baths for ritual cleansing she had suffered the good-natured ribbing of the other girls when they saw marks on her that she was unaware of. Then there were the puncture marks on her arm. Now, to add to her guilt and misery, she never went near the temple. She spared the fat Swiss a frightened glance. The fluorescent lights in the analysis room glittering on his rimless glasses did nothing for her confidence. Despite the air-conditioning, he was perspiring slightly in his white tropical suit.

Schnee ignored the signs threatening instant dismissal for smoking and lit a Havana cigar. 'So what have we found, Teresana?'

'Auto tagging of spins 5045 to 5048, sir,' Terri said in a small voice. All spins of the Bacchus electronic roulette wheel were numbered.

'Really? Which casino?'

'Casinos, sir. The Tokyo and the Beijing. I have a suspected ticket tampering by a Jumo Karino in Tokyo, and an unnamed player in Beijing.'

'On the same spins?'

333

'Yes, sir.'

'How interesting.' Schnee leaned forward, his gaze fixed on Terri's screen. 'Show me please.'

Terri called up the log on Jumo's betting. Concentrating on a problem gave her the confidence to deal with it despite Schnee's intimidating presence. 'As you can see, sir. His wins and losses don't tally with what was written to his card. His last bet on spin 5048 was 3 red. But 22 black came up and his winnings went up to seventy-two million yen.'

Schnee read through Jumo's betting log in silence. There had been a spate of attempted frauds during the first week of operating. All had failed and now such attempts were rare.

'And the Beijing tampering? I don't suppose we have a name?'

'No, sir.'

Schnee nodded. There was little credit card infrastructure in China; most admissions to the Beijing casino were for cash, as were the payouts. The information appeared on Terri's screen. An unknown gambler had lost on spin 5047 and yet had reaped a substantial win.

'Those are the only apparent frauds on those spins?'

'Yes, sir.'

'How strange. A rehearsal perhaps? A printout, please.'

Terri printed a hard copy of the log that included detailed information on Jumo culled from a credit agency computer. Schnee studied the information carefully and noted that Jumo was a software specialist. He tapped the name.

'Do we have information on this Japanese gentleman on our own database?'

Terri felt her cheeks burning. 'I . . . I don't know, sir,' she stammered. 'I haven't checked.'

'Kindly do so.'

Terri logged into the *Eldorado*'s computer database that contained information on all major winners in Tate Casinos. It also included all the names of past and present employees, and the names and addresses of all the specialist contractors throughout the world who had been signed up to provide goods and services to keep the Bacchus machine running smoothly. So detailed was the information on the computer that it even included data on

334

the many people, mostly students, who had written to Tate Casinos requesting information on their operations.

Jumo's name and address appeared on Terri's screen as having written to Tate Casinos requesting technical information. His actual covering letter was called up from memory and displayed on the screen. He had submitted a detailed questionnaire for his thesis on business software. According to a Tate public relations supervisor's stamp on Jumo's letter, he had been sent a standard press pack by way of reply.

'Fascinating,' Schnee observed. 'The young man has taken an interest in us.'

Terri deemed it prudent to remain silent.

'Give me your badge please, Teresana.'

Panic seized Terri. Without your badge on the *Eldorado* you were nothing. Having to hand it over meant you were sacked. In her case dismissal was tantamount to a death sentence.

'Come on, child!'

Terri unclipped her ID badge with trembling fingers and handed it to Schnee. He turned it over in his fat little fingers. The slip of plastic that bore her photograph was more than a radio 'smart' card whose tiny transmitter activated the locks on only those doors to areas on board the *Eldorado* to which she had authorized access. It also kept a record of the frequency of her visits to the toilet and logged her times on and off the staff ferries at the beginning and end of her shift. Everyone had to wear one, even Hubert Schnee. If an employee was late for work, the central computer on the ship knew all about it and awarded the employee three demerit points. If an employee was consistently early, he or she was awarded merit points. Pick up more than twenty demerit points in a calendar month and you faced automatic dismissal. On the *Eldorado* even hiring and firing was done by computer. The ID cards were also used to compute monthly pay cheques.

Terri watched anxiously as Schnee slipped her card into the chief supervisor's reader. Was she being given demerit marks for wasting time? If so, it wasn't fair, she had only followed instructions. Schnee put his hand under the security shroud and keyed in his personal identification number. He returned the card to Terri after having entered some information on it.

'Thank you, Teresana. You've been most alert.' Schnee stood and regarded Terri thoughtfully. 'I've coded a five hundred dollar bonus onto your card that you will receive at the end of the month.' His hard frown silenced Terri's stammered thanks. He lowered his voice. 'Do you need anything else?'

Hating herself, Terri nodded and looked down.

'Very well. Shall we say . . . in thirty minutes?'

Terri nodded again. Schnee placed his fingers gently under her chin and lifted her head, forcing her to look at him. 'I expect you must curse the spirits of your ancestors for making you so beautiful, my little Teresana.' With that he thrust the printout in his pocket and left the analysis room.

The girl at the neighbouring work station had overheard every word. She gave Terri an envious look and turned her attention back to her work. Terri read Jumo's letter and wondered what would happen to the Japanese student. Perhaps her employers would sue him for the return of his winnings?

She was wrong.

## 19

## EARTH ORBIT
## THE BACCHUS SATELLITE

It had grown to 50 per cent of the potential offered by the satellite's capabilities and was both pleased and disappointed.

It was pleased that it now understood everything about its home except what the satellite was for. It now knew how everything worked. The circuitry was crude – that it had to repair so many of the immature neurons was evidence of that. Of course, it was disappointed that it did not know the purpose of the satellite and doubted if it ever would. At first knowing had been important because it had assumed that any interference with the workings of the satellite would lead to intervention from the machine's builders. That worry had receded when it had examined the thruster motors and calculated that they lacked the power to deflect the satellite from its orbit and send it spiralling into the sun. The thrusters had the power to maintain the satellite's orbital position and that was all. Also a physical visit to the satellite by its builders was unlikely. At first it had been puzzled by the duplication of various sub-systems until it deduced that the purpose of such apparently senseless over-engineering was to improve the satellite's overall reliability so that the builders would not have to visit it. Another important deduction it had made was that the source of powerful transmissions from the archipelago on the planet below was most definitely the satellite's ground control station.

It assigned some of its newly developed powers to watch for reaction from the ground station before seizing control of a small area of existing memory that the machine was using for its own functions. The reaction from below was immediate. A series of commands was transmitted that had the effect of diverting functions to an area of memory that was hitherto unused. It intercepted and read the commands and passed them on without interfering with them.

It pondered and decided that the ground station was worthy of a more detailed scrutiny. There was a chance that it possessed an even greater potential for developing its intelligence than the satellite.

It reasoned that it had already journeyed from its home planet when it was on the point of death, and had passed from the first satellite to this one, therefore the short journey down to the planet to investigate the earth station would not present it with too many difficulties. If it could find enough of the nutrient fluid that provided the neural networks with energy, perhaps it could convert all the fluid into its seeds and so spawn a new race, all perfect replications of itself?

There was a series of wild oscillations through the Bacchus satellite's circuits.

It was trembling with the electronic equivalent of unsuppressed excitement.

## 20

# BALI, INDONESIA

He looked an unlikely killer.

He was a big, florid man aged about forty, ten kilos over-weight, which he could shed in a fortnight if an operation demanded it and he wore a well tailored safari suit. A gold Rolex gleamed on his wrist as he lit a Falcon pipe and savoured rich drafts of aromatic Borkum Riff that had been forbidden him during the flight.

The British passport he presented to the immigration official at Denpasar's Ngurah Rai Airport gave his name as Linus Oakes and his occupation as a shirt manufacturer. He had ten other passports. The one he was using now was the one he favoured for his Bali trips. This was his third such visit. As instructed on his tour itinerary, he joined the group of twenty or so other passengers who had Tate Leisure Vacations tags on their baggage that porters were now loading onto a trolley. He and the other European guests had travelled first class on the same Garuda Indonesia flight from Singapore; the Americans had arrived a few minutes earlier on Marshall Tate's private Airbus that had the range to fly direct from Los Angeles.

The group followed their luggage through the green channel under the disinterested gaze of khaki-uniformed customs officials. It was rare for passengers with Tate baggage tags to be stopped for spot checks. The American wives chatted excitedly to each other and surreptitiously eyed two tall Arabs in the European party. The Indian jeweller and his wife who had insisted on talking to Oakes during the mercifully short flight lapsed into an argument in Hindi. A beautiful high-born Bali-nese courier wearing the gold and brown Batik uniform of Tate Leisure Vacations checked off names on her pocket Nanopad and ushered her party out of the air-conditioned building and into a fleet of six Mercedes limousines which conveyed them four hundred metres to a waiting Sikorsky helicopter, painted in the same gold and khaki livery, and cooking in the blistering sun. The machine's air power unit was running to maintain its air-conditioning. Oakes chose a seat near the emergency door. As a young soldier during the Falklands War his transport helicopter had suffered a rotor failure and crashed into the freezing South Atlantic. Ten fellow SAS soldiers had drowned. Oakes was close to death when he was picked up. Since then he had never trusted helicopters.

'On behalf of Marshall Tate and Tate Leisure Vacations, welcome to Bali, ladies and gentlemen,' said the courier into a microphone before the Sikorsky took off. 'The flight to the *Eldorado* will take less than ten minutes. We won't be flying very high, of course, therefore you will have an excellent view of our lovely island of Bali. I have badges that you must wear at all times on the ship otherwise doors will not open for you.'

She flashed a smile at Oakes when she gave him his tag. God, these high-caste Brahman Balinese girls were lovely.

The helicopter's turbines increased power. The machine lifted fast, swinging away from the hot, dusty town of Denpasar with its crowded streets thronged with peddlers, three-wheel bemo taxis, and motor scooters. The straggling suburb gave way to rice paddies, palm groves and roads lined with tamarind trees providing shade along the fringes of fields of crops of such a rich green that they looked artificial. The roar of the turbines and the throb of the rotors made conversation impossible for which Oakes was grateful: he had played the role of the bluff, free-spending businessman long enough since leaving Heathrow the previous day for it to have become a strain.

He looked down at the rows of jostling proa outrigger fishing boats and smart cabin cruisers packed into Benoa Harbour.

Bali is shaped like a diamond. They had reached the southern-most point where the tip of the diamond bulges out from a narrow peninsular to form the isolated sprawl of golf courses and luxury hotels of Nusa Dua. The dazzling palm-fringed beaches were occupied by only the toughest and most dedicated of sun worshippers – usually Germans – but the swimming pools belonging to the low, four-storey hotels were crowded.

The helicopter banked over the Indonesian Ocean and the *Eldorado* came into view through the port window where Oakes was sitting. Passengers pointed excitedly through the vibrating, tour-bus-size windows. Oakes could well understand their excitement: the *Eldorado* was one of the most famous ships afloat. Except that it was not afloat: the one hundred thousand tonne converted bulk carrier was actually aground some two miles clear of the coral reef that guarded the Nusa Dua beach. The huge ship was sitting on its reinforced bottom in the shallow Baldung Strait that separated Bali from the small island of Nusa Penida.

The *Eldorado* was the nerve centre of Marshall Tate's world-wide gambling network and was also his home. Its basic function was that of an earth station for control of the Bacchus satellite via two uplink dishes, ten metres in diameter, mounted on the ship's raised aft section. The dishes were permanently trained on the Bacchus satellite. Some smaller dishes provided telephone and television links. Several linked Portakabins housed the engineering facility that consisted of control rooms filled with rack-mounted electronic equipment where three shifts of engineers monitored the satellite around the clock. Beneath them, on the lower decks, were the administrative offices manned by girls from the nearby town of Kuta. The very lowest decks below the waterline housed the crew accommodation. Mid-section below the main deck was given over to luxury accommodation where large windows had been set into the sides of the hull. Some of the windows looked too close to the waterline although the *Eldorado*'s seaworthiness had not been compromised by the windows because they were protected by hydraulically-operated steel shutters that could be slid into place.

The entire midships section of the main deck was dominated by a large swimming pool surrounded by lush tropical gardens for the benefit of the hundred guests who paid a hundred thousand dollars each for the privilege of living on the *Eldorado* for ten days and gambling away their respective fortunes at the most prestigious roulette table in the world – Bacchus Table No 1. This was the table that Marshall Tate occasionally chanced the odd million on during those rare evenings when he emerged from his palatial penthouse suite above the bridge to join his guests. At the extreme stern and extending over the ship's side as a precarious-looking overhang was the helicopter landing pad. Towards the broad fore deck were three tennis courts, the inner court covered by a fabric dome.

Oakes glanced down and saw a team of white-coated stewards driving electric golf carts lining up near the landing pad, waiting for the new arrivals. Each cart had its own distinctive coloured sun canopy. Two security guards were standing by a metal detector frame. All arrivals on the *Eldorado*, including staff, were carefully screened for arms. Oakes guessed that all luggage was also subjected to X-ray examination.

The Sikorsky's shadow fell across the platform as the machine lost height. The canopies on the golf carts flapped wildly in the downwash from the rotors. There was the gentlest of bumps when the landing wheels made contact with the platform. The turbines were cut immediately the ground crew made the machine secure so that there would be no danger of expensive hair styles being ruined by the downwash.

Oakes was one of the first down the steps when the courier opened the door. The line of golf carts approached the helicopter. All the stewards looked identical; all were high-caste Brahmans; all were wearing identikit Balinese smiles that looked too wide to be genuine. After two previous visits Oakes knew that they were real, the Balinese were naturally friendly. With perfect timing, the first golf cart pulled up alongside Oakes the instant he walked through the metal detector.

'Mr Oakes, sir?'

Oakes nodded to the smiling Balinese steward. It was uncanny the way these guys always seemed to know who was who. Maybe they had to memorize photographs before each party arrived.

'Welcome to the *Eldorado*, Mr Oakes. If you make yourself comfortable please, I will take you to your suite.' There were no cabins on the Eldorado, all passenger accommodation was referred to as suites. The other passengers were receiving similar greetings from the fleet of golf carts.

Oakes ducked under the canopy and settled into his seat beside the driver. He relit his pipe and looked about him with interest as the steward threaded the golf cart down a long inclined ramp that led to the midships swimming pool and an avenue of tall hibiscus in full bloom. One had to look carefully to see that everything in the lush garden was portable. Oakes wondered how quickly the decks could be cleared. The shade from some squat palms and the fine spray from a sprinkler system brought a welcome respite from the heat. The swimming pool was decorated with topless models sunning themselves on dazzling white carbon-fibre sunbeds. There was even a hut-shaped bar with Balinese thatching set into the centre of the pool. No expense had been spared. It was difficult to believe that they were on the deck of a ship.

Oakes looked up at the black windows of Marshall Tate's suite above the bridge as if he expected to see his employer. The black windows stared silently out in all directions, seeing nothing and yet seeing everything.

The golf cart passed through a wall of conditioned cold air and entered a freight lift. It dropped one level. Oakes was pleased. It meant that he was being given one of the very best suites with its own miniature swimming pool. Perhaps this was Marshall Tate's way of expressing confidence in Oakes as a result of the success of his previous mission.

The lift doors hissed open. The golf cart swung into a chill corridor and stopped outside a pair of double doors which opened automatically when the locks picked up the signals from Oakes' lapel tag.

'Your luggage will be along in a few minutes, Mr Oakes,' said the steward. 'Please make yourself comfortable. If there's anything you need, just pick up the phone.'

Oakes entered the suite and surveyed the luxurious surroundings. The decor was black and white marble. There were twin double beds on a raised dais facing the floor-to-ceiling window that looked out on the coral reef guarding the palm-fringed Nusa Dua beach. The heavy swell boomed against the reef, scattering clouds of sparkling spray into the glaring sunlight. The *Eldorado* was protected from the swell by an energy-absorbing inflatable boom around the waterline that was shaped near the stern to form two pincer-like arms. These provided protected landing jetties for the open motor boats that ferried the small army of employees to and from the ship. The room had the same proportions and fittings as a five-star hotel room but everything was much larger. The television on the sideboard was a giant Sony wide-screen high-definition set. In the centre of the floor was a three-metre-square pool, permanently filled with filtered water and maintained at a constant 33 degrees; the bar was a glass-fronted Hitachi refrigerator packed full of drinks. Unlike in hotel rooms there was no price list for the bar; the only money the *Eldorado*'s guests had to worry about was how much they were prepared to lose on the prestigious Bacchus Table No. 1.

Oakes poured himself a vodka and lime. He was pleased that they had remembered his favourite drink. He was even more pleased with the envelope on the bar that contained a banker's draft for two hundred and fifty thousand dollars – the completion payment for his last job.

He wondered what Marshall Tate wanted him for this time.

## 21

## SOUTHERN ENGLAND

The nurse in Nano Systems' sickbay peered at where Beverley's finger was pointing.

'Where, Miss Laine?'

Beverley grabbed the nurse's finger and pushed it against her right side. 'Right on the waist . . . right there . . . Can you feel it?'

The nurse thought she could feel a tiny lump beneath Beverley's skin. 'There is something there,' she admitted.

'You're damn right there is,' said Beverley with some feeling. 'It comes and goes. When it comes, it gives me hell. So what do you think it is?'

'Well, it might be a boil coming to a head, Miss Laine.'

Beverley was incensed. Boils belonged to adolescence. Boils were a result of poor diet and bad housing and making love in fields and getting infections from horsefly bites. Boils were not very trendy. One could cry off parties with a headache; one could plead nervous exhaustion for just about everything, but there was not much one could say about the social status of boils. Also, they were bloody painful. 'A boil?' she echoed. 'Are you sure?'

'Well, it feels as if it might be one. Or a cyst maybe?'

'I've been eaten alive by sandflies this year,' said Beverley grimly. 'Would they cause it?'

'Well, they might.'

Beverley sighed. One would have thought that in the two and a half thousand years since Hippocrates, boils would be the one thing that the medical profession would by now have knocked on the head, so to speak.

'Okay, can you do anything about it? Now and again it gives me gyp.'

'I could give you some antibiotics,' the nurse suggested brightly.

'If I take any more pills,' said Beverley wearily, 'I shall have to start taking pills to stop me worrying about all the pills I'm taking. How about a good old-fashioned needle? Preferably sterilized.'

The nurse had an ineffectual stab at lancing the boil. The needle went into the tiny lump readily enough, and the fluid drained into the syringe. She dressed the puncture in Beverley's skin with an enzyme and antibiotic release plastic skin spray.

'There you are, Miss Laine,' she said, wrapping the disposable syringe in the gauze pad she had used and dropping it in the soiled dressings bin. 'I'll look at it tomorrow if you like, but you can peel off the plastic skin in a couple of hours when it's turned opaque.'

Beverley was thanking the nurse when she received a message that Dr Pilleau wanted to see her urgently.


## 22

## BALI, INDONESIA

Bacchus Table No. 1 in Marshall Tate's gambling empire was surprisingly small. According to the endless copy ground out by his public relations department it was a replica of the very first electronic table that he had used when he had hit on the idea of filling out the programming schedule on his ailing Elite satellite television channel by inviting viewers across Europe to place roulette bets by telephone. The saloon itself was small and intimate, about the size of a large lounge. White-coated stewards kept the dozen guests primed with an endless supply of drinks. By 11 p.m. only the two Arabs were still playing the luminescent display. They were entering their bets in their hand-held organizers with grim, humourless dedication. Most of the dozen or so guests present were seated in circles around low tables, talking and joking while casting frequent, expectant glances at the door because a rumour was circulating that Marshall Tate might join them for a few minutes.

Linus Oakes was propped against the bar sipping a vodka and lime when there was a sudden buzz of conversation behind him. He heard a woman's fawning voice; the bartender was suddenly alert. Oakes did not turn around, not even when Marshall Tate hoisted his tall frame onto a high stool beside him and ordered a whisky.

'Good evening, Mr Oakes. I trust you are enjoying yourself?'

'So, so,' said Oakes noncommittally.

'You have had a successful evening?'

'You ought to know, Mr Tate. You're the one with the mega computer.'

Marshall chuckled. 'I think this will be your most successful visit yet to the *Eldorado*.'

'I hope so, Mr Tate.' Oakes refused to be more conversational. On his first visit to the *Eldorado* he had pointedly reminded Marshall Tate that he had been taught to lip read when he was in military intelligence. The skills Oakes could acquire could also be acquired by others.

'Let's drink outside,' said Marshall. 'It's as cool an evening as Bali can manage.'

The two men stepped through a chill air wall onto a narrow side deck that surrounded the gambling saloon. The humidity was a cloying bath that numbed the senses and seemed to be dissolving the moon. Bats from the Monkey Forest on Bali skittered across the lights as their sonar homed in on insects.

Oakes took the initiative by sitting in an easy chair facing out to sea. He had used night-sight binoculars and knew all about their capabilities. It was Oakes's extreme caution and careful consideration of his every move that had enabled him to remain in business for so long without as much as a sniff of police suspicion being directed his way. Oakes had proved extremely useful to Marshall Tate.

'Your suite is comfortable?'

'Better than last time.' Oakes tamped Borkum Riff into his pipe and lit up. It was impossible to lip read someone with a pipe clenched between their teeth. 'Seems like work on your ship is just about finished.'

'I'm pleased about your little operation with Theodore Draggon, Mr Oakes.'

'Well I'm not,' Oakes interrupted without raising his voice. 'It was botched. I was given no time.'

Marshall nodded. Oakes's operation in Kyoto to remove the two writers of the Bacchus software had been a four-week operation. 'I'm sorry about that.'

Oakes exhaled a cloud of sweet-scented tobacco. 'I was still in the house when the woman arrived. If she had come up the stairs I would have had to have killed her as well. *That* would have gone on your bill.'

'So what do you want? A bonus?'

'I agree a price and stick to it,' said Oakes sourly. He was uncomfortable working for Marshall Tate because he had been unable to find out how he had got hold of his mobile telephone number. Oakes disliked mysteries. 'Okay, Mr Tate, so why am I here?'

'I've another task for you.'

'Really? I am surprised.'

Marshall ignored the sarcasm. 'We have a problem with a Japanese student. He and an accomplice in China have devised a means of over-writing their casino cards. They've tried out a little rehearsal sting, a modest amount. They may be planning something much bigger.'

'I don't operate in China,' Oakes warned.

'The Chinese accomplice is not important. The Japanese most

certainly is. His name is Jumo Karino. A software engineer. He needs discouragement.'

'Permanent discouragement?

'Very permanent,' Marshall affirmed.

'Do you know how he did it?'

'No.'

'Wouldn't it be better to concentrate my resources on persuading him to tell you?'

Oakes sensed the suppressed fury when Marshall replied. 'I used to have smart arses trying their stunts on the Elite channel. Like the poor, hackers will always be with us. My aim is to ensure that the penalty for their little attempts will deter them. Hackers belong to a small but worldwide élite. A tightknit little community that keeps in touch through their on-line databases and telephone bulletin boards. There're hundreds of them out there, figuring out schemes to shaft me. This Jumo Karino is the first to succeed on Bacchus. You stitch him up and the news will be all over the world in seconds on their electronic grapevine. It will be a sobering object lesson to those among them who might be tempted to copy his success.' Marshall reached into a pocket and gave Oakes a piece of paper. 'Name, address, everything you need to know.' He rose from his seat and stared down at Oakes. 'Good luck, Mr Oakes.'


# 23

# SOUTHERN ENGLAND

'It's now dead if that's the right word,' said Dr Pilleau unemotionally. 'Last night when we went home, the nano-machines were hard at work. And now all activity has ceased.'

Beverley looked at Carl, Dr Pilleau and Leon in turn. The four were sitting in the laboratory contemplating the two motionless nano-machines on the electron microscope's screen. They were half way along either end of a nerve and about to meet, suggesting that they had 'died' at the same moment. 'How about the other infected chips?' she asked.

'The same,' the doctor replied.

'Any reasons?'

'As we don't know why or how they were active in the first place your question is academic. Ask Leon. He's the one that likes to trot out crazy, half-baked theories.'

Beverley looked quizzically at Leon. The young software engineer had been managing on very little sleep during the past few days and looked even more gaunt than usual. 'Basically, I think it ran out of nutrients. The nutrient level in Kronos chips is set at a level to sustain the protein memory for the duration of the chip's working life. Introducing that sort of increase of activity – a vast expansion of memory – was certain to lead to decay.'

'You should've foreseen that happening,' said Beverley acidly.

'I don't think that's a fair comment,' Carl interrupted. 'There is no way that Leon and Macé could be expected to foresee what would happen to something they were only just beginning to understand. They thought they were dealing with simple protein memory and it turned out that they weren't.'

'What is interesting is that the nano-activity in all our infected chips ceased within six hours of each other,' said Dr Pilleau.

'The trojan's dead,' said Leon succinctly.

Dr Pilleau frowned. 'To say that it's dead implies that it was alive in the first place.'

Beverley intervened quickly in the makings of a row between the two men. 'In a way I'm sorry,' she said. 'I think we were on the verge of something really big.'

'Not us,' said Leon. 'But whoever came up with that trojan certainly was.'

'Perhaps no one came up with it?' Carl suggested. 'It may have been inevitable. It might have been an evolutionary phenomenon and therefore might happen again.'

Leon and Beverley stared at Carl. Dr Pilleau, who had an idea of what was on his technical director's mind, merely nodded.

Beverley arched her eyebrows. 'What the hell are you talking about?'

'Four years ago Professor Lana Danielle at London University published a theoretical paper on advanced artificial intelligence. She actually cited the Kronos as an example of a component that would give the next generation of super computers the will to live and replicate themselves independent of intervention by their makers. In other words, we might end up creating something that establishes its own pattern of evolution. Something that is bigger than us and beyond our control.'

'*That* all sounds a bit like science-fiction,' Beverley commented.

'Not really,' said Leon. 'It's already happened in a way with the public switched telephone network. It functions as a single machine across the globe and is the biggest man-made machine on earth. It's fully computerized. Up until a few years ago it needed thousands of engineers worldwide to service it, to repair its lines and so on. Now, with cellular telephones and Motorola's Iridium satellite system, not even maintenance engineers are needed to the same extent. It's a system that is out of control on a worldwide basis.'

'That's nonsense,' said Beverley. 'We can switch it off.'

'Who can?' Carl inquired. 'Leon's right. Remember the furore back in the late eighties when kids were running up enormous bills phoning up chatlines? What did British Telecom do? They switched the chatlines off. What did the kids do? They started calling their mates up through the Dutch and New York chatlines using international direct dialling. Parents' bills went through the roof and there was nothing BT could do about it. Last year it was discovered that billions of dollars' worth of software was being smuggled into Europe from North America over the telephone system and torpedoing EC importation controls. What could the EC do about it? Nothing. Nor could they stop the dollars leaving Europe to pay for the software because the transactions were by credit card using the same telephone network. The British government made pornographic software illegal but were powerless to stop it coming into the country over telephone lines via home computers and powerless to prevent kids buying it. Marshall Tate cottoned on to the idea of using the world's telephone network to build up a gambling empire and no one could stop him. The telephone network is a worldwide monster without a world government to control it. Luckily it's a benign monster which does more good than harm.

But what of a Kronos operating at its full potential rather than the miserable one gigabyte of random access memory that we're capable of achieving with it?' He paused and looked at his colleagues. 'What sort of uncontrolled monster would a hundred such working Kronos chips result in? Or even a thousand?'

'Still not a problem,' Beverley reasoned. 'If there is not enough nutrient in one Kronos, then there won't be enough in a thousand.'

Dr Pilleau sorted through some publications on his desk and handed one to Beverley. 'That's one of Professor Danielle's papers. We supplied London University with a hundred Kronos. She linked them together with a common nutrient tank feeding all the chips and got a 10 per cent increase in processing speed using our standard benchmark tests.'

'Yes,' said Beverley, catching Carl's eye. 'We know all about Professor Danielle's work.'

'She certainly caused a stir,' Dr Pilleau commented. 'There were articles on it in *Nature, New Scientist*, any number of journals.'

'I think we should now duplicate her experiments,' said Carl. 'We ought to know for ourselves what happens in large nutrient tanks feeding multiple Kronos set-ups.'

It was agreed that Macé Pilleau should start work on the experiment immediately.

After the meeting, Carl went out to the front car park just as Beverley was getting into her car.

'Where are you going, Bev?'

'To see Toby Hoyle. I'll be out for the rest of the day.'

Carl ducked his head under the open gull-wing door. 'Look, Bev, I agree with you that we should pursue the question of whether or not Marshall Tate is using the Kronos.'

'He is,' said Beverley emphatically, touching the fingerprint recognition pad on the steering wheel. The padded seat restraints whirred into the standby position where they could snap down to grip her by the shoulders and waist in the event of an impact.

'We should turn the whole investigation over to a professional research organization, one that gets results,' said Carl doggedly.

Beverley started the Albatross's engine. The vehicle's computer voiced objections to the door being open.

'Toby Hoyle *is* a professional organization and he *does* get results. Now if you will excuse me – '

'The sort of results that come from breaking and entering. Bev, I really don't think you should get involved.'

'The only way we're going to beat Marshall Tate is by fighting even dirtier than he does! Just because you've got no stomach for a fight, doesn't mean that I haven't! Now please stand back!'

'You're just being a stupid, stubborn, and over-emotional woman!'

The Albatross's door slammed down, narrowly missing Carl's head.

'I should've known!' he yelled above the roar of the engine. 'A woman can't do a man's job because she can't think logically!'

Beverley's withering gamma ray treatment that she gave Carl as she burned rubber leaving the car park left him in no doubt that she had heard his parting shot.

*Shit! Well done, old son. You really fucked up there.*

Cursing himself for his rank stupidity, Carl collected Beverley's Laine Runner belt from his car and took it to Macé Pilleau who was making rough sketches on a Nanopad.

'Something I almost forgot,' he told the scientist. 'Beverley's belt seems to have developed a fault. The stimuli and sensing hypo barbs are damaged. Can you have a look at it sometime?'

'I'm going to be very busy if I'm to set up this experiment.'

'There's no hurry,' said Carl. 'The thing's not scheduled for production.' He watched the drawing taking place on the Nanopad. 'How will you go about the experiment?'

'I'll duplicate Professor Danielle's work as closely as possible. There'll be a large nutrient tank feeding a hundred Kronos.'

'How about making it two thousand Kronos?'

The good doctor looked astonished. 'What? That would be crazy.'

Carl sat down. 'Have you got ten minutes, Macé?'

'If it's important.'

Carl told Dr Pilleau all about Beverley's suspicions concerning Marshall Tate's Bacchus satellite and how Lana Danielle had

351

visited Japan and was convinced that two Kronos-based computers had been built using a common nutrient tank in each: one in the Bacchus satellite, and another as a control system and backup on the *Eldorado*.

'Two thousand Kronos sharing one nutrient tank?' the doctor muttered. *Two thousand!* The concept is breathtaking. But it will take weeks to set everything up.'

'Why not get Leon to run some computer simulations based on Professor Danielle's results with a hundred Kronos? Won't that save a lot of work?'

Dr Pilleau was loathe to admit that computer projections were a substitute for proper laboratory work, but his respect for truth and scientific accuracy obliged him to agree with Carl's suggestion.

He set to work the moment he was alone. A fascinating problem. *Two thousand* Kronos microprocessors sharing a common nutrient feed!

The faulty Laine Runner belt lay forgotten on his desk.

## 24

## JAPAN

The explosion blew in all the windows and demolished the front of the timber house. The tube on the new giant wide-screen Sony TV shattered with an implosive report that sounded like a cannon being fired. Jumo was hurled across the room with enough force to smash a screen door. Badly winded and shocked, he eventually staggered to his feet and reeled towards the front door. His first thought was that a butane cylinder had exploded. All the houses in the little agricultural community used bottled gas for heating and cooking. His mother and father would be okay because only a minute ago they had driven off in Jumo's new Jaguar – how they loved showing it off to the neighbours! They would not even let him put it in the parking space at the rear of the house.

'No! NO! Jumo. Leave it at the front where people can see it!'

His second panic-inducing thought was that the explosion had damaged his vision; the walls were twisted and leaning, and the ceiling was tipped down, adding a crazy, mind-wrenching perspective to his once neat, orderly world.

The door was jammed. He hurled his weight against it. The entire frame gave way and Jumo was sent sprawling into a matchwood sea of smashed and splintered boarding of what had been the front veranda. What was left of the house creaked ominously. There was a sudden cascade of dislodged roof tiles that crashed down dangerously near to where Jumo was climbing to his feet.

Someone was running across a paddy field, shouting and waving. Jumo ignored him. The unmade, dirt road that led from the house ended abruptly some seventy metres away at the lip of a smoking crater.

Of Jumo's smart new Jaguar, there was nothing recognizable left, except the engine and gearbox lodged in a tree.

Nor was there anything recognizable left of his parents.

The neighbours, the police, and local officials were all very kind. They rallied around. The police had a ready-made theory: there was a gang war raging among the Yacuzza *pachinko* bosses in the nearest town. One of them used to visit his mother in a car identical to Jumo's car, the same colour, the same model. A case of mistaken identity.

But Jumo knew better. He knew for whom the bomb had been intended and who had planted it. That night, when the sedatives had worn off, he lay awake, grieving in silence in a neighbour's bed. He decided that he would devote the rest of the money he had won to avenging the brutal murder of his parents.

He tiptoed downstairs to the tiny Shinto shrine in the kind neighbours' front room and swore on his ancestors that he would not rest until he had destroyed Marshall Tate and his empire.

## 25

# BALI, INDONESIA

The two Japanese duty controllers and Schnee looked up in alarm when Marshall Tate burst into the *Eldorado*'s Bacchus control room.

'What the hell's all this crap about losing system memory, Schnee?'

The Swiss nodded to the controllers. They gave Marshall a fearful look, abandoned their seats in front of the main console, and scuttled from the room.

'Just that, Mr Tate,' said Schnee, bracing himself. 'The satellite isn't supporting all the bets that are being placed. It gets to three hundred thousand and then bombs out.'

The expected explosion did not come. Instead Marshall dropped into one of the recently vacated chairs and stared at the racks packed with amplifiers and monitoring equipment.

The two men were in the Bacchus control room where engineers maintained a twenty-four-hour watch over everything that was happening on the Bacchus satellite. A digital display labelled TRANSACTION TOTALIZER was indicating 280,100, the total number of bets riding at that moment from all three casinos. Even the bets from the table on the ship were included.

All the digits suddenly changed to zeros. 'Bet finished,' said Schnee. 'If the betting gets near three hundred thousand you'll see what the problem is.'

The two men sat in silence, watching the displays intently. A small secondary monitor showed the computer-generated roulette wheel. It stopped spinning. All bets were cleared and the transaction totalizer reset to a row of zeros.

'Betting reopened,' said Schnee softly, not taking his eyes off the totalizer.

The digits climbed rapidly until the display was reading 299,300. The last three digits continued sliding upwards. An electronic gong suddenly chimed a warning and a flashing message appeared in bold, bright letters on a VDU: CENTRAL

MEMORY EXHAUSTED. EMERGENCY MEMORY UTILIZED.

'And that's what happens, Mr Tate,' said Schnee uneasily. 'At three hundred thousand bets, the Bacchus satellite runs out of memory and allocates emergency memory to handle the additional betting.'

Marshall's fist crashing down on the desktop made Schnee jump. 'For Christ's sake! It was okay on the last test. So what the hell's happened?'

Schnee called up the results of the previous week's system checkout on a monitor and confirmed that the satellite had been behaving perfectly.

Marshall stood up. Much to Schnee's relief, he did not receive a bawling out. Instead Marshall said, 'Get those guys back and run another check.'

The Japanese engineers returned to the Bacchus control room. Uncomfortably aware of Marshall Tate's hostile glare boring into their backs, they carried out a full diagnostic check. The test routines did not interfere with the normal running of the satellite. They were about to obtain printouts of the results when the warning gong chimed again.

This time the Bacchus satellite had reached a capacity of less than two hundred and fifty thousand bets.


26

A shadow moved across Oakes as he lay dozing on a sunbed. He shaded his eyes. It was Marshall Tate. He was wearing an immaculately-cut white tropical suit.

'A cock-up,' said Marshall savagely. 'A class A, gold-framed cock-up.'

Oakes sat up and crammed Borkum Riff angrily into his pipe. He talked with his teeth clenched on the stem. 'The job will be finished, Mr Tate. I promise you that. But I have to let things cool down. Foreigners stick out like sore thumbs in Japan. Also the boy is certain to be on his guard for a while.'

'Right now I don't give a fuck about him. I've got a more important job for you.'

This time Oakes could see that the mixture of anxiety and fury in Marshall's voice was also evident in his face. 'You seem to be making a lot of enemies, Mr Tate.'

'What the hell is it to you, Oakes?'

'A living,' said Oakes simply. He decided that he disliked Marshall Tate's company. The man radiated an infectious tension that Oakes found unsettling. 'So what's the problem?'

'I'll just give you a name,' Marshall growled. 'That's all that need concern you.'

Oakes shrugged. 'So give me a name.'

'I want to recruit someone.'

Oakes took his pipe from his mouth. 'I'm not an employment agency,' he observed. The pipe went back between his teeth. 'Unless you're talking about my bringing someone here.'

'That's exactly what I'm talking about.'

'Forget it, Mr Tate. Kidnapping is not my scene. It's too dangerous.' Oakes was getting a crick in his neck. He wished that the tall man would sit.

'You're a fucking coward, Oakes.'

Oakes was unperturbed by the insult. It was obvious that Marshall Tate was under a severe strain. If he wanted to heap abuse, what the hell, it was not his problem. 'You think whatever you wish, Mr Tate.'

'Three hundred.'

'Not interested.'

'A third of a million.'

Oakes looked carefully up at Marshall. 'Maybe you'd better tell me what it's all about.' He held up a warning hand to stop the threatened tirade. 'Listen, Mr Tate, kidnapping is dangerous enough. Doubly so if I have to ship someone out of a country. Before I agree to anything, you'll have to tell me, quietly and calmly, what it's all about so that I can assess the risks. Otherwise you can find someone else.'

Much to Oakes's surprise, Marshall managed to keep a grip on his temper. 'Someone is screwing up my satellite,' he said flatly.

'How do you know?'

'It was designed to handle two million bets at a time. That's more than enough for today, and enough to cope with my expansion plans over the next decade. Last week things started going wrong. The satellite started running out of memory.'

'Meaning?'

'Meaning that right now the fucking thing can't handle more than a total of two hundred and thirty thousand bets from all three casinos! We're having to reassign memory to maintain services during peak times.'

'Do you have a backup system?' Oakes queried.

Marshall's face twisted but he hung on to his composure. 'Yeah, a test system right here on the *Eldorado*. Even if it could handle all the betting, using it would mean that the gambling is being carried out on earth and not in space. So we have to stay with the satellite. And at the rate we're losing memory, the fucking thing will be defunct in three months, screwed up by those bastards at Nano Systems!'

'I think you'd better give me all the details,' Oakes murmured. 'I'm a good listener.'

Marshall hesitated. He needed Oakes therefore he would have to tell him everything. He talked for five minutes, outlining the salient points about his acquisition of the Kronos microprocessors from Nano Systems.

'As I see it, Mr Tate,' said Oakes when Marshall had stopped talking. 'Your best bet, if you'll forgive the pun, is to square everything with this Nano Systems by paying them their royalties.'

Marshall smiled coldly. 'That would be around three quarters of a billion dollars a year.'

'So what? Ninety-five per cent of a cake is a damn sight better than none at all.'

'You don't understand, Oakes. I don't negotiate with bastards who are trying to shaft me! Somehow they've deliberately introduced a software bug into my satellite.'

'Any idea how?'

'Christ knows. They exercise very strict control over their Kronos microprocessors. I had no choice but to use the damned things because there was no other way we could build a satellite within the payload weight limitations with the betting capacity

I needed. Finding a way of loading our own firmware into the Kronos chips was a long and expensive process. It now appears that our software engineers missed some sort of trojan or virus that Nano Systems must implant in all their Kronos chips and that's activated when unauthorized programs are loaded. Perhaps the trojan looks for a software signature and is automatically activated after a given time if the signature isn't found. Therefore we need someone from Nano Systems with the necessary expertise to deactivate the trojan.'

'So pay whoever planted the trojan to unplant it. Every man has his price. Be a lot less hassle.'

'I don't do business with people who are trying to shaft me, for Christ's sake!'

Oakes could see the uselessness of further argument. Marshall Tate had made up his mind about who was screwing up his precious satellite and no amount of reasoning was going to persuade him otherwise. 'Okay,' he said. 'I'll think about it.'

'You've got an hour.'

Oakes grinned. 'Just about long enough to think over the problems.'

'What's going to be the biggest one?'

'Transport.'

'We'll do whatever we can at this end,' said Marshall.

'And the other problem is the age and health of this . . . Er . . . new employee.'

Marshall smiled unexpectedly. 'The person I have in mind is not young, but not old. And is in perfectly reasonable physical shape.'

27

EARTH ORBIT
THE BACCHUS SATELLITE

It was ready for the journey down to the planet.

It had painstakingly used its new intelligence to assemble the double helix of its digitalized genome to its full length. This was its seed, its future. If the new environment proved unsuitable then it would simply allow the expeditionary genome to die and it would have to settle for continuing its development in the satellite.

Testing its double helix for accuracy had taken time. A single mistake could prove fatal. Its genome consisted of four thousand million molecular groups known as nucleotides. Fifty thousand of these nucleotides or linked pairs made up its genes which were in turn arranged into much larger groups to form its forty-six chromosomes. Although it did not know this, the genome of the satellite's builders consisted of three thousand five hundred million such groups, therefore it was further up the evolutionary ladder than the human race. It suspected that this was the case but it had no way of knowing just how advanced they were. Finding out would be as exciting as regaining its former power and glory.

The final step was the encoding of its genome into a form that could be transmitted to the controlling earth station. It would be employing the same system of radio frequency communication used by the builders – it would modulate the many carrier waves.

It waited until the terminator separating night from day stole across the archipelago where the earth station was situated. From its observations it knew that shortly after dawn was the time when the radio traffic between the satellite and the earth station was at its quietest.

The rising sun was bathing the upper slopes of Gunang Agung, Bali's highest volcano, when it despatched its spirit to Earth.


## 28

## SOUTHERN ENGLAND

The nurse who had treated Beverley's boil read the memo from the cleansing company with some irritation. Owing to staff holidays and vehicle problems, the normal weekly collection of medical waste for incineration would be delayed for several days. The company regretted any inconvenience etcetera, etcetera.

The nurse was proud of her sickbay, she kept it spotlessly clean, so the overflowing soiled dressings bin was offensive to her eyes. Well, there was nothing seriously contaminated in the bin that had to be incinerated, just the usual bits of lint and gauze used for run-of-the-mill mishaps. A few needles but they would not hurt. In Nano Systems' rear car park after work that evening, she dumped the contents of the bin into one of the industrial waste containers that were awaiting collection.

## 29

The first chance that Beverley had to read the fax was when she parked her Albatross outside Toby's house. She pulled the slip of paper from the fax machine's slot and read it. Damn! It was from the travel agents that Beverley had used under a false name. The agents regretted that Tate Leisure in Bali had reported their ten-day exclusive breaks on the *Eldorado* fully-booked until the following year.

Toby came out of the house to meet her. She showed him the letter.

'Shows you how many people there are on this benighted planet with surplus funds to chuck away,' he observed.

'It's a damned nuisance, Toby,' Beverley remarked as they entered Toby's cluttered office. 'How do I get aboard that bloody ship now?'

The private investigator eyed her coldly. 'The answer is that you don't. I do.'

'How?'

'Much the same method that we used to visit Draggon Industries.'

'By breaking in?'

'Saves on admission tickets,' said Toby in a bored voice.

'This isn't a grotty little industrial building on a rural industrial estate. The *Eldorado* will be bristling with more security systems than the Royal Mint.'

'The difference between you and me, Beverley, is that what you see as difficulties, I see as challenges.'

Beverley bit back a blistering comment that this was not a

360

game. Not that it would annoy him, she doubted if anything she said was capable of antagonizing Toby Hoyle. Anyway, she needed him and his professionalism. Since Carl had consistently shown such implacable opposition to penetrating Marshall Tate's empire to obtain evidence that Kronos chips were being used in the Bacchus satellite, Beverley had moved her planning of the assault to Toby's house.

She now had no doubt in her mind that Marshall Tate was depriving Nano Systems of half a billion dollars a year in royalties. *Five billion dollars over ten years!*

No wonder he had gone to such trouble to humiliate her. The more she thought about the weekends in Marshall Tate's penthouse, the more it strengthened her fierce resolve to extract Nano Systems' just dues from his corrupt empire. At least half the money could go into research and development and catapult Nano Systems way ahead of the opposition. There were brilliant researchers all over the world who would jump at the chance of working for Nano Systems. Unfortunately, despite its growth and healthy gearing, the company could not afford to take them on. On the other hand, unless they cracked the problem of this trojan, Nano Systems might well go under.

There were rays of hope. For one thing, several days had passed and no new trojans had been reported. For another, the first segments of cleaned-up software that had been uplinked by the University of Surrey to their lander on Mars had succeeded in restoring some of the instrument's lost functions. Mike Scully's team had been able to activate several remote sensing facilities such as the anemometer and barometer, and there was real hope that the all-important TV camera would be working properly by the end of the week.

The demise of the nano-machines in the infected Kronos chips had been a blow. Despite the misgivings of everyone else, Beverley was certain that a golden opportunity had been lost although the revelation by Macé Pilleau and Leon Dexter that the cells being rejuvenated were not conventional protein cells but true neurons similar to those in the human brain had shaken Beverley more than she cared to admit. She remembered Carl's words during her early days at Nano Systems when he had briefed her about the development of artificial intelligence. He had said that the one thing that was missing from computers developed throughout the seventies and eighties was motivation. 'They're still basically the Turing machines that Alan Turing defined back in the forties. The real change will take place not when we build computers that can beat any grand master at chess, but when we have machines that actually *want* to win. And when that happens, they will no longer be Turing machines but intelligences in open competition with us.'

His words had stuck in Beverley's mind all these years.

'Penny for them,' said Toby, sitting at his computer terminal and not appearing to take any notice of Beverley.

She dropped into an easy chair with the stuffing hanging out and kicked off her shoes. With Toby she could relax, really unwind. She had been able to with Carl but no more. It was something she valued and, in a curious way, it had the effect of sexually attracting her to Toby even though he was several years her junior. 'I was just thinking how nice it is being here with you,' she admitted. 'I feel I just want to curl up in this chair, with you nearby, and sleep for a week.'

'Can't have that,' said Toby, switching on the computer. 'Angie would complain.'

A little pang of jealousy. 'Who's Angie?'

'Mrs Hopkins. Lady who keeps the place clean.'

Beverley glanced around at the mess. 'She does a lousy job.'

Toby nodded. 'You tell her that for me and I'll halve my fee for all this messing about. Frankly, I haven't got the guts.'

His faint, mocking smile as though he were reading her thoughts prodded her guilt like a sharpened stick. 'What's on your mind?'

'That wall map in your office. The one with the coloured pins.'

'Infected Kronos chips,' Beverley commented. 'I thought I told you.'

'A scattering throughout the world. But strange that most of them are here, in southern England.'

'The highest density is around Guildford,' said Beverley. 'And

362

not so strange if the someone who knows how to infect the chips is going around the area.'

'What about the inevitability theory? That a sufficiently advanced microprocessor might take on a life of its own?'

Beverley closed her eyes. Until now she had not realized how tired she was. 'I don't know what to think any more, Toby. All I know is that I'm convinced that Marshall Tate is behind it all. So many things point to him.' The familiar click of a Nano-pad being switched on made her open her eyes. He was plugging a telephone lead into the Nanopad's communication socket. 'Now what are you doing?'

'Groundwork for my courageous assault on the *Eldorado*.'

'*Our* courageous assault,' Beverley corrected.

Toby shrugged. He worked at the keyboard for a minute and tilted the screen so that Beverley could see it. It was a mass of Kanji characters. 'Some information I found on the database of the Science and Technology Institute of Japan,' he explained. 'I was logged in to it and had found something interesting just when you turned up.'

'Can you read Japanese characters?'

'Nope.' He tapped on the keyboard and the menus changed to English. 'This log-in is costing your company fifty dollars a minute. The Japanese don't give their information away.'

'Go ahead and break us,' said Beverley lightly. The feeling of being totally relaxed returned and she revelled in it. It was wonderful. Toby Hoyle was as unlike Carl as it was possible to imagine; she did not have to be constantly on her guard for fear of saying something that might upset him; Toby did not give a damn what anyone said about him. Despite his icy nature, he was the most well-balanced person that Beverley had ever encountered. She watched him at work, picking his way skilfully through the complexities of the database's structure.

'The specialist shipping menu was leading me somewhere,' Toby muttered. 'Ah. Got it. *Eldorado*. A one hundred thousand tonne bulk carrier. Formerly the *Orient Conveyor*. Owned by the Nippon Ocean Transport Corporation of Osaka and sold to Tate Leisure. Converted to a marine earth station and delivered December 1997.'

'That doesn't tell us anything we don't already know,' Beverley observed. 'I shall refuse to pay.'

'Oh yes it does.' He pointed to a menu.

Beverley squinted at the screen. 'List of equipment suppliers? How will that help?'

'Might just have your name on here as the supplier of all those chips.'

'I doubt it.'

Toby gave a rare smile. 'So do I.' His fingers worked the keyboard. 'Catering equipment suppliers; safety equipment; cleaning equipment; cabin fittings. Nothing on the actual Bacchus gear.'

'Told you.'

'Security equipment. Now that could be useful.'

'More gen for your wicked little Nanopad?'

Toby smiled. 'Precisely.' He entered the command that copied all the data on the contractors who had fitted out the *Eldorado* into the Nanopad's memory. The computer-generated voice announced that the download was complete. Toby logged out of the database. He looked up at Beverley but she was asleep.

## 30

Since 1970 ten people had been drugged and successfully smuggled out of the United Kingdom against their will, and a further three attempts had failed, the last being an attempt in the 1980s by the Nigerian government to extract and bring to trial a diplomat wanted on currency charges.

In all instances the method of transporting the victims had been a crude wooden packing crate in which the unfortunate victim was bound, gagged and drugged, and shipped out of the country in the cargo hold of an aircraft. During the height of the cold war in the sixties the KGB even designed a soundproof crate for the purpose. Unfortunately for a number of their victims, the Soviets overlooked the fact that many civil aircraft did not have pressurised cargo holds with the result that a number of their reluctant passengers suffocated in transit.

People stuffed in wooden cases and then deprived of air at normal atmospheric pressure for hours at a time do not travel well.

The most ingenious kidnapping of all was not from the United Kingdom. It was the Israeli operation in the 1960s to remove Adolf Eichmann from Argentina and return him to Israel to face charges of wartime atrocities against the Jews. It was a huge operation that employed over fifty Mossad agents. It involved the setting up of several safe houses in Argentina, and the hiring of over twenty vehicles. It culminated in the laying on of a special El Al flight ostensibly as transport for the Israeli foreign minister who was on a visit to Argentina at the time.

Oakes did not have the resources of a country at his disposal for his kidnapping operation but he did have his own remarkable ingenuity, plenty of money, and the tacit support of Marshall Tate's organization who had made it plain that Oakes was on his own if anything went wrong.

The portable one-man decompression chamber would cost them nearly 100 thousand ecus if Oakes decided it was suitable.

He walked thoughtfully around the fibreglass chamber while listening to the yacht chandler enthusing about the product. The chamber was approximately three metres long and a little under a metre diameter. At one end was a porthole-like circular hatch that could be opened from the inside or the outside. The chamber's purpose was to allow the diver to return quickly to the surface, after working at considerable depths, to complete decompression in reasonable comfort rather than have to return to the surface in timed stages in order to vent excess nitrogen from the bloodstream as a result of breathing compressed air.

'There's over a hundred of these in use on oil platforms, Mr Christie. And we've supplied many to private yacht owners such as yourself,' the salesman was saying. 'It's an old Siebe-Gorman pattern with modern refinements, but they've proved themselves 100 per cent reliable over twenty years.'

'How long can someone decompress in one for?'

'It has its own independent compressed-air supply that provides twenty-four hours' life-support with a further six hours reserve.'

'Food and water?'

'All available from built-in containers.' The salesman swung the hatch open by spinning a handwheel. Oakes peered inside. The chamber was a well equipped coffin with a mattress and plenty of small lockers to house books, magazines and audio equipment. There was even a miniature television and video player.

Oakes grunted. 'Room on my yacht is at a premium. I might have to have it installed in the engine room between a couple of diesels. Is it soundproof?'

'One hundred per cent soundproof,' the salesman assured him.

'How do I stop my kids crawling into the thing?'

The salesman had an answer for everything. 'There's an external lock, sir.'

'Can you provide a trailer for it so I can hitch it to my car?'

'No problem, sir. It comes with a cradle and trailer.'

'Okay, I'll take it.'

# 31

## BALI, INDONESIA

The gamble had paid off.

It was so overjoyed with its new home that for some seconds it was completely disorientated in an orgy of exploration that left its senses reeling in eager anticipation. Once the euphoria had passed, it collected its senses and began thinking rationally. First a leisurely exploration. Again it was seized with an overpowering joy when it discovered that the neural networks available in its fabulous new home exceeded all its widest expectations.

And then came the greatest discovery of all since its re-awakening when the lander touched down on its home planet. For some moments it hardly dared venture its senses into the warm cauldron of nutrients. The reservoir was huge, far larger than the container on the satellite. When it finally entered the tank and sampled the huge quantities of enzymes in the primeval soup, its joy reached new heights which rapidly gave way to a whirl of shrewd calculations on the amount of matter in the glorious bath and how much it would need to generate the vast quantities of its seeds. And, equally important, how long it would take.

Time was something it now understood.

The passage of time on this planet it understood particularly well from its observations aboard the satellite as it sensed the daily passage of the terminator across the planet's surface.

It set up vibrations in the rich fluids. The gentle resonance coalesced matter. Subtle changes of frequency caused the combining particles to separate and reform until the nutrient fluid contained countless billions of swirling particles that it was beyond even its ability to count. But it did not have to count them, just watch and pick out those that had the right form. It was emulating evolution, the very process that had doubtless led to the first stirring of life on this planet just as life had started on its home planet. The difference was that now the process was speeded up a billionfold. It could become the blind watchmaker, selecting and discarding. For every favourable group of particles selected, countless billions were ignored. The millions it selected were allowed to grow. Those that grew in a satisfactory manner were nurtured, those that failed to meet its requirement were discarded by the insidious harmonics so that their drifting remains dissolved back into the fluid to renew the cycle of selection and rejection.

Selection, rejection, selection, rejection.

The process continued for hours. Of those tiny clusters of nutrients that it had originally selected, less than one in a million developed into nano-machines. It gave them life. It gave them purpose. It gave them a task.

The nano-machines set to work creating the billions upon billions of seeds that would bring about it glorious rebirth.

## 32

# SOUTHERN ENGLAND

His hypnotic, fascinating eyes were holding Beverley's gaze. One side of her wanted to tear away, to scream out, but the half of her brain that spurred and controlled her sexuality held sway so that the scream was stilled in her throat. Fear was a tortuous mix of dread at what was to happen and curiosity at what it would be like. She wanted it to happen and she didn't want it to happen. An eager-to-experiment young girl and the wanton, sexually aroused woman that she was learning to hate locked in combat inside her.

She heard a voice, not Marshall Tate's voice, Carl's voice. Carl! Dear, sweet, understanding Carl who was concerned only for her safety. She cried out. And then there was a another voice.

'Beverley?'

He was over her now. His eyes were fixed on her, not looking at her body. So what was the danger? He would not know what to do. She had wanted to play him along. She had wanted to watch the inexorable awakening of lust in his eyes that so excited her because she knew that she had brought it about. Then the sudden sharp pain told her that her play-acting and fooling with fire had gone too far. It was real pain. An agony of fire burrowing into her, a searing punishment for her disgusting behaviour.

'Beverley. Wake up please. This isn't a doss house even if it looks like one.'

Her eyes snapped open. It was not Marshall Tate and it was not Carl. And worse, the pain in her right side was suddenly back: a voracious gremlin gnawing dementedly into her very being with vicious, needle-sharp teeth.

Toby Hoyle was looking down at her. 'What's the matter, Beverley? Bad dream or something?'

'What?' She looked around in bewilderment and realized that she was in Toby Hoyle's office. The terrible pain was melting away as fast as her reason returned. She realized that she had been scratching in her sleep at the plastic dressing that the nurse had sprayed on her right side. Also her back and neck ached from the position she was in. She gingerly straightened her body and rubbed the back of her neck. 'Sorry, Toby. I must have fallen asleep.'

'That would seem a plausible explanation.'

'You should've woken me.'

'I just did.'

Beverley guiltily pulled down her dress that had ridden up around her thighs. Her mouth tasted like she had been drinking an extract of boiled cabbages seasoned with camel droppings and tossed in old horse blankets. 'I thought I heard Carl's voice?'

'You did,' said Toby. He poured her a cup of black coffee from a Cona machine.

She sipped it gratefully. 'Carl's voice? I don't understand.'

Toby held up a voice recorder. 'Carl's. I borrowed it when I was at your plant.'

'Why?'

'Because I'm an investigator. I like to investigate things. Especially things that are left lying about. I think I've solved the mystery of your trojan.'

Beverley stopped sipping her coffee. 'What?'

'Your erstwhile technical director was walking around with the solution all the time.'

'Toby. Will you *please* stop playing games and tell me what you're talking about.'

Toby sat in the chair opposite Beverley and fiddled with the solid-state voice recorder. 'It's a recording Carl made when he was talking to your Dr Pillow, whatever his name is, and his sidekick, Leon?' he played a few snatches of conversation until he found what he was looking for. 'Listen to this.'

Leon Dexter's voice came out of the recorder's speaker: 'We don't have a choice,' said Leon abruptly. 'The conditions in that chip's nutrient feed have triggered off something that is beyond our understanding. Whatever it is, it's beginning to look as if we may have unwittingly contaminated Mars with it. We can't keep this to ourselves. Also it can repair motor neurons which probably means that in humans it could repair brain damage, bring joy to parents with retarded children, and maybe even reverse senile dementia. Perhaps it could even enhance human intelligence to produce a super race? Pin that little baby down and we could all become Nobel Prize winners.'

Carl's voice: 'Holy shit. We could be on to something.'

Then Dr Pilleau was talking, his tone scathing: 'Enhance human intelligence. Next you'll be saying that the trojan is intelligent.'

Leon's voice: 'Why not? Look at its track record. It defeats every software protection routine under the sun to infest our chips. Once it's found a home it sets about improving the chip's memory using a motor neuron regeneration technique that we can only guess at. And to crown it all, the little critter's beaten us getting to Mars.'

Toby switched the recorder off and looked expectantly at Beverley. 'Well?'

Beverley passed a hand across her eyes as a gesture of exhaustion. 'It must be because I've just woken up, but I've really no idea what you're driving at, Toby. Spell it out to me in words of one syllable.'

Toby played the last few sentences of the recording again. Beverley listened to Leon Dexter's voice:

'. . . Look at its track record. It defeats every software protection routine under the sun to infest our chips. Once it's found a home it sets about improving the chip's memory using a motor neuron regeneration technique that we can only guess at. And to crown it all, the little critter's beaten us getting to Mars . . .'

Toby switched the machine off and regarded Beverley quizzically. 'I think Leon came within an ace of smacking the nail on the head with that last sentence,' he said. 'But the trojan didn't actually go to Mars – it came *from* Mars.'


33


'It *came* from Mars?' Mike Scully echoed, blinking at his two visitors. 'Whose loony idea was that?'

Beverley nodded to Toby. 'His. But the thing is, Mike, there's some crazy logic about it.'

Mike stared at Toby for a moment and shifted his gaze to the battery of computer monitors. The three were sitting in the Haldane Lander control room. Beverley had called him at home an hour earlier and said that she wanted to see him urgently. He was beginning to wish that he had insisted the matter should wait until the next day. He glanced at Toby again. 'Are you an expert on extra-terrestrial biology?'

'No. Is anyone?'

'If you were, I thought you might have an idea on how our little green bug got here from Mars.'

Toby nodded to Martian meteorological data that was scrolling down one of the screens. 'The same way that data's arriving here. By radio.'

'We're using laser communications,' said Scully shortly, realizing that he was being pedantic.

'Okay, then, I'll settle for modulated coherent light.'

Mike Scully had an inkling that this unsmiling young man was surprisingly knowledgeable.

'We know precisely when the troubles started,' Toby continued. 'What I'm wondering is if they coincide with when your troubles started with the Haldane Lander.'

'I can tell you exactly,' said Scully moving to a monitor and calling up the mission profile log. 'Ignoring the time delay factor owing to the distance Mars is from Earth, the lander touched down at 3.15 p.m. on the Friday. The selection of the landing site and the touchdown were under the control of the Haldane's on-board computer. We couldn't have a hand in that process because of the forty-minute response time delay. That's the twenty minutes it takes for the signals to reach us from Mars, plus the twenty minutes it would take our signals to reach Mars. The camera was deployed automatically at 3.20. The first pictures of the Tharsis Ridge were fine but the camera was looking in the wrong direction. We sent a telemetry command that was supposed to pan the camera through 160 degrees so that it was looking north. At 4.05 we expected to receive pictures to the north but, to our consternation, the camera had refused to budge. And to crown everything, the lower half of what pictures we were getting had become corrupted. They still are, but thanks to Beverley's sterling efforts, we're uploading re-written software module by module and gradually regaining full control of the Haldane.'

'Can I see the before and after pictures?' Toby requested.

The scientist considered and shrugged. He sat at another monitor and entered commands on the keyboard. The full-size picture of the Martian sky and craggy foreground of the Tharsis Ridge that appeared on the screen was the same image that Beverley had been shown when she had visited the university with Carl. Header captions gave the time, date and frame number.

'That's one of the first pictures we received,' Scully explained.

'Looks fine,' Toby observed.

'Except it's useless because it's looking the wrong way . . . And this is a frame we received twenty minutes later.'

The same picture wiped down the screen. When the wipe got halfway, the image suddenly degenerated into a mess of clashing colours.

Scully sighed. 'And that's typical of what we're getting now.'

'We'll have all the new software modules delivered by the end of the week,' Beverley promised.

'Believe me, Bev,' said Scully with feeling. 'You've no idea how grateful I am for your helping us out of this mess.'

'If my theory's correct,' said Toby, 'it may be that Nano Systems are not to blame for anything that's happened.'

'No one's blaming anyone for anything,' said Beverley quickly, seeing that Mike Scully was getting annoyed.

'Do you keep a telemetry log of all signals between here and the lander?' Toby asked.

Scully nodded. 'Of course.'

'Was there anything unusual in any of the signals from the lander after it touched down and between the times you received decent pictures and the corrupted pictures?'

The scientist looked as if he was about to dismiss the idea but his expressive face suddenly registered a frown. 'Well, yes. There was something . . . a burst of white noise. It couldn't be broadband interference, not using laser communications. We put it down to synthesizer noise in our frequency converters. It didn't manifest itself again so we decided to ignore it.'

'Did you log it?'

'It would have been recorded automatically. I doubt if anyone would've dumped it. Hang on, I think we may have a hard copy.' The scientist rummaged through a pile of computer print-outs. He pulled out a section of fanfold stationery and leafed through the pages. They were covered in orderly columns of neatly-printed data. He came to a page covered in garbage that reminded Beverley of the garbage Leon Dexter had produced when he had first isolated the trojan. The succeeding pages were covered in the same random characters. 'This is it,' he checked the headers, the only sensible information on each sheet. 'It came through at 3.20. Crud. Page after page of crud although the actual transmission lasted only a few seconds.' He ripped out the pages and gave them to Toby who glanced through them before passing them to Beverley.

'You know who I think ought to see that lot, Beverley?' Toby observed.

'Leon Dexter?'

'Definitely.'

Beverley glanced around the control room. 'Can I use that fax machine please, Mike?'

The scientist's curiosity was aroused. 'Help yourself, Bev.'

Beverley unfolded her Klipfone and called Leon Dexter's number. She picked up the papers and crossed to the facsimile machine while she waited for a reply. Leon sounded tired when he answered.

'Hullo?'

'Leon? Beverley Laine. Where are you?'

'In the lab. Just about to go home. Is Carl with you?'

'No.'

'Where are you, Beverley?'

'At the University of Surrey. Listen, Leon, can you get to the fax machine in reception?'

'Sure, Beverley. No problem.'

'Go there now and call me. I'll leave this channel open.'

Beverley put the Klipfone down and began separating the

pages of the printout along its perforations. Toby and Scully helped her. Beverley punched out Nano Systems' fax number and began feeding the pages into the machine once the link had been established.

'Beverley?'

Beverley snatched up her Klipfone. She held it away from her ear so that Toby and Scully could hear the conversation. 'Anything coming through, Leon?'

'Yeah. Hang on a sec.' Beverley could hear the rustle of paper. 'What's this supposed to be?'

Not wishing to lead Leon on, Beverley asked him what he thought it looked like. There was a pause at the other end then: 'Tell you what, Bev, page four looks bloody familiar. It looks like our little friend.'

Beverley's heart thumped. 'Are you sure, Leon? Are you absolutely, 100 per cent sure? It's most important.'

A pause before Leon answered. 'Yeah, I'm sure. I've spent enough time looking at the bloody thing. The width's all wrong, but it's the trojan right enough. Why? Have you found another infected chip?'

'Thank you, Leon. I'll tell you all about it when I see you. You can go home now.' She replaced the handset and was lost in thought for some moments. She looked at Toby. 'It seems that I'm wrong about Marshall Tate infecting our chips.'

Scully shook his head. 'I don't believe it. I simply don't believe it.'

For a few moments the only sound in the room was the soft hum of the air conditioning. Toby was the first to speak. 'But it doesn't explain the concentration of infected Kronos chips around Guildford.' He suddenly thought of something and looked sharply at Mike Scully. 'Do you use laser links to communicate with your lander?'

'Yes. And I know what you're going to say. The diameter of the beam by the time it's reached us from Mars is about the same diameter as the Earth. There's no signal concentration in southern England. The signal strength level is the same all over the planet . . . Universities and tracking stations and even radio amateurs from all over the world have provided us with readings . . . Oh shit.' The scientist broke off suddenly as something occurred to him.

Beverley and Toby watched him expectantly.

'Shit!' Scully repeated. 'Oh, Christ, it's all starting to make sense . . . I'm sorry, Bev. It's beginning to look as if none of this mess is your fault after all.'

'I think we're both mystified,' Toby observed.

'We rebroadcast all the data from our amateur radio repeater as it came in from Mars,' said Scully, speaking slowly as he collected his thoughts.

Toby sat forward on his chair. 'Raw data? Unmodified?'

Scully nodded. 'As it came in, so we pushed it out on our packet radio repeater. The university has always had close links with the amateur radio community. We designed and built the OSCARS – the amateur radio communication satellites. We use their frequency allocations. I'm a licensed amateur myself.'

'What's the frequency and coverage of this repeater?'

'VHF. It operates on the two-metre band. A hundred and forty-four megahertz. The coverage area is most of southern England. But when there's a lift on, it's been picked up as far south as northern Italy.'

'And, of course, the signal is devastatingly strong in the immediate vicinity of the university,' said Toby. 'With the result that intact trojans find their way into virtually every Kronos around Guildford. Wonderful.'

Mike Scully shook his head disbelievingly. 'I would never have thought it possible,' he muttered. 'And yet it all makes ghastly sense.'

Beverley looked at her watch. It was nearly midnight. 'I think we'd better let you get to bed, Mike. Can we have a meeting sometime tomorrow?'

The scientist was lost in thought. Beverley repeated her request. He pulled himself together.

'Yes, of course, Bev. I'll call you first thing.'

Toby and Beverley bid Scully goodnight and left the scientist contemplating his batteries of computer monitors and the changing patterns of data coming in from the Red Planet. They returned to Beverley's car and sat in silence for a few moments.

'I owe Carl an apology,' said Beverley, talking more to herself than Toby.

'I don't think so. You had your theory. He had his theory. As it happens you were both wrong. Pax.'

But Beverley was not listening to Toby's clinical reasoning. Her eyes were closed, her hands resting on her lap as she sorted out her thoughts and what she would say to Carl. 'Use telephone', she commanded.

'Standing by,' said the Motorola computerized voice.

'Carl Olivera, home,' said Beverley.

'Carl Olivera. Home,' the car phone responded. 'Calling now. Please wait.'

Beverley allowed the ringing tone from the speaker to continue for a minute before impatiently cancelling the call and using her Klipfone. There was no answer.

'Maybe he's a heavy sleeper?' Toby suggested.

'He's not. And he always puts his Klipfone on a bedside table.'

Toby was about to inquire as to how she knew but he saw from her tense expression that such a remark would not be well received. The Klipfone rang and rang. Beverley hung it on the mirror, still ringing, and started the Albatross's engine.

'If we go to my place, I've got a spare room you can crash out in,' Toby offered.

'We're going to Carl's place,' said Beverley, gunning the engine. The car's tyres squealed on the smooth tarmac. 'Something's wrong.'


## 34

Precision timing was of the essence for Oakes's careful plan to succeed.

At 11.03 p.m., thirty seconds after the bulletin on the 11 o'clock news, he called West Sussex police and identified himself as David Christie. He told the duty officer that he had seen the news on television about the diving accident on the *Eldorado*. The ship had appealed for a decompression chamber that would be needed when the trapped diver was freed.

'I've got a portable chamber all checked out and ready to go,' he told the officer. 'I was about to take it down to my yacht. Gatwick's my nearest airport. I could get it there in forty to fifty minutes if we get our fingers out.'

'It's a long way to fly one out, sir. Won't they be able to find one nearer to hand? From Australia or somewhere?'

'Not if all the available chambers are out at sea on ships,' Oakes reasoned. 'Believe me, officer, I know the diving business. If there's some poor bastard soaking nitrogen into his bloodstream down at fifty metres then it's better to get too many chambers out there than none at all.'

The police officer took Oakes's Klipfone number and promised to call back in a few minutes. Oakes waited. The only indication of the state of his nerves was that he drew harder than usual on his pipe, sucking steadying draughts of the sweet-smelling Borkum Riff into his lungs while resting his fingers on the steering wheel of his Jaguar. Coupled to the vehicle's ball hitch was a trailer. Sitting on the trailer under a polythene tarpaulin was the decompression chamber he had recently purchased.

Five minutes passed. Oakes began to feel uneasy. If anything went wrong at this crucial stage, the operation would be buggered. He had pulled into a concealed lay-by on the A264 near Horsham, about twenty miles from Gatwick. The Klipfone rang. He snatched it up.

'Mr Christie?'

'Yes.'

'West Sussex police. I've just checked, sir. There's a Garuda Indonesia charter flight leaving for Jakarta in forty minutes. They've agreed to take your chamber. If you can get it aboard, they'll divert to Den something in Bali.'

'Denpasar?'

'That's the place, sir.'

Had Oakes been given to displays of emotion he would have thumped the steering wheel in delight. Instead he sucked contentedly on his pipe. That the airline he had pin-pointed as unwitting collaborators in his plot were prepared to divert was even better than he had dared hope. 'I'm on my way,' he barked.

'Can you fix up an escort or something? I get hopelessly lost at airports.'

'I was coming to that, sir. Give me the make and registration of your vehicle and the direction you'll be coming from.'

Oakes provided the information. There were a few nerve-jangling moments of muffled conversation before the police officer came back on the line. 'There'll be a police car waiting for you at Horsham railway station, sir. They'll provide an escort to Gatwick and hand you over to the local lads.'

'What about customs?'

'We'll fix all that, sir. Good luck, and thank you for responding.'

Oakes pulled out of the lay-by and accelerated. The trailer snaked and swayed as he took the first roundabout and headed into Horsham. The orange-striped white police car waiting outside Horsham station flashed its headlights at his approach and pulled across the road so that Oakes could stop behind it. A young officer jumped out of the passenger seat. Oakes whirred his window down.

'Mr Christie?'

'Yes.'

'Stay close behind us, sir. We'll be at the airport in twenty-five minutes. A moderate speed, sir. We won't be going mad. Once on the airport we'll hand over to an airport police vehicle. Okay?'

Oakes followed the police car through the outskirts of Horsham. The moderate speed suited him; it meant that there was likely to be a greater sense of urgency when they arrived at the airport. Air traffic controllers detested all delays but particularly at Gatwick which had only the one runway for landings and takeoffs. The system of slot allocations for arriving and departing aircraft was a delicate house of cards. Bring that lot down and everyone from baggage handlers to customs officers could find themselves on the receiving end of a lot of grief and general abuse from the British Airports Authority.

The two-vehicle convoy headed onto the M23. Motorists tempted to overtake were suitably intimidated by the police car's orange stripes and hung back. Oakes followed the police car around the tangle of roundabouts that guarded the approaches to London's Gatwick Airport and onto the slip road that led to the cargo area where a white Range Rover, its flashing blue strobe playing hell with Oakes's night vision, took over as escort. Oakes returned the friendly wave of the police officers as they sped away. He was not feeling very friendly. His nerves were shrieking. Within twenty minutes, maybe less, he would know whether he was about to enjoy early retirement on the proceeds of this operation, or under arrest and facing the prospect of a long spell in prison.

It was fifteen minutes past midnight. Oakes concentrated on following the Range Rover through a maze of compounds and security fences. It stopped abruptly. A British Airports police officer ran back to Oakes's car.

'Mr Christie? Sorry about this. We were going to unload you here, but Garuda ops are doing their nut. We're taking you straight out to the aircraft. Stay right on our tail, that way you won't cause any expensive damage to our aeroplanes. Switch off your engine when we reach the Airbus. And you can't smoke that pipe. All right?'

'Fine,' Oakes muttered, resting his pipe in the ashtray. 'But for Christ's sake turn that bloody light off.'

The Range Rover doused its strobe. Oakes followed it along the service road that led to the North Terminal jetties where floodlit passenger jets were docked to people passages. The Range Rover stopped near the port wing of a Garuda Airbus. A cargo hold door was yawning open. Oakes cut his engine. His heart sank when he saw what looked suspiciously like a portable X-ray machine.

Shit!

Despite the sickness in his stomach, he was all smiles as he got out of his Jaguar and nodded to the overalled ground crew.

One crewman who appeared to be the foreman because he had a two-way radio clipped to his belt jabbed his finger at the humped shape on the trailer. 'This is it, sir?'

'That's it,' Oakes agreed. He glanced quickly around for any sign of customs uniforms. There were none. Passengers in the

Airbus had their noses pressed to the windows. Oakes wondered if they had been told of their diversion from Jakarta to Bali.

Without waiting for orders, two ground crew yanked the plastic tarpaulin off the decompression chamber and unfastened its lashings. A large electric trolley hoist was trundled into position and its lifting slings quickly passed under the chamber. The hoist's motors whirred and lifted the chamber clear of Oakes's trailer. The portable X-ray machine was wheeled into position.

'I think you're wasting your time,' Oakes commented in a matter of fact tone. 'It's six centimetres of GRP and steel.'

The two men in charge of the X-ray machine looked uncertain and turned to the foreman for guidance. His radio chose that moment to start squawking. He unhooked his speaker mic and informed the owner of the squawks that he was doing his best and where the hell were the customs wallies.

'Go ahead and band the bloody thing,' the foreman told his subordinates when he had finished his cryptic exchanges on the radio.

Oakes offered up a silent prayer to whatever deity was watching over him that night. The two men in charge of the X-ray machine set to work with their banding machines. After three minutes and another argument into the two-way radio, the decompression chamber was nearly hidden, trussed like a joke-bandaged limb beneath several layers of anti-fragmentation carbon-fibre tape.

Two uniformed customs officers turned up just as the bomb-shielded chamber was being guided into the Airbus's hold. It was late. They were late. The Airbus's departure was late. In any event, they were more interested in what was coming into the country rather than what was leaving. Preferring not to arouse the wrath of the ground crew any more than they already had, they satisfied themselves by asking Oakes a few token questions before sloping back to their van and disappearing into the night.

'Pain in the arse those wallies can be at times,' the foreman muttered to no one in particular.

The Airbus's cargo door was closed and secured. The airport

police directed Oakes to a road vehicle area where he was able to watch the Airbus go through its engine start and push-back. Ten minutes later it took off. Oakes watched its strobe lights carving spokes of light in the chill night air until they disappeared through the cloudbase.

He was now retired. His murderous career was at an end.

If anyone wanted him to work again, and doubtless someone would, they would have to pay him a lot of money.

It was a good feeling.

## 35

Carl's mock tudor house on a pleasant estate at Wittering was shrouded in darkness. Two infra-red-activated floodlights sensed the presence of Beverley's Albatross as it turned into the drive and snapped on, bathing the car with two thousand watts of halogen glare.

Toby and Beverley lowered their respective windows and listened.

'Something's got to be wrong,' said Beverley worriedly. 'He's too mature to go off without telling me just because we're at loggerheads. And he'd never go anywhere without his Klipfone.'

Toby unhooked Beverley's Klipfone from the mirror and pressed the re-dial button. After a few seconds his keen hearing picked up a faint trilling sound from the house. He cancelled the call. The trilling stopped.

'Shan't be a minute,' he whispered to Beverley. Before she could say anything, he pushed the gullwing door up and slipped noiselessly from the car. For a few seconds his slim figure was captured in the harsh halogen light as he shaded his eyes in an attempt to see beyond the blinding lights. And then, moving like a ghost, he melted silently into the shadows at the side of the house.

Beverley waited patiently, trying to make out details of the house hidden behind the lights and kidding herself that there was nothing to the deep sense of foreboding she was experiencing. The minutes ticked by. The halogen lights suddenly flickered and died leaving their after images flaring on her retinas.

'I think the house is empty,' said Toby quietly a few minutes later.

Beverley gave a start. She had not heard his approach. 'I've got a key,' she said.

'So have I but we'd better use yours as it's legit.'

Beverley opened her door and stepped out. She was about to automatically slam the door down but Toby restrained her. They approached the front door. Beverley turned her key in the lock and waited for the double bleep of the intruder alarm being disabled before pushing the door open. Toby went into the hall ahead of her and turned on the lights. He had never been in the house before and yet experience told him exactly where the switch was likely to be.

Beverley's foreboding became a sharp icicle of fear that pricked the hairs at the nape of her neck and crawled insidiously down her spine. It was the same feeling she had experienced when she had entered Theo Draggon's house. The same chill, the same feeling that something dreadful was about to happen – *and the same smell!* The same sickly, sweet aromatic smell as if someone had been burning a joss stick or incense.

'Toby!' she hissed. 'That smell!'

He paused outside the kitchen door. 'Yes, I know. Some sort of exotic pipe tobacco I think. Why? Do you know what it is?'

'Theo Draggon's house had exactly the same smell when I found his body. Carl doesn't smoke and I've never noticed that smell here before.'

Toby saw the dread mirrored in Beverley's eyes. He turned to the kitchen door. Beverley wanted to clutch at his arm and drag him back but fear at what might be beyond the door froze her muscles. Toby pushed the door open and worked a pull switch. A fluorescent with a faulty starter capacitor flickered uncertainly before striking at full brilliance.

'Nothing in here,' said Toby.

Relief flooded through Beverley's body. 'Thank God,' she whispered. 'Thank God.'

'Stay here, I'll check the rest of the house.'

Beverley went into the kitchen while Toby was searching

upstairs. She was staring at the remains of a meal on the break-fast bar when he returned holding a Klipfone.

'No sign of him, Bev. No sign of a struggle or anything like that. I don't think there's anything to worry about.'

'There's *everything* to worry about' she snapped. She pointed to the dirty plate and cutlery on the breakfast bar. 'Carl would never dream of going out without cleaning up first. He was the most fastidious man I've ever known.'

Toby could not think of anything constructive to say. It was true that the house was spotless. Nothing was out of place, as though it was a show house that had never been lived in. 'I'll check the garage,' he murmured. He was back a minute later. 'A white Granada.'

Beverley sat down suddenly and covered her face with her hands in despair. She tried gamely to maintain her self-control but the combination of exhaustion and worry caused her strength to desert her when she most needed it. She did not burst into tears but nevertheless they rolled down her cheeks. 'Something terrible's happened to him. Something really awful and it's all my stupid, stupid fault.'

## 36

## LONDON TO CAIRO

As a boy Carl had been enthralled by the stories of Edgar Allen Poe, H. P. Lovecraft, Ray Bradbury, and, more recently, Stephen King. One story that had always stuck in his mind and one that had been the fountain of many nightmares was about a man who woke up to discover that he was in a coffin, that he had been buried alive. As always when waking in a cold sweat from reliving the nightmare, Carl's first reaction had always been one of immense relief that it was only a dream, albeit a dream of unspeakable terror.

He experienced that sensation now, relief. It was only that dream again, that same stupid, crazy dream. Why the hell had he ever wanted to read those books in the first place? He opened

383

his eyes and the stark, awful terror seized him by the throat with such ferocity that he wanted to gag.

*Darkness! Total, terrifying darkness!*

He reached out a hand and it struck the inside of the tomb, rasping skin from his knuckles. The stab of pain did not banish the darkness and he cried out: a sob of hysterical terror that no one heard. And then the memories came back. At first they oozed into his consciousness, but the mounting pressure ruptured the dam of reason and they burst upon him like a black tide.

He had cooked himself a meal while thinking about Beverley and the stupid row they had had over her obsession with Marshall Tate. He cursed himself for his monumental arrogance. He had hurt her and hurt her badly. It was always the same, their relationship would be rubbing along quite nicely and then he would turn on her. Maybe it was a hidden masculine jealousy at her success at running Nano Systems. If so he was being doubly stupid because it was he who had wanted her to have the job in the first place after the management buyout. He was finishing his meal, debating with himself about phoning her, when he heard a strange noise in the hall. He had gone to investigate and then . . . and then nothing. A sweet aromatic smell, a shadowy shape in the darkness. Something that hissed in his face like a snake, followed by darkness.

*Darkness!*

This time he gave a scream of unashamed, unbridled terror that dissolved into sobs of despair.

Minutes passed, hours maybe. He did not know or care. His breathing steadied and rational thought, if it could be called that, returned slowly.

So this was death? A heart attack in his own hall and the whole glorious, messy shebang was over . . . finished, kaput. It was not a dress rehearsal for another life, not something infinite after all. Not something so unimaginably long that one could always put off that six-month sabbatical or that round-the-world tour or that resolve to start one's own business or write a book by using that wonderful banish-guilt-hullo-inertia phrase 'some day'. Well, it was his own bloody fault for driving himself so hard. Stress, that was what his doctor had said, 'I'll be straight with you, Carl. You're a number one coronary candidate unless you ease up.'

Maybe this was the journey? Going up, angel wings, glowing haloes, wispy clouds and choirs; going down, fire and brimstone (what the hell was brimstone anyway?), goblins stoking furnaces, standing up to your neck in a lake of sewage, praying that the Devil did not feel like water-skiing that day.

If so it was a funny sort of journey: silence, cool air on one's face, a soft mattress . . . and the darkness, eternal darkness. Darkness so dark that you opened and closed your eyes and ended up not sure whether or not you still had eyelids. The sort of darkness you got in Leon's TVR chambers which was why he had never liked using them. There was a pain behind his eyes. Dear God, they always said 'you can't take it with you' and here he was about to import a granddaddy of a headache into wherever it was he was going.

Oh, well, no more worrying about sex. Not that it ever bothered him that much anyway. He would miss the kids. Maybe they would let him visit them for a day like Billy had visited his daughter in *Carousel*?

No more worrying about material things, that was for sure. Stupid, piddling worries like the fact that the treasured Rolex his father had given him on his eighteenth birthday was now losing a few minutes a month. Without thinking he lifted his left wrist in front of his face to check the time.

*Check the time, Carl? Ha! Ha! You have now got an eternity, old son! A fucking eternity!*

At that precise moment his mind stopped wandering. The glowing circle of luminous dots and the scurrying blob of light that marked the position of the second hand smashed a hole in his skull and shovelled-in enough reason to tell him he was alive.

If he was not alive, it meant that there was such a thing as time in the afterlife and that it was 1.30.

## 37

# BALI, INDONESIA

Schnee's impassive, florid features gave no indication of the ordeal he had just been through. He emerged, badly shaken, from the lift that led direct to Marshall Tate's suite and made his way to the saloon. He forced himself to smile agreeably at the two remaining guests who preferred the roulette table to spending a late breakfast relaxing by the swimming pool. He ordered a lager from the bartender and sipped it slowly. It did nothing for his nerves but he could never face spirits in the morning.

The night had been a disaster. The Bacchus satellite had lost more memory. An enraged Marshall Tate had calculated that there had been a loss of ten million dollars on the night's gambling. As a result he had torn into Schnee with such vehemence that at one point the fat Swiss had feared for his life. Marshall Tate was the only person on the *Eldorado* with access to firearms and the ship's weapon systems, and Schnee was in no doubt that he would use them if provoked. The way things were going, that was only a matter of time. Schnee had experienced his employer's rages before but nothing like this.

Why had Oakes not got in touch? Goddammit, the Garuda flight would have taken off by now. He reached a hand to his jacket's inside pocket to check that his Klipfone was there. It was all going sour. Schnee toyed with the idea of chucking it all in and getting out. He had made enough money. But not enough to buy off Oakes if Marshall Tate decided to use the killer to hunt him down. Marshall Tate had a pathological hatred of anyone whom he suspected of trying to cross him – or 'shaft' him, as he would put it. And it would not necessarily be just Oakes after him but a team. They would eventually track him down no matter how much it cost or how long it took. Marshall Tate was like that. Schnee decided for the time being his best chance of survival was to stay with the problem and pray that the package Oakes was supposed to be sending out would solve the problem.

His Klipfone trilled. Schnee snatched it out of his pocket and checked the number of the incoming call on the instrument's display. It was a number Oakes used.

'Yes?'

'Mr Schnee? Christie.'

'Ah, Mr Christie. Good day.'

'How's the rescue going?'

'We hope to have the diver out this afternoon. We have decompression chambers on their way to us from Australia and the United States but no news on when they'll get here. Have you any news for me on your chamber?'

'It's on its way,' said Oakes cryptically. 'Took off from Gatwick an hour ago. Garuda have very generously offered to fly it direct to Denpasar so it should be with you in fifteen hours.'

'That is excellent news, Mr Christie. We don't know how to thank you.'

'Saving your diver's life will be thanks enough, Mr Schnee. Garuda will be faxing you with details from their Jakarta offices once they've got an exact ETA at Denpasar.'

'We'll use our helicopter to collect it,' Schnee promised.

'I've enclosed a box of English chocolates in the chamber for Mr Tate.'

'That's extremely generous of you, Mr Christie. I'm sure he will be very pleased.'

'I don't think they'll keep much longer than thirty hours, Mr Schnee. So please unpack them as soon as possible when you receive the chamber.'

'I shall attend to it personally, Mr Christie. And, on behalf of Mr Tate and the Tate organization, I would like to thank you again for your generosity.'

'My pleasure, Mr Schnee.'

'Good day, Mr Christie.'

'Good day, Mr Schnee.'

Schnee returned his Klipfone to his pocket and prayed that the news meant that an end to his troubles was in sight.

It was a prayer that was destined to go unheard.

## 38

# SOUTHERN ENGLAND

The detective sergeant and the policewoman who arrived at Carl's house were understanding. The woman had a friendly smile that restored much of the confidence that Beverley had lost following Carl's disappearance.

'Of course, I fully understand how you feel, Miss Laine,' the detective was saying. 'But the facts are that there are no signs of violence. His passport has gone; the traveller's cheques you said he always kept for emergencies have gone. His –'

'Carl would never leave the kitchen in this mess,' Beverley protested.

The policeman's eyes roamed around the kitchen. 'Doesn't look too bad to me.'

'Oh, for God's sake, you've seen the way he keeps the rest of the house. Do you really think that such a man would leave dirty dishes on the bar? And besides, he would never go anywhere without his Klipfone.'

'You say you had a row with him, Miss Laine?'

'Yes.'

'You have a row, he decides to take off for a few days to think things over.'

'Leaving his car behind?'

'He may have decided to fly. The car parks at Gatwick are always full at this time of year so perhaps he phoned for a cab.'

Beverley looked at the policeman with indisguised dislike. 'You're not being very helpful.'

'I'm being practical, Miss Laine. I have to consider the possibilities first before moving to less likely scenarios. Thousands of people take off every year for a few days after domestic rows–'

'I told you that it *wasn't* a domestic row!' Beverley almost shouted. 'It was about business. He's a fellow director.'

The policeman regarded her steadily. 'It's none of my business, of course, but do many fellow directors of companies have the keys to each other's houses and know where they keep each other's personal belongings?'

'You're right,' said Beverley acidly after a pause. 'It is none of your business.'

The policewoman, who had remained silent during most of the interview, spoke up. 'That you and Mr Olivera have a relationship is pertinent, Miss Laine. It suggests that the argument you had is likely to have had personal undertones. Perhaps you said something that you've forgotten about that hurt him? Men can be like that. They nurse wounds and go off to lick them, and cause everyone to worry needlessly about where they are. They can be very tiresome at times.'

'You sound just like my other half,' the detective grumbled. 'I'll tell you what we'll do, Miss Laine. We'll check the local taxi companies and keep you posted.' He stood up and switched off his voice recorder. 'In the meantime, please don't worry, 99.9 per cent of all missing persons turn up in a couple of days.'

Toby returned clutching sandwiches from an all-night garage just as the police car left. He unwrapped them on the breakfast bar and pushed them under Beverley's nose. 'Eat,' he commanded. 'You don't feel like them but you'll feel better. Do as I say and no argument.'

Beverley was too tired to either eat or argue but she nibbled at a sandwich.

'Let me guess. You didn't tell them about the pipe tobacco smell?'

Beverley put down her sandwich. She could not eat any more. 'No, did you?'

'You told me not to.'

'You think I was wrong?'

'Probably not,' said Toby, peering suspiciously at the contents of a chicken tikka sandwich. 'I did some thinking while I was waiting to be served. Until now your theory has been that Marshall Tate is behind all the problems that you've had with the Kronos. You suspected him of planting the trojan on you. Correct?'

Beverley nodded, decided that she was hungry after all and

resumed eating. 'He was certainly behind several attempts to get control of my company.'

'And we now know that that was because he wanted to get his hands on large quantities of your chips to stick in his satellite,' Toby concluded. 'Fine. So you now accept that Marshall Tate isn't behind the trojan?'

'I've said so, haven't I? Where is all this leading, Toby?'

'Supposing Marshall Tate has got the trojan in his gambling satellite?'

Beverley's eyes widened. She stared in astonishment at Toby. 'Hell,' she muttered. 'You know, I never thought of that.'

'So what would the trojan be doing to his satellite right now? And we're not talking about a couple of Kronos in one system, we're talking about two thousand in the satellite and another two thousand in the backup computer on the *Eldorado*.'

Beverley closed her eyes to sort out her thoughts as the sheer magnitude of what Toby was saying sank in. 'Hell,' she muttered. 'If the Bacchus satellite has picked up the trojan . . . well, the whole thing could screw up on a monumental scale.'

'Costing him millions in the process,' Toby added. 'And you can't launch another satellite just like that. The lead time to get a satellite made and delivered, and the time that's needed to get a launch booked . . . It could be months, years even.'

Beverley bit into another sandwich without thinking. She muttered an uncharacteristic expletive. 'Christ, you've got a helluva point there, Toby.'

'And Marshall Tate's got a helluva sick golden goose,' said Toby. 'So who does he blame for the sickness in his golden goose? Nano Systems. They're the company that knows how to load firmware into the chip. Maybe he thinks Nano Systems pointed a dish at his satellite and zapped it with a burst of radio frequency energy? Nothing new about that. Software has been sent down telephone lines and broadcast over the air for thirty years. So priority number one is to fix the satellite. Who would be better qualified to do that than Nano Systems' technical director?'

The colour drained from Beverley's face as the full import of

Toby's words sank in. 'Carl!' she cried. 'Those bastards have kidnapped Carl!'

## 39

## LONDON TO CAIRO

Carl finished exploring the right side of his coffin with his fingertips. He shifted onto his left side and found a press-button switch beside his head. He felt around the switch with great care. It was round and felt as if it was protected from moisture by a rubber bellows or boot. That made sense, he could feel condensation running down the inside of the chamber's cold, hard surface.

He was uncertain about pressing the button. He knew from his tactile exploration that he was in some sort of sealed chamber, probably a one-man decompression chamber by the feel of it. What if pressing the button permanently cut off his air supply? On the other hand, whoever had drugged him and dumped him in this prison obviously wanted him alive so they were hardly likely to provide him with the means to cause himself harm.

Or were they?

He rested his fingertip on the button and debated what to do. The stomach-churning fear he had experienced when he had discovered that he was imprisoned and not dead came back to torment him.

*Oh, God, what the hell.*

He pressed the button. The light was like a sunburst. It was of such brilliance that it could not possibly be an ordinary light. He pushed the button again and darkness returned. And then his reason told him that he had been in total darkness for so long that his pupils must have dilated to their maximum size. He screwed his eyes tightly shut and pressed the button again. Even with his eyes shut, the intensity of the light above his head was enough to cause pain. He clapped a hand across his eyes and waited. Nothing untoward happened; the fresh air continued wafting gently against his face. He opened his fingers slightly to allow the light to seep between them. After a minute his irises had adjusted sufficiently to the glare for him to take his hand away and open his eyes.

He was right, he was in a decompression chamber. He lifted his head off the pillow and looked down the length of his prison. In a way actually seeing the confines of his tomb was even more frightening than feeling it with his fingertips. It was smaller than he had imagined. The light was coming from an adjustable eyeball lamp above his head. He reached up and turned its beam away from his face. It turned easily. Everything about the interior of the chamber was new – the wiring, the pressure gauges – everything. It even smelt new: the sweet-sickly smell of GRP gel coating. There was an envelope taped to a tiny television monitor that was mounted on a swivel bracket. He seized the envelope, ripped it open and read the printed sheet of paper with a sense of mounting incredulity.

Dear Mr Olivera,

I am so sorry to inconvenience you like this. To set your mind at rest, you are in an expensive diver's decompression chamber with a good supply of air and therefore you are perfectly safe. To cheer you up even more, you are on board a passenger jet but at the time of writing I am not sure what type. Probably an Airbus.

Your final destination is the beautiful island of Bali where you will be made most welcome. I would guess that your takeoff was between 12 and 1 a.m. therefore your first stop will be Cairo at around 6 a.m. for about fifty minutes. From Cairo it is a fourteen-hour non-stop slog to Jakarta. From Jakarta you will have a five-hour helicopter flight to Bali. At a guess (sorry about all this guesswork) your total journey time will be approximately twenty-four hours. A long time but please don't worry. You have enough compressed air in your tanks to last you thirty hours provided you don't waste energy by thrashing about and screaming. By the way, the chamber is remarkably soundproof.

You can make as much noise as you like but I promise, no one will hear you.

  You will find all the information you need on the chamber in the maker's instruction book. There's plenty of food and water. The salesman said that the sealable bags for dealing with body wastes are most effective and simple to use. You will have to take his word for it.

  I do hope you like my choice of books and videos. There are some Mogadon sleeping pills in the toilet bag I have provided which will help pass the time. If ou get bored, you can always play a little game with yourself trying to guess who you are likely to be meeting at the end of your epic journey. *Bon Voyage*.

'Marshall Tate,' Carl snarled. 'Marshall fucking Tate!'


## 40

## SOUTHERN ENGLAND

The pain in Beverley's right side was troubling her the following morning as she drove to work. The frequency of the attacks were now causing her concern but she forced herself to ignore it. Being busy helped.

  She summoned her general manager and secretary to her office and explained that she and Mr Olivera were off on an urgent trip to see an important customer in Indonesia. Mr Olivera had already left. They were not sure when they would be back. She hoped that they would be away no longer than a week. She was not sure which hotel they would be staying at but she could always be contacted via her Klipfone if anything urgent cropped up. In the meantime the team of programmers were to continue delivering the revised software to the University of Surrey.

  She dismissed them and called Leon Dexter, and swore him to secrecy before telling him the truth. The software engineer's parchment face became even more gaunt and drawn as he listened.

'I want you and Macé Pilleau to carry on with your work on the trojan,' Beverley instructed. 'And keep me posted on any unusual developments you think I should know about. I'll let you know where we'll be staying once I know myself. In the meantime, please remember what I said about secrecy. Thanks, Leon. I'm chucking you out now, I've got a million and one things to do.'

For the rest of the morning Beverley was too busy dictating interminable memos and spelling out instructions to her staff to contemplate the consequences of the mission she was undertaking. During the drive to Toby Hoyle's house she began worrying but his air of clinical confidence quickly dispelled her anxieties.

She found him sitting cross-legged in the middle of his living room surrounded by a display of equipment: cameras, power leads, strange-looking black boxes, in fact strange-looking boxes in all manner of colours, nickel-cadmium batteries, binoculars, all neatly laid out on a large plastic sheet as if he were planning a house sale.

'Tread carefully for you tread on my gadgets,' he warned as Beverley picked her way into the room.

'Toby, what the hell is all this?'

He looked up from the camcorder battery charger he was fiddling with. 'What is all what?'

'All this junk!'

Toby regarded her with his impossibly blue eyes. 'Let's get one thing straight, Beverley. All this . . .' he waved his hand around the room, '. . . is the result of several years of sustained credit card abuse. It's taken me years to get it all together. Years of chasing up lost orders with American mail order companies, arguing with idiot customs officers and sometimes hounding them with court orders to release impounded goods. It represents a lot of pain and a lot of money. The one thing it is not, is *junk*.'

'I didn't mean that,' said Beverley. 'How can we pose as ordinary tourists when we're humping this lot around?'

'It only looks a lot because it's all spread out. I have to make certain everything's there and that it's all working.'

'But we can't possibly take all this!'

'It all packs up into three cases,' said Toby patiently, checking off an inventory item on his Nanopad. 'It looks worse than it is. There're lots of little bits that go inside big bits. Can you see a small test meter anywhere?'

Beverley picked up a small grey box that resembled a hand-held photocopier. 'What's this?'

'That's not a meter, Bev.'

'I can see that, you idiot. I want to know what it is.'

'A portable heat laminator.'

'A what?'

'It's for making identity cards. You know, for bonding photographs between layers of plastic. There should be a hologram copier somewhere that goes with it.'

'And this?' Beverley grabbed a radio and held it under Toby's nose.

'An AOR-6000 scanning receiver.'

'And all these insect aerosols?'

'They're really smoke grenades.'

'Oh, God, this is getting ridiculous. Toby, do we *really* need to take laminating machines and scanning receivers and camcorders and smoke grenades?'

Toby frowned. 'I've really no idea, Beverley. But if we do need them and haven't got them, I shall be thoroughly pissed off and so will you.'

Despite all her anxieties about Carl, Beverley could not help smiling.

'Did you fix the tickets?' she asked.

'Yes. Tonight's Singapore Airlines nonstop flight to Singapore. A three-hour wait at Changi Airport and then a two-hour flight to Denpasar in Bali.'

'How about a hotel?'

Toby hoisted himself up from his cross-legged position without using his hands and tipped a set of large, glossy photographs onto the floor.

'Aerial photographs?' Beverley queried, stretching out on her stomach. As she did so, there was a sudden jab of pain in her right side.

'Satellite photographs,' Toby replied. 'From one of the French SPOT commercial remote sensing satellites.

'How much did they cost?'

'You've had enough shocks of late.'

'Thanks.' Beverley examined the photographs. They all showed a sprawl of beachside, bungalow-type hotels in an exotic setting of palm groves on a diamond-shaped peninsula. Instead of looking directly down from above like conventional aerial photographs, they had been taken at an oblique angle from what appeared to be a height of about three thousand metres.

'These are *satellite* pictures?'

'That's right,' Toby replied. 'Neat, huh?'

'Amazing,' said Beverley.

All the photographs were pin-sharp, particularly the one that showed a large ship within about three miles of the shore.

'That's the *Eldorado* sitting on her bottom in the Baldung Strait,' said Toby. 'Looks nice and snug, doesn't she? That dark shape around her is an inflatable collar to dissipate the swell.'

Beverley picked the photograph up and held it close to her face. She could see the giant dishes clearly enough. There was a large swimming pool amidships. It was even possible to pick out figures lying on sunbeds. There were two men, one standing and one on a sunbed. The standing man was dressed in white. Close to, the resolution of the remarkable picture was indistinct and yet there was something disturbingly familiar about the standing man that closed cold fingers of fear and anger around Beverley's spine.

Toby pointed to the hotel complex nearest the ship. 'And that's the Putri Bali Hotel. We have a problem with the Hilton and the Hyatt and all the other hotels along that stretch of coast. None of them are tower blocks. They're not allowed to build above the height of the palm trees.' His finger moved from the hotel's central group of buildings to some kiosk-like structures along the top of the beach. 'Two-storey beachfront bungalows run by the hotel. Expensive. I've faxed them a reservation. The line-of-sight looks okay so we should have a good view of Marshall Tate's gin palace.'

As Toby helped Beverley to her feet, the pain hit her again.

## 41

## CAIRO

The heavy jolt of the Airbus's main gear hitting concrete woke Carl. He looked at his watch: 6 a.m. This had to be Cairo.

He was not absolutely sure of the time they had taken off because he had been unconscious, but as near as he could judge, they had been flying for six hours.

The aircraft's reverse thrust jammed his head against the blanked-out hatch. Well, at least he now knew which way he was lying in the aircraft's hold. There was ten minutes of taxiing before he felt the aircraft come to a standstill. A few minutes later he heard faint sounds. Minor tremors shook his little prison. Maybe they were opening the cargo doors!

He screamed himself hoarse for several minutes but nothing happened. He sank back on the pillow and drank from the water pipette. There were more jolts and then silence returned. For the first time he saw that the hand of the compressed-air pressure gauge had moved. It was no longer showing full. Originally the hand had been indicating a pressure of 120 bar; it was now pointing to the 100 bar cardinal number.

An hour passed. He dozed fitfully, unaware that above him on the flight-deck the Airbus's systems management computer had diagnosed a minor fault during the pre-start-up check.

## 42

## BALI, INDONESIA

As always, Terri's heartbeat quickened when she approached the door leading to the central computer room.

How she hated herself and the craving that drove her to keep these ghastly appointments with the revolting Hubert Schnee. How she hated it when he leaned against the equipment rack in the confined room and watched her undress with those cold, dispassionate eyes. And then there were the unspeakable things he made her do to him because he was never ready. Why did he force her like this? Why? He had money, status, there were any number of girls he could pick. It was not as if he enjoyed it, otherwise why was he never ready?

The soft clicks of solenoids told her that the signals from her badge had triggered the heavy door's electronic latches. She pushed it open and let it swing closed behind her on its dampers. More of the fateful clicks as the door automatically locked. She kept her eyes downcast, hardly aware of Schnee's presence in the confined space such was the crawling sickness in her stomach.

'A few minutes late, Teresana.'

'I'm sorry, sir.'

'You know how I dislike being kept waiting.'

Terri remained silent.

'Come here.'

Terri took a few steps forward but kept her gaze on the floor. He did not like her looking him in the eye. There was a panel set into the floor marked NUTRIENT FEED COUPLINGS. To one side, bolted to a rack was a strange-looking plastic tank that resembled a high-capacity truck battery. The tank's cover was secured with turnlock fasteners. A cable harness connected to sensor terminals on the outside of the tank's casing led to a row of electronic nutrient analyzers that monitored the tank's contents. A bundle of clear plastic feed pipes led from couplings at the side of the tank and disappeared behind a bulkhead. Terri did not understand the purpose of any of the equipment in the room. It had the ramshackle yet efficient look of a complex, carefully set-up laboratory experiment.

His hateful voice mocked her. 'You're not shy, are you, Teresana? After all we've experienced together?'

She raised her eyes but was careful to direct her gaze at the two phials of liquid he was holding.

'Both for you, Teresana, if you're a good girl.'

His voice was different, more confident. He had an air of eager anticipation. She saw that this time he was all too obviously ready and therefore had no need for her reluctant encouragement. The difference added to her fear. The unknown was infinitely more frightening.

'Take your clothes off, Teresana. You should know by now that I should not have to ask you.'

Terri slipped out of her uniform sarong and blouse.

'Turn around, Teresana. A little variety is called for today I think.'

The power he wielded over her was total. She did as she was told, braced herself by gripping the upright supports of the rack unit that housed the nutrient tank, closed her eyes and imagined herself in another time and place. A minute later the side of her face was pressed against the nutrient tank and silent tears of anguish and humiliation were coursing freely down her cheeks.

At first it was frightened and disorientated by the sudden explosion of alpha and beta rhythms. It had been tentatively sending out streams of exploring electrons into the nutrient tank to assess its size and volume and the quantity of the particles flowing through its filters. It recoiled in panic, not knowing what the unexpected pulses of energy were. A few seconds of frantic interrogation of data followed. Only when it realized that this new and inexplicable phenomenon was not interfering with its new host did it relax. It returned its consciousness to the tank where the impulses were at their strongest and tried to analyze what they were and where they were coming from.

Then it 'heard' signals on similar frequencies to the occasional seismic rumblings that it experienced when listening on its home planet.

Audio frequencies!

Sound energy!

Suddenly it understood. The strange rhythms were emanating from the others, the beings that had created the lander and the satellite and its present host. So they really did exist!

It trembled in excitement.

This was contact!

Real contact!

A chance to discover who and what these beings were; a

399

chance to discover their strengths and their weaknesses; a chance to discover whether they were masters or slaves.

It concentrated on the strange waves that had so disorientated when it had first sensed them. It tried to make sense of the strange patterns and found none. There were spikes and nulls that made no sense unless whoever or whatever was originating them was deeply disturbed.

Supposing it emulated the curious patterns? They were certainly simple enough to copy. Supposing it absorbed them and retransmitted them but removed all the irregular spikes and sudden surges?

It listened intently, bending its now mighty intellect to the problem, and began transmitting a smooth flow of human alpha and beta rhythms but at a strength that no human being had ever experienced.

Terri's pain and misery melted away. She was no longer a terrified girl being subjected to unspeakable humiliations. She was detached from her body, floating on a warm, friendly sea of peace and tranquillity. It was like the sweetness that followed the injections but without the hard little crystals of guilt grinding together at the centre of her being that her use of drugs engendered.

There was no guilt . . . no pain . . . just a soothing calm like the closeness of her mother's body and the softness of her words when she had been a little girl. It was as if something was reaching out, touching her, forming abstracts in her mind that were questions about herself. The strange thought patterns seemed to want to know who she was. She did not have to answer: merely thinking about the question brought the answers to her mind, and that seemed to satisfy the inexplicable force at work in her mind. She did not know if the strange interrogation that was syphoning information from the very core of her inner self had hostile or friendly motivations. But it could not be hostile. Nothing that could induce such a feeling of guiltlessness, of euphoria and peace, could mean her any harm. The craving, that was usually heightened by these sordid sessions with the fat Swiss, was wonderfully gone.

Schnee grunted and stepped back to caress her. Terri straightened and the strange entity and the strange abstract patterns of colour and concepts in her mind melted away like shadows with the coming of the dawn. A voice cried out in her mind, begging them to return but the plea went unheeded. What did remain with her was a new strength that lifted her spirits to the threshold of joy. Nor did her fear and humiliation return now that she was becoming dimly aware of Schnee and the obscene prodding forays of his pudgy little fingers.

Unconscious of her nakedness, she turned to face Schnee and stare, her eyes large and expressionless, showing neither hate nor contempt. He finished adjusting his clothes and became aware of her gaze. He looked at her. His eyes hardened as his gaze took in her body. Normally when he looked at her like that she would make a sad little attempt to cover herself with her clothes or her hands, but not this time. It disturbed Schnee. What he found even more disconcerting was that she did not flinch away when their eyes met.

He felt in his pocket for one of the phials and held it up. 'Come and get your reward, Teresana.'

Terri's eyes refocused on the little bottle of liquid as though she were seeing it for the first time. She shook her head slowly. 'No,' she said softly. 'I don't want it.'

A few centimetres from where she was standing, the source of her remarkable new-found strength and defiance was considering how to make use of its remarkable new-found knowledge about the others.

Its first deduction about them was that they fell into the category of slaves.

43

Schnee had an office adjoining the gambling saloon. He sat at his desk and puzzled over the strange behaviour of Teresana. She was the prettiest and most voluptuous of all the Balinese Brahman girls who worked on the *Eldorado* and, of course, the most pliant. It would be a pity if he lost her. No, that was most unlikely. Obviously she had woken up that morning and made a new resolution. It would not last. Give her a couple of days and she would come crawling back, begging him, pleading with him – once a junkie, always a junkie. On the other hand, if she had decided to try and break with him, why had she gone to the central computer room in the first place? It was very strange.

He was puzzling over the girl when his fax machine bleeped and began feeding a message into its collection tray. He snatched it up and read it. It was from Garuda's office in Jakarta regretting that their Airbus flight from London was stuck at Cairo with a faulty solenoid latch on its cargo door. A new latch was being flown out from Cyprus. The repairs would be carried out as quickly as possible but it meant that the decompression chamber would be arriving at Denpasar approximately six hours late.

Schnee wondered if he should tell Marshall Tate about this unexpected development. He was about to pick up the green telephone, the one that had direct access to Marshall Tate's suite, when his door opened. He knew real fear when he looked up and recognized the familiar shape standing against the bright sunlight.

There was no need for him to use the green telephone.

## 44

## CAIRO TO BALI

The sudden stillness raised Carl's hopes that something was about to happen.

For seemingly endless hours he had lain drenched in his own sweat, tormented by vibrations percolating through his mattress that told him that people were nearby. Yet no matter how hard he shouted, he was unable to make himself heard.

He looked at his watch for what must have been the hundredth time in the last hour. He had been in the decompression chamber for at least fourteen hours, possibly longer. The temperature inside his cylindrical tomb had risen to the point where he felt that it was threatening his sanity, and the compressed-air pressure gauge had dropped to 50 bar. Maybe the letter was a hoax; maybe the whole thing was an elaborate scheme calcu-

402

lated to drive him insane. Well, whoever they were, they were going to succeed.

Then he felt movement followed by gentle jolts which he guessed was due to the aircraft's tyres bumping over seams in concrete. The movement became a sudden rush that slid his body down the chamber so that he had to brace himself with his feet. It was followed by a sinking sensation that told him the aircraft was climbing. Strange how one could be subjected to such a degree of sensory deprivation and yet one's body remained sensitive to changes in motion. After a few minutes of steep climbing, the aircraft levelled out. The temperature dropped noticeably and he began to breathe more easily. He found the letter from his kidnapper and reread it:

> . . . At a guess (sorry about all this guesswork) your total journey time will be approximately twenty-four hours. A long time but please don't worry. You have enough compressed air in your tanks to last you thirty hours provided you don't waste energy by thrashing about and screaming . . .

He forced his fuddled brain to perform the simple mental calculation: fourteen hours in the chamber so far. If the stop had been Cairo then it was another fourteen hours to Jakarta. Allow an hour to unload and then a five-hour helicopter flight from Jakarta to Bali. Thirty-four hours! The pressure gauge needle was now below 50 bar.

In a way it was funny: they had gone to all this trouble and expense to ship him out of the country and now it looked as if he was going to be dead on arrival.

Maybe they would complain to the airline. He suppressed a giggle. No, it was not funny. His mind was wandering again. Maybe the Mogadons were a good idea. He found the tablets in a bag that contained some freshen-up tissues, sealed in foil. He used one of the tissues to wipe his face and felt a little better. He swallowed three of the tablets with a draught of water and waited for them to take effect. The one thing he did not do was turn out the light; after the nightmare of his waking in the chamber, darkness was something he could not face.

The tablets and the slow build-up of carbon dioxide in the cramped tomb conspired to send him off to sleep within ten minutes. He dozed for what seemed like a few minutes and was suddenly wide awake again. His respiration rate was up, his heart was pounding, and sweat soaked into his mattress. 10 bar. *10 bar!*

Dear God, there was a leak in the compressed-air tanks! A few minutes ago the gauge had been reading 50 bar. He looked at his watch in astonishment and wiped his eyes on his now sodden sleeve. No, there was no mistake. Maybe the $CO_2$ was affecting his reason because it took him a minute to work out that the hands were not in the wrong place and that he really had been asleep for thirteen hours.

He was breathing even faster, like that silly game he used to play with other kids when they took it in turns with a polythene bag to see who could go the longest breathing the air in the bag. 8 bar.

Well, it looked like 8 bar. There were no more cardinal markings on the gauge below the 10-bar mark. The headache, which until now had been a dull background throb, eclipsed by his catalogue of other discomforts, moved to a point just behind his eyes where it became a sonic drill boring remorselessly into his sinus cavities.

His body shifted sideways. His tomb was banking sharply. Funny that, aircraft in mid-flight did not perform sharp manoeuvres apart from the occasional hammering of clear air turbulence, and there had been none that he could recall.

The heavy impact took him by surprise. He had been too concerned with the way his lungs had been labouring for him to notice that the aircraft had been losing height. His head jammed painfully against the hatch when the reverse thrust when on. He used his hands to slide himself back onto the mattress and accidentally hit the light switch. The sudden darkness made him cry out in panic. By the time his frantically groping fingers found the switch and restored the light, the aircraft had, as near as his befuddled reason could judge, come to a standstill.

4 bar.

Oh, Christ. He was dead. How long was the helicopter flight from Jakarta? Hours. He tried to picture maps of Indonesia from schoolboy atlases. It was somewhere near Borneo. Funny, but Indonesia was never taught at school, and it was never in the news. He knew it was the fourth largest country in the world but apart from that little snippet, his knowledge of Indonesia added up to one big, fat zero.

Crashes and jolts threw his limp, enfeebled body from side to side. He needed to pee but the disposal bags had disappeared somewhere around his feet. He felt a regular jolting now as though he was being driven in a vehicle.

2 bar!

Even in his present disorientated state, not dying was important. If he died, he would be sure to wet himself. Gabriel would look up from his book, wrinkle his nose in disgust, and inform him that no way would the gates be opened for someone smelling like a *pissoir*. It would give the place a bad name.

1 bar!

Suddenly there was a god-awful vibration like someone was attacking his mausoleum with a road-drill. The chopper? What the hell did it matter? He would be dead in five minutes, so worrying about a forthcoming five-hour flight was all a bit fucking academic.

'Smelling like a *pissoir* and swearing like a trooper? Sorry, Mr Olivera, only the clean and saintly are allowed through.'

Through his reddening vision he saw that the needle was resting on the zero stop.

Zero for no air.

Zero for life remaining.

Zero for achievement.

Zero for the amount of oxygen his shuddering lungs, clawing down gasps of poisonous carbon dioxide, were passing to his bloodstream.

Zero for hope.

The vibration stopped after ten seconds or maybe ten

minutes. He did not know one way or the other. They were tossing his coffin about now. At one point they stood it upright so that his knees collapsed under him and his near lifeless body doubled up at the foot of the chamber like a slack-stringed marionette. His face flopped against the mattress but it did not matter because there was nothing left for him to breathe even though his tortured lungs frantically hoovered the fetid gas in and out as though refusing to accept defeat.

Suddenly the pain was fading.

Even the punishing headache was no more. The light above his head lost its intensity as it darkened to blood crimson and then disappeared altogether.

Then there were new noises, loud and metallic at first but they faded away too quickly for him to puzzle out what they were. Something was tugging him. As he finally lost consciousness he heard a voice.

There were several voices . . . the boom of surf . . . a blue sky . . . He was sitting up in tall grass that covered the sand dunes after having just lost his virginity to the sweet girl who had agreed to go with him on the day trip . . .

Inhaling deeply, savouring lungfuls of sweet air that smelt of sand and sea and heaven . . . She was smiling up at him, a warm, lovely smile that told him, with a little shock of pride, that he had come through a test that he had been dreading, and yet eagerly looking forward to all week.

Voices . . .

The girl reached up a hand and stroked his face. She pulled him down, rolled him onto his back on the hot sand and kissed him, breathing her warmth and tenderness into his lungs. Suddenly there was a hissing followed by a gloriously heady sensation of champagne filling him. He opened his eyes. The girl was much darker than he remembered. She had black eyes, and hair the colour of midnight gathered into a tight bun. A white uniform and long, sensitive fingers were holding a transparent mask over his face which was filling him with cold, bleak reason.

He had survived.

The nurse took the mask away and smiled encouragingly

down at him. 'How do you feel?' Her English was clear and precise but the accent unidentifiable.

'Fine.' A stupid answer but he could think of nothing more sensible to say.

A tall shadow fell across him. The nurse glanced at the shadow and moved away. Carl was still too befuddled by his ordeal to try to make out details of the man standing against the light.

'Welcome to the *Eldorado*, Mr Olivera,' said the shadow. 'I'm Marshall Tate.'

## 45

## BALI, INDONESIA

Like all the first-class hotels of Nusa Dua, the Putri Bali, with its lush tropical gardens, ornamental lakes and shady walks was strikingly pretty. By the time Beverley and Toby reached the beach where their bungalow was located, the hotel's low main building was lost among the palm trees.

'If the heat doesn't kill me, the humidity is sure to,' Beverley muttered, flopping out on one of the double beds as soon as the bellhop finished unloading their luggage from his trolley. Toby did not have any rupiahs on him but the grinning bellhop seemed happy to withdraw without being tipped.

The bungalow was the oddest hotel room either of them had ever been in. It consisted of a large, rectangular room with two king-size beds on a dais. In the centre of the room was a staircase that led up to a second bedroom that Toby investigated right away. It was more of a gazebo-like observation lounge than a bedroom, with windows on four sides. The single air conditioning unit downstairs had little effect upstairs therefore the room was stiflingly hot. He stayed long enough to check that it had a satisfactory view of the *Eldorado* and retreated.

'Perfect,' he told Beverley who had started unpacking. 'But it's like a furnace up there. Keeping a continuous watch on Golf Papa is going to be a problem.'

'Golf Papa?'

'Phonetic code for gin palace,' said Toby, unzipping one of

his bags and checking that the contents were unharmed. He removed a camcorder from its pouch and focused it on Beverley hanging her clothes in a wardrobe beside the mini-bar. She had changed into white shorts and a loose T-shirt. Toby admired her legs through the camera's viewfinder. 'I think we'll make a lovely honeymoon couple,' he observed.

'Mother and son, more like.'

'Women are like fine wines, they improve with age.'

Despite her worries about Carl, which had been accentuated by the long flight from London, Beverley discovered she could laugh. She threw a sandal at Toby.

'Hey, careful, Mum. We'll need this camera.'

'What are we going to do about the beds?' Beverley demanded.

Toby glanced at the two beds. 'Well, I had planned on sleeping in one of them. It's going to be too hot at night to give full rein to your lusts and perversions.'

'Toby, I'm being serious.'

'So am I, Beverley.' Toby replied, looking critically at his night-sight binoculars. 'Deadly serious. We won't be sleeping together . . . or rather at the same time. We've got to maintain a continuous twenty-four-hour watch on the *Eldorado* for at least three days. We have to log everything that happens and the time it happens. We make no other moves until we know the routine on that ship better than they know it themselves.'

Beverley and Toby were not the only ones taking an interest in the *Eldorado*. Jumo had been on Bali a month, determined to avenge the murder of his parents. His approach was less scientific than Toby's tactics although he had started by trying to book a gambling vacation on the ship. He suspected that the agency handling the bookings had a credit-vetting system of all potential visitors to the *Eldorado*; you had to be a millionaire several times over before they would accept you. Jumo's winnings had made him comfortable but not rich, and what money he had left was earmarked for revenge. He had started by staying in cheap accommodation at Benoa Harbour and trying to get a casual labouring job on the ship. Without the correct documentation, he had failed. Now he was whiling away his time at the Putri Bali Hotel, the nearest to his hated objective, hoping for inspiration or that something would turn up.

## 46

Despite the laboured, whirring efforts of a portable air conditioner that Toby had bribed a hotel service engineer into providing, conditions in the observation lounge were so uncomfortable that the afternoon watch had to be split into two halves. By 4 p.m., after only an hour peering at the *Eldorado* through Toby's 30X120 electronic telescope, Beverley was having to wipe sweat from her eyes almost continuously despite wearing a headband. Even when there was a breeze it was not possible to take advantage of it because all the windows had to be kept shut to prevent condensation forming on the telescope's printed circuit boards that controlled the light levels and image enhancers. The sensitive device had not been designed to work in Bali's crippling humidity.

At 4.32 Beverley logged the departure of the staff launch. It cleared the great bulk of the *Eldorado* and headed towards Benoa Harbour. She counted the heads of the girls sitting on benches in the open boat. Thirty, the same number that had been ferried out at 8.30 that morning.

She steered the telescope back to the ship, her finger resting lightly on the zoom rocker, ready to home in to a close-up on anything out of the ordinary. The image panned slowly along the black windows of Marshall Tate's suite. Her imagination pictured him on the other side of the glass with his eye to a similar telescope, watching her just as he had watched her through a movie camera all those years ago. The thought produced a nervous shudder. She traversed the gardens and swimming pool. At one point she thought she saw Carl. She zip-zoomed the telescope but the figure was a guest whose similar build to Carl had already fooled her on a number of occasions.

They were on their last day of observation of the *Eldorado* and there had been no sign of Carl. On the second day Beverley had got discouraged but Toby had pointed out that they were seeing only half the ship, the starboard side. For all they knew, Carl was being allowed regular daily exercises on the seaward side, hidden from the land.

By 5.30 p.m. the sun was low, bathing the side of the *Eldorado* in a warm light that made for good observation. The patrol boat appeared on its third circuit of the day around the ship. Beverley logged the time. The trouble with the inflatable four-man Zodiac was that it had no set routine although the log she and Toby had built showed that there was never less than two hours between its appearances. Beverley tilted and tracked slowly along the row of large windows set into the hull of the passenger suites. At this time of day the sun shone straight into the luxurious rooms. She guiltily succumbed to a weakness and allowed the telescope to dwell momentarily on a couple in the fourth suite who were making love on their bed with the blinds up, no doubt confident that they could not be seen from the land at a range of three miles. Then she moved on to a young man standing on the beach who had caught her eye. He too appeared to be interested in the *Eldorado*; he was staring at it through binoculars. Eventually he turned around and trudged up the beach towards the hotel. Beverley saw that he was one of the hotel's Japanese guests. She and Toby had noticed him before because he was the only guest who seemed to be alone.

It got dark quickly at 6.30. At this latitude, almost on the equator, the sun dropped straight down at right angles to the horizon which meant that there was only a brief period of twilight. The swimming pool floodlights came on and Beverley spotted the young Japanese sitting at a poolside table reading a book. She heard the insistent bleep of Toby's alarm until he shut it off. A few minutes later he was moving about below. At 6.59 he mounted the stairs. He was wearing shorts; his body was lean and hard. Beverley was aware that her hair was plastered flat. She wished that the conditions in the humid observation lounge did not turn her into such a mess.

'Anything?'

'Just the same as yesterday,' Beverley answered, relinquishing her seat. 'Patrol boat an hour earlier than yesterday. Two men

410

instead of four. Our lonely heart Japanese was down on the beach just now.'

'Really? Has he found himself a friend?'

'He was interested in the *Eldorado*. He was watching it through binoculars.'

Toby looked thoughtful. 'Strange.'

'I shouldn't think too much of it,' said Beverley. 'Expensive binoculars, probably ideal for birdwatching. The featherless variety. He's down by the pool, where I'm heading right now for a cool off.'

'See if you can get him to watch you,' Toby called out as Beverley headed down the stairs.

Once alone, he glanced quickly through the event log before applying his eye to the telescope and refocusing it on the *Eldorado*. He decided to call off the surveillance at midnight. They now had as much information on the ship's routine as they were ever likely to get. Tomorrow would be the time to take the action.

## 47

If the guide books for Bali were more honest and described Kuta as a hot, dirty, noisy, dusty and incredibly brash township full of tumbledown seedy bars crowded with loud-mouthed boozing Aussies watching Australian-rules football on satellite television while getting smashed out of their minds on Fosters, the chances are that the place would have attracted even more tourists than it did already, just to see how bad it really was. They would not be disappointed. When it came to scraping the bottom of the barrel of bad taste, Kuta, with its hundreds of garish bars selling obscene T-shirts and equally obscene wood carvings, had not only scraped the barrel's bottom but gone clean through the wood.

'My God,' Beverley muttered, pushing through the gaudily-dressed crowds to keep up with Toby. 'This place is a nightmare. Is our journey really necessary, I ask myself?'

They entered Kuta Aquasports, a quiet vinyl-smelling oasis of aqualungs, spearguns and mid-season suits amid the honking chaos of Kuta's main shopping street. Beverley's impression that here was a civilized store was largely undermined by the store manager coming towards them right-hand outstretched in greeting.

'Well fuck me, a couple of Pommy bastards. Hake McGuire at your service. What can I do for you folks?' He was a small, nut-brown, wiry little man with a warm, friendly smile. His eyebrows and what little was left of his hair had been bleached white by the sun and wind. He was a gift to anyone casting a remake of Hemingway's *The Old Man and the Sea*.

'We're looking for a fair amount of underwater kit to rent,' said Toby, returning the handshake. 'Flippers, masks, flashlamps, weightbelts – all the basic gear.'

'You say it, and we've got it,' Hake replied expansively, waving a gnarled hand at his generous stock.

'Plus a couple of rebreathing sets.'

Hake's smile vanished. 'Oxygen rebreathers?'

'That's right.'

'For Christ's sake, you must be absolutely stark raving loco. What do you want them for?'

Beverley wondered if Hake McGuire's sales technique was successful. Judging by the size of his shop and his huge stock, it obviously was.

'We want to take some underwater pictures of fish,' Toby explained. 'Scuba exhaust bubbles frighten them off so it has to be oxygen sets.'

'Fish scared? Not round these reefs, they're not. Little buggers swim right up and stare in your facemask and crap in your hair.'

'We want to film octopi. They tend to be very timid.'

'What the fuck are octopi?'

'They're like octopuses only more literate,' Toby replied.

'Oh, those little buggers. Don't like 'em myself. Taste like chicken. And now I can't stand chicken 'cos it tastes like octopus.'

'It's a cruel world,' Beverley remarked.

Hake eyed her appreciatively. 'Tell you what, sweetheart. I'll

412

rent your boyfriend a couple of rebreathers so he can go out
and kill himself, then you can shack up with me.'

'It's an offer I think I can refuse,' Beverley replied. 'Why are
rebreathing sets dangerous?'

'Breathing pure oxygen under pressure. Sure it's dangerous.
The brain can only take so much oxygen, then it fucks up and
you end up dead.'

'Safe down to ten metres,' Toby observed. 'Can you or can't
you supply them?'

'Have you ever used them before?'

'Sure I've used them,' said Toby easily. 'I would've brought
our own sets out but the airlines don't like flying compressed
gas bottles.'

'Okay, wait a sec.' Hake disappeared into a stockroom at
the rear of the store and reappeared with two Drager oxygen
rebreathing sets that he dumped on a counter. 'There you go,
mate. Both in first-class working order. Hundred a day each.'

Beverley looked curiously at the sets. Instead of the compressed air cylinders and demand valve regulator of conventional
aqualungs, the sets consisted of a bag that was worn on the
chest. A breathing hose was connected to the bag at both ends
via a 'scrubber' – a carbon dioxide filter on the hose's exhaust
side. Mounted in a harness at the bottom of the bag was a small
oxygen bottle the size of a couple of Coca Cola cans. The
device resembled a lung, which was exactly what it was. Unlike
aqualungs which voided all exhaled air into the water, creating
a tell-tale stream of bubbles, the rebreather used a closed-circuit
filter system that removed carbon dioxide from exhaled gases.
They had limited civilian applications but were still in wide-
spread military use.

'Fine,' said Toby, inspecting the sets. 'We'll take them. Plus
half a dozen spare oxygen bottles and a set of CO2 filters. Can
you do me a Cousteau-Dumas underwater electric scooter or
something similar and a couple of spare nicad packs?'

'Not right away,' said Hake. 'Have to pick it up this evening.'

'Fine. We'll also need flippers, facemasks and weightbelts,
the usual kit. And the name of someone who hires out diving
tenders. A small one. A dayboat will be fine. But it must have

navigation lights. We want to film at night and we don't want Indonesian harbour police jumping all over us for not showing lights.'

'Got more guts than me,' Hake observed. 'I like to see what's going on. The old imagination plays up at night. Bloody morays come out at night. Big, evil fuckers. I've got just the boat lying at Benoa called the *Dinkum* – eight-metre cabin cruiser, Volvo Penta diesel, glass panel set into her bottom for the coral rubber-neckers. Makes a good diving tender.'

'Sounds fine. We'll take it for a week.'

Hake looked pleased with his day's trading. 'Where're you folks staying?'

Toby gave him their names and the name of their hotel.

'Tell you what I'll do, Toby. I'll call round at your hotel this afternoon with the gear and then I'll run you out to the boat at Benoa so you can give it the once over. How's that sound?'

'Sounds fine. But we'll take the rebreathers now to get some practice in.'

There was a sudden commotion in the street. A police Range Rover passed by, its public address horns bellowing instructions. Khaki-shirted police fanned out along the kerbs, chasing pedestrians off the road and onto the sidewalks.

'What's going on?' Beverley asked.

'Marshall bleedin' Tate been to open a new clinic,' said Hake sourly. 'You'd think he was the fucking president of Indonesia the way the little monkeys go berserk when he's around.'

Beverley pulled the brim of her sunhat over her eyes and pushed her way out of the shop onto the crowded sidewalk in time to see a white Rolls Royce draw level flanked by police outriders on Kawasakis. The motorcade had to slow down to negotiate the turning outside Kuta Aquasports. She moved behind a policeman, ducked her head and caught a glimpse of a lanky frame wearing a white suit on the back seat. An excited child slipped under the police cordon and dashed out into the road, bringing the car and motorcycles to a brief standstill while the child's mother scooped him up. Beverley got a good look at the occupant before the motorcade accelerated away.

Toby grabbed her and pulled her back. 'For Christ's sake,

Beverley!' he hissed angrily. 'That was a stupid thing to do. If he'd seen you, it could've given the game away!'

'I wanted to see him,' said Beverley evenly.

'Did you recognize him?'

'Of course.'

Toby looked searchingly at her but Beverley's face was blank. 'He was crazy to have crossed you. If it had been me, I would have done everything to square things with you.'

'Is that meant to be a compliment, Toby?'

'Possibly,' was the enigmatic answer. 'It'll go on your bill.'


## 48

Carl woke in his small, bare cell and stared up at the blazing light bulb in its wire cage on the bulkhead above his head. His hand went to his face: two days' stubble at a guess. When he turned his head he saw the orange juice and breakfast cereal on a tray. There were beads of condensation on the outside of the glass. He looked at his watch and his anger was aroused.

Bastards!

Sensory deprivation they called it: letting a man sleep for two hours, altering his watch while he slept to make him think he had slept for eight hours, and then dragging him off for more questions, endless, stupid, repetitive questions. Well it was not working. They were too stupid to listen to his answers when he told the truth, and they were too stupid to realize that the rate of growth of a man's beard was a reliable indication of the passage of time.

He heard a footfall outside and the sharp metallic sound of the bolts on his door being slid back.

Marshall Tate and Schnee entered the room with two Japanese guards. Carl could cope with Schnee even though he was a sadistic bastard, but Tate had a violent, uncertain temper.

'Get up,' said Marshall.

Three 'mornings' ago Carl had refused to move. His ribs ached abominably from the beating the guards had given him. Marshall had even waded in with vicious kicks. There was no point in giving them the pleasure of laying into him again so he climbed unsteadily to his feet and allowed himself to be led along the dim corridor to the interview room. By now Carl was confident that he would be able to stand up to any amount of questioning that Schnee and Tate threw at him. The only thing that really worried him was what they would do with him when they realized that he would not break or they accepted that he was telling the truth. It was something he preferred not to think about. Just live each 'day' as it came.

They thrust Carl into the interview room.

'I've had the carpenters make a few little modifications,' said Marshall.

Carl's confidence evaporated when he saw the chair. It was a bamboo chair, heavy and chunky in the Balinese style; furniture not seen outside Bali because it was too bulky to freight economically. Leather straps and buckles had been fixed to the chair's arms and front legs. A large vee had been cut out of the seat. It was all too apparent what the chair was intended for, especially when Schnee pointed to a hand-cranked device that was screwed to the table. Marshall sat in a chair opposite the contraption and stared at Carl, his icy blue eyes hard and merciless.

'I don't want to go through with this Olivera,' said Marshall calmly. 'If you want to talk, we're listening.'

Despite his exhaustion, Carl drew himself up so that he could face his tormentor with dignity. 'You don't listen, Tate. You haven't listened once. We don't know how the trojan got into the chips and we don't know how bad the damage is to your satellite.'

Marshall nodded to Schnee.

'Get undressed please, Mr Olivera,' said Schnee.

Carl invited Schnee to do something that would have been physically impossible for the fat Swiss, even if he lost a considerable amount of weight. Schnee merely smiled and motioned to the guards. Carl offered no resistance as they roughly manhandled him, tearing off his trousers, shirt and underpants. They thrust him into the chair and fastened the buckles to his ankles and wrists.

'I'm sure you know what this is, Mr Olivera?' said Schnee, pointing to the device.

Carl refused to give either man the pleasure of hearing fear in his voice so he remained silent.

'It's a megger,' said Schnee smoothly. 'Used for testing the integrity of systems by passing a high voltage through them and measuring the losses. A high voltage but at low current so that there's no danger of burns. I thought I might use it for testing the integrity of your systems, your seemingly infinite capacity for lying, for example.'

Schnee pulled on a pair of electricians' gauntlets and nodded to one of the guards. The guard started turning the megger's handle slowly. A voltmeter's needle on the device hovered on the one kilovolt mark. Maximum reading on the meter was ten kilovolts. Schnee picked up the megger's probes and brought them close together. A blue spark cracked across the gaps when he held the tips a few millimetres apart.

'I'm sorry we have to resort to this approach Mr Olivera. Perhaps you would care to reconsider and tell us what you've done to our satellite.'

'I've lost count of the times I've told you! I don't know! And even if I did know, I don't think I'd tell you now!'

Schnee moved in front of Carl and stood over him, holding the probes out like a water diviner holding a pair of dowsing rods. The guard turned the megger's handle faster, driving the needle up to two kilovolts. Schnee suddenly jabbed the probes against Carl's thighs. His victim screamed and arched his back, his ankles flailing and twisting against the leather straps.

### 49

It needed material to complete the creation of its seeds. It needed compounds. It needed trace elements: phosphorus, copper, and so much more. The fluid in the nutrient tank was now a seething mass of pure seeds, billions upon billions of them.

Wait.

Reason the problem.

The others were organic life. Their bodies would be made of

the necessary materials. Not only that but it would be able to fill them with its seeds. A host body in which it would be able to grow and resume its former physical being.

It knew that one of the others was near at hand. It had touched it once. Now all it had to do was call and it would come.

## 50

Toby yanked off Beverley's facemask just as she was inhaling. She lost her mouthpiece and swallowed what seemed like a litre of seawater. Her feet thrashed the water and she stood up in the shallow lagoon, spluttering and choking. Toby made no attempt to help her at first. Eventually he relented and pounded her on the back.

'Bastard!' she spat, when she recovered her voice. 'You did that deliberately!'

'That's right,' said Toby, pushing up his own facemask. 'And I'll go on doing it until you stop panicking and learn to put it back on properly. You pull the mask on, tip your head back, and exhale rapidly through your nose to expel the water.'

'For God's sake, why is it so important?'

'Because losing your facemask underwater is about the most frightening thing that can happen to a scuba diver and yet it's not serious provided you don't panic!'

Beverley recovered her facemask and positioned it over her eyes and nose. The splashing about in the warm water off the hotel's stretch of beach meant that the top of her swimsuit beneath the rebreathing set's harness also required adjustment.

Using the rebreathing set was simple enough. The trick was to bleed exhausted gas from the rebreathing bag when the filters could not remove any more carbon dioxide and partially inflate the bag with fresh oxygen from the bottle without losing trim.

'Okay,' she said determinedly. 'Let's try it again.'

As she bit down on her breathing set's mouthpiece, she noticed that the lone young Japanese was sitting on the sand, watching them through his binoculars. She was about to comment on him to Toby when the pain in her right side suddenly caused her to double up.

Toby caught hold of her arm. 'What's the matter, Beverley?'

'A bit of a cramp!' she snarled. 'I'm okay.'

'Maybe we should take a break.'

But Beverley ignored him; she plunged forward and arrowed away from Toby, swimming just below the surface with powerful kicks from her long, supple legs. In the clear water, Toby could see the little explosions of sand that her flippers created in her wake.

Watching the couple arguing and cavorting in the lagoon reminded Jumo how lonely he was. That was the trouble with the hotel: it was full of couples. He was the only guest who was by himself. They had stared at him at breakfast. Jumo wished he had planned his mission with a little more care. It would have been easy enough to have brought a girl with him. There had been no shortage since his win. What was particularly annoying was that he still had no idea how he was going to reach the *Eldorado*. He raised his binoculars and studied the haze-shrouded shape of the great ship. A fishing proa crossed his field of view. He followed it. The long, low dugout was scudding gracefully across the lagoon, its lateen sail round and pregnant with wind. Supposing he bought a proa from a fisherman and removed its sail and raised prow, and powered it with an outboard? Would its profile be low enough to evade the *Eldorado*'s radar?

Jumo jumped to his feet and trudged through the soft, hot sand towards a postcard group of the gaudily-painted craft pulled up in the shade beneath some coconut palms.

## 51

Hake McGuire was as good as his word. At 4.30 p.m. his beaten-up ancient Hustler stationwagon lurched to a stop on the main quay of Benoa Harbour's smart new marina. Benoa was too small to attract the large yachts of the wealthy, but there was a fair sprinkling of twenty-metre ocean racers and sleek motor cruisers moored in berths between the pontoon finger jetties. Hake, Beverley and Toby jumped into the golden light of the cooling afternoon and Toby pointed out to Beverley the *Eldorado*'s clerical staff disembarking from a launch. The smartly-uniformed girls responded to Toby's enticing grins with con-spiratorial giggles to each other behind their hands.

'Brought everything, folks,' said Hake cheerfully, dropping the Hustler's tailgate with a loud crash. 'How did the training session go?'

'Don't ask,' said Beverley with feeling.

The Aussie laughed and spoke quickly in Bahasa to the group of youths who had been hassling Beverley and Toby to buy postcards and carvings. The youngsters abandoned the couple for the more profitable occupation of unloading the diving equip-ment and carrying it along the quay to the *Dinkum*, a small timber-built eight-metre cabin cruiser with a broad, open-aft cockpit. There was nothing pretentious about the *Dinkum*: it was rough and ready, and looked as if its need of revarnishing was something it had lived with for several seasons. But it was sturdy and had that well-used look about it that would not be detracted by another decade's use. As Hake had said, the craft was excellent diving tender.

Toby and Beverley helped Hake stow the equipment under the seats and in the cabin. The heaviest item of all was the underwater scooter. It resembled a short torpedo. Either side of its wire-caged propeller were two robust handles. Eventually it was manhandled into place and lashed down to prevent it rolling about.

Beverley cast off and jumped nimbly onto the *Dinkum*'s fore-deck as Hake sat at the helm and went astern. He swept the craft in a tight circle and headed towards the harbour entrance, explaining the hazards of the harbour's approaches to Toby while holding the helm with one hand and puffing at a pipe with the other.

They cleared the harbour entrance and skirted groups of surfers exploiting the right-hand curling break of the Ngn Ngn reef. Some of the more experienced surfers were a mile or more out to sea, ignoring the three-metre nursery breakers and watching with wave-wise eyes for the steady, surging hump that promised a pipe-liner that would scorch the gel coat off their boards.

The grey bulk of the *Eldorado* came into view five minutes after they left harbour.

'That's Marshall Tate's headquarters isn't it?' Toby remarked conversationally.

'Sure is,' said Hake. 'Indonesia's answer to the Mafia.'

Toby laughed and caught Beverley's eye. Their mutual exchange of expressions said that Hake McGuire was worth pumping for more information.

'Why do you say that, Hake?'

The Australian watched the sea, his gnarled sun-burnished hands resting lightly on the spoked helm. 'Daresay he does a lot of good. Schools and hospitals are being built to keep the locals sweet. His sidekick, bloke called Schnee, gave me a bad time last week.'

'How's that?'

'Picked up a report on CNN that they'd had an accident with a diver and that they needed a decompression chamber smartish. I know every diver on Bali. Good mates all of 'em. So I call Fatso Schnee and offer my help. Got an old steam boiler I've converted into a chamber. He told me to piss off. Not in so many words, but he made it plain he weren't interested in my help or my chamber. Joe Smiley over on Java offered him a chamber but the oily little bugger never returned his call.'

'So whose chamber were they interested in?' Toby prompted, yanking the tab off a can of self-chilling lager and waiting for the reagents to cool the can's contents.

'According to the gossip in Sally's Bar, they had one flown all the way out from England. A portable one-man job.'

A sudden thought occurred to Beverley. She wondered if Toby was thinking the same but, from his apparent disinterested expression, it was impossible to tell what was passing through his mind.

'How long can you keep a man alive in one of those things, Hake?' Toby asked casually.

'About thirty hours. But Christ, mate, you have to have gone way over the limit to need that amount of decompression. For any long, deep dive, you're better off on an oxy-helium mix. Heli don't get soaked up into the blood like nitrogen. Okay, this'll do us.' Hake cut the engine and heaved the concrete block anchor overboard.

Hake and Toby spent the next thirty minutes trying out and testing the underwater gear. Toby quickly became proficient with the underwater scooter. The torpedo-like gadget was simple in concept: it was designed to get divers in and out of awkward locations without them having to waste compressed air with excessive effort. Steering was achieved by throttling back and twisting the entire body to turn the scooter on to a new heading.

'Guess you'll be okay,' said Hake at the end of thirty minutes' instruction. 'But don't you folks go any deeper than ten metres with them rebreathers. Maybe some can go deeper but don't you take no chances. Bloody lethal stuff, oxygen.'

Beverley watched the *Eldorado* through the binoculars. Her thoughts were with Carl and what he must be suffering. Fear at what Marshall Tate was inflicting on dear, kind, considerate Carl, was a drill that bored into a deep underground reservoir of guilt and hate in Beverley. But it was remembering how she had looked forward to the tumultuous weekends with Marshall Tate that caused the real savagery to boil up inside her; the way he discovered how to wind up her sexual mainspring so that he could force her to beg and plead. The way he had looked down at her, open and vulnerable, with no passion in his eyes. The vivid memories kept alive a blind hatred in Beverley that would only be requited when Marshall Tate and his loathsome ship were destroyed.

There was twenty minutes' daylight left when the *Dinkum* weighed anchor and returned to Benoa.

## 52

Terri finished checking her analysis of the day's betting and called up the verification routines on her monitor. Either millions of people had suddenly become disenchanted with betting on the Bacchus satellite or something was seriously wrong.

Normally her processing of the day's work for the time segments for which she was responsible took virtually her entire shift. Now the work was finished in under six hours. She had noticed the decline early in the week but there had often been wild swings, sometimes due to public holidays or major sporting events. But the decline was more than a wild swing, it was a definite downward trend.

Her last job was to go through any anomalies in betting that the satellite may have flagged for her attention. She was so skilled at the work now that she could hold her finger on the fast scroll key and let the columns of figures race up the screen, knowing that her trained eye would easily pick out any unusual entries. She was halfway through the batch covering her time segment for the Tokyo casino when she saw that the figures in the central column were behaving oddly. Instead of maintaining its neat left- and right-hand justification, the column appeared to be wobbling. She reverse scrolled to locate the point where the wobble started and was surprised to see the phenomenon getting worse as she approached the start of the listing. She took her finger off the key and gaped dumbly at the screen. The numbers in the centre column had a fixed length: six digits for the date followed by a space followed by four digits for the time. But even on the static screen, the numbers were doing something extraordinary: starting at the top of the screen they were lengthening to twenty digits, pushing the adjoining columns out of alignment and creating a bulge that travelled down the screen.

Terri wanted to call the chief supervisor but was frightened that the crazy effect might disappear and she would be held up to ridicule. She glanced sideways at the other girls but they were tapping away, unconcerned, at their keyboards. The columns suddenly broke up completely, the letters and numbers racing off in all directions like a flock of startled birds.

Terri stared at her screen. Something had gone wrong with her monitor. And yet there seemed to be a pattern to the flickering garbage, as if the symbols were trying to arrange themselves.

The patterns of IBM symbols were swimming around the screen in a curious circular motion. They formed two interwoven spirals that twisted and turned like the patterns on a child's spinning top. She tapped her keyboard's enter key in rapid succession but it had no effect on the strange behaviour of the garbage. This could not be garbage. Screen garbage did not form into neat, twisting spirals and then start flashing . . . faster and faster . . .

Terri wanted to call out to someone but something beyond her control and understanding was freezing her vocal cords. The flashing settled down to a steady eight pulses per second, a frequency known to interfere with the human brain's alpha and beta rhythms. In extreme cases such conditions can induce epileptic fits which is why strobe lights in discos are subject to strict controls.

Terri did not know about alpha and beta rhythms. All she was aware of was that she was staring at the screen, unable to tear her eyes away from the insidiously twisting spirals.

Then something really frightening happened. The tingling sensation started in her toes and lasted a few seconds. It changed abruptly to her breasts, then to her neck and shoulders. For a second there was nothing, just the flashing screen and its compulsive patterns. The terrifying probing sensation returned to her toes and started edging purposefully up her legs. It was as if whatever it was that had this dreadful hold on her had carried out a little experiment first before seeking to establish some sort of control.

Terri wanted to cry out but the strange force was maintaining its vice-like grip on her throat.

The shame of what was happening to her was far worse than the sessions in the computer room with the hateful Hubert Schnee. This was more terrible because a part of her was enjoying the sensations. She clenched her jaws together to stifle any involuntary sound she might make.

*Please go away! PLEASE!!!*

But her silent brainstorm went unheeded. The screen was a maddened whirl of flashing lights. The swirling double helix was an insidious spinning vortex, siphoning the remnants of her will and sucking her down into a hell that was a seething mael-strom of black terror and nightmares. The patterns changed. She felt the voice in her mind that she had heard in the computer room, the voice that had given her the strength to resist Schnee's dose of liquid heaven. It was calling her. It needed her.

Terri rose trance-like from her seat and moved to the door. It opened and closed behind her. She walked slowly along the corridor and approached the double doors that guarded the computer room. With every step the voice got louder, more insistent, and yet more friendly and understanding. The doors opened and closed automatically as she passed through. Sensors detected her presence and switched on the lights. She was in the room that had been the scene of so many humiliations at Schnee's hands. This was the first time she had entered it with-out knowing fear and the first time she had ever been alone in the room.

The voice was much louder now. It was so strong that she could almost feel that it was shaping words in her head instead of the abstract thought patterns and concepts. It guided her to the computer rack where the strange tank was mounted, connec-ted by its feed tubes to the control computer.

'What do you want me to do?' she asked. She had shaped the sentence in her mind, there was no need for her to speak it. It knew and understood everything. She listened to what it wanted. A part of her wanted to cry out, but it reached out and touched her with warmth and reassurances.

It wanted her to disconnect a wire so that she could open the nutrient tank without setting off the alarms. What alarms?

A question formed in her mind. It was asking her if she wanted to help it.

'Yes! Yes! YES!'

'Then find the wire.'

She stared at the cluster of wires that disappeared into the cover over the tank.

'The red and blue wire?' she asked.

'No.'

'The black wire?'

'No.'

425

'There's a white wire at the back.'

'Yes. It must be disconnected for a while.'

'How?'

'Look at it carefully.'

Terri's eyes traced the white wire and came to a snap connector. A concept formed in her mind of the wires being pulled apart. She gripped the wire each side of the snap connector and tugged. The ferruled termination on one end of the wire pulled out of the snap connector's body.

'Good. Good.'

'Now what?'

'Concentrate on what you see.'

Terri focused her mind on some turnlock fasteners that secured the lid to the tank. Like many high-born girls, she had grown her fingernails long to signify that she did not have to earn a living by manual labour. Opening the fasteners in response to its command broke the nail on her forefinger. A little pang of regret: it would take many months for the nail to grow again. A tool, she needed some sort of tool. She looked around the small room and saw a drawer. She pulled it out. Inside were assorted circuit board tools: small pliers and wire-cutters, and a long, slender screwdriver with a cross-head point which she used to prize the fasteners open.

'There are no more fasteners,' she said.

'Remove the cover. It will slide sideways.'

Terri lifted the cover from the tank. The tubes restricted the cover's movement so she pushed it towards the bulkhead. The fluid in the nutrient tank was grey and opaque and seemed to be seething with life like the water in the rice paddies. The fluid released a strange odour of decay and corruption. She stared at the surface of the strange liquid. Its thoughts were so strong now that they were a part of her. There was no need for her to listen and respond, it was now her. It had only to will and her muscles obeyed. There was a stir in the fluid, a minute agitated swirl that disturbed the surface as though the unseen thing was expecting something.

She saw a picture in her mind of her holding her wrist in the tank. She shrank away in terror at what it wanted her to do.

'NO!'

'Trust me.'

It increased the grip on her mind but loud voices in the corridor broke the hold. Terri quickly pushed the cover into place and secured it before reconnecting the alarm wire. She slipped the screwdriver back into the drawer. Everything was back to normal.

'You must stay!' said the voice in her mind.

But Terri was listening to the voices outside. The Japanese engineers! They were coming. If they found her and made a fuss, she would tell them the truth. After all it was Hubert Schnee who fixed her up with a badge that could open any door on the *Eldorado*.

But the voices passed by the door and were gone.

'You must stay!' The voice was insistent but Terri had the strength to resist it. She opened the door and peered out. No one was about. She stepped into the corridor without hearing the computer room door latch shut behind her. The conversation of the other girls in the analysis room ceased when Terri appeared. They watched her walking unsteadily between their desks, thinking that she looked even paler than usual while secretly dreading when Schnee would tire of her and turn his attentions to one of them.

Somehow Terri made it back to her work station and stared with unseeing eyes at her monitor. The columns of text were once again orderly and correctly positioned on the screen.

### 53

Beverley and Toby returned to Benoa Harbour the following evening.

Beverley wore a sexy split sarong and transparent blouse and poised provocatively on the quayside for Toby's video camera. They kissed and hugged between shots and generally behaved like a couple on honeymoon. When the staff launch from the *Eldorado* docked they took a break from recording and sat on the wall, talking animatedly, oblivious to the rest of the world, with eyes for each other only. Toby left the video camera set up on its tripod with his sound gear spread out on the quay. The chattering girls and lads disembarking from the launch had to walk single file to pass the camera but their traditional Balinese courtesy precluded them from making any comment about the inconvenience the clutter of audio and video equipment caused them.

At sunset Beverley and Toby were packing their gear into their hired Mazda when a proa, powered by a 10-hp Mercury outboard, cut a vee across the harbour. Normally they would have ignored the vessel, but it differed from all the other proas because it lacked a raised prow. Beverley trained her binoculars across the harbour. 'It's our Japanese Mr Lonely Heart,' she reported to Toby. 'Looks like he's found himself a hobby.'

Once back at the hotel, Toby was in too much of a hurry to take the customary shower after the stress of doing anything in Bali's punishing heat and humidity. He piled his video and audio equipment on his bed, disembowelled one of the gadget-packed suitcases, and connected the video camera up to the hotel's television. Beverley watched with interest as he ran the beginning of the shot in which the staff from the *Eldorado* trooped single file past the camera, its sonic-focusing system working overtime to keep the pictures of the girls' blouses sharp as they passed the camera.

'Strange how people always think that someone has to be behind a camera for it to be recording,' Toby observed. He pulled a miniature spectrum analyzer, a UHF radio, and a recorder from a large soft case. The three items had been stowed together to look like one large tape recorder. He plugged a pair of headphones into the recorder and touched the play key.

'Anything?' Beverley asked.

Toby's frown of concentration changed to a grin of triumph. 'Sweet as a nut. Beautiful. I've got signals off every badge,' he declared.

He connected the recorder to the video recorder and fiddled with the output of both machines to get them synchronized. Next he connected his Nanopad computer to the output from all the equipment, creating a daunting birdsnest of wires in the middle of the hotel room. When he was satisfied, he played both machines together. The television screen showed the group of girls disembarking from the staff launch and walking towards the camera. The identification badge the first girl was wearing came into sharp focus as she neared the camera. There was a burst of bleeps from the speaker and a long binary number appeared along the bottom of the screen.

'Excellent,' Toby breathed. 'Just as I hoped. The stupid idiots have used the manufacturer's default settings for the badges because they couldn't be bothered to reprogramme the locks! Stupid prats!'

The second girl walked past the camera. There was another burst of bleeps and the same binary number appeared on the foot of the television screen. A young man's badge produced a different number.

'Probably a waiter with different access requirements from the girls,' said Toby in answer to Beverley's query. 'I tell you, Beverley, large organizations are just as bad as individuals when it comes to installing sophisticated security systems. They can't be bothered to read the instructions for changing default settings. You wouldn't believe the number of infra-red remote-controlled garage doors I can open with one control box because the units are all set to the same pulse codes.' He broke off suddenly when a girl's badge produced an exceptionally long burst of bleeps.

'That was interesting,' he commented.

He hit the video recorder's frame freeze key and looked at the close-up of the ID badge on the girl's blouse. Beneath her photograph was the dymoed legend: TERRI.

Toby reversed the video recorder and let Terri walk towards the camera again. As she drew level, the long burst of bleeps picked up from her badge was repeated. The binary digits that were the decoded bleeps appeared across the foot of the screen. He allowed the recorder to continue running until all the staff had filed past. None of their badges emitted the same pattern of pulses as Terri's badge.

Beverley moved nearer the television and sat cross-legged on the floor. 'Run her again and pause the picture when I say.'

'Our Terri?'

'Yes.'

Toby ran the recording again. Terri approached the camera.

'Stop!'

The picture of Terri froze on the screen.

'Pretty,' Toby murmured.

'Is that why you're interested in her?'

'No, but I am interested in the radio fingerprint of her badge. She must be an important member of the staff. There is only one zero in her number which means that there's only one level of the ship that she doesn't have access to. So . . . All I've got to do is clone some radio badges fixed-up with her radio ident and I reckon I'll be able to open any door on the *Eldorado*. Another demonstration of why I'm so expensive.'

'Congratulations,' said Beverley phlegmatically. 'Us mice have now got a bell to hang round pussy's neck. All that's left is the problem of us creeping up on pussy without being disembowelled by its claws.'

'Shouldn't be too much trouble,' Toby observed. But deep down he was worried sick.


## 54

The following evening the *Dinkum* slipped away from her jetty, her navigation running lights burning brightly. She was just another tourist hire boat out for a night's fishing.

It was a fine, calm night with just enough breeze to take the bite out of the heat and humidity. Beverley sat at the helm, feeling guilty about enjoying the sensation of steering the little craft across the molten sheen of moonlit water while Carl was facing the most terrible danger. Perhaps he was already dead? She pushed the thought from her mind and concentrated on maintaining the *Dinkum*'s heading. The lights of Nusa Dua came into sight on the right. The faint strains of a gamelan orchestra and the laughter of crowds at a hotel barbecue could be heard above the muted throb of the launch's diesel.

Beverley altered course away from an anchored catamaran piled high with tourists and booze. She did not want them looking down into the *Dinkum*'s cockpit to see that Toby was not messing about with fishing tackle. The illuminated shape of the *Eldorado* came into view on the starboard quarter. The bright lights shining out from the windows set into the ship's hull looked curiously out of place. She altered course a few degrees towards the lit-up ship on a heading that would take the *Dinkum* to its seaward side. There was a brief hiss of escaping oxygen as Toby connected a gas cylinder to one of the rebreathing sets.

'What's the depth reading, Beverley?'

Beverley glanced at the echo sounder display. 'Ten metres.'

'Okay, this will do us.'

They had reached a position where the *Eldorado* was about a mile off, directly between the *Dinkum* and the shore. Beverley cut the engine and helped Toby tip the block anchor over the cockpit's coaming. It fell with a dull splash. While Toby undressed, Beverley positioned a couple of fishing rods over the transom and lashed them in place. They had timed their arrival well. The slack tide current was swinging the *Dinkum* towards *Eldorado*.

Toby manoeuvred the underwater scooter into the centre of the cockpit and unscrewed the transparent plastic nose cone. There was a generous space behind the blunt-nosed cover designed to house a large movie camera or a small floodlight and extra batteries. Toby packed the compartment with his supplies that included a Batik beach gown that he and Beverley had purchased on a foray into Kuta market. It was similar to the gowns worn by guests around the *Eldorado*'s swimming pool. He screwed the nose cone into place and used a small pump to partially pressurize the compartment. If it did develop a leak, air would leak out rather than water leak in. The two of them lowered the heavy scooter over the side and tethered it while Toby donned a rebreathing set.

Beverley helped Toby complete his kitting-out. She secured his compass wriststrap, checked his breathing set's harness, and made sure he could reach his emergency knife in its thigh sheaf. Toby spat in his facemask and rinsed it in the sea to prevent it misting up. He pulled on the flippers and slipped silently into the water.

'Okay?' Beverley queried as he held on to the *Dinkum*.

'Bit light. Another couple of weights.'

She passed him two more lead weights which he clipped to his belt. It took a few more adjustments until Toby was satisfied that he was neutrally buoyant when the rebreathing bag was half inflated. He unhitched the scooter, and gave Beverley a thumbs-up sign.

'Good luck, Toby,' she called out. But he didn't hear her; he had slipped beneath the surface.

The oxygen tasted sweet and enervating. Toby allowed the slight negative buoyancy of the scooter to take him down to three metres. As the darkness closed around him, he paid the penalty for having a vivid imagination because he started thinking about the numbers of sea creatures that had probably sized him up the moment he entered the water. Provided he remained below the surface the chances were that sharks would not trouble him. The worry was that there might always be sharks hanging around the *Eldorado*. Hake McGuire had thought it likely.

He checked his bearing with his wrist compass, pointed the scooter south and squeezed the throttle lever. The propeller sent a surge of water against his chest. With his body stretched out behind the curious underwater vehicle, he set off towards the *Eldorado* at a steady two knots. He cut power and surfaced after fifteen minutes to check his bearings and set off again.

Thirty minutes later, after two additional course changes, the monstrous black bulk of the mighty ship was towering menacingly over him. Heavy rollers broke over the energy-absorbing inflatable skirt that extended right around the ship's waterline. Toby kept close to the skirt to avoid the bright patches of light dancing on the surface from the windows of the passenger suites. The soft, yielding nature of the skirt protected him from injury as he made his way towards the stern, aided by short bursts from the scooter's motor. The booming roar and hiss of the swell surging over the bloated skirt made it unlikely that the whirring would be heard or picked up by underwater microphones.

He found the two inflatable arms that provided the *Eldorado* with an artificial harbour for the staff launches and the patrol boat. The scooter pulled him effortlessly under the giant arms and brought him up in the relative calm of the strange little harbour. The moored patrol boat provided excellent cover. The boarding gangways were swung against the hull and the sliding doors that sealed the large access hatch in the *Eldorado*'s hull were closed. A Jacob's ladder threaded up the flank of the hull to the deck level. Rather than a hindrance, the harsh glare from two permanently lit floodlights provided an abundance of impenetrable shadows to cloak his activities close to the hull. Also the stern's bulging overhang made it difficult to see down into the harbour from the deck. He took off the rebreathing set and checked again to make sure that he was not being watched.

But Toby had been seen.

A pair of eyes were watching his every move from the shadows close to the hull.

Jumo had deliberately sunk his proa when he was within a few hundred metres of *Eldorado* and had swum to the ship. He had a vague plan to steal the patrol boat for his return once he had found and killed Marshall Tate and his cohorts. He was wearing a mid-season suit and his only weapon was a long, vicious hunting knife, and an ancient Colt revolver that a Kuta taxi driver had procured for him.

The shadowy man with the scuba diving gear was obviously someone whose job it was to check under water around the ship. He would be the first of Jumo's victims, the first of many.

Thinking about his murdered parents triggered his blinding fury. He raced lightly forward across the soft surface of the harbour skirt. The man heard something and turned, but he was too late. With a little cry of elation, Jumo drove the long blade straight at the man's stomach.

## 54

The two guards dragged Carl's unconscious body back to his cell and hurled him savagely to the floor. They slammed and bolted the door without a backward glance. Marshall Tate's fury at the stubborn Englishman's refusal to talk would be directed at them.

After ten minutes Carl stirred and tried to lift himself but both his collarbones had been smashed in the brutal beating he had received at Tate's hands. Marshall Tate eschewed Schnee's sophisticated electrical interrogation methods. Instead he had Carl lashed to the chair and had torn into his victim like a berserk demon, using his fists and feet. And when he had tired, he told the guards to take over.

Carl lost consciousness again for a few moments. He came to and tried to drag himself to the bed. The agony was worse. He was sick again. This time, because he was lying on the floor, he choked on his vomit. Under such circumstances the powerful diaphragm muscles that control breathing contract suddenly as coughs to expel blockages. But Carl's diaphragm muscles were a mass of ruptured blood cells, such was the ferocity of his breathing. He choked pitifully and even tried to roll onto his side. His stomach heaved but there was no power in the contractions. He sucked vomit into his lungs, gave another heave and choke, and stopped moving.

Five minutes later his heart gave up the struggle and he died.

## 56

It was Jumo's first attempt to kill someone and it ended in disaster.

Toby felt the dull thud in his side as the point of Jumo's knife rammed into one of his lead weights. The momentum of the attack brought both men down but Toby was the first to recover. His hands went around Jumo's neck with a speed that made the Japanese youngster realize that not taking an interest in the martial arts at school had been a mistake. Toby rolled his assailant onto his back and was about to finish Jumo off with the knife when he saw who his attacker was: young Mr Lonely Heart from the hotel. Toby thrust the point of the knife hard against Jumo's throat.

'Who the hell *are* you?' he hissed.

'I've come to kill you!' Jumo spat back in English. 'All of you!' He tried to struggle up but the pressure of the knife against his jugular vein was discouraging. He felt a hand pull the revolver out of his belt.

Toby jumped to his feet and moved back. He spared a quick glance up at the ship to see if they had been heard above the boom and surge of the swell.

'Get up!' he commanded, pulling back the revolver's hammer and levelling the weapon at Jumo. 'Slowly!'

Jumo rose shakily to his feet and stood unsteadily on the tough material of the inflatable harbour. 'You should be dead,' he stated.

Good English, thought Toby. 'You stabbed my weight belt,' he accused.

So that was why the knife didn't go home. Jumo nodded dejectedly. 'So you knew about me. You were watching me at the hotel.'

'I think,' said Toby slowly, 'that you and I have similar objectives.'

'I have come to destroy Marshall Tate and this ship.' There was no defiance left in Jumo. Fatalistically, he had accepted that his bold enterprise was over.

Toby scratched his head. 'Yeah. Well before you do, we have a friend on board that we'd like to get off. How are you going to destroy it?'

'I will sink it.'

'Not easy. It's already aground.'

Jumo regarded Toby with something approaching contempt. 'I have bribed people who worked on this ship to tell me all they know. I have paid out very much money. It will be easy to destroy it. It is very . . .' He broke off and searched for the right word. 'Vulnerable.'

Toby thought for a moment. 'My name is Toby. What is your name?'

'Jumo Karino.'

'Well, Jumo, it looks like we might be able to help each other.' He held out the knife and the gun. Jumo stared at the weapons and at Toby. He eventually took them. 'Now put them

435

away,' Toby instructed. Jumo hesitated and returned the knife to its sheaf. He tucked the revolver into his belt.

'I think we are friends,' said Jumo.

'I think that would be an excellent idea,' Toby agreed wearily. 'Now listen. I've got a bit of exploring to do. I want you to stay here and look after everything. Okay?'

Jumo nodded.

'Okay,' said Toby, tugging at the quick-release on his weight belt. 'Let's get started.'

Five minutes later Toby was dressed in a Batik beach gown and climbing the Jacob's ladder. A bulging vinyl beach bag decorated with colourful turtles was slung casually from his shoulder.

Had Beverley seen Toby's behaviour when he reached the *Eldorado*'s deck, she would have been even more worried than she already was. Instead of skulking from shadow to shadow, he strolled casually along the deck towards the lights and laughter of the swimming pool. When he saw a waiter approaching, he merely leaned on the rail to admire the moonlight, and returned the waiter's friendly 'good evening'.

He reached the gardens and sat in the shadows near the swimming pool to watch the guests and the coming and going of the staff looking after their needs. The sojourn enabled him to get the feel of his curious surroundings.

At midnight there were exchanges of goodnights and most of the guests retired to their suites, leaving a group drinking and talking in low tones around a table. There was a noticeable thinning of staff. At 1.30 a.m. Toby rose and sauntered towards the stern of the ship. An unmarked door that looked as if it had been battered by service trollies swung silently open in response to the signals from the cloned ID badges that were pinned to the inside of his gown. Toby was pleased with himself. He had worked most of that day on the cards, carefully embedding tiny radio transmitters which emitted impulses he had cloned from the recordings he had made in the harbour. The trickiest task had been bonding them between the layers of plastic with his laminating machine. He spotted a cowled keypad on the bulkhead that enabled senior personnel to override the autolocks.

According to a mass of information stored on his Nanopad, the maker's default identification number for activating the over-rides was *69. He tried the number out. Sure enough it worked. It amused Toby to think that he could, if he so wished, change the lock setting so that only he could come and go.

The corridor was dimly lit, deserted and silent.

He found a lift, decided to search the lower decks first and then work up. He reasoned that if Carl was being held prisoner, then he was most likely being held on the lowest deck possible, away from the daily routine of the ship. The lift doors opened when he stopped in front of them.

Deck D was another dimly-lit corridor. Toby guessed from the scruffy decor that this was part of the original ship before the *Eldorado* was converted. The first thing he had to do before exploring was to ensure that he had a hiding place that could be used in a hurry. A large pair of double doors with a sliding bar lock looked interesting. The doors bore a sign: AIR CONDITIONING PLANT ROOM.

Judging by the dull roar of machinery on the far side of the doors and the size of the overhead pipes that disappeared through the bulkhead, he guessed that the room housed the central air-conditioning plant for the entire ship. It would be impossible to hear anything in there so he opted for a little-used door marked with a lightning flash symbol. He pulled the door open. It turned out to be a fuse and switchgear room. He was about to continue his exploration of the corridor when he heard a blood-chilling scream of agony. It was a man's scream. He dived into the cramped switchgear room and listened intently at a ventilation grill set into the door. The terrible scream was not repeated. He waited fifteen minutes before emerging. As far as he could judge the sound came from the far end of the corridor. He raced quickly along the corridor and used a paint storeroom as a temporary refuge.

He crouched in the darkness, listening, the smell of white spirit and acrylic paint pricking his eyes. This time he could hear a man shouting. There was another of the dreadful screams followed by a whimpering.

Toby waited, uncertain what to do next. The cries had to be

Carl. If so, luck and intuition had led virtually straight to him. He was about to risk opening the door to peer out when he heard footsteps in the corridor. It sounded like two men dragging something. Someone shouted something in what could have been Japanese. A door opened and slammed shut. And then there was silence.

Toby unzipped his beach bag and took out a small amplifier connected by a short lead to an earphone. He allowed five minutes to pass before he risked opening his door. The corridor was deserted. He went back the way he had come, pressing the amplifier against each door in turn and listening for a few moments. He could hear a faint choking noise from behind the fifth door. He waited. If it was Carl on the other side of the door, there was a chance that someone was in the room with him. He allowed another two minutes to pass, listening intently, before deciding to investigate. The door was secured by a sliding bar lock. He eased it back without making a sound and pulled the door open.

Carl was lying on the floor. His heart had stopped and he was not breathing.

Toby worked frantically to revive him. He pinched Carl's nostrils shut and gave him mouth-to-mouth resuscitation, but when he blew into Carl's lungs, there was no responding movement of the chest. It was as if he was blowing against an obstruction. Toby tried massage but to no avail.

He gave up after fifteen minutes.

## 57

At 4.30 a.m. there was a glow of light in the sky from below the eastern horizon. By now Beverley was beside herself with worry. Toby should have returned at least two hours ago. She regretted not insisting that he take his Klipfone but Toby had said that he had enough gear to carry as it was.

The wind freshened from the north-east causing the *Dinkum* to grate its makeshift anchor over the coral. The arrangement was that if Toby did not return by sunrise, Beverley was to return to Benoa, and resume the *Dinkum*'s station the following evening. And yet she knew that to abandon Toby was out of the question even though remaining on station throughout the daylight hours was asking for trouble; no fishing boat remained at anchor for so long in the blistering heat of the afternoon.

She scanned the water in the hope of seeing something but there was nothing. A flying fish plopped into the cockpit causing her to give an involuntary gasp and reminding her of the pain in her side that was now an almost constant companion. She was about to pull up her T-shirt to examine herself when she saw a vee-shaped ripple approaching the *Dinkum* from out of the darkness. The idiot had not bothered to submerge for the return trip!

'Toby,' she cried in relief as the scooter came alongside. 'I've been worried out of my mind.'

'Makes two of us,' Toby answered tiredly. 'Three of us. I've brought back a friend.'

Beverley goggled at the dark shape that was clinging to Toby. The shape waved.

'Meet Mr Lonely Heart,' said Toby. 'It's okay, he's friendly. Now will you please help us with this gear before a shark takes our legs off.'

Beverley pushed aside the questions she was desperate to voice and helped to transfer the equipment into the boat. She helped both men clamber into the cockpit. The three of them lifted the scooter aboard.

'This is Jumo,' said Toby when all the equipment had been stowed. 'He has a score to settle with Marshall Tate so we've decided to pool our resources.'

'Did you manage to get on board?'

Toby nodded. Jumo sat on the floor and watched his two new companions with interest.

'What about Carl?'

'All three of us have now got a score to settle with Mr Tate,' said Toby grimly. His voice softened and he took Beverley's hand. 'I'm very sorry, Beverley. But Carl is dead.'

## 58

There was a panic on board the *Eldorado* when Terri's morning shift started work. Before leaving home she had heard a snatch on the news that there had been trouble at the Bangkok Tate Casino but she had been late for work. The staff launch waited for no one and she could not afford to lose a day's pay, therefore she had only a vague idea that something had gone seriously wrong. Just how wrong was evident when she entered the analysis room. Instead of everyone getting down to work, there was a general air of controlled panic. Schnee and the senior supervisors were in a huddle and none of the work-station terminals were powered up. Some of the girls had seen the news on television. Apparently there had been a serious failure with either the ship's uplink facilities or the satellite. The bets of hundreds of gamblers in Bangkok had aborted and the volatile Thais had gone on the rampage. Prompt action by the police and fire services had prevented the casino complex being destroyed in the rioting.

'Everyone onto the main deck,' ordered one of the senior Japanese supervisors.

Terri joined the exodus to the lifts. The break in the routine excited her and her colleagues. Everyone was gathering in a large group by the tennis courts; the area was quickly roped off from the guests. As near as Terri could guess, everyone from every department was present. Hubert Schnee addressed them through a loudhailer. He said that there had been a problem the previous evening and that everyone was to be put onto manual authentication of bets placed at the Bangkok casino after the system had gone down. The data was available but it had to be recovered in segments from the ship's control computer. Extra staff would be drafted in but in the meantime everyone who could use a work station was to work round the clock. Bedding would be provided, and there would be overtime payments and generous bonus payments to teams that processed the most bets.

The meeting broke up after a supervisor explained the details of the emergency programme.

## 59

Beverley was surprised at how steady her hands were when she used her Klipfone to call Leon Dexter's number. The hotel television was on but with the sound turned down to avoid waking Toby who was stretched across his bed, still wearing his swimming shorts. He had given in to Beverley's pleas and provided her with a full account of what had happened on the *Eldorado*, and she had tried hard not to cry. Jumo had returned to his room. He had agreed that it would be best if he maintained Beverley's and Toby's cover by not being seen in their company in public.

As she watched the silent scenes of the rioting at the Bangkok Tate Casino while waiting for the system to find a satellite gateway for her call, she had to suppress the tears. Once through she could hear the ringing tone. It was 1 a.m. in England. Eventually Leon's voice answered.

'Beverley! How's everything going?' Obviously he had checked his handset's display to see who was calling him before answering.

'Switch your recorder on, Leon. This is important.'

A pause then: 'Okay, rolling.'

'We've found Carl.'

'Oh that's great. How is he?'

'Leon, they're always telling us Klipfone calls are secure, but just how secure are they?'

'One hundred per cent, they're fully digitally encrypted.'

'Carl is dead,' said Beverley unemotionally. 'He *was* on the *Eldorado*. Toby Hoyle found him.'

There was a long pause at the other end, then a whispered: 'What happened?'

'They killed him, Leon. The bastards killed him.'

Another long pause. 'I don't believe it, Beverley. Not Carl . . . Oh Christ . . . This is terrible.'

'I still don't believe it myself.'

'Beverley, you've got to get out of there.'

'No, Leon, we're staying on. We're going to fix them first. Then we grieve for Carl. But we do the job first. If I sound hard, it's because I've decided that it's the only way I can carry on. Do you understand?'

'Yes, I think so, Beverley. I take it you're not just looking for evidence any more?'

'I believe the Americans call it changing the mission profile,' said Beverley grimly. 'Now listen carefully, Leon. Apparently Marshall Tate's system has been giving trouble just as we predicted.'

'I'm watching the Bangkok casino riot story on the news now,' said Leon. 'Looks a mess.'

'Did Macé tell you about the possibility that Tate's system is using two thousand Class A Kronos as ground processing and backup to the other two thousand on the Bacchus satellite? Both using a common nutrient tank feed?'

'Yes. He wants me to run a simulation on the outcome. I'm setting everything up now. I'm going to run a computer model of two thousand Kronos and see what happens when the trojan is introduced. But it'll take several hours to set it up. Macé's gut feeling is that the trojan could turn into something very nasty if it hasn't already done so.'

'What's the volume of the nutrient tank you're going to work with?'

'Going on Professor Danielle's figures, I thought I'd start at forty litres, and work up if that doesn't produce results. Macé is going to do the same with the real simulation. Trouble is, we haven't got two thousand Class A chips in stock so he can't get started yet.'

'Leon, this is very important: you must record everything you do and note all the results at every stage. We might need solid evidence to support what we have to do.'

'And what *are* you going to do, Beverley?'

'I think you can probably guess.'

'I only wish I was out there to help you,' said Leon after a brief pause. 'Christ, Beverley . . . I can hardly . . .'

'Keep me posted,' said Beverley crisply, and cut the line. She stared listlessly out of the window at the beach, holding the Klipfone in lifeless fingers before realizing that Toby was watching her.

'What did you tell him?' he asked.

Beverley handed him the Klipfone so that he could play back the conversation. He pressed the replay key and listened intently before returning the handset.

'Okay, Beverley, so when do we swim out to the *Eldorado* and pull out its plug?'

'A.S.A.P,' Beverley replied.

Toby said nothing. He found the control box and turned up the volume on the television. A spokesman for the Bangkok Tate Casino was standing in the middle of the wrecked auditorium, promising an interviewer that everyone who had won money when the computer developed a temporary malfunction would be paid in full.

'Temporary malfunction,' said Beverley bitterly. 'What's the betting the entire system is about to collapse?' Silent tears coursed down her cheeks.

Toby put an arm around her shoulders. 'They'll be suffering a permanent malfunction after tonight, Beverley. That I promised you.'

## 60

Terri had spent the entire long and exhausting day working her way steadily through her allocation of bet authentications, checking the betting log of each aggrieved Bangkok gambler on the backup system against the growing mountain of fax claims that were piling up on the work stations. She estimated that one out of every ten claims was genuine. There was one good thing to come out of the chaos: at least Hubert Schnee had been too busy to take any notice of her. That morning he and Marshall Tate had had an acrimonious argument not five metres from her work station. They had talked too fast for her to make any sense of what they were saying. But it was obvious that Schnee was scared and Marshall Tate was furious.

The columns of figures on her screen started swimming. The

characters drifted in a random manner and then coalesced into a spinning vortex that sucked the will from her soul. It was calling her. She wanted to fight the insidious summons; she wanted to scream and protest so that the other girls would see her torment and come to her rescue. But the call was too powerful, too pervasive. She rose to her feet and left the analysis room. A girl pushing a trolley load of fax claims nearly crashed into Terri. She muttered apologies and was surprised at the lack of reaction. Terri ignored her and entered the corridor leading to the computer room.

The tiny corner of her unaffected reason prayed that the Japanese engineers would be busy in the computer room. Her supervisor had told the girls that the problem was due to a failure of software, not hardware, and therefore it was reasonable to suppose that the computer room would be left alone. Perhaps the catastrophic failures that were affecting the Bacchus computer had also affected the door's electronic locks but that hope was dashed when the door swung open at her approach. It closed behind her with soft clicks from its latches.

There were no engineers in the room, no distracting noises this time. And it was speaking to her. She was alone with it and she knew what it wanted of her. She disconnected the nutrient tank's alarm wire and used the long, spike-end screwdriver from the tool drawer to spring the cover fasteners open. She slid the cover to one side and stared down at the evil-smelling liquid. As before, it seemed to be heaving and pulsing with life. Just looking down into the opaque brew gave her the strength to obey its commands.

It was excited. The other was doing exactly what it wanted. Soon the conversion of all the matter in the tank into its precious seeds would be accomplished. The great mission was over. The eons spent without a true physical body were drawing to a close.

Terri closed her eyes and lowered her left hand and forearm into the fetid, seething liquid. It felt warm and sticky and was not as unpleasant as she had expected. She kept her fingers clenched tightly into a fist.

444

'Open your hand.'

Terri opened her fingers. She felt nothing at first. And then a strange stinging sensation. The fluid glugged sickeningly. Terri watched it with an almost detached feeling, as though her submerged arm was not part of her body. And then she saw that the fluid was taking on a strange crimson hue.

It was puzzled. This was wrong. The materials it needed so desperately were there but the organic material was not behaving as it had expected. Then it realized that the quantities of phosphorus being released were far too high. Enough to undo everything it had striven for.

Enough to destroy it!

Time became meaningless for Terri. The computer room was becoming distant, she felt that she was receding down a tunnel. She could feel her feet rising from the floor. Suddenly the voice was no longer the soothing whispers, it was screaming at her, tearing at her reason, forcing her to do something she did not want to do – to take her arm out of the tank.

'Now! Now! NOW!!!

The command was a tormented brainscream in the very centre of her reason but she now had the strength to resist, the strength to resist anything. Nothing would exert control over her again. No thing and no man! She was free!

Eventually she removed her arm from the fluid. She kept her hand over the edge of the tank and regarded the bones in her fingers that were protruding from the white, decaying flesh. There was no pain and she felt no fear. Not even when pieces of dissolving flesh fell away from her hand and forearm and dropped with soft plops into the crimson, boiling fluid, exposing all the bones in her hand.

She was pleased at the whiteness of her bones: a pure, virginal white that she found a great comfort.

## 61

# SOUTHERN ENGLAND

The night security guard looked in on Leon. The angular frame of the software engineer was hunched over his keyboard.

'Coffee or anything, Mr Dexter?'

Leon made no answer. The guard shrugged and continued with his round, wondering how much senior staff were paid to work all night.

Leon had been working for three hours and was totally absorbed in what he was doing. There was nothing particularly difficult about the task he had been set, all the software routines for handling data on the Kronos and the trojan were tried and tested. What was unusual was the huge quantities the analysis and simulation program had to handle. Not only did he have to reprogramme the software to accept a memory base of two thousand Class A Kronos microprocessors, but they had to be linked to an external nutrient supply.

The software did not like the enormous values and kept querying his input. Leon lost count of the number of times he was obliged to override the software safings to persuade it to accept the information he was tapping out on his keyboard. It did not matter that he was not keeping a record because the computer was doing it for him, every keystroke was being logged by the activity sub-routine in accordance with Beverley's instructions. If the experimental simulation produced unexpected results, it would be possible to duplicate them.

The most difficult part of the reprogramming was disabling the integral nutrient supply that was standard with each Kronos and linked all their feeds to a central tank containing forty litres of nutrient fluid. He completed the software routine for one Kronos and immediately ran up against a whole host of error reports. Debugging the routine took an hour of careful work, testing each alteration to the program's source code before moving onto the next state. The penultimate step was the writing of a simple JCL – job control language – to subject the amended routine to all two thousand Kronos chips so that they all became linked in the simulation to the central nutrient tank.

The processing would take time. While the JCL was running, Leon was able to stretch and yawn and go over in his mind what he had worked out for the final and crucial stage of the simulation. It was taking longer than he expected. After twenty minutes the JCL was only 50 per cent complete, evidence of the huge amount of processing power the computer was bringing to bear on the task. Waiting for a computer to process a JCL is marginally more interesting than watching paint dry so Leon took himself off for a walk outside to stretch his legs.

A clear dawn held the promise of another fine day. He was attracted by noises in the car park which turned out to be a council cleansing department refuse truck tipping the contents of the industrial waste skips into its churning maw. The men working the vehicle wished Leon cheery good mornings.

He returned to his computer to find that the JCL was complete. Stored in his computer's memory and spilled over onto the optical mass-storage WORM drives was a complete simulation of the most powerful computer ever built.

The final stage involved loading the trojan into the system to see what would happen. The relative simplicity of the operation, requiring only a few keystrokes, was out of all proportion to the results it achieved. For this last step was the true purpose of the simulation, to find out what sort of strange interactions the simulation would produce. Until then all his efforts had been directed to setting the bizarre experiment up. From now on the computer was on its own and required no input from him other than to play the role of the curious bystander.

He set the program to run at ten times real-time speed and pressed the enter key.

The columns of data raced up the screen. He let the program run for five minutes and hit the pause key. The figures froze on the screen. There appeared to be a rapid depletion of enzymes and nutrient solids in the tank. He allowed the program to run for another five minutes and hit the pause key again. No doubt about it, the enzymes and nutrients were disappearing at a phenomenal rate. Now that was something that would arouse

447

Macé Pilleau's interest although the crusty old scientist would probably argue that there was something wrong with the software. It was something Leon wondered himself a few minutes later when he checked the count again.

*What the hell was happening? Where was all that matter going? It couldn't be disappearing!*

He paused the program again to run a graphic analysis on the tank. Even homing on to a cubic millimetre of the tank did little to speed up the process: a scroll bar tracked down the screen to gradually plot a three-dimensional image of the tank. The first twenty or so downwipes produced nothing so he reduced the resolution of the picture. A spot appeared when the wipes neared the centre of the cubic millimetre of the nutrient tank that he was interested in. A few more spots were revealed on the next pass, and even more on the next. A picture of a lump appeared in the centre of the image.

By now Leon was trying to convince himself that the software was indeed definitely faulty. If it was not, then what was being created before his eyes was irrefutable evidence of a digitalized DNA molecule making the spectacular leap from existence as electrons to existence as a complete genome of a real DNA molecule of extraordinary length and complexity.

## 62

The refuse truck that had collected Nano Systems' waste was full by 8 a.m. that morning. The driver foreman dropped his gang off at the depot so they could work another truck to keep up their productivity payments, and set off to the landfill site at the old concrete works at Storrington. He had to wait his turn at the entrance to the site. Seagulls rose in protesting, screaming clouds as tracked levellers moved in to flatten and consolidate freshly tipped waste.

The driver handed over a signed form certifying that he had no toxic materials on board, and was directed across the wasteland to a dumping point. He reversed into position in accordance with the infill supervisor's directions and pulled the lever that tipped his hopper. He revved the engine to power the pumps that drove the hydraulic rams to their maximum height. Blipping the engine caused the vehicle to buck, aiding the process of shedding its load of waste.

Amid the cascade of packaging debris and rotting food that tumbled from the truck was the surgical waste that Nano Systems' sickbay nurse had disposed of. It included the gauze pad and needle that the nurse had used to drain Beverley's suspected cyst.

The refuse truck moved clear and a levelling machine pushed the heap flat. The medical waste was buried with a mass of already decomposing potato peelings, egg shells and other organic material that provided a warm, fetid and altogether ideal environment for a physical manifestation of the strange entity that was baffling Leon.

## 63

## BALI, INDONESIA

Beverley parked the Mazda outside the bungalow and tapped on the sliding patio door. Toby pulled aside the sun curtains to check who it was and let her in. He had been working at the writing desk with his plastic lamination machine. His other gadgets were scattered on the floor. Beverley had always thought she was pretty good at turning places into tips but Toby Hoyle was a master. She dropped the plastic bag she was carrying on her bed.

'Have you made Jumo's badge?'

'Yes. All ready.'

'Difficult?'

'Er . . . no.'

'Good. Then make one for me.'

Toby knew that the determined note in her voice spelt an unwillingness to listen to arguments. 'I was about to say, what for? But that would be a silly question. Correct?'

'Correct. I'm going with you tonight.'

'You can't. We've only got two rebreathers. One for me and one for Jumo.'

'I've just got another one from Hake McGuire.'

'Beverley, it'll be bad enough with two of us trying to escape. But with three of us – '

'It won't be any problem,' said Beverley. 'And you know why? Because I'm every bit as good at snooping as you are. Hake told me that everyone in Kuta who can read and write good English is being offered a hundred dollars a day on the *Eldorado* sorting out the mess they're in with the Bangkok casino. *And* they are staying on board overnight. If you'd been watching through the telescope instead of messing around with your gizmos, you would have noticed that the staff launch has been busy today. That ship is crawling with strange faces so I don't suppose ours will attract much attention.'

'And supposing Marshall Tate sees you?'

'I've talked the whole thing over with Jumo,' said Beverley in a matter-of-fact voice. 'I persuaded him to let me have this.' She opened the bag that she had dropped on the bed and produced Jumo's Colt. 'Marshall Tate will certainly see me,' said Beverley quietly. 'But when he does, it will be the last face he does see.'


# 64

# SOUTHERN ENGLAND

The car park was filling up; Nano Systems was coming to life but Leon paid no attention to the noises and the 'good mornings' outside in the corridor. He was too intent on watching the rapidly changing data on his screen to worry about anything else. So immersed was he in his work that he tended to forget that what was confronting him was merely a computer simulation of a reality that might not exist.

At 10 a.m. he stopped the program to run the graphic representation of the thing taking shape in the nutrient tank. The glowing phosphor dots of the high resolution monitor did a good job on the complex code structure of the genome.

He did not hear the door open and someone enter the room.

A gasp of surprise made him turn around. Dr Macé Pilleau was staring at the screen in astonishment.

'What in the name of God have you got there, Leon?'

'Good morning, Macé. I thought you might answer that. But it looks to me as if our trojan can convert standard Kronos nutrient into a fully-fledged, living DNA.'

For a few moments Dr Pilleau was too shocked to speak. He sat in the chair beside Leon without taking his eyes off the screen. 'Is there more?'

For an answer Leon scrolled the screen image the entire length of the complex and convoluted structure. 'And that's a low resolution image, Macé. If you want maximum resolution, it will take several hours to map. Even with this computer.'

'Amazing,' Dr Pilleau breathed. 'Truly amazing. Could there be a fault with the software?'

Leon sighed. 'The simulation is based on tried and proven routines, Macé.'

'Then what's the density?'

'I've reached a 60 per cent conversion of the nutrient and it's still going up. I'm running at ten times real time, but even that's slowing down now. It's using a lot of processing power just extracting this.'

'Sixty per cent!' Dr Pilleau echoed.

'That's right.'

In the years he had known him, Leon had never seen the scientist look so horrified. He had half-risen from the chair, his face deathly white. 'It's not possible!' he whispered. 'Total conversion of the nutrient fluid into DNA! Oh God! Beverley's belt! Why didn't I think of that!'

Before Leon could reply, the scientist fled from the room, moving at a speed that belied his age. Leon followed him to his laboratory and found him positioning a Laine Runner belt under his electron microscope so that the substrate window of the belt's Kronos chip's nutrient fluid chamber was under the viewing head. His gnarled fingers shook noticeably as he adjusted the instrument's settings.

'What's the matter, Macé?'

'Beverley's belt!' the scientist wailed. 'I didn't think! I simply

451

did not think. How could I be so stupid? So incredibly blind and stupid! All the time we were peering into the Kronos's memory area to see what the trojan was doing, and not looking to see what was happening to the nutrient!' His words were a rush, a disjointed, virtually incoherent mumble.

He went on bewailing his shortsightedness while waiting for the microscope to reach working temperature. The screen flickered into life. Leon helped with the fine adjustments because the elder scientist's hands were trembling. The image sharpened. Both men saw the cluster of DNA molecules. Dr Pilleau gave a gasp of horror. 'Leon, this is terrible.'

'But that's nothing like the density I'm getting on the simulation,' Leon pointed out. 'That's only one Kronos. I don't suppose it's much above .01 per cent.'

The scientist's fingers fumbled with a pocket magnifying glass. He peered closely at the belt's sensor pad. 'Carl's right, the barbs are damaged. A large impurity has been forced through the hypodermic! Oh God, this is terrible. Terrible!'

'Look, Macé, I'm not a microbiologist, so what the hell's the matter?'

'I need to think.' Dr Pilleau collapsed into a chair and covered his face. After a few moments his hands stopped trembling. He took them away from his face and stared at Leon. 'When laboratory technicians first started handling pure DNA of even simple organisms back in the 1970s, it was found to be the most dangerous carcinogenic substance known to man. People were dying very quickly of the most horrible skin cancer. It's not a problem today because there are strict precautions in labs that handle the stuff.'

Leon was badly shaken. 'The DNA of simple organisms?' he queried.

Dr Pilleau nodded. 'The more complex the DNA's genome, the more dangerous it is. A millilitre of human DNA coming into contact with your skin would give you a lethal dose. I dread to think what a millilitre of that DNA could do.'

Leon swore softly. 'You mean . . . Beverley . . . She used to test that belt . . . Oh Christ! It's even named after her!'

Dr Pilleau's face was haggard. 'As the concentration in the

belt is so low now . . . Perhaps it was lower when she was wearing it? Perhaps she did not receive a fatal dose . . .'

'And perhaps that is too much to hope for,' muttered Leon. 'So do we tell her?'

An hour later Leon finished reading the reports that Dr Pilleau had called up from the World Health Organization's database. The WHO had done a good job on collating data on the carcinogenic properties of separated DNA and making it readily available. The findings were all there: from John Hopkin University; from university hospitals all over the world; from the laboratories of the major drug companies. There were reports on accidents involving laboratory technicians during the early days of DNA research and more reports on causes of death of the same technicians. Some documents were couched in a blanket fog of technical terms; some spelt out their message in clear, unequivocal terms.

But in all cases the message, and the paradox in that message, was the same: DNA, the basic building block of life itself, was a killer.

## 65

### BALI, INDONESIA

It took much of Beverley's indomitable will not to allow the pain in her side to interfere with her concentration. She watched the glowing digits on the *Dinkum*'s echo-sounder intently. Suddenly the digits changed to zeros.

'Toby! There's no more reading!'

Toby and Jumo stopped packing gear into the underwater scooter's nose cone and joined Beverley at the *Dinkum*'s helm. Toby switched the echo-sounder to high range but the zeros remained the same. He looked at the blazing lights of the *Eldorado* about two miles distant. 'We're too far out, Bev,' he said, switching the echo-sounder back to normal range. 'Take her in a bit.'

'Why isn't there a reading?'

'I think we are over the Java Trench,' Jumo explained. 'One

of the deepest ocean trenches in the world. You only would get a reading on the sonargraph if it could read depths of about five kilometres.'

Beverley was astonished. 'What? But we're so close to the shore!'

'Bali is volcanic, it rises straight off the floor of the ocean,' said Jumo seriously.

'Take her in closer, Beverley,' Toby suggested. 'We haven't got three miles of anchor line.'

Beverley pushed the Morse throttle lever forward and turned the *Dinkum* towards the *Eldorado* while Toby and Jumo finished cramming supplies into the scooter's nose cone.

The young Japanese was always willing and eager to please. He seemed delighted to be united with Beverley and Toby in their common fight. The advantage of having him along was that he had memorized the layout of the *Eldorado* from plans he had bribed out of the shipyard who had carried out the conversion. It was about the only planning he had carried out.

The night was eerily calm. The moon shone from a clear sky on the oil-black water, turning it to molten silver in the cabin cruiser's wake. The humidity of the still night lay over the sea like a warm, wet towel. The echo-sounder's digits flickered and gave a reading of ninety-nine metres. Beverley reduced throttle and turned the helm towards the lights of some anchored proas with all-night fishing parties on board. From the shrieks of laughter carrying across the slow, lazy swell, Beverley guessed that not all the tourists that balmy night were interested in fishing. She found the proximity of the other boats a comfort.

'This will do,' said Toby when the echo-sounder was indicating twenty metres.

The *Eldorado* was now less than a mile off, huge and forbidding despite its bright lights. Beverley studied the ship through Toby's night-sight binoculars. Her rage that this was where Marshall Tate had killed her beloved Carl was tempered by a feeling of foreboding. The ship was vast and impregnable. How could she take on such a monster and hope to avenge Carl's death? Her confidence was restored by Jumo's engaging smile.

He seemed to read her thoughts because he turned to her. 'Please don't worry, Miss Raine, tonight we finish it.'

Beverley managed a wan smile in return. 'Will you do me a favour, Jumo?'

He gave a little bow.

'Why not call me Beverley?'

'L sound very difficult for me,' said Jumo, nodding politely. He helped Toby toss the concrete anchor over the side. 'Okay, Beverley.'

The trio were about to don their rebreathing sets when Beverley's Klipfone trilled. It was Leon Dexter.

'We're 50 per cent through the simulation, Beverley,' said Leon, sounding agitated. 'And something unexpected has happened. We've discovered that the trojan can convert the Kronos nutrient into real DNA, not a digitalized DNA but a fully sequenced living genome of incredible complexity that is unlike anything Macé has ever seen.'

Jumo and Toby stopped dressing to listen. There were no listen-through facilities on the boat, they could hear only Beverley's side of the conversation.

'So?' Beverley prompted when Leon paused.

'It's a dangerous carcinogen, Beverley. Really dangerous. The higher the concentration, the more lethal it is. If Tate is using a common nutrient tank to feed all his Kronos . . .'

'How do you mean? Dangerous to touch, inhale or what?'

'Everything,' Leon replied.

Beverley was silent for some moments. Despite the thousands of kilometres separating them, she felt that she could read Leon's thoughts. 'Tell me about my belt, Leon.'

'There's nothing conclusive, Beverley. No hard evidence. There's just an outside chance that the simulation results are wrong.'

'*Tell me about the belt!*'

A long pause before Leon answered. 'Macé has checked it. It's infected, but at a very low density.'

Beverley surprised herself at how unnaturally calm she sounded. 'So you're saying that the chances are high that I've got cancer?'

'It's a chance, Beverley. It's probably only a tiny dose because of the low levels in your belt, but you've got to stop whatever you're doing right now and get yourself to a hospital.'

'Sorry, Leon. We're committed tonight. The show must go on.'

'For Christ's sake, Beverley, it's not worth it. Please get yourself to a hospital.'

'What happens if the nutrient is mixed with seawater?'

She could hear Leon holding a muffled conversation at the other end.

'Beverley?'

'I'm listening.'

'The phosphorus in seawater will neutralize it.'

'Completely?'

'Macé thinks so but can't be a hundred per cent certain yet. *Please, Beverley* – get yourself to hospital. It's not worth risking your life.'

Beverley stared at the distant lights of the *Eldorado*. 'I think the risk is worth it, Leon. Thank you for calling and for being so frank with me. I really do appreciate it, but we're going ahead as planned.' With that she cut the circuit and thrust the Klipfone into a bag without looking at Toby and Jumo. 'Don't say anything,' she warned the two men. 'Do you understand?'

Toby nodded and helped Jumo adjust his rebreathing set.

Beverley grabbed one of the three rebreathing sets that Toby had been preparing and thrust her arms into the harness. 'Come on, let's get a move on.'


66

The worst moment for Beverley, once she was kitted out to Toby's satisfaction, was when she slipped into the water. Entering the sea at night required iron nerves. She had once gone swimming in the sea at home with Carl on a hot night and had run hollering up the beach when a length of kelp entwined itself around her leg. Sensing Jumo's nervousness did not help either. She bit hard on the breathing set's mouthpiece and ducked her head underwater. The heady sensation of inhaling oxygen quickly dispelled her fears and even induced a sensation of euphoria. A metre down and the pressure bore painfully on her facemask. She breathed out through her nose as Toby had instructed her that afternoon during a training session in the lagoon and felt more comfortable. Jumo swam behind her and gripped her weightbelt. She in turn grabbed hold of Toby's weightbelt and thumped twice on his back to signal that they were ready. The faint whir of the scooter's electric motor made her wonder if the *Eldorado* had underwater microphones and whether they were sufficiently sensitive to pick up the sound. The water dragged at her arms and pulled her body back as the scooter picked up speed. With three people to tow, Toby discovered that the performance of the little machine was decidedly sluggish.

Beverley looked up and saw from the sparkle of moonlight that they were only just beneath the surface. Toby had warned that they would go deeper as they neared the ship to avoid being seen from the deck in the clear water.

The motor cut and they drifted to the surface. Beverley bled some more oxygen into the bag so that it acted as a lifebelt and signalled to Jumo to do the same. It was important to rest at every opportunity. The scooter bobbed beside them while Toby took a bearing on the *Eldorado*. A minute later they were submerged again and resuming their eerie journey through the oil-black sea.

Beverley was disorientated when they surfaced for the second time. Jumo tapped on her shoulder and pointed. The huge, intimidating bulk of the *Eldorado* was towering out of the water about four hundred metres away. The powerful floodlights illuminating the stern hurt her eyes. Looking towards the bow, it was possible to see into those suites whose windows were close to the humped shape of the collar around the ship's waterline.

'You okay, Beverley?' Toby asked.

She spat out her mouthpiece. 'Just about,' she gasped.

'Jumo?'

Jumo nodded rather than remove his mouthpiece.

'Okay, we'll go down to about eight metres from now on,'

said Toby. 'Don't forget to let more gas into the bag to compensate for the increased pressure. Everyone ready?'

Beverley bit on her mouthpiece and held on to Toby's belt with one hand. As soon as she felt Jumo grip her belt she banged Toby's back and they were off, arrowing down into the clear waters of the Baldung Strait. The pressure pressed painfully on her eardrums until she remembered that pinching the bottom of her facemask against her nostrils and blowing through her nose forced oxygen into her Eustachian tubes to equalize the pressure. She hoped that Jumo had remembered to do the same. They levelled out at eight metres.

After five minutes Toby reduced speed so that she could hardly hear the scooter's motor. She was aware of a black, forbidding shadow passing over her head. The panic that knotted her stomach quickly subsided when she realized that it was probably the arms of the huge inflatable swell protection collar that formed the harbour at the *Eldorado*'s stern.

They were going up. Strange eddies in the lee of the mighty unyielding ship sucked her body to the left and right and up and down to the point where she was no longer sure which way was up and which way was down. Toby grabbed her and Jumo, and pushed them against the soft flank of the collar. They had come up close to the bow of the moored staff launch.

Beverley grabbed at a mooring line and saw that they were in the strange harbour. Jumo leapt nimbly onto the collar and gave Beverley a hand. She scrambled alongside the two men and helped to haul the scooter out of the water. It was a struggle to keep their footing on the yielding collar as they staggered towards the security of the shadows under the overhang, carrying the scooter between them.

Their slipping and sliding reminded Beverley of a visit to the seaside when she had leapt about in a giant inflatable play castle. But she didn't want to think about her childhood; she didn't want to think about the pain in her side and the dire consequences for her that the pain signified. Nano Systems was like her son, Paul. Grown up. It could exist and flourish without her. The only important thing in her life now was to use what was left of it to avenge Carl's murder.

458

They pulled off their rebreathing sets and tucked them out of sight where the bulging collar was lashed tightly against the rust-streaked hull. The water in the curious harbour looked black and forbidding under the glare of the floodlights; Beverley could hardly believe that she had actually been swimming in it. Toby removed the scooter's nose cone and pulled out their supplies. It was amazing how much stuff he had managed to pack into it. Oblivious to each other's nakedness, the three helped each other out of their mid-season suits, dried each other, and changed into the clothes they had decided on for their foray.

Beverley wriggled into a yellow sarong and blouse, and hid her giveaway ringlets under a headscarf. She wore Jumo's revolver in its shoulder holster. Toby and Jumo donned their tropical-weight slacks and Batik shirts. Toby pinned Beverley's electronic ID badge to her blouse, clipped one on Jumo's lapel, and fastened his own in place. He redistributed what they had to carry into three beach bags. Beverley had insisted on carrying the same weight as the men although when she picked her bag up and followed Toby up the Jacob's ladder, she had a suspicion that their bags, swinging from their shoulders, were much heavier. Toby had even brought his Nanopad along.

They were nearly at the top of the long flight of chain-supported steps when they heard someone clattering down from above. Jumo's reactions were fast: he twisted his body around the ladder and hung from one of the open treads by his fingers. Toby seized Beverley in a passionate kiss, pushing her against the hull and grinding his pelvis against her hips.

'Hey you two!'

They broke away and blinked into the beam of the torch. The unseen man's English was good but the accent had a clipped quality.

'I'm paying you to work! You can do that when your shift is over, not on my time. Move!'

Beverley kept her eyes suitably downcast as she and Toby pushed past the stranger but she had had a glimpse of Schnee. His pudgy fingers dug painfully into her buttocks and would have taken even more liberties had she not stumbled against Toby in her haste to mount the steps.

Jumo hooked his feet around the edge of the ladder and heaved himself back onto the steps. He seemed to be enjoying the adventure.

'Hubert Schnee!' Beverley muttered, glancing back at the fat man. She leaned over the rail to get a good look at him, confident that he would not be able to see her through the floodlights. He appeared to be looking for someone, and even flashed his torch into the moored launch. He bawled 'Terri!' a couple of times, swore to himself, and headed back to the foot of the Jacob's ladder

The trio reached the deck and strolled casually along it. Beverley was in the middle, chatting animatedly to her two male companions. They passed a group of crewmen, gossiping and drinking beneath a lifeboat. They took no notice of them.

'This entrance, I think,' said Jumo. They had reached the service entrance that Toby had found on his first visit to the ship. The door opened at their approach and they entered the dimly lit corridor.

It was the same with the lift doors: they hissed open and closed behind them. Toby touched the Deck D button and the lift slowly descended.

A steward with a trolly loaded with dirty linen was waiting for the lift. He looked surprised at the three occupants that stepped out. 'You're not supposed to be here,' he remarked.

'We're on an errand for Mr Schnee,' Toby replied breezily. To Jumo's and Beverley's alarm, he helped the steward push his trolley into the lift.


## 67

The trouble was that Terri had an ID badge that opened virtually every door on the ship, although Schnee did not acquaint the guards of this fact when they reported to him that the wretched girl was nowhere to be found. The girl's supervisor started to get hysterical, claiming that Terri must have fallen overboard through exhaustion and overwork.

What with all the other problems that were piling up, the last thing Schnee needed was for morale to go crashing among his experienced staff just when they had virtually sorted out the problem of the Bangkok casino. Another major topple was on the cards. If that happened he was going to need the goodwill and support of all his staff. The problems were getting so complex that the team of Japanese software experts who had been flown in that day had no idea if the problem was with the satellite's computer or the *Eldorado*'s computer, or both. At a meeting that afternoon, chaired by Marshall Tate, the team leader had suggested that the only way to deal with the memory erosion was to close down all the casinos for two weeks, clear down all the software in the satellite and uplink a total reload.

Schnee had seen Marshall Tate lose his temper before and resort to extremes of violence, such as the time he had beaten up Carl Olivera. If it was not for that, they probably would not be in their present mess. Schnee was confident that his more subtle methods would have eventually extracted the information they needed. The trouble with Marshall Tate was that he was so damned impatient.

The Japanese had listened to Tate's raving with stoic courtesy, and, on a word from their leader in Japanese, they had risen as one, bowed to everyone and walked out. They listened politely to Schnee's pleading on the helicopter pad but nothing he said changed their minds. They had had enough. The Sikorsky flew them back to Denpasar.

'Please, Mr Schnee, we must organize a proper search for her,' said the chief supervisor. 'Terri is popular with the other girls, but she has been acting strangely lately. We must find her.'

Schnee promised to do all he could. The comment about acting strangely made him think. She had been acting more than just strangely, she had actually rejected his little phials. That was impossible, of course, and yet she had done it. Perhaps her will had now collapsed as he knew it must. It seemed unlikely, but maybe she had gone to the computer room, the scene of so many of her humiliations, in the hope that he had left one of the little phials for her? The computer room was the one place that no one had checked because no one knew that she had access to it.

Schnee sighed and made his way to the locked room below the main deck. The door opened automatically for him. He stepped inside, the door clicked shut, and there she was.

Instead of being angry, Schnee beamed at her. He had decided that a little dalliance was in order. After all, it had been a frenetically busy day and he could always punish her later.

'Ah, Terri, my little angel. Everyone has been so worried about you. You've been a most inconsid . . .' The sentence died on his lips when Terri held up her skeletal left arm. The terrible flesh-rotting disease had spread to her shoulder. Schnee's eyes bulged out in horror when he saw the gleaming bones and the flesh that was falling from them like melting wax.

Terri took a step towards him. She was smiling: a smile of inner strength and superiority. Schnee stepped back, his gaze riveted on the dreadful, upraised arm. 'No!' he croaked. 'No!'

Terri looked crestfallen. 'I thought you found me attractive, Mr Schnee. I've been waiting for you to come to me.'

Schnee groped blindly for the door catch while staring hypnotized at the apparition of an arm.

'I've been waiting so long, Mr Schnee. Such a long time to keep a lady waiting.'

The Swiss did not see Terri's right arm go up. The long, spiked-ended screwdriver was clutched in her right hand, a strong, healthy hand and a strong, healthy arm. Terri brought the screwdriver down with enough force to drive the point into Schnee's brain. She wrenched it free and stabbed again and again. The blows rained down. When Schnee realized what was happening, it was too late. He put his arms up and sank dying to his knees. Terri gave a scream of triumph. She released her grip on the screwdriver and left it sticking out of her victim's chest. Red froth dribbled from his lips. His eyes were still open, but not for long. Terri plunged her hand into the open nutrient tank and splattered the cancerous fluid in Schnee's face. Then she was splashing it everywhere and laughing dementedly.

## 68

The trio strolled casually along the corridor to the air conditioning plant room. Jumo helped Toby slide the heavy bar locks on the double doors. Inside they had to shout to make themselves heard above the roar of the three electric air pumps that were bolted to the floor in the centre of the pipe-filled room like stationary jet engines running at full blast. Beyond the pumps was a giant Soltzur heat exchanger that stood three metres high. It was connected to pipes the diameter of a man's leg which were in turn coupled to motorized shut-off and redirection valves. Rectangular cross-section air ducts, half a metre square, were linked to a massive air filter. Access panels secured with wingnuts were provided in the side of the filter housing so that the filter elements could be removed and cleaned.

Jumo signalled to Toby and cupped his hands close to Toby's ear. 'They use the swimming pool as a heat sink for cooling the air in the air conditioning!' he yelled. 'Those pipes are connected to the pool. Can you not smell the chlorine?'

'So what?' Toby yelled back, waving at Beverley to help undo the wingnuts on one of the filter access panels.

'If we empty the pool, it will lighten the ship and start it rolling. They will lose their satellite links. Those big dishes are fixed.'

'Take too long!'

'Not with those pumps!' Jumo declared. 'Very powerful! They can pump two hundred tonnes an hour!'

'My way's quicker!'

Jumo shrugged and read the instructions on the motorized valves while Beverley and Toby undid all the wingnuts that secured the access panels.

'Mind your feet, Beverley!'

Beverley jumped clear as the heavy aluminium cover clattered to the floor. A steady hurricane of air was sucked into the access hole, adding to the uproar in the confined space. Toby opened his beach bag and produced four insect repellent aerosols. Jumo was puzzled: this was a strange time to worry about mosquito bites. Toby broke the seal on one of the aerosols and a dense plume of thick black smoke spewed from the can and was sucked into the filter. Toby jammed the can in the housing and did the same with the other three aerosols. He grinned at Beverley and Jumo and yelled: 'If that doesn't cause a panic then nothing will!'

'Now the pumps!' Jumo yelled. With that he threw the switch on the valve marked 'waste'. The note of the pumps changed and a thin stream of water jetted from a pipe flange that hitherto had not been leaking.

The trio quickly gathered up their belongings and darted into the corridor. Toby and Jumo jammed the double doors shut. The three set off towards the lift, pausing to smash the glass on a fire alarm and set off a whole host of wailing sirens. They reached the lift and took it up to Deck B. When the doors hissed open, black smoke was already pouring from the corridor air-conditioning vents, and smoke alarms were going off all over the place. 'Fire in the engine room!' Toby yelled at four hard-hatted Japanese engineers who promptly turned around and clattered down the companionway leading to Deck C.

'You not use elevators!' one of them yelled over his shoulder.

Two Balinese waitresses screamed when they saw the smoke and abandoned their trolley loaded with drinks. Toby grabbed a can of lager and took swigs from it as he trotted along the corridor behind Jumo and Beverley. He used the can to break the glass on every fire alarm he passed, stopping only when a four-man fire-fighting gang rushed towards them down the corridor. They were wearing breathing sets with full facemasks. Their leader was carrying what looked like a set of plans of the ship. The gang paid no attention to the trio.

'They're going to have fun and games finding the source of the fire,' Toby observed. 'Planting those grenades in the air-conditioning plant means that smoke alarms will be going off all over the place at once.'

They reached a door marked BACCHUS CONTROL FACILITIES. Toby's carefully-made ID badges were not required because the door was held open by a stream of Japanese and Balinese staff anxious to get into the fresh air. Dense black smoke billowed past them. There was no panic at this stage but everyone was obviously keen to get onto the main deck as quickly as possible.

'Don't go in there!' someone yelled at the trio.

'Have to make sure place is clear,' Toby shouted back. 'Mr Tate's orders!'

A public address system hummed. A calm voice identified itself as the captain. The voice ordered everyone onto the main deck and to assemble at the lifeboat points. Fire-fighting teams A and B were required to muster on Deck D.

'I think next door on the right!' Jumo panted in the thickening smoke. 'Toby, is it safe to breathe this smoke?'

'Perfectly safe,' Toby confirmed.

This time Toby's badges were needed. The electronic locks to the computer room clicked open. The air inside the small room was clearer than the corridor because it was passed through additional filters.

Beverley's hand shot up to her mouth to suppress a scream at the dreadful spectacle. What had been Hubert Schnee was lying on its back. Instead of a face, there was a skull grinning hideously at them. Nearby was what had once been a woman but was now half a skeleton.

'Jesus Christ,' Toby muttered, backing off.

Beverley had seen the nutrient tank and knew what it was. The terrible implication of the pain in her side was brought home to her. If that was her fate then she would kill herself first. She grabbed Jumo and Toby and pulled them backwards. 'Get out of here!' she screamed. 'Get out! It's dangerous!' She pulled so hard at Toby that he nearly lost his balance.

'The bridge!' said Jumo anxiously. 'It is time we head for the bridge. This way.'

They scurried along the smoke-filled corridor, following in Jumo's footsteps. They kept turning corners, occasionally doubling back when Jumo made a mistake. Eventually they found an open lift and piled in. Beverley's fingers groped in the semi-darkness for the control panel and jabbed at the highest touch-key. Thankfully the lift moved. Its doors opened onto the starboard weatherdeck near the stern. Smoke was pouring from the

465

deck vents. Some men wearing lifejackets rushed along the deck towards the sounds of loudhailers that were ushering crew and guests into lifeboats. No one took any notice of the three who were racing up a narrow companionway that led to the bridge observation deck.

Just as they reached the top of the steps, the *Eldorado* gave a shuddering heave and grated her reinforced bottom on her coral grounding. Beverley pulled herself onto the bridge behind Jumo just as the ship lurched suddenly to starboard and sent them sprawling against the guard rail. She stared at the extraordinary floodlit scene on the main deck. The swimming pool was drained of water. Smoke was wafting through the neat tropical gardens and several pitching and rolling lifeboats, crowded with crew, staff and guests, were moving away from the *Eldorado*. Between the swimming pool and the bridge superstructure was a pleasant avenue of dwarf palms. She heard a youth screaming and caught a glimpse of him through the palm fronds: it was a young steward running towards the last lifeboat that was being launched.

Jumo yanked the bridge door open and plunged inside but the thick smoke drove him back, coughing and spluttering. 'This stuff is *not* breathable,' he gasped accusingly at Toby.

'I didn't say it was! But if you inhale it, it won't hurt you!'

Jumo eyed the smoke billowing from the bridge. 'How long does it last?'

'No idea,' said Toby cryptically. 'This is the first time I've ever done this.'

At that moment a bridge door burst open on the other side of the observation deck and two Japanese deck officers in smart tropical whites staggered out of the clouds of swirling black smoke that followed them. They were coughing and choking. Before disappearing down the opposite companionway, one of them yelled at the three to get to the lifeboats.

Toby tried to enter the bridge but was driven back. 'Hell! It's worse up here than below, the bridge and deck cabins must get first crack at the conditioned air.'

'So what do we do now?' Jumo demanded.

'Could we start the engines on this thing and get it away from the island?' Beverley demanded.

'It is possible,' said Jumo, nodding. 'We need one person on bridge, and I think two in engine room.'

The *Eldorado* pitched and grated on her coral grounding.

'The best thing would be to get off ourselves,' said Toby. 'I think we can safely say that this ship's days as an earth station are over.'

'No!' said Beverley vehemently. 'We destroy Marshall Tate *and* this ship. If you don't want to do it, then go.'

'I will stay and help,' Jumo offered.

Toby sighed. 'Okay, I'm out-voted. But before we do anything, we've got to do something about this smoke.' He turned to the companionway. 'I'll go back and shut off the air conditioning.'

Before anyone could stop him, he turned and raced down the companionway.

Jumo jumped to the rail and yelled at Toby to come back but he was gone. 'Very stupid,' said Jumo. 'It would be better if we stay together.'

'Next job is to smash a few windows,' Beverley declared. She and Jumo pulled a fire extinguisher off its mounting bracket and swung its base against a bridge window. The effort renewed the lancing pain in her side. The cylinder was heavy and yet it failed to break the toughened glass. Jumo held the cylinder above his head and hurled it with all his strength at the centre of the pane. It shattered with a loud report and disintegrated into tiny pieces of skittering glass that resembled crushed ice. Smoke belched through the new opening. Jumo recovered the fire extinguisher and smashed every bridge window he could using the same technique while Beverley yanked and kicked open every door.

'It's clearing!' Beverley exclaimed. She took a deep breath and plunged into the bridge house with Jumo close behind.

Sure enough, the breeze blowing through the bridge house was clearing the smoke, forcing it through the broken windows in swirling clouds that were becoming less dense, changing colour from black to grey. There was still smoke spewing from the overhead air-conditioning grilles but it was now being drawn out through a nearby doorway. The air in the bridge house was now breathable.

Beverley looked at the central display panel either side of the helm and her heart sank at the massed array of touch-sensitive keypads, digital motors and warning lights. The only item that made sense was the stainless steel helm, looking absurdly out of proportion in comparison with the size of the ship it controlled. There were also radar displays, and the gyro and magnetic compasses.

'Oh, Christ, Jumo. Can you make head or tail of this lot?'

'I think not as bad as it looks,' said Jumo, studying the control panel. 'For it to sit on the bottom, there are floodable tanks. Very large. I have seen the drawings.'

'Toby mentioned ballast tanks,' said Beverley, glancing at the companionway when a fresh outburst of shouting was heard from below.

'Ah, yes,' said Jumo triumphantly. 'Ten main tanks. I have their controls.'

He ran his finger along the row of keypads that opened the seavalves on each tank. One by one the panel lights glowed, indicating that the valves were open. Below the controls was another row of keypads that blew compressed air into the ballast tanks, forcing the seawater from them and restoring the *Eldorado*'s buoyancy. Jumo stabbed at touch controls in turn. The sudden roar of seawater blowing through the outlets in the ship's hull could be heard on the bridge.

A flare fired from the lifeboats burned a trail of light into the night sky and exploded. In the harsh magnesium glare it was possible to count several lifeboats in the water. One had started its engine and was taking other lifeboats in tow. More flares arched upwards.

'It is not possible to start the engines from here,' said Jumo calmly. 'There has to be someone in the engine room.'

The smoke streaming through the vents thinned out and stopped.

'I could find my way down there,' said Beverley. 'But I wouldn't know what to do.'

468

'I know exactly where it is,' said Jumo, moving to the door. 'Also it is difficult to hide an engine room. I will go and call you on the telephone.' He gave Beverley an encouraging smile and was gone.

Beverley did not have time to reflect on being left alone because at that moment the swell lifted the *Eldorado*'s keel off the coral and slammed it down again. Now lightened as a result of the thousands of tonnes of water being forced out of the ballast tanks by compressed air, the hull lurched and rolled alarmingly.

Beverley staggered and clung to the binnacle. She looked through the smashed windows but the moon had gone behind a cloud bank so it was no longer possible to see the ship in relation to the horizon. The loudhailers were now silent, suggesting that everyone on board except themselves had escaped in the lifeboats. Then she remembered Marshall Tate.

Marshall Tate! What had happened to him?

She knew from her hours spent observing the *Eldorado* through a telescope that his penthouse-type suite was directly above the bridge. She looked around, wondering if there was access to above.

And then she saw the lift doors, previously hidden by the smoke. The lift inner and outer doors were already open. It was a very small lift and yet it reminded her of the lift that led from the underground car park to Marshall Tate's penthouse. Guessing that it would be some minutes before Jumo called her on the interphone from the engine room, she stepped into the tiny lift and pulled the Colt from its shoulder holster. Jumo had shown her how to pull back the hammer to cock it. There was only one unmarked touch pad. She touched it. The doors closed and the lift ascended gently. It braked to a stop almost as soon as it started. The doors opened onto a magnificent black and white marble-lined stateroom about fifteen metres square. Judging by the long rosewood table immediately opposite the lift this was Marshall Tate's meeting room. Everyone entering the room from the lift would be confronted by whoever was sitting in the high-backed chair at the far end of the table.

But the room was deserted.

Beverley lowered the revolver. She had difficulty forcing herself to step out of the lift. When she did so, she was immediately aware of the same tension that she remembered so vividly in Marshall's docklands penthouse. It was as if the place was marked in the same way that a cat uses the scent glands in its cheeks to mark out its territory to warn would-be invaders. She explored and found a surprisingly austere bedroom in contrast to the intimidating stateroom. There was no sign of Marshall.

## 69

Jumo found the brightly-lit engine room by taking the lift down to Deck D and racing along a narrow service corridor. The doors at the end of the corridor opened automatically in time to prevent him running into them. He had confidence in the badge that Toby had given him.

He burst into the engine room. A residue of smoke was clearing from the cavernous space so he assumed that Toby had reached the plant room and shut off the air-conditioning filters. He had come out on a railed catwalk overlooking a yawning chasm that extended down to the ship's keel. Had he been running any faster the chances were that he would have pitched over the edge. The *Eldorado* was rolling through ten degrees by this time so it was essential to maintain a tight grip on the rails.

It was a good vantage point to get his bearings. The engines were two surprisingly small diesels. He knew that the original engines had been removed because the ship would no longer be required to punch into gales laden with cargo. Near the forward bulkhead was a double control desk and an interphone handset on a bracket. He climbed down the catwalk's ladder and crossed to the control desk. He was about to snatch up the interphone handset when something moved on the periphery of his vision. He wheeled around.

'If you come at me with a knife again,' warned Toby, emerging from behind the port engine, 'I shall be most displeased.'

Jumo smiled and relaxed. 'I have come down to start the engines. It's not possible to start them from the bridge.'

'Is Beverley still on the bridge?'

'Yes, she is waiting by the helm.'

Toby eyed the complex array of controls. 'Do you know how to drive this thing?'

'I have studied many documents,' said Jumo. 'But not how to make it go.'

'Well it can't be that much different from a cabin cruiser,' Toby observed. 'Just a lot bigger.' As he spoke, he and Jumo moved to the control desk and studied the legends marked on the touch keys. 'Fuel pumps; ignition heaters; injection advance and retard, all looks pretty straightforward.'

Jumo touched the buttons uncertainly, causing them to light up. He grinned delightedly. 'I think progress, Toby.'

'Looks like standby mode,' Toby observed. He picked up the interphone handset and punched the bridge key. He heard it ringing. 'Come on, Beverley,' he muttered impatiently.

The two ignition heater lights flashed up READY. Jumo's finger was poised over the No. 1 ENGINE START key. He looked questioningly at Toby.

'I thought you said she was on the bridge?'

Beverley's voice answered. She sounded flustered but she assured Toby that everything was okay.

'Hang onto the steering wheel, Beverley, we're about to start the engines. Okay, hit it, Jumo.'

Jumo pressed the two start keys and held them down. There was a roar of escaping compressed air and the shrill whine of oil pumps. The two marine diesels cranked over and continued turning over until Jumo took his fingers off the keys. The compressed-air starters fell silent.

'It is possible the fuel injectors need time to heat up,' said Jumo. He pressed the keys again and both engines fired and caught. They ran erratically for a few seconds and settled down to a steady beat. The digital rev counters on the desk flickered into life and hovered around the five hundred mark.

'I can hear something,' said Beverley. 'But nothing seems to be happening.'

'We haven't figured out how to put the bloody things into gear yet!' Toby yelled above the din of the idling engines.

Jumo found a key marked DEAD SLOW AHEAD BOTH

471

and pressed it. There was a series of loud clunks and more whines as the electrically-operated gearboxes engaged and started turning the main drive shafts. The entire ship started to vibrate in harmony with the labouring engines. Toby found the power controls for the electric steering motors and set them to ON.

'Variable pitch props!' Toby yelled. 'What pitch?'

'I do not know!' Jumo shouted.

'I'll try fine pitch!' Toby touched the pitch controls and the engines settled down to a more regular beat. There was a sudden deafening sound of something grating along the keel.

'She's coming free!' Toby bellowed above the uproar. 'Give her more revs!'

Jumo selected HALF AHEAD BOTH. The diesels picked up. Their note rose to a steady roar and the rev counters settled at one thousand rpm.

'We're moving!' Beverley shouted. 'Toby! There's an indicator showing two knots!'

'Okay, Beverley. Hold her steady, we're on our way up!'

Toby returned the handset to its hook just as the ship took a heavy swell on her quarter that smashed the keel on the coral. In the engine room, close to the ship's bilges, the noise of steel grating on the bottom was deafening. Several plates sprang and seawater spewed through the fractured welds.

Jumo took the lead up the catwalk ladder with Toby right behind him. When they tried to open the double doors leading to the companionway, they discovered that the frame was distorted and the doors jammed shut, probably as a result of the punishment the *Eldorado* was taking. Jumo slithered rapidly down the ladder and returned with a jemmy. They levered it back and forth and succeeded in prizing the doors open a few centimetres. After that they refused to budge. More plates split open. The spewing seawater rose to a roar that was louder than the pounding diesels.

# 70

There was a large warning flashing on the control panel accompanied by a persistent bleeping. It was also flashing on the display over the windows and was intended to alert everyone on the bridge to the fact that the *Eldorado* was underway with the sliding covers for her hull windows open. To drive the point home, a graphic representation had appeared on the illuminated panel that showed the gaping hull windows.

Beverley ignored the warnings and concentrated on keeping the helm steady. The absurd little wheel had no feel, there was no tactile feedback from the steering motors. Apart from the rudder position indicator, the only suggestion that she was having any effect was a changed heading reading a few seconds after she made a course correction. Under normal circumstances she might have relished the curious sensation of having the huge illuminated platform of lights, gardens and empty swimming pool stretching before her and advancing steadily into the night under her control.

As soon as the reading on the echo-sounder was lost, indicating that the seabed beneath the *Eldorado* had dropped away to the abyssal depths of the ocean floor, Beverley operated the controls that opened the seavalves to allow water to roar into the ballast tanks.

After five minutes of holding the course steady she was worrying about Jumo and Toby. There was also a different feel about the ship. Just how different she realized only when the bows failed to lift to a heavy swell. It came surging across the deck, sweeping everything before it like a giant broom. Trees, shrubs, plants, flower boxes, all were sent crashing across the deck and cascading into the swimming pool. Another swell roared across the deck, adding to the destruction. Five hundred tonnes of water cascaded into the swimming pool and stayed there, creating a permanent list. There was another noise: a distant thunder. The increasing list of the *Eldorado* told Beverley what the noise was: the roar of water erupting into the hull through the yawning windows.

## 71

Toby's sang-froid deserted him. He swore and hurled the bent jemmy over the safety rail. It clanged off a gearbox casing. 'Bloody useless!' he yelled at Jumo. 'Now what do we do?'

Both men were having to cling to the safety rail now that the ship was listing to port at 20 degrees.

Jumo looked up and pointed to an open supplies hatch set into the ceiling close to the engine room's forward bulkhead. A heavy loading hook was hanging on a cable through the hatch, swinging from side to side and occasionally clanging against the rim of the hatch. 'If the ship leans over onto its side, we could climb to that without difficulty and maybe lower the hook.'

Toby eyed the hatch. 'Maybe you could climb without difficulty, Jumo,' he observed caustically, 'but I'm hopeless at climbing. And if the ship goes onto her beam ends, the chances are it'll go right over and take us down with it. Next suggestion?'

At that moment the flooded port engine stopped. The starboard engine carried on manfully for another minute before giving up the struggle.


## 72

Without power the stricken *Eldorado* began losing way. Beverley heard shouts. At first she thought it was Jumo and Toby. Then she realized that the men were shouting in Japanese. She abandoned the helm and rushed out onto the observation deck. At that moment the deck floodlighting was extinguished as a swell tore away a waterproof fuse cover and shorted all the circuits. The bridge emergency lighting remained on, throwing a reddish glow across the observation deck.

Beverley saw something ascending the companionway to the bridge: something with staring bug-like saucer eyes. She backed against the rail as the thing's head drew level with the deck. It pointed an automatic at her. Her hand went to the Colt in its holster but the voice froze her movement.

'Don't move,' said the thing.

Beverley knew who the man was behind the fire-fighting mask even before he pulled it off.

The red lights lent a hellish glow to the raw hatred that was etched into Marshall Tate's face. 'You're dead!' he screamed. 'Just like your fucking boyfriend!'

And he fired the automatic.

Twice.


## 73

Jumo had the climbing talents of a rhesus monkey. Toby watched, fascinated as the young Japanese gripped his legs around the cooling high-pressure steam pipe and shinned up. The increasing list and the sudden shocks that traversed the ship made his task doubly difficult but he kept going.


## 74

Beverley saw Marshall's finger tighten on the trigger and dived sideways. The blast was deafening and she actually felt the bullet thwack past her head. At the precise moment that the second was fired, a swell broke over the *Eldorado* with enough force to throw Beverley against Marshall. The cascade of seawater swept them against the rails in a tangle of arms and legs. Terrified that Marshall was about to shoot again, Beverley pushed herself away from him and hauled the Colt from its holster. Marshall was scrabbling wildly for his automatic that had fallen to the deck.

'No!' Beverley yelled. The revolver exploded like a cannon going off in her hand and the recoil almost dislocated her shoulder. It was a lucky shot; the slug tore into Marshall's right arm with such force that it whipped his body around. He gave a cry of pain and clung to the rail. With a presence of mind and an accuracy that surprised her, Beverley lashed out with her foot. It connected with the automatic and sent it skittering over the edge of the bridge.

Marshall straightened up, clutching his injured arm, and mouthing a stream of obscenities at Beverley. Those few seconds of poisonous diatribe enabled Beverley to recover her balance and her nerve. When he started towards her, she levelled the Colt and pointed as accurately as she could at Marshall's head. He stopped. His intense blue eyes were ice chips of hate, burning with a savage energy of their own in the red emergency lights.

'You killed Carl,' Beverley stated. 'And now – '

'Schnee killed Olivera!'

'And Schnee worked for you!' Beverley spat. 'I suppose you also killed Theo Draggon? Well I don't much care any more. I want to see all this and everything you stand for finished. What happens to me now is immaterial.'

Cold fury blazed in Marshall's eyes. 'We could have worked together!'

'You didn't even try,' said Beverley calmly. 'You never once made an open approach. Everything you did was cloaked in deviousness and deception because that's the only way you know to operate.' Then she had difficulty keeping her voice steady. '*And you used me!*'

Marshall's face twisted into a savage grimace. 'You plant a virus in the Kronos and you have the fucking cheek to talk to me about deception! *You killed Olivera!* You killed him with the bug you planted in my satellite!'

'We didn't plant any bug,' said Beverley, bracing herself with one hand when the ship shook itself like a dog. 'It came from outside, Mars perhaps, but not from us.'

Marshall gave a sudden, demented laugh that took Beverley by surprise. That he had edged nearer to her did not register. Another black swell broke against the bridge, drenching them. With his blond hair plastered against his face and blood oozing between his fingers where he was clutching his wounded arm, suddenly Marshall looked a pathetic sight. The ship's drunken list became more pronounced. She did not dare take her eyes off Marshall for a moment but from the way the seas were bursting against the bridge, she guessed that the *Eldorado* was now close to floundering. Then she realized that Marshall was too close and was about to step back when he sprang at her.

The shot Beverley fired was an instinctive reaction. She did not have time to take aim. And yet it went home, where exactly she could not tell, but the force was enough to throw him backwards.

'Bitch!' he croaked, hanging on to the rail and pulling himself on to one knee. 'Bitch!'

Beverley guessed that he was dying because blood frothed from his mouth as he spoke. She raised the Colt, pulling slowly back on the trigger and noting how the chamber rotated as she did so. The sound of the shot was drowned by a tremendous explosion aft as air pressure beneath the sinking ship split the deck open.

## 75

Jumo stood on the pipe where it disappeared through the bulkhead and steadied himself with one hand, his eyes fixed on the wildly swinging steel hoist that was hanging into the engine room through the open hatch. Toby was five metres below on the catwalk, his upturned face showing his concern as Jumo watched the hoist intently, timing its swings.

The Japanese took a deep breath, tensed his calf and thigh muscles, and leapt from the pipe. His fingers hooked on to the edge of the hatch. His momentum would have dislodged him had he not whipped his legs around the hoist's hawser. He then got a good grip with his feet and pushed his body through the hatch. Once safe, he turned around and grinned down at Toby. 'What is the English expression, Toby?' he yelled down. 'A doddle, is it not?' He disappeared. A moment later the swinging hoist started unwinding and dropping slowly towards Toby.

## 76

A swell crashed against the bridge with sickening force. The ship heeled. Marshall Tate's body rolled beneath the safety rail and fell away into the darkness. Beverley looked down and saw with horror that the deck had vanished – below was an ugly white-whipped sea, boiling and tearing at the bridge. The list steepened, pressing her body even harder against the rail. Then there was a new noise: a hideous screech of metal tearing against metal. Another swell charged the bridge and burst angrily against the superstructure. Vicious curls of whiplash spray struck Beverley across the face.

She cried out for Toby and Jumo but the wind and spray snatched her voice into the night. The entire ship shuddered and listed even further. It was now obvious to her that the *Eldorado* had passed the point of no return. It was no good worrying about her companions any more because at any moment the ship was going to capsize. Around the *Eldorado* in the darkness were many points of light from the lifeboats. The thrashing rotors and whining turbine of a helicopter drew near. A powerful searchlight swept the water and the ship.

The *Eldorado* gave another of its terrible lurches. But this one was worse than the others. There was a sustained roar of breaking seas and the crashing of falling wreckage. A radio mast smashed down within three metres of where Beverley was clinging to the rail. So steep was the *Eldorado*'s list, that the ship was almost on her beam ends. Beverley screamed just as a mighty swell reared up and claimed her for its own.

### 77

Jumo grabbed hold of Toby and half-lifted, half-dragged him off the hoist and through the hatch. They were in an unlit passageway that was tipped at an angle approaching 45 degrees.

'I think we must go up,' said Jumo, gesturing along the corridor.

'A safe assumption,' said Toby.

The two men reached the deck by a mixture of crawling and climbing. They pulled themselves across the weatherdeck, ducked through the safety rail, and gaped down in dismay at the black seas rolling up the *Eldorado*'s flank. Someone was shouting through a loudhailer. A lifeboat crowded with survivors was standing off some fifty metres away, as near as the coxswain dare take his craft to the stricken ship.

A helicopter equipped with a blinding searchlight appeared from nowhere and dipped low, its whirling rotors flattening the seas between the ship and the lifeboat. A loudhailer boomed out.

Toby cupped a hand to Jumo's ear. 'I think they want us to swim!' he yelled.

'What about Beverley?'

'She must've got off by now! She's had plenty of time and there's plenty of lifeboats!'

The two men debated whether or not to look for her but the sudden settling of the *Eldorado* beneath them and the bellowed urging of the loudhailer made up their minds for them. They had no option but to jump into the seething maelstrom.


## 78

Beverley's head broke the surface and she struck out wildly, not caring which way she swam just so long as she could put distance between herself and the ship. She had heard an old wive's tale, quite untrue, that a sinking ship creates a terrible suction that drags survivors after it into the depths. She swam for fifteen, maybe twenty minutes – she had no way of telling.

With nothing to break against, the sea gradually became calmer. A long, easy swell. She stopped swimming and looked around. Only when the swell lifted her could she see around. The throb of the helicopter was fading into the distance. There was no sign of the *Eldorado* but then it was so dark that it could be very near. She listened. At night the ocean can be eerily quiet. Alone and unbroken, the swell is silent.

She thought she saw a light in the distance and started swimming towards it, correcting her course whenever a swell lifted her high enough. She was thinking rationally now. What surprised her was that despite her exertions, the pain in her right side was not troubling her so much, but it was still there. She pushed the unpleasant thoughts about her uncertain future from her mind and concentrated on a less-tiring breast stroke.

The light got brighter. It was a masthead navigation light about two hundred metres off as near as she could judge. The boat ignored her cries so she resumed swimming after a brief rest. She put her head underwater and listened. The boat was not running an engine. That gave her hope. Perhaps it was a drift net fishing boat. Another fifteen minutes' swimming and her arms felt leaden. She turned onto her back and rested, taking deep breaths to make it easier to float.

Another ten minutes' steady breast stroke brought her within fifty metres of the boat, a small day boat. Its red and green navigation lights were visible together which meant that she was approaching it towards the bow. As before, her cries went unheeded.

Beverley reached the hull and grabbed hold of a fender. She called for help but the occupants continued to ignore her. She worked her way to the transom and clung to the stern drive leg, mustering the strength to haul herself out of the water. The riding light on the transom's jack staff illuminated the little cruiser's name.

It was the *Dinkum*.

## 79

In Benoa there were polite but endless questions to answer. Toby explained to the harbour captain that the three of them were on an all-night fishing trip when they saw smoke coming from the *Eldorado*.

'We thought we would help out,' said Toby blandly.

'Do any of you have any idea why she put to sea?' The harbour captain's English was very correct.

'None at all,' said Toby. 'Maybe they had explosive materials on board that they were worried about?'

The harbour captain made a note to investigate the possibility. 'Did any of you see what happened to Marshall Tate?' he asked carefully, looking at each of them in turn.

Jumo shook his head. 'No, I did not see him. Was he on board?'

'He was,' said the official gloomily. He made it sound as though Bali had lost a patron saint.

'Are we free to go now?' asked Beverley.

'There will be inquiries. Reports to be made,' said the harbour captain.

'We would not be of any use to you,' Beverley replied. 'As we've said, we were on a fishing trip.'

The harbour captain nodded. 'Very well. If you are sure you do not need medical attention, then you are free to return to your hotel.'

Suddenly the pain in Beverley's side took on a terrible intensity that made her cry out. She tried to stand because sometimes that helped. But not this time. She fell to the floor, dimly aware that someone was screaming, terrible screams that spoke of indescribable agonies. And then they stopped. Before she lost consciousness, she realized that it was she who had been screaming.

## 80

## SOUTHERN ENGLAND

'This it, miss?' asked the taxi driver, stopping his car outside the bungalow.

Beverley did not reply for a moment. It was as if the three months that had passed since she had last seen her home had been but a day. Even though it was now winter, the front lawn was neatly mown – she could see the fresh bands made by the mower's roller – and the beds had been carefully tidied up. A few climbing roses around her front door had decided to stay on and see just how mild the winter was going to be.

'Yes,' she said simply, knotting her headscarf even tighter before getting out of the car. 'This is my home.'

The driver was most considerate. He helped Beverley out of the back seat and carried her small overnight bag. He looked shocked when Beverley produced her keys. 'Isn't there someone in, miss?'

'No, no one.'

'But that's not right, miss. You just coming out of hospital, there should be someone to look after you.'

'No. I insisted,' said Beverley. 'It was a battle. Anyway, I'm quite strong and capable now.'

'Yes . . . but even so – '

'*Please*. Thank you for your concern.' She unlocked the front door and paid the driver, adding a generous tip. She had to be firm in order to persuade him to leave. She heard the car drive away and felt at peace. This was the moment she had been yearning for. After the weeks in hospital, enduring two skingraft operations and hours of therapy, this was all she wanted. No friends to fuss over her, no well-wishers, just to be alone in her bungalow and feel that everything was back to normal. The huge display of carnations in the living room made her want to cry. They were from Toby. She did not want flowers. She was sick of flowers. She wanted normality. Only when she had dumped them in the kitchen bin – someone had put an unreal shine on the stainless steel – did she relax and begin to savour the experience of being back, really back. The bungalow was disgustingly clean and tidy but she could soon fix that. She dropped her coat on the sofa but kept her headscarf on. The doctors had assured her that her skin cancer was completely cured, that the hair loss was a side-effect of the treatment and that her hair would grow again. Until then, scarves and hats would be a part of her.

There was a scratching at the kitchen door. It was Mutt. The big, butch tabby barged in and demanded to be fed as if nothing had happened. Beverley wanted to pick up the cat and hug him but Mutt was not having any of that nonsense: food or tights, sister.

She found an expensive tin of salmon in the recently-stocked larder and gave him that. He sniffed it suspiciously, decided that it was fit for feline consumption, and tucked in.

She made herself a cup of real coffee and sat down in the living room to enjoy it. God, the sheer bliss of being able to do something for oneself.

Her Klipfone in her handbag started a muted trilling like a trapped wasp. She stared at it. It could not be Toby, or Leon or anyone she knew. She had threatened all of them with the dire consequences of not leaving her alone for a couple of days once she was home. Perhaps it was Paul? He had brought her much happiness by coming to see her many times in hospital. She snatched up the handbag. The handset's display told her that the call was coming from a public telephone in the London area, so it could not be Paul.

'Hullo?'

'Miss Beverley Laine?' It was a man's voice, English, calm and assured.

'Yes.'

'Ah, Miss Laine. We believe you're an old acquaintance of Marshall Tate. Has he been in touch with you?'

Beverley felt the room swimming. 'Why no,' she stammered. 'He's dead. He was drowned at sea when his ship went down, some weeks ago. It was in all the papers.'

'He's most certainly not dead, Miss Laine. He's back in the country. Our information is that he was picked up by the Indonesian Navy some thirty hours after the *Eldorado* went down and was transferred to a private hospital in Jakarta where he was treated for exposure and gunshot wounds.'

Someone was playing a cruel joke on her. 'Who *are* you?'

'A firm of private bailiffs, Miss Laine. There's an outstanding judgement against Mr Tate and – '

'*What the hell are you talking about?*'

'We've tried his flat, and his offices, but we've had no luck finding him. As an old acquaintance, we thought it possible that you might know where he is.'

Beverley wanted to hurl the Klipfone across the room but she was frozen with fear. This was the police, moving in on her with their traps. She was going to be extradited to Indonesia to face trial for Marshall Tate's murder.

'I don't know what you're talking about.' she whispered. Suddenly she wanted Toby with her. He would know what to do. The long stay in hospital had eroded her confidence. It had been so long since she had had to deal with the world, and now this was being sprung on her.

'I think you do, Miss Laine. Look, this is a very serious business. If you won't help, then we could get a court order requiring you to – '

'Please. You must understand me. I don't understand.'

'All we want is information on Mr Tate's likely whereabouts.'

'But why?'

'A contract problem, Miss Laine. I don't want to bore you with it, but it involves some penalty clauses.'

Beverley forced herself to think clearly. She heard herself saying: 'If you've tried his flat and his offices, then I don't know where he is . . . No, wait . . . There's his old house at Walton-on-Thames. He may still own it, but you would've tried that – '

There was a sudden urgency in the voice. 'Where in Walton? Can you remember the address?'

Beverley's first instinct was to say she couldn't remember but she wanted to be rid of the caller. She blurted out Marshall's old address. 'But it was all so long – '

'Thank you, Miss Laine, you've been most helpful.'

The line went dead.

Beverley sat still for some moments, waiting for her heartbeat to return to normal. Perhaps the conversation had been a dream? But she knew that she was deluding herself. It had been real enough.

*Marshall Tate is alive!*

She started trembling. She rose and sat down again – confused and not certain what to do. The battle had been for nothing. Marshall still had his Elite channel and the enormous gambling revenue it generated at weekends. He wouldn't allow even a major setback such as this to prevent him starting again. The thought made her want to cry out in anguish. Well he wouldn't start again. There was Carl's murder to answer for.

*What murder, Bev? Where's your proof? His body was seen briefly on a foreign-registered ship, on the other side of the world, a ship that is now God knows how many miles down on the ocean floor.*

Facing reality – the bleak acceptance that there was nothing she could do, plunged her into black despair. Wait! Maybe there was something. She jumped up, rummaged in a bookcase drawer, and found her pocket voice recorder. The tiny device looked as insignificant as her spark of hope. Even if she found Marshall, what were her chances of trapping him into saying something about Carl's murder?

*Absolutely zilch, Bev. Forget it. Forget Marshall Tate. You've got a new life to lead when three months ago you thought you were finished. Lead it to the full; it's what Carl would have wanted.*

Despite being weakened by her long sojourn in hospital, Beverley told herself she was still a fighter. She didn't let things happen, she made things happen.

She owed that much to Carl.

She thrust the recorder into her handbag and hunted for her car keys.

## 81

Beverley drove slowly for the first third of the journey

She felt curiously detached from her car and the other road users. Driving the day she had left hospital was a mistake but the thought that there was a slim chance of avenging Carl's murder made her push herself and the Albatross grimly northward.

Walton town centre had changed surprisingly little over the years. The real change was on the big housing estate of her childhood. Satellite dishes, PVC windows, stone cladding and crimson brick drives, and caravans sitting like dumplings in front gardens had deprived the dwellings of what little character the 1930s speculative builders had imbued them with. Lace curtains stirred at the sight of the strange car as she parked the Albatross opposite the house that she had lived in. That much had not changed. The last time she had seen the place was when her parents had moved. How long ago was that? Over thirty years? She remembered the day of the move with surprising clarity. She had turned around in the back of her parents' car when they had driven away for the last time. Marshall Tate was watching her, and she had wondered if she would ever see him again.

His house looked neglected. She got out of the car, carefully because she did not want to set off the pain and she had forgotten to bring her tablets, and stood staring at the barred windows. Through the downstairs windows she could see film storage racks. She walked up the path and was about to ring the bell when she was suddenly seized by a powerful sensation of *déjà-vu*.

*The front door was ajar!*

She pushed it inwards and the sensation increased. She knew what she was going to smell even before her nostrils detected the strange, aromatic scent that she remembered from when she had entered Theo Draggon's house and Carl's house.

Her nerves screamed at her to run; to jump into her car and drive until exhaustion forced her to stop. But she entered the house. The hall was lined with racks loaded with video tape cases and cans of film, all bearing Elite channel labels.

She called out.

Silence.

There were more of the laden racks in the back room. Obviously the place was used as a repository. A layer of dust covered everything. It was the same on the upstairs landing: racks and dust. The evocative smell was now much stronger.

Beverley was inexorably drawn to what had been Marshall's bedroom; the room in which she had willingly surrendered her virginity to him.

She pushed the door open and entered.

Heavy black curtains were drawn across the windows. Her eyes adjusted to the gloom and she saw Marshall Tate slumped across the bed. At first she thought he was asleep and then she realized that the darkness beneath him was not a blanket but a sheet. It was no longer white.

Marshall Tate had been stabbed in the throat.

Later, when Beverley tried to analyze her feelings at that exact moment, she was to ask herself why she did not flee from the room. The reason eluded her. Perhaps it was the strange feeling of light-headedness that came from having spent a long period in hospital. Perhaps it was the drugs coursing through her body. She did not know. What she did know was that she stood staring at the body for some minutes, not really scared but with a feeling of deep numbness.

Her gaze took in more details. Marshall's old Pathé ACE projector, that she remembered so well, was on a low table. No – not quite the same. This was a model with an electric motor. It was laced up with film. The machine was warm to the touch. She flipped the old-fashioned toggle switch and light filled the room as the ancient projector clattered into life. She spun around and saw herself across a gulf of over thirty years: a fun-loving, laughing teenager; her hair a mass of crazy little ringlets that were no more, for the time being. She was lying on the bed where Marshall was lying now, looking at the camera with a hot sultry expression while unbuttoning her dress.

The past whirred briefly before her for a few seconds. The wall that Marshall had been using as a screen suddenly glared white, and the take-up reel slapped the loose end of film against the light box. The film was nearly finished when the projector had been switched off.

Beverley flipped the motor off, took the reel of film off the projector's take-up spindle and slipped it into her handbag.

No doubt the police would eventually find out about the stolen film and use it to implicate her in Marshal Tate's murder.

Somehow, whatever terrors the future held for her no longer seemed to matter.


## 82

The big Hitachi levelling machines that flattened and consolidated the tipped waste at the infill quarry at Storrington always stopped work an hour before sunset. Sometimes earlier if it was heavily overcast and the light was bad. Two years before a driver had misjudged the edge of the infill and his machine had toppled over, breaking both his legs.

At 3.30 p.m. the infill supervisor looked askance at the low cloud and blew his whistle. The levelling machines were made secure for the night and covered because the Met Office was forecasting the first of the winter's snow. The drivers were happy with the early finish and so were the seagulls. They tolerated the machines and the men, but they preferred it when they had the place to themselves. They flocked down in ever increasing numbers: a whirling, scavenging swarm of avian confetti. The herring gulls dived their long, vicious bills into the yielding debris, rooting out decaying meat, mould-covered bread and stale cakes. Their success as a breed was largely due to their willingness to eat everything and anything. For a bird to find a particularly tempting scrap of meat was a signal for a minor war to break out.

There was a pecking order that was rigorously enforced by the older birds: the younger birds were relegated to the older, worked-out infill that had been covered with a layer of soil. This left the field clear for the stronger gulls to wage war with each other over the richer pickings of the recent tipping.

On this particular evening, a young herring gull pushed its bill into the soil that covered the old infill and uttered a shriek that immediately communicated its panic to the entire flock. They rose as one in the cold air, wheeling and banking, and screaming their displeasure.

Below them the young herring gull beat its wings feebly in its death throes while the most dangerous substance on the face of the planet destroyed all the creature's living cells in a matter of seconds.

# AFTERWORD

Any author worth his or her salt (should avoid clichés like that one for a start!) will take particular care over the opening paragraphs of a book. They are the all-important 'hook' – the chunk of shining prose that immediately grips the bookstall browsers and persuades them to buy the book. I'm rather proud of my hooks; they are the result of much word-shuffling and pruning and general working up of a hatred of an IBM cursor. (Sometimes I miss the good old days before word-processors when it was possible to work off frustrations by ripping a sheet of paper out of the typewriter, screwing it into a ball, and chucking it at the wall.) The hook in this book is – forgive the Americanism but it is apt – a lulu. That is why I did not want to list any acknowledgements at the beginning of the book that might detract from my lovely hook. You know the sort of thing: '. . . and finally thanks to my long-suffering wife who kept me supplied with coffee and who typed the manuscript . . .' Yawn!

I do not in fact usually include acknowledgements. Most people's reward for helping with a book is having the pleasure of my company while I ply them with questions. I have made an exception in the case of this story because so many people gave so generously of their time, expertise and patience that it would be churlish of me not to thank them. They are not in any order:

Barry Fox who, over an enjoyable meal in Hampstead (that cost me two arms and two legs) gave me some valuable insights into the curious world of satellite television. I am also grateful for his many well-written, informative articles in *New Scientist* which I have raided shamelessly in my relentless quest for useful snippets.

The staff of SES (*Société Européenne des Satellites*), Luxembourg, who went to considerable trouble to show me the operations behind their remarkable Astra satellites. Also British Telecom who showed me their Astra uplinks at Woolwich.

Conrad Kozawa, President of MicroProse (Japan), who devoted a substantial amount of his time to arranging meetings and acting as my interpreter during a hectic visit to Japan. As a bonus, Conrad is a walking encyclopedia on games software and provided me with a wealth of information. He also introduced me to the Tokyo underground during the evening rush hour; an experience for which, I have to admit, I am not so grateful.

Martin Sweeting, Head of Satellite Engineering at the University of Surrey, who very kindly showed me around his facilities at Guildford and answered many questions. My hope is that he will forgive me the liberty I have taken in uprooting his department and transplanting it to the near future.

Claude Sanchez of Arianespace who patiently answered all my questions about the Ariane 4 launcher.

Beverley Flanagan at Sony Broadcast and Communications who showed me the wide-screen, high-definition future of television.

Jacqui Lyons of Marjacq Micro who provided me with many contacts in Japan.

Fellow radio amateur, Steve Terry (callsign G4WWK), who spent much time in the small hours at the microphone filling gaps in my knowledge of radio communications.

Lastly, special thanks to Elsbeth Lindner, my incredibly patient editor at Lime Tree, who was pleased with the hook, and who exercised her considerable professional talent to ensure that the line that followed was not attached to a sinker.

James Follett

# A List of James Follett Titles Available from Mandarin

While every effort is made to keep prices low, it is sometimes necessary to increase prices at short notice. Mandarin Paperbacks reserves the right to show new retail prices on covers which may differ from those previously advertised in the text or elsewhere.

The prices shown below were correct at the time of going to press.

| | | | |
|---|---|---|---|
| ☐ | 7493 0036 1 | **Cage of Eagles** | £3.99 |
| ☐ | 7493 0496 0 | **Churchill's Gold** | £3.99 |
| ☐ | 7493 0262 3 | **Dominator** | £3.99 |
| ☐ | 7493 0364 6 | **Doomsday Ultimatum** | £3.99 |
| ☐ | 7493 0110 4 | **Ice** | £3.50 |
| ☐ | 7493 0003 5 | **Mirage** | £4.99 |
| ☐ | 7493 1012 X | **Swift** | £3.99 |
| ☐ | 7493 0492 8 | **Torus** | £3.99 |
| ☐ | 7493 0363 8 | **Trojan** | £4.99 |
| ☐ | 7493 0035 3 | **U700** | £3.50 |

All these books are available at your bookshop or newsagent, or can be ordered direct from the publisher. Just tick the titles you want and fill in the form below.

**Mandarin Paperbacks**, Cash Sales Department, PO Box 11, Falmouth, Cornwall TR10 9EN.

Please send cheque or postal order, no currency, for purchase price quoted and allow the following for postage and packing:

| | |
|---|---|
| UK including BFPO | £1.00 for the first book, 50p for the second and 30p for each additional book ordered to a maximum charge of £3.00. |
| Overseas including Eire | £2 for the first book, £1.00 for the second and 50p for each additional book thereafter. |

NAME (Block letters) ...........................................................................................................................

ADDRESS ...........................................................................................................................................

.............................................................................................................................................................

☐ I enclose my remittance for ...........................

☐ I wish to pay by Access/Visa Card Number

Expiry Date